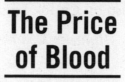

The Price
of Blood

Also by Chuck Logan

Hunter's Moon

THE PRICE OF BLOOD

CHUCK LOGAN

HarperCollins*Publishers*

HarperCollins books may be purchased for educational, business, or sales promotional use. For information please write: Special Markets Department, HarperCollins Publishers, Inc., 10 East 53rd Street, New York, NY 10022.

FIRST EDITION

Designed by Ruth Lee

Library of Congress Cataloging-in-Publication Data

Logan, Chuck, 1942–
    The price of blood / Chuck Logan. — 1st ed.
      p. cm.
    ISBN 0-06-017492-7
    I. Title.
    PS3562.04453P75   1997
    813'.54—dc21   96-47519

97 98 99 00 01 ❖/RRD 10 9 8 7 6 5 4 3 2 1

For Sofia Pieri Logan

And the chief priests took the silver pieces, and said, it is not lawful for to put them into the treasury, because it is the price of blood.

And they took counsel, and bought with them the potter's field, to bury strangers in.

Wherefore that field was called, The field of blood, unto this day.

Matthew 27: 6–8

1

BROKER'S HOUSE WAS FALLING INTO THE RAVINE.

The problem was the sloping yard and the exposed limestone foundation that had pushed out in two of the corners. Spring rains had turned the mud basement into a storm sewer, and now a gravel-toothed ditch stretched from the foundation down to the ravine like an Okie's Dust Bowl nightmare. This condition had undermined the back of the house and caused the buckled linoleum floor in the kitchen to pitch ten degrees and, back when he smoked, Broker could lay a cigarette on the table and watch it roll due east.

When he'd moved from St. Paul he'd bought the house for the lot, which had a clear view of the St. Croix River. Property was taking off in Stillwater and someday they'd pave the street and bring in city water and sewer to the north end. Someday he'd jack up the original 1870s row house, slap in a solid foundation, tear off the screwed-up kitchen addition and put in a real kitchen that some yuppies fleeing the Minneapolis–St. Paul Metro would pay big bucks for. Then he'd sell it and invest in the resort his folks owned up north . . .

But that was a retirement plan and, for now, grass went knee-high in the steep, eroded backyard and the neighborhood cats and nocturnal raccoons could prowl through it unobserved, while his crop of dandelions threatened to mutate into sunflowers. And the lilac hedges were headed for jungle and the rain had caved in the footings he'd put in to pave the dirt driveway.

His dust-busted '87 Ford Ranger was parked in the back and angled downhill, trusting in the emergency brake and two cobble-stones jammed under the front wheels to keep it from rolling off the lot.

On a mild spring morning in the last week of May, Broker opened his eyes, squinted, and figured that his life was headed into the ravine along with his house and truck.

Phil Broker, long divorced and never remarried, and with little visible means of support, rose late, threw cold water on his face, brushed his teeth, and did not shave. Barefoot, he walked his slanting stairs and floors down to the kitchen and put on water for coffee. While it heated he stared at the envelope from Publisher's Clearing House that lay on his kitchen table and declared in two-inch type: WIN TEN MILLION DOLLARS!

As he spooned Folger's instant into a cup and poured in boiling water he reminded the envelope that he didn't need the whole ten million. Two hundred and fifty thousand was the figure he had to hit.

Still barefoot and wearing only a pair of jeans, he took the coffee into the backyard and sat in a patch of thin sunlight on a distressed metal lawn chair. Through the steam curling up from his coffee cup he studied a whimsical rainbow the sun painted in the gloomy pan of oil he'd emptied from his truck the day before.

Buck up, kid, his dad would say, you still got your health.

Which was true. Broker looked younger than his forty-three years. He stood six feet tall and weighed 180 pounds and he figured that was just the right size for a man; being strong enough to stand your ground but still lean enough to run away. Barechested, with thick dark hair worn long and pulled back in a ponytail, he cultivated the aspect of a well-preserved biker who had almost turned to honest labor. His rugged face and neck and his arms below the biceps were T-shirt–tanned from working outside, in contrast to his torso and shoulders, which were pale, with plump blue veins marking the packed muscle. He'd spent a lot of time in the sun once and he didn't associate tans with beaches.

His quiet green eyes were flecked with amber and deep-set below thick, striking black eyebrows that met in a shaggy line across his unlined forehead. Young children liked his eyebrows and tugged on them, reminded of a friendly wolf toy.

Three sips into his coffee, a car pulled into his driveway—too fast—and he heard the spitting gravel hit the peeling wood siding on his house. He sighed and added a few pennies of menace to his gaze and his eyes shaded to the color of a dirty dollar bill.

Rodney in his Trans Am had to lean on the gas one last time to hear the engine roar before he cut the ignition. Broker shook his head that it had come to this. He listened to the car door slam. Too loud.

"Broker? Where are you?"

"In the back."

Rodney, a world-class asshole who lifted weights at a health club, swaggered around the house with his pocked skin damn near orange from a tanning booth fire. He had short, spiky blond hair and fried video-arcade blue eyes. He looked around and said, "What a fucking dump."

Broker had been to Rodney's cheap condo in Woodbury. There was green fur growing in the swimming pool.

"It's an investment," said Broker.

"You insured? I could torch it for you, no extra charge."

"Where is it?"

"In the trunk."

"Bring the car back here."

"First I want to see some money."

Broker pulled a wad of currency from his Levi's and dropped it on the peeling lawn table that, like the chair, was stricken with white paint leprosy. Rodney reached. Broker covered the cash with his hand. His square hand looked like he'd preferred to go without gloves last winter. Rodney judiciously took a step back.

"Bring the car around. Don't take it out in the driveway on a public street," said Broker.

Rodney's derisive laugh sounded like birds burning up in high tension wires. Again, Broker shook his head. More and more he had to deal with assholes like Rodney who failed to grasp basic emotional math or elementary physics. It genuinely frightened Broker that Rodney worked a day job as a machinist for Northwest Airlines. More and more, he worried that guys like Rodney were out there being air controllers or running the dials at nuclear power plants.

Rodney went back for his wheels and gunned down the drive and parked next to Broker's truck. He got out and popped open the trunk.

"One Power Ranger's toy," said Rodney, throwing back a flap of olive drab army blanket and revealing the full auto, military M16A/203. The one with the grenade launcher grafted ominously under the barrel.

"Ammo for the launcher?" asked Broker.

Rodney dug in the blanket and palmed three blunt 40mm high

explosive rounds. Like butter-tipped baby dinosaur teeth.

"Just three?" Broker raised his eyebrows.

"Three should be enough for the customer to see if the goods work. Take it or leave it. Got some other folks interested." Rodney grinned his skin cancer grin.

Broker squinted, unconvinced.

"I shit you not. These gang-bangers in north Minneapolis are up to battalion strength and put out some feelers." Rodney's grin broadened. "I said this magic word to them: *grenade*."

"Bullshit," said Broker. Rodney was in the reserves and liked to make with the military terminology.

"This deal sours, the future is over north," said Rodney. By future, Rodney meant the many guns he intended to pilfer from Uncle Sam.

"North Minneapolis isn't exactly my territory," said Broker.

Rodney glanced at Broker's shit-kicker truck and laughed. "Yeah, you best stick with your wood-niggers up in Stearns and Pine counties."

"It's their money. I'll call you tonight, after six. I'll set the deal for tomorrow at twelve noon," said Broker.

"They coming down here?"

"I'm not giving them a choice. Bad enough I have to drive up thirty-five east with one machine gun. I ain't doing it with five more of them."

"And I get to meet them?"

"Yeah, Rodney, you meet them and deal direct from now on. I'm not real hot on this gun stuff."

Rodney strutted to the lawn table, snatched up the bills, and counted. He stopped in midcount, staring.

"It's all there," said Broker.

Rodney's eyes jittered on two mourning doves that delicately executed a feeding ballet atop a birdfeeder set into the lip of the ravine. Unlike everything else in the overgrown, eroded yard, the feeder showed a caring hand, sanded and varnished and shaped with an elegant flair for craftsmanship. A zigzag stuck in Rodney's eyes as he tried to extract a thought. Out of place.

"Birds," he said.

"I got nothing against birds," said Broker.

2

BROKER ATE A BOWL OF SPECIAL K, DRANK A GLASS OF orange juice, and filled his Thermos with coffee. Then he changed into a clean black T-shirt and pulled on Wellington boots, a Levi's jacket, and a long-billed black cap. He threw a nylon hideout holster that held a Beretta compact into his glove compartment along with a cell phone. Then he clipped on his pager.

The sky was bright but burnished with an unseasonable chill so he grabbed a loose polo shirt to disguise the pistol if he had to strap it to the small of his back. He tucked Rodney's rifle into the false floor of his truck bed and rearranged his tools.

He ran an ad in the local paper for landscaping and handyman jobs. Sometimes he cut and hauled firewood. He had a talent for landscaping and kept a Bobcat on a trailer up north. One of his big limestone jobs was even photographed for the St. Paul paper.

But . . .

People still had a line on him from the old days. So he augmented his income periodically, ferrying marijuana and speed from up north down to the river valley. It was the speed that got him onto Rodney. There was this lab up in Pine County run by some skinheads who had swastikas and machine guns on the brain.

Broker shook his head and studied his work-battered hands. A long time ago he had vowed to never get trapped working inside in an office. So now . . . machine guns.

He artfully rearranged his tool trove so that anything he needed was always in a steel tangle on the bottom. But it was good camouflage. Nobody would want to get dirty nosing around in the intimi-

dating pile. He locked the rear door to his camper and got in and
slowly drove out his driveway.

He pokeyed up the dirt streets at the city limits and climbed the
North Hill until his tires picked up cement. He passed nicer homes
that abutted the golf course and turned south onto North Fourth
Street. He craned his neck when he passed the bed and breakfast
that the movie star had just bought and was remodeling. She was
nowhere in sight. Slowly, he rolled down a gauntlet of three-story
woodframe homes with Rococo gingerbread trim. New tulips
punched up in the flower beds. Lilac and bridal wreath were busting
out. He passed the Carnegie Library, built in 1902, and the city hall
and turned left on Myrtle and drove three blocks to Main Street.

He pulled into the FINA station and gassed up. With a dry hitch
in his voice he asked the clerk for six pick-five lotto tickets. The
Powerball drawing tonight was for 32 million bucks. He pocketed
the tickets, a couple packs of beef jerky, and hit the road.

He drove north, up State 95, through cuts in the river bluffs and
listened on A.M. radio for a weather report. The day would remain
clear but with a kicker. Frost was possible tonight across the northern tier suburbs. His eyes were fixed beyond the tree lines ahead.
Still cold up north.

North was more than a direction. As life in the Cities took a definite seedy turn, he could always count on one last clean place—deep
winter up along the North Shore where he'd been raised. He
replayed a memory from last November, during deer season.
Strapped in snowshoes, he'd plodded the frozen shore of Lake
Superior on a night so cold that sap exploded in the trees. Orion glittered down and solid bedrock buoyed him from beneath the clean
snow and he had felt locked in place by a harsh beauty that was
older than God. He wanted to get back to that moment. Leave the
city lights behind.

He tapped in F.M. on the radio and listened to a luncheon program from the National Press Club on Public Radio: Andy Rooney
reminiscing about World War Two. The Big One.

He had never thought big enough. His ex-wife, Kimberly, had
diagnosed the problem on her way out of his life and on her way to
the spa to read *Money* magazine on the Stairmaster and to lose eight
pounds, the better to run down the type-A attorney who did think
big. Kim'd probably think highly of Rodney, who dreamed of being
an international arms dealer. Rodney had figured out how to rip off
military M16s from Fort Snelling. When Rodney talked about guns

and dope in the same breath he sounded like Archimedes. Eureka. He'd found the lever that moved the modern world.

Rodney had approached Broker at a gun show, six months ago, directed by someone with loose lips. Rodney had done his homework and had a description of Broker as a former large-quantity dealer who now had scaled down to a low-profile conduit for the "white man" dope—speed and grass—that traveled between northern Minnesota and the eastern suburbs. But the dope trade had gotten too rough and crazy. More and more he was mixed up in illegal arms.

Broker did credit Rodney with organizational skill. He had put together a group of reservists throughout the state. Like him, they were armorers who worked in supply. Like him, they over inventoried weapons parts. Slowly they were assembling their own illegal armory out of spare parts. What Rodney needed was a man who could connect him to a market. Quietly.

Like his ad in the Stillwater *Gazette* said: "BROKER FIXES THINGS." One thing led to another. But Broker was a cautious man. He'd insisted on meeting Rodney's crew, to check them out in detail.

He turned west on Highway 97, drove through Scandia, and hooked up with Interstate 35 outside of Forest Lake. Now he was rolling north at 65 miles an hour.

He drank some coffee and ate one of his beef jerkys and continued to think about Rodney, who had this idea about a big score at Camp Ripley when the guard went up to train for the summer. He had stoned dreams of villas on the Mediterranean, sailboats. Rodney wanted to sell tanks.

Broker shook his head. Once he'd barreled through the Black Hills with a semi full of grass and stolen Harleys. He wondered if a Bradley armored vehicle would fit in the back of a semi.

The people he was on his way to meet fantasized in such terms. But mostly they made do with semi-automatics: AKs, Mini 14s, and Colts. But this one guy, Tabor, the money guy, hinted that he had pieces of a .50 caliber and someday maybe he'd let Broker take a crack at getting that baby up and cooking.

It was business. He didn't share in the dialogue with his clients. Tabor had hired Broker to rewire his house on the side. By the time Broker was done he'd fixed the washer and the dryer and built a screened porch. All the time Tabor was making with the far-right sounds.

Broker told him. *Lookit. I used to run a little product into the Cities but*

I didn't like it after the demographics started to change and cars full of heavily armed Zulus from Chicago and Detroit started appearing out of nowhere so now I do something else. I'm in it for the money—but mainly when things get busted, I fix it. And then Broker would wiggle his fierce eyebrows and give his wolf smile.

Tabor owned a Ford dealership and a ton of land in Pine County and regularly attended church. He didn't approve of Broker selling dope. Broker pointed out that he'd been introduced to Tabor by a bunch of neo-Nazi wackos who cooked speed in the piney woods, so lay off the pious crap. And Broker wasn't real comfortable hanging around with Tabor's buddies, who dressed up in soldier suits and played with guns out in the sticks. After the Oklahoma City thing he'd seen those guys on "Nightline" talking to Ted Koppel about the same kind of ideas about county rights that Tabor spouted. Since that federal building went up, the feds had a purple erection on. A bust had just gone down in the Cities. It was on the news. Regular alphabet soup. DEA. ATF. FBI. Minnesota BCA. Five, six counties.

But Rodney and Tabor had agreed to a one-time gig to be connected. On a touchy deal involving military rifles Broker could expect $500 per piece. So three grand for six weapons. His toe eased off the accelerator. With a machine gun in the back maybe it was a good idea to drive the speed limit.

3

HE TURNED OFF AT THE HINCKLEY EXIT AND WENT DOWN THE road until he saw the cantilevers of the Grand Casino flared against the fir and spruce. The Ojibwa's Revenge, it looked like the Flying Nun's hat getting ready to take off. Just for lunch, he told himself as he wheeled into the lot. He walked into a campfire cloud of tobacco smoke and felt the electronic surge of the slots.

The patrons were mostly weathered retirees; smokers with lined faces from fifties television. Like an indigenous cargo cult, they bent to the machines in disciplined ranks and made a collective wish. If they all hit the right combination, VE and VJ Day would come pouring back in a silver avalanche.

He put a few dollars' worth of quarters in the poker slots, cast an envious eye at the high stakes black jack tables, lost his quarters, had a hamburger and a vanilla shake, and left the casino with a sugary jingo-jango rushing in his veins.

Back on the road he headed east into the wooded back country. Out of habit he worked a jigsaw on the gravel roads, weaving in and around some lakes. He fiddled with the radio, lost the signal from the Cities and finally turned it off and just cruised, kicking up a trail of dust. He skirted the St. Croix State Forest and came up on his destination, a small general store and tavern that Tabor owned on a crossroads. He rolled by the store, checking the cars parked outside. Tabor's new Ford Bronco, several pickups. He turned around at a logging road and on the way back he tested the pager to make sure it was working. Then he parked in front of the tavern.

Jules Tabor sat at the wheel of the Bronco. He motioned to Broker to pull his rig around to the back of the building. Tabor parked in front of a large pole barn. He got out, worked a combination lock, pushed open the doors, and waved Broker in.

Tabor pulled the door closed behind Broker's truck. Broker got out and they shook hands. Broker always noticed this archaic ritual. Most of the people he dealt with were way past guaranteeing a deal with a handshake.

Tabor had a face like rare prime rib as befits a K-Mart country squire and member of the Chamber of Commerce. Broker figured that, like a lot of serious right wingers, Tabor had solid half-truths pumping in his big fatty heart. His political allies, unfortunately, had leaked out of a Bosnian Serb circle jerk. Broker took it in stride. He'd dealt with passive-aggressive hippies and rabid pseudo-anarchists, lethal pint-sized Hmong mafia, and frothing Black nationalists. Geekers, all of them, with their IQs wired directly into their assholes, as far as Broker was concerned. So now here was potbellied Jules Tabor with a graying mass of hair and skidmarks of clandestine reverse John Brown zeal streaked in his blue eyes. He wore a white short-sleeved shirt and a tie with a trout on it and his chest pocket bulged with pens clipped into a plastic holder stamped with the logo of his car dealership.

Tabor's eyes swelled with gun hormones.

"Got it right here in the back," said Broker. He dropped his tailgate and rummaged in his tools. Tabor winced disapprovingly at the disorder. Broker opened the hinged door to his false bottom compartment and slid out the mean black rifle and handed it to Tabor, who held out his arms like a man picking up his grandson for the first time.

"I gave him your money. It's all yours," said Broker.

Tabor cradled the rifle/launcher in his arms and looked at Broker in anticipation. Broker handed over the three rounds for the launcher.

"Those are high explosive, you can get illumination, smoke, and buckshot," said Broker.

"I got to try it out," said Tabor.

Broker rubbed his hands together and warily glanced around.

"I mean I'll take it back on my land. Give me an hour," said Tabor. It was a statement not a request.

"You, ah, know how to load it?" asked Broker.

Tabor grinned. "Got a manual." He wrapped his new possession in the blanket, stuffed his pockets with 40mm high-explosive rounds and left the pole barn.

Broker closed the doors and waited a few minutes to make sure he was alone. Then he opened the door to his truck, rummaged under the seat, and pulled out a frayed copy of the *Peloponnesian War* by Thucydides. His line of work, he always did kind of identify with Alcibiades.

There was an old easy chair in the barn and he sat there, drinking the rest of the coffee from his Thermos, reading with one ear cocked. Twenty minutes later he heard three spaced, faint crumps. Half an hour after that, tires crunched outside the building. Broker stuck his pocketbook back under his seat.

Now for the hard part. "You want the other five and the ammo it'll be three thousand apiece and another thousand for two hundred rounds of HE. So sixteen grand. Then you guys split my fee. At my place. Tomorrow," said Broker.

Tabor squinted. "I thought it was like this time, you carry."

Broker shook his head. "I agreed to connect you. Now he's seen your money and you've seen a gun. I don't want to carry any more money or guns on this deal."

Zeal departed from Tabor's blue eyes. A shrewd car dealer took over. "I don't know—"

"Look, I drive up the interstate with a truck full of machine guns and grenade rounds, it's a risk."

Tabor folded his big arms over his barrel chest. "I don't like going down to the Cities—"

"Stillwater ain't the Cities." Broker worried the gravel with the toe of his boot. "We got a problem. Look, there's other people interested in this stuff."

"Who?"

Broker shrugged. "I don't know, some gangs over north in Minneapolis, so my guy says."

"You'd sell military weapons to the niggers?" Tabor frowned.

"Well, naturally I don't want to . . ."

Tabor sucked on a tooth, reached in his hip pocket, and took out a pocket calendar, flipped it open, sucked his tooth again. "What time tomorrow?"

"Around two in the afternoon."

"Sixteen thousand," said Tabor.

"In cash."

"Okay. And I'll bring the two guys who want to meet your supplier. Like we talked about."

Broker shrugged carefully.

"What time was that?" asked Tabor.

"Two P.M. sharp."

Broker winced because Tabor, the small businessman, was actually writing it down in his calendar. Probably in detail. Five machine guns, meet Broker, 2 P.M. in Stillwater. Praise the Lord and pass the ammunition.

"Deal," said Tabor, extending his large, firm hand. Feeling odd, Broker took the handshake and got back in his truck. He left Tabor standing in his pole barn rotating an empty 40mm shell casing in his large fingers with that weird light in his eyes like he was going to free the oppressed white slaves.

Things were going so well that Broker briefly entertained the notion that he was in step with luck. He couldn't resist stopping at the casino on the return trip. In ten minutes the dollar slots gulped down a hundred bucks of his own money in a hiccuping slur of electronic chimes. So much for luck. Grumbling, he walked to a phone and dialed.

A very ill-humored black voice answered. "What?"

"Rodney's on for noon. The buyers are on for two P.M."

"Check. What's with the bells. Where the fuck are you?"

"The Grand Casino."

"You been out there too long, Desperado."

At ten in the evening, Broker sat in his living room in front of the TV and wrote down the winning Powerball numbers and methodically checked his thirty tickets.

Thirty losers. He tore up the tickets and threw them at the TV. Then he reached for the phone and punched a 218 area code and a number north of Duluth.

"Cheryl, it's Broker. Let me talk to Fatty."

Fatty Naslund's voice came on the line as lean and trim as cold hard cash. "Yeah, Broker, I figured you'd be calling."

"Where we at, Fatty?"

"Thirty days. I can't hang my ass out there exposed longer than that on a quarter mil note."

"Thanks, man, how's my dad doing with it?"

"Mike? You know. Stoic. Like his son."

4

RODNEY HAD COME AND GONE, BUT NOT WITHOUT SOME difficulty. So far it was running smoothly. Broker hummed "Everything's Coming Up Roses," an old habit from the dope deal days, as he straightened up the living room.

Two in the afternoon. Sunlight filtered through the dusty venetian blinds on the living room windows and cut mote-filled stripes across his couch. He was proud of his couch, a garish fabric design that resembled burning tires in black, yellow, and green. He had found it on the I-94 shoulder about a mile west of the Hudson Bridge. Must have fallen off a Goodwill truck. Broker was on it, had it in the back of *his* truck in a minute flat.

He had a Goodwill armchair to go with the couch and that did it for the living room unless you counted the stripped down Harley chopper frame that sat on a poncho with its steel innards neatly arranged around it and smelling faintly of gasoline. And the hunk of marble that perched on a beer case for a coffee table.

And the whole wall of books in cheap pine shelves, used paperbacks, mostly, that he'd bought by the crate from the bookstores that lined Stillwater's main street.

Besides the five dully gleaming M16A2/203s lined up in a row on the couch and the ammo boxes stacked to the side, the books were the only orderly objects in the whole damn house.

Broker smiled in anticipation. Antsy for it to get over.

Right on time, a brown Econoline van with tinted windows and—hello—*Alabama* plates pulled to the curb in front of his house and Tabor stepped from the passenger side wearing powdery soft stonewashed jeans and a matching jacket, an oatmeal colored sweatshirt, and a pair of blinding white Nike crosstrainers. Looks like a coach. Broker tested the battery in his beeper. C'mon, coach, it's game time, baby.

So Tabor's buyers were out of state and they packed some muscle. The driver had arms like he juggled railroad ties and a beer-pudding belly filling up a loud red T-shirt. As they came up the steps, Broker read the slogan on the shirt spread around the silhouette of an assault rifle.

MY WIFE YES
MY DOG MAYBE
MY GUN NEVER!

The other guy, who'd been riding in the back of the van, was lean, with close-cropped silvery hair, and he wore a nylon running suit. He carried an attaché case. *Yes.* He was the guy to watch. He looked like he'd been seriously trained at sometime in his life and had kept up the habit.

Broker met them on the porch steps. Tabor introduced his companions. Red beer gut was Andy. Running suit was Earl. Earl took Broker's hand and pierced him with pale blue lifer's eyes and said "Howdy, pleased to meet you," in a deeply sincere southern accent.

Earl did not let go of Broker's hand. He had vicegrips for a forearm and the more Broker saw of Earl the more Tabor looked like a balloon with the air going out of it. Okay, so Earl's the man. So he wasn't surprised when Earl gave orders in a quiet drawl. "Andy, you go in there and take a look around."

Andy nodded. "Most ricky tic, Earl."

"Hey," said Broker, breaking Earl's hold with a sharp twist of his hand, "Tabor, what is this?"

Tabor smiled. "It's their money."

So. Okay. Broker wondered if they would try to take him off. In his previous dealings with handshaking Jules Tabor that eventuality had not occurred to him. But Earl was a kind of dangerous cottonmouth with a soft voice and cold swampwater in his veins. What the hell was Earl doing up here in the recently unfrozen north? *Why, shopping away from the federal heat down south. Fucking machine guns. Where is my brain. Should have stayed with grass.*

Broker and Earl deciphered each other for two minutes and silently agreed; they were natural enemies. Broker's face was relentlessly northern European, an angular German forging under the lobo eyebrows, with a touch of his mother's stormy Norwegian melancholy informing his eyes. Earl's face was a True Believer knot, cracked with stress, yanked way too tight. But Broker detected dangerous reserves of strength seething in Earl's pale eyes. Like he'd grown up breathing poisonous ideas.

Andy came back to the front door. "He's all right, Earl, keeps a messy house but seems all right. Stuff's in on the couch. Nobody else here."

"Where's the guy?" Earl asked.

Broker tapped the pager on his belt. "He calls in half an hour, leaves a number. If everything's cool, he drops by, you meet. I get paid and you go off and develop a business relationship."

"Suppose that's sensible," said Earl. Everyone smiled.

Broker let his surface relax. "You boys had me going for a while there. C'mon in and have a beer."

That's when two cars rounded the corner. The first, an airport cab, pulled up right behind the van. With a soft squeal of tires, the second car, a green Saturn, pitched forward on its suspension and suspiciously backed up and disappeared around the block. Everyone halted in midstride on Broker's squeaky porch steps.

He saw who was in the cab and, given a choice, at this precise moment, Broker would have preferred to see a nuclear fireball blossom on the North Hill of Stillwater, Minnesota. And he just fuckin' knew. His life was about to spectacularly blow up right in his face.

Again.

5

*N*INA PRYCE!

She was intense and she was not bad looking and she had been famous once for a few brief days and she was a goddamned freak who trailed a guidon of tragic purpose. And she was getting out of the airport cab.

Broker groaned. Quicksand. Under his feet.

A pair of seriously athletic thighs and calves hinged by perfect carved knees swung from the car door followed by a lithe young woman in an outrageous apricot miniskirt, sandals, and a flimsy tan top that had these string things holding it up. Bare shoulders and a bronze cap of short hair caught spears of sunlight.

Her big gray Jericho eyes were danger deep and nothing but intelligent—problem was, they fed current into a challenge to the world to knock them down. And he saw the spidery, brand-new skull and crossbones tattoo that grinned a merry fuck you on the supple, defined muscle of her left shoulder. And—*aw God*—she stood up with that sinewy ramrod presence that couldn't be disguised in the trashy good-time-gal duds she wore.

There is a quality that is scary enough in a man. Broker found it mildly terrifying in an attractive woman. The Germans, naturally, had a word for it. They called it *Stramm*.

The rest of the world called it military bearing.

She'd be about twenty-nine now. Five eight and put together, in her case, like a brick latrine. As she paid the fare and slung her bag over her shoulder and hauled out a suitcase, Tabor, Earl, and Andy put their eyes on Broker. Broker smiled. It was his innate smile and revealed his soul and the lessons of his life in a flicker through the grate of his rugged features. The smile said: *Fuck me dead.*

Broker did the only thing he could do, he laughed.

He'd always thought that she was nice to look at as long as she didn't move. Nina in motion suggested the Waspish grace of training events that involved guns, swords, and horses. And she was moving and she glowed with an unhealthy excitement that looked to Broker like the moral pollution of some big city. Down South, judging from her surface tan and her clothing. She paused on the sidewalk and plunked down her suitcase. Twenty feet away and she radiated the energy of Excalibur plunged into the cement.

Earl, impressed, removed his hat.

Broker blurted, "You heard of the telephone?"

"Aw, Broker, if I would have called you would have split on me, just like last time." Slang didn't ride well on her clear, chiseled diction. Broker stared: deceptive tiger-kitty freckles, ascetic slightly sunken cheeks that bespoke hours of sweat hitting varnished gym floors, gray eyes, and a straight tidy nose. Full lips, but set in a straight, austere line. Way too clean for present company.

And he cringed further because she was trying to slip into a raunchy vernacular that didn't fit her erect posture. Nina knew what Broker did for a living, but she got her ideas about it from books and movies.

As if to allay his fears, she lifted a pint of whiskey from her purse, held it up like a prop, unscrewed the cap, and took a long drink. The tendons of her throat struggled with the gulp, but she got it down and her smile brightened. Maybe she figured she'd come off less obvious when drunk. The problem was, she didn't drink. The quicksand was about to his knees.

She came up the steps and Earl gallantly went to help her with the suitcase. And her miniskirt and sandals were a million raunchy miles off from Minnesota in May and she was a lot exhausted and she smelled of cognac and a night of insomnia and nicotine and a musk of travel that needed a wash and she was definitely in the wrong place at the wrong time and the edge in her gray eyes took in Broker and the scene he had going and it was clear she couldn't care less.

"You can't be here . . . *now,*" he fumed.

"Got no place else to go." She shot a glance over her shoulder. "And there's some creep following me."

Broker backed up a step and dry-swallowed.

"Guess you guys scared him off." She shrugged and started for the door. Earl and Tabor scanned the street defensively. Andy moved to block her, big hands out, warding.

Nina cocked her head and took a stance that really annoyed Broker because, right now, he didn't need any utter fearlessness of youth bullshit. She read the sentiment on Andy's gross belly. "You married, Sport?"

"Yeah, so," said Andy.

"If I was your wife and I caught you wearing that I'd wait till you were asleep and lump you good with a cast-iron frying pan."

Andy looked past Nina. "Earl?"

"Who's following you?" asked Earl.

"This New Orleans cop," said Nina. "Don't worry, he's a dirty New Orleans cop. Off the force."

"Why's he after you?" asked Earl.

"I stole something from his boss, okay? Jesus, what is this—a Boy Scout meeting?"

"Let her go," said Earl. He turned and peered into Broker's eyes. Broker's shock was real, it couldn't be faked. He removed his cap, scratched his sweaty hair, and glanced up and down the street, finishing with his arms out, palms up.

They went in. Broker grimaced when Nina sang out from the living room, "Holy shit, Broker. You're not selling grass to college kids anymore."

"Ah, Earl," said Andy with a touch of gruff alarm in his voice.

Nina had kicked off her sandals and stood barefoot on the stained hardwood floor holding one of the fierce-looking weapons up and inspecting it. There was no other way to say it, even though it was not correct in circles Nina wouldn't be caught dead in. She didn't hold a gun like a girl.

Earl, Andy, and Tabor noticed this instinctively.

"Nina, what are you doing?" demanded Broker.

She smiled. "Haven't handled one of these in a while."

"Where?" asked Earl, quietly fascinated.

"Where what?" Nina placed the rifle back in its place on the couch.

"Did you handle one of those?" finished Earl.

Nina shrugged. "In the Gulf."

"You were in Desert Storm?" asked Earl.

Nina drew her fingers through her sunstreaked hair and cocked her head and her hips and purred in a honky-tonk drawl. "Honey, I *still* got sand leaking into my shorts."

Broker clamped his eyes shut and grimaced. When he opened

them he saw Earl studying her with a queer reverence, like she was alien royalty or a deadly new virus. Earl wasn't sure. He shrugged and looked intrigued. "It's possible. There were women over there." He squinted. "You look kinda familiar."

"You get up to Michigan much?" asked Nina.

"I been to Flint."

"Ann Arbor," said Nina. She flopped into the easy chair and picked up the pint bottle of Hennessey cognac from where she'd left it on the floor.

Broker's wince deepened. *Her dad's label.* Nina took a pull on the bottle and narrowed her eyes.

"Nina, you never could drink," stated Broker. "No drinking. Go clean up."

"Let her be," puffed Earl. "If her New Orleans cop shows up it's his tough luck. Hell, she alone's worth the trip up here." He turned to Andy. "Check 'em out," nodding at the military hardware. Then Earl swung the briefcase up on the marble slab.

"Aw right," breathed Broker.

"First why don't we look in the lady's purse and suitcase, just to keep the game friendly," said Earl. "Jules, check it out."

While Tabor went into Nina's things, Earl paced the room. He stopped at the bookcases and scanned the titles.

"You read a lot for a guy who fixes washing machines," he said flatly.

"The dude I bought this place from left them."

"Uh-huh, he liked history."

Tabor wheezed and stood up. He tossed items from the purse on top of the briefcase. "Airline ticket. Northwest flight from New Orleans landed not over an hour ago. Two thousand, three hundred, and change in cash. Another two thousand in travelers checks. College ID from the University of Michigan. Driver's license issued to Nina Pryce, Ann Arbor, Michigan. Picture matches."

Earl raised his eyebrows. Nina swigged on her pint and shrugged. She lit a cigarette like she'd watched too many French movies and almost coughed when she inhaled. "The suitcase," said Earl.

"Clothes, travel things, toothpaste, makeup, and *this*." Tabor stacked a pile of manila folders and a roll of paper on the coffee table.

Broker's sternum vibrated like a wishbone being cranked back for a big wish. He stared at Nina hard. She held his eyes with an unshakable conviction that was out of place in this room, at this moment, with these people.

Earl riffled the pages in the top folder and squinted at Nina. "Very interesting," he breathed. "Xeroxed copies of some kind of classified military inquiry. Fort Benning, July 1975. Just gets curiouser and curiouser, don't it?"

He paged through the folders and studied the contents of a slender one. He held up a photostat for Jules and Andy to see. "Copy of a police report on a Cyrus LaPorte. For misdemeanor assault in a federal prison."

Broker groaned out loud.

Earl squinted and his lumpy jaw muscles rippled, mulling as he rolled open the map. "This what you stole?"

"Yep," said Nina.

"Isn't LaPorte the retired general, the one with the boat?"

Nina smiled and crossed her legs. They were the kind of legs that laughed at nylons, and they sliced the air like scissors.

Broker, not known for attacks of nerves, felt a mild panic corkscrew up his spine. He had to take control of the situation. "We're through with the preliminaries. Nina's going to walk down to the corner for a pack of cigarettes—" he said.

"Uh-uh. I kinda like having her around," said Earl. "Go ahead. Open it." He nodded at the briefcase.

Broker stooped and shot back the latches. Hello, sixteen grand. He opened the top and stood upright, tensed, hands floating at his sides. "What the fuck is this shit?"

The briefcase held a King James Bible, a video cassette tape, and a .45 semiautomatic Colt pistol. The pistol butt was a vacant cavity. Empty. In the ominous silence, Nina giggled. Broker felt the raw nerves in her giggle tickle him like poison ivy. He saw she was starting to lose it to the booze. *Damn.* Broker started to sweat.

"I thought I was dealing with Tabor, who are you, coming in here like this," he seethed at Earl, "with this . . . bullshit."

Earl reached over, acquired the pistol, brought a magazine from the pocket of his jacket, inserted it and racked the slide. He did not set the safe. With the pistol hanging casually in his hand he proposed in a calm voice, "We all sit here for a few minutes and get acquainted and see if anything unusual happens. We already got notice of one cop in the area. Let's see if a million Yankee cops come through the door."

Across the room Andy methodically worked down the row of weapons, clearing bolts, checking chambers, toggling with the breech of the launchers. A cold metal snap and precision clacked in the tense room.

Nina leaned forward and looked into the briefcase and plucked out the cassette and studied the label. In the process she spilled a little of the cognac. The amber liquid splashed lightly on her knee and trickled slowly between her thighs.

"The truth about the alleged Holocaust. Lectures by Rev. Earl Devine," she read. Broker watched her eyes, The cloudy shiver in them. Little muscles at the corner of her lips twitched. "You gotta be fuckin' kidding," she said.

"Watch it, pottymouth," said Andy. "Earl's an ordained minister. Just thought you should know."

"You need a bath, Nina," said Earl. "I can smell you."

"Not as good as I can smell you, *Elmer*."

Earl chuckled. "Andy, Jules tells me that Mr. Broker carries a nine mil Beretta in a hideout over the crack of his ass under that baggy T-shirt. Take a look."

Broker put up with a rough hand stiff arming his neck, another frisking his back. "He's clean, Earl."

"Check his socks." Andy did.

"Take the battery out of that pager," said Earl.

Andy unclipped the device and dumped the battery to the floor. *Uh oh*, thought Broker. Then Andy tossed the pager to Earl who placed it on the marble slab next to the briefcase. With a casual show of force he raised the butt of the .45 and smashed the plastic device.

"This isn't going to work. My guy won't show unless he beeps a number," said Broker. "Deal's off. And you people are outta here. Nina, get upstairs."

"I'm enjoying my conversation with Elmer here," she said. There was murder in her eyes, way more complicated than these good old boys could ever know. It was time to pull the plug. Fuck the money.

Andy giggled at Nina's defiance. "Nice for a man to be taken so seriously in his own house."

"You just shut up, Broker," added Earl with a thin smile. "This lady don't add up and she's got some explaining to do. The kind of explaining that might take all night," said Earl with a thin smile.

Broker shot a poison look at Nina. The anger in his voice was real. "What the hell are you doing here, goddammit!"

Nina tipped the bottle up, swallowed, and sneered.

"Gawdamn," grinned Earl, "do that again, honey, I love the way you swallow."

"I just want my fucking money," muttered Broker. Earl waved him silent with the big Colt.

6

THEY WAITED. SWEAT RAN DOWN BROKER'S RIBS AND POOLED in his shorts. He paced, shadowed by Andy. Jules Tabor stood at the window and watched the street. Earl went upstairs, found Broker's pistol, came down and scouted the backyard; then he brought a chair from the kitchen and sat facing Nina, knees almost touching, and read through the dossier material that had been in her bag. He glanced up. "What good is this? Most of it's crossed out."

"That's the Freedom of Information Act for you," said Nina as she suicidally finished the pint. Then she picked up the video cassette and studied the blurb on the back.

Earl set the dossiers aside and spoke to Jules. "Go out to the van, check out the street for about five more minutes then pull in back. We'll load up there. Andy, look around for some rope to tie them up."

"Hey—" Broker started to protest. Earl snapped the .45 on him.

"Sorry, Broker, I came to do business with an arms dealer and I wind up with a redheaded chick with a suitcase full of government documents. You lose, buddy." He grinned at Nina and his voice lowered, husky, thick in his throat. "So we're going to take you folks for a ride. Get to know you a little better."

Broker wasn't believing this. Standing there on razor blades and Earl was blushing. Where's the goddamn money? He had to *see* the money and the guns together.

It was strange in the room. The five rifles lined up. Earl's dry rustling breath. Andy rummaging in the kitchen. The skeletal Harley frame like a boned-out steel cheetah.

Nina wasn't impressed. She curled her lip and tossed the video cassette into Earl's lap. He twitched pleasurably.

"You write that copy on the back?" Nina mused. "The Jews made it all up, huh. The SS. The death camps."

Earl cleared his throat and said in a reasonable voice, "There's eyewitness accounts that the camps were built after the war. It's a side of things that should be heard."

Broker watched her bunch into a sinewy coil in the chair. He could feel the lances of adrenaline advance out of her pores.

"Hey, Earl," said Andy, coming in with a roll of duct tape, "come away, man, the bitch is drunk."

Broker heard the van engine start, listened to the sound move from the street along the side of his house into the back yard. Andy ripped off a length of tape. Like fingernails on a blackboard.

Then Nina's voice took on the flat meter of the army officer she had been for six years. "Be advised, mister, *my dad* liberated one of those nonexistent camps . . ."

Broker tensed when he saw her eyes cloud with holy wrath. *Aw God*, here comes "The Battle Hymn of the Republic."

"And he told me the GIs were so damn . . . taken by what they saw that they wouldn't even shoot those guards. They killed some of them with their . . . bare . . . hands!"

Nina Hour. Broker wasn't fast enough. She came up from her hip with the pint held by the neck and swung it in a backhanded chop like a cleaver across Earl's nose.

Glass and bones cracked. Andy dropped the tape and went for his pocket and pulled out a thick bone-handled gravity knife and started to flick it open with his big thumb. But some tape was tangled on his fingers and that gave Broker a precious second. First he had to deal with Andy. He pivoted and smashed an elbow in Andy's surprised face but then he had to go after Earl, who had sprung from the chair with blood pouring from his swelling nose. Earl, raging, growling, and evidently in shock that he had been struck by a woman, dropped the .45 and plucked the shattered bottleneck from his chest and threw it at Nina, who ducked, and it crashed through the window and, with the breaking glass and Earl's roar, Broker finally felt it start to happen outside.

7

TABOR SCREAMED IN THE BACKYARD. A STAMPEDE OF RUN-
ning feet shook the house. Earl, oblivious in rage, raised his hand to
slap Nina—which was a real serious culture-bound mistake on Earl's
part. She leaned back and Earl's open hand swatted thin air. She
rebounded like a piston and forked a rigid arc formed by her right
thumb and the knuckle of her index finger up under Earl's chin. Earl
instinctively tucked his neck into his hunched shoulders. The force
of Nina's blow was absorbed in the powerful tendons of his neck,
not the vulnerable throat.

Tires squealed and the reek of burning rubber torched in from
the street; car doors slammed and the back door slammed. They
were coming in with all their usual tact of bull elephants. Andy
went past Broker running for the kitchen and Broker went for Earl
who now had his hands on Nina.

Andy screamed when he saw a tall black man, whom God had
made without a waist, so that his pumping hips and thighs jointed in
a power train to his ribs, doing a hundred-yard dash across Broker's
grubby kitchen straight at him.

St. Paul Det. Jarrel "T-Bone" Merryweather was pure onyx black
and his shirt was an ivory off white and his tie of expensive silk. J.T.
came on screaming at the top of his ex-drill-sergeant lungs, manag-
ing to smile at the same time because he really ate this shit up. J.T.
didn't take the time to vest up because he knew there was only one
way to get through a door, which was first and fastest, because
Broker had taught him how to do it. He held a 12-gauge Remington
riot pump steady before him with the muzzle gaping like an open
onrushing manhole straight to Redneck Hell: "Freeze—you fuckin'

piece of shit—I'll blow your mother-fuckin' head loose from your fat cracker ass!"

Broker heard a groan as Andy collapsed to his knees and somewhere Tabor was yelling how he wanted to see his lawyer and other people were in the room giving Andy his rights but he was giving his full attention to Earl and Nina was getting in the way trying to step in and kick Earl and catching Broker in the ribs a couple of times and Earl had this confused little boy lost look in his eyes as his cheeks popped like chicken bones because he'd strayed too far from home in Alabama, and—ha, mother fucker—Brokers from Minnesota had met Alabamians before, in July 1863, at a place called Cemetery Ridge and, like his ancestors before him, Earl had come too far north and walked into the remorselessly moving parts of Det. Lt. Phillip Broker of the Minnesota Bureau of Criminal Apprehension.

But then Earl rallied and, with an insane red-and-gray bloodshot flapping in his eyes, surprised Broker by clamping the edge of Broker's left thumb in his teeth, as he mashed down and Broker felt the teeth sink into the skin, the muscle, and the bone of the top joint.

Earl's jaw muscles pulsated through the blood running down his face and Broker screamed when J.T. butt-stroked Earl with the 12-gauge to make him let go. The jarring pain traveled—electric, incandescent—up his arm.

"Don't," screamed Broker.

Earl wouldn't let go. He growled even though he was covered with cops grabbing at him, and his neck and jaw continued to surge, leathery and lethal as some damn snapping turtle.

Five pairs of hands searched for a hold on Earl's face. Fingers clawed in his nostrils, yanking back, while Earl growled and shook his head and Broker screamed.

Procedure went to hell in the bizarre circumstance. "Phil, don't move," shouted Ed Ryan, the ATF agent in charge. "Grab that fucker's head. Stabilize it. Don't let him shake like that, he'll *bite it off.*"

Somebody in a vest and black cap was cuffing Nina.

"J.T., keep her close," Broker yelled, rolling his eyes toward Nina, and Merryweather, who'd been taping the caper off the wire in Broker's pager, pushed the officer away from Nina and took the guy aside, explaining. And Broker was sure that the terrible crunching sound that he heard with his ears, but also was hearing *inside* his body traveling up his arm, was his thumb being bitten off.

A dozen officers, Robocopped in black body armor, bore down in a twenty-four–handed grab-ass all over Earl who continued to growl and tried to thrash. They sought leverage on the bulging muscles of Earl's neck and jaw, experimentally jabbed him in the eyes; one guy had a wooden spatula from the kitchen and was trying to pry between Earl's teeth. Earl had these serious teeth. The spatula broke.

"Man will not *let go*. I'm gonna have to cap the sucker," said J.T. Merryweather loudly for effect, resigned, dubiously setting down the shotgun and drawing his pistol.

"You can't shoot a guy for biting somebody," a voice yelled.

"Hell I can't, he's attacking an officer. Just shoot him a little bit, to make him stop."

A woman deputy from Dakota County wondered aloud, academically, "Where *exactly* would you shoot him?"

Sweat poured into Broker's eyes. The pain was incredible, immobilizing, and it was just a *thumb*.

Several paramedics pushed through the house, which was now crawling with men and women wearing badges and armed to the teeth and the Washington County SWAT team was there and they were all pumped up on adrenaline and the smell of sweat and fresh blood and everybody was talking at once and the radios were crackling.

And voices. "Who's the chick? What's she doing here?"

And "Secure that money on the floor."

And Nina. "That's *mine*."

Broker floated in an excruciating fog, wrapped in fiery cotton candy that dripped sticky red from the mangled knuckle that was locked in Earl's jaws. Somebody blurted on a radio, "No shit, one of the assholes *bit off* Broker's thumb."

They eased him off his knees to the floor so that Earl, stretched out like an alligator, lay between Broker's spread legs, breathing in short snorts, with worms of snot crawling on his upper lip. His face had turned a demented purple and orange with some parts showing through the blood a horrible fish-belly white and the engorged veins popped out on the twisted crimson cables of his neck muscles.

"Got a doctor coming," yelled a medic. His cohorts quickly took wood splints from their bags and jammed them between Earl's teeth. As they worked, Broker noticed the contents of Nina's purse, which lay scattered beneath him. He reached down with his good hand for the pack of Gauloises. *Like the cognac, her father's brand.* He found the lighter in her purse and lit it. Despite the pain, the bright pink airsacs in his lungs collected in a happy banzai charge and ran straight for the nicotine.

The medics carried on in awed, too-loud voices. A spirited professional discussion about the problem Earl presented.

"I've read about this, surge of adrenaline, ancient survival mechanisms—"

"Strongest muscle group in the body—"

"Stuck together. I thought that meant intervaginally?"

"Bad joke. Bad joke."

They had worked the splints between Earl's teeth to buy Broker time but debated that they couldn't pry the jaws apart without risking a surge that would take Broker's thumb with it.

A medic shouted into an emergency radio. "We can't bring him in. They're attached. Sure we're trying to keep him calm . . . whad'ya mean, don't let him wander around. He's not in shock, he's fucking being *eaten.*"

The medic handed off the radio and knelt beside Broker. "Okay. It's a tricky one so the doctor's coming with a shot. We gotta keep his neck immobilized, we've stabilized the biting pressure, but if he gets to whipping his head around . . . Hey, the guys got serious neck muscles." Another medic, a husky blonde wearing a Washington County Paramedic jacket, narrowed her eyes at Broker. "You shouldn't be smoking," she lectured, just like a good Minnesotan.

"Fuck you! Get him offa my hand!"

Nina was there, watching him. Broker peered into her merry, adrenaline-drunk, gray eyes. Speckled blood blended naturally with her freckles. A slight bruise darkened her left cheekbone. She stifled an absurd laugh.

"What?" Broker demanded.

"I can't help it," she sputtered. "It's . . ." She glanced at the spectacle of Earl trying to eat the thumb. "Just too weird." She broke into contagious laughter.

"Don't," gasped Broker. "It hurts when I laugh." The insane hilarity subsided and he drilled her with tormented eyes. "What the hell are you doing here?"

Nina shrugged. "You said if I ever needed help I should come to you. Well, here I am."

Broker groaned. Earl's lips curled back and his teeth gleamed, socketed in Broker's blood—his eyes were pure Pickett's Charge. The hollow growl emanating from back in his throat sounded like the sound effects in *The Exorcist.*

8

THE DOCTOR LOOKED LIKE BEN FUCKING CASEY, WITH COPI-ous chest hair sticking out of his green scrub shirt. He sauntered like a deeply tanned visitor from Olympus on a slum tour through the seedy mayhem of the house. He smiled, amused at the macabre ban-ter circulating among the heavily armed law enforcement types forming a brawny huddle over Broker and Earl.

He snapped on thin rubber gloves and tapped a bulging vein on Earl's red, swollen neck and said, "Hmmmm." John Eisenhower, the Washington County sheriff, walked into the room. Broker had worked undercover with Eisenhower years back in St. Paul. Eisenhower proceeded to study the situation, alert blue eyes in his blunt blond features. Broker knew the look. John was learning something . . . new.

"What are you going to give him?" asked Eisenhower.

The doctor held a syringe in one hand, a vial in the other. "Ketamine," mused the doctor. "The question is how much."

"Knock him out," urged J.T. "Fast."

The doctor shook his head. "Give him too much, he could go into spasm. Cardiac arrest."

"So?" J.T. was impatient. He gestured with the big black Glock automatic in his hand.

The doctor smiled, enjoying himself. "There's a liability ques-tion," he said.

"Stick him," ordered J.T.

"What if his teeth are loose and he swallows one and chokes?" speculated the doctor, inserting the needle in the vial, playing with the pressure on the plunger, estimating his dose.

Broker, his eyes pin dots in a waterfall of sweat, muttered, "Nothing wrong with his fuckin' teeth."

"I could get sued," pondered the doctor.

"All these nervous coppers, you could get shot," explained J.T.

Ed Ryan squatted next to the doctor. "I'm the ATF special agent in charge. Give the shot. Now."

"Yeah, but who backs me up if I get sued?" replied the doctor.

"Now," said Ryan, in an icy voice.

Earl, imprisoned in a dozen pairs of hands, shied back from the needle. The doctor pointed to Earl's upper right arm. Earl's shirt exploded away in J.T.'s hands. It reminded Broker of a bunch of cowboys and cowgirls hog-tying a steer. Earl snorted as the needle popped into his deltoid. He seemed to levitate, thrashing in the imprisoning hands. There was an audible snap. A huge ATF guy spoke up apologetically: "Sorry 'bout that."

"A wrist," offered a calm detached female voice. Nina.

"About three minutes to kick in," said the doctor. He smiled. "One possible side effect of ketamine is that he could go into a psychotic delirium for as long as twenty-four hours."

"Nice touch," admired J.T.

"I thought you'd like it," said the doctor.

Broker puffed mightily on the cigarette and watched the drug seep into Earl's mad eyes. Everyone took a strong hold and waited. Earl tried to beat the clock. Tried to grind through the wood splints. Broker flashed on *Jaws*—watching the shark come over the transom. Nina wiped sweat from his forehead. She held his free hand.

Finally, Earl's snarls began to moderate into a ghastly yawn. Slowly the pressure on Broker's thumb cranked back. Earl's eyes fluttered and the steely muscles of his face drooped. Broker felt a gruesome suckling sensation as Earl's loose, bloody lips slipped over his thumb. Earl made a sound like a drooling baby. Ga ga goo.

Earl began breathing in anesthetized, blood-smeared dopery. "Aha," said the doctor serenely as he removed something from Broker's bloody thumb. "Did someone hit this guy in the mouth before the bite?"

"You could say that," said J.T. Merryweather.

"Loose canine," said the doctor, holding up Earl's tooth. "That's probably what saved your thumb." One of the medics moved in and irrigated the wound with stinging disinfectant. "Move it," the doctor ordered Broker.

Broker gritted his teeth and sent messages into the gashed flesh. The digit moved.

"Okay, we have intact tendons. Don't know about nerves. Clean it like hell all the way to the ER. The human mouth is *the* dirtiest thing there is."

Squads and unmarked cars from the Washington, Dakota, and Ramsey counties' Task Force jammed the brick emergency entrance portico of the Riverview Memorial Hospital. Rodney, who'd been arrested at Broker's house—Broker had been arrested with him to keep his cover consistent—sat cuffed in the back of one of them, forgotten for the moment. But as Broker climbed from an ambulance, aided by cops, Rodney raised his cuffed hands and aimed an index finger, cocked his thumb. Through the window Broker saw his lips form a "Bang."

Word got out over the radios that one of the assholes had bitten off Broker's thumb. Security got lost in the scramble to come and gawk. It was a real mess. His cover was blown to smithereens. Nina squeezed his good hand and smiled helpfully. Through a veil of blue curtains, Broker saw Earl wheeling by, thrashing against restraints on a gurney. "Mama, Mama," he screamed. "There's snakes in my poop!"

A pissed-off ER surgeon and his team shooed the rubbernecking cops from his triage. "Out. It's a bite. No big deal. So get the hell out of here."

Nina refused to budge.

"She stays," said Broker.

"You'll get some time off work now," said Nina in a matter-of-fact voice, eyes fixed on Broker's wound.

"Huh?" Broker watched needles. Tetanus in his butt. Then Novocain in his thumb, then this curved job that strung catgut through what looked like a torn flap of extra-large pigskin glove attached to the palm of his left hand.

"You see, I'm in a little trouble and I could use a guy like you," said Nina.

"Wonderful." Broker watched, resigned, as the doctor stitched and tied.

9

BROKER DIDN'T WANT TO HEAR IT.

They gave him Dilaudid and put him in a hospital bed. He needed rest, they said. Fat chance. With Nina curled up on a chair at his side, alternately sleeping and watching him.

She was his doppelganger, come haunting.

It was about her dad. It was always about her dad. She still didn't get it. Ray Pryce had stranded him in a real tight spot and almost got him killed. But it wasn't like that at the beginning. Dilaudid dripped into the adrenaline void and the memory flickered like slow-motion cinema.

May Day 1972, QTC—Quang Tri City—
Stalingrad South

North Vietnamese regiments supported by tanks and artillery fought South Vietnamese regiments supported by the U.S. Air Force in the rubble of Quang Tri City. The rubble had been pounded to gravel. The North Vietnamese regiments had won.

The tank was a low-slung Russian T–54, with a smooth round turret like a green steel igloo, from which protruded the biggest cannon Broker had ever seen. Dozens of other North Vietnamese tanks picked through the junky bricks on the muggy summery morning. Except this one had just pushed a wall over on 2nd Lt. Phil Broker, who had become separated from his unit and who was now pinned under a slab of cement and imprisoned in a bristle of rebar whiskers. Stuccoed in mortar dust and twenty-one years old, he was for sure going to die because he was dumb enough to get caught in a losing battle in a lost war.

A hatch opened on the turret and a tanker shouldered up and removed his goggles, a smile broadened across his insect-tough Tonkinese face. The treads clanked back, grinding masonry; and the tank realigned, beetle fashion, as the cannon barrel moved left and then down, probing the air. Broker experienced one of those acoustic shadows he'd read about. A roaring battle was winding down all around him but he could clearly hear the hollow shouts coming from the interior of the tank. Happy shouts of the victors.

Helpless, pinned in the rubble, his rifle crushed, his radio broken, out of grenades, Broker watched the guy looking out the hatch engage in a spirited discussion with his crew mates about how best to squash this most stupid of long-nosed foreign dummies.

And then, through eyes teared to glue by brick dust and sweat, young Phil Broker witnessed a scene from a 1950s newsreel out of Budapest. A gaunt figure in dusty American olive drab sprinted up and across the rubble. He clutched a smoking wine bottle cocked back in his right hand.

At first the North Vietnamese tanker laughed at this puny intruder but then very quickly he popped back into his steel shell as Lt. Col. Cyrus LaPorte came straight in at a dead run, let out a chilling rebel yell as he hurled the Molotov.

Broker watched the bottle arc gracefully through the congested air and splash into flame against the side of the T-54. He inhaled an explosive rush of basic American gumption and gasoline.

The flames jump-started a machine gunner in the tank, who went seriously to work. LaPorte danced for a moment, in very uncolonel-like glee for a fortyish West Pointer, as rounds sprayed the loose bricks around his feet, drawing the fire away from Broker.

Then the turret cannon poked in LaPorte's direction. That's when Major Pryce's square body appeared over a collapsed wall thirty meters away with a LAW on his shoulder. The back blast raised a cloud of smoke and dust. The antitank round slammed into the T-54. A tread cracked off. The tank wallowed, stymied in the debris. Pryce waved to LaPorte, tossed off the Law canister, and swung his M-16 from his shoulder to cover the burning tank. LaPorte unslung his rifle and scanned the smoking concrete wasteland for NVA infantry.

And Staff Sergeant Tarantuna, Adonis-tall and athletic, weighted down with his bag of explosives, broke through the smoke, running in tandem with a short wiry South Vietnamese in tiger-stripe fatigues.

Broker heard human sounds chorus quickly to a shriek inside the burning tank. The hatch flipped open. A boil of oily smoke obscured his line of sight. Pryce's rifle squeezed off laconic semi-automatic rounds.

But then Sergeant "Tuna" and Colonel Trin were scrambling across the rubble and kneeling next to him. Tuna grinned as he heaved his bag off his shoulder. "I say fuck him. He's just a brown bar lieutenant."

"He's got the radio," said Trin, also wearing a deranged blood sport grin.

"Radio's busted," croaked Broker, who was newer to this war business than they were and who definitely wasn't grinning. He'd been thrown to these wolves in a little town named Dong Ha up on the DMZ before the offensive. About two weeks after he arrived he looked through the mist on Good Friday morning and saw thousands of NVA and hundreds of tanks coming straight at him. They had been coming nonstop for a month.

"Then fuck him," said Trin in the perfect unaccented English he'd acquired as an undergraduate in America.

"Actually," said Tuna, "we figured you'd had it after we got split up. But you know Mama Pryce and Trin here, they insisted we come back to look for you."

But Broker was awed, far gone in distracted shock, watching LaPorte. The colonel danced a tight little victory jig in front of the burning tank and shook his fists at the smoke-stained sky. "All my life I wanted to do this. Nail a fucking Russian tank with a gas bottle. I feel like a fucking . . . Hungarian."

"Where the hell you get the Molotov, Cyrus?" yelled Pryce.

"Over there, some collapsed hooch. There was a can of gas and a wine bottle. So I shredded a battle dressing for a wick. Worked like a dream." A triumphant grin knifed across LaPorte's lean Creole face. The whole front had collapsed, a rout was in progress. LaPorte was smiling.

Then, his local celebration spent, he swung his pale eyes to where Broker was entombed in cement. "Area's crawling with NVA. How bad is it?" he yelled.

Tuna studied the slab of concrete angling down over Broker. "Looks to me like he's got a ton of cement pinning his legs."

"I can wiggle my legs," Broker said hopefully. "It's like I'm stuck."

"How is he?" yelled Pryce, jogging up to the knot of kneeling soldiers.

"He's stuck," crowed Tuna as he spread out gobs of plastic explosive, primer cord, and detonators with blinding dexterity, his brown eyes checking the slab, the angles, the position of Broker's trapped legs.

"He's stuck?" LaPorte laughed like he was delivering a punch line to a really old joke. "Check that out." He pointed through a cloud of smoke. South of the ruined town a flight of American Hueys rocked through the air, dodging small arms fire on their landing approach.

"Last American choppers that'll ever be seen in Quang Tri Province," observed Pryce philosophically.

"You can still make it to the landing zone," said Trin grimly. "I'll stay with Phil."

And Broker watched the three older Americans refuse to dignify Trin's suggestion with a verbal response. They wouldn't leave him. Or Trin. Tuna bent and fussed with his explosives. The others stood guard. There was a nervous moment when some infantrymen came tumbling over the rubble. Trin's men. The only organized resistance left in the town.

LaPorte, Pryce, Tuna, and Broker were all that was left of the advisory team assigned to the South Vietnamese regiment commanded by Nguyen Van Trin.

Now the American advisors were being airlifted, leaving the South Vietnamese to survive as best they could. There was still time for LaPorte, Pryce, and Tuna to make it out.

"Can you do it, Jimmy?" asked LaPorte.

Tuna gnawed his lip. "It's a tricky one." He jammed small lumps of explosive at one end of the slab, squinting at the configuration.

"Jesus," muttered Broker.

Pryce put a steady hand on his shoulder. "We'll get you out, son." Then he removed a French fag from the gold cigarette case he always carried in his chest pocket, lit it, and stuck it in Broker's lips.

Fighting in the ruined town they had all acquired a sidelong nervous aspect— heads constantly rotating, eyes sliding to the edges of their sockets. Broker had come to think of them as three stern uncles. LaPorte being the brilliant one and Pryce the older, wiser, steady one. Tuna was the dark indispensable joker, with a bag full of magic, who would give you a hot foot.

And Trin was the strangest man Broker had ever met.

"Okay," said Tuna. "Now, after the bang, this hunk of shit is going to levitate two feet in the air on this end, turn ninety degrees on the fulcrum of the other end, and fall to earth three feet from your right boot."

"Right," said Broker in a shaky voice because they had all taken off their flak vests and were packing them around his face and torso and crotch.

"Young man," LaPorte encouraged, "if you had a hard on, Jimmy could blow your left testicle past your dick without disturbing it and put it through the hole Pryce punched in the side of that tank."

"Absolutely," grinned Jimmy Tuna. "But we will all step back a few paces and watch from a safe distance."

So what do you do when you have time to watch yourself die. You lick your dry caked lips and you whisper the Lord's Prayer, except when you see the snaky hiss chase down the det cord fuse you shut your eyes and scream . . .

The shock put both of Broker's legs to sleep. When the smoke cleared the huge piece of cement was exactly where Jimmy said it would be. Broker reached. His testicles were still attached.

"Now what?" asked Major Pryce as he and LaPorte lifted a dazed Broker and dragged him along, one of his arms over each of their shoulders. Trin's men threw an infantry screen around them as they plodded toward a column of refugees and retreating ARVN soldiers.

"What have we got left, Trin?" asked LaPorte.

"A battalion, plus all the stragglers we can round up," said Trin.

"There's some time. The fuckers are consolidating after taking the town. We have to mount a rear guard so these refugees can get south to Hue City," said LaPorte. In the distance they all saw the flight of helicopters take to the air, lifting out the American advisors. "Pussies," sneered LaPorte softly.

Trin had his map out. Strung between LaPorte and Pryce, Broker watched them decide on a chokepoint: a bridge on a river a mile south of the town. And that's exactly what they did. For twenty-four mad hours they held Highway One south of the smoking pile of bricks that had been Quang Tri City. Thousands of refugees and dispirited ARVN soldiers crossed that bridge to an illusion of safety. Then Jimmy Tuna blew it under the first T-54 stupid enough to attempt to cross.

They walked to Hue City with barely a hundred men, all that remained of Trin's regiment. Back home the public didn't know. They didn't care.

The army knew. LaPorte's Stand added another flourish to his legend. They said he was on a fast track to being General of the Army. A West Point maverick out of New Orleans, he vowed to stay in Vietnam to the very end, with Tuna and Pryce and Col. Trin. And it was at the very end that Broker was invited back into the company of these "Last Dogs" to aid in the Evacuation. And that's when LaPorte's career was virtually destroyed and Broker, Tuna, and Trin narrowly missed dying.

Nina's father brought them all down when he went into business for himself and died in dishonor.

Broker had been briefly stationed at Fort Benning with Ray Pryce and had met his family and had supper at his home. After Pryce's death, in the awkwardness of youth, and believing that the sins of fathers should not be visited on children, Broker had tried to be a comfort to the dead man's family when all their other friends shunned them.

After that visit, Nina kept track of him. She'd written long tortured letters to him throughout her adolescence. Then she'd run away from home in Michigan at sixteen, hitchhiked to Minnesota, and presented herself in the midst of Broker's falling marriage. With her mother's permission, he gave her shelter for the entire summer before her senior year in high school. J.T. Merryweather pointed out that the gawky teenage girl was the straw that broke the bitch's back and sank Broker's marriage. J.T. thought it was a good thing—Broker got free and Nina straightened out. For a while.

Smart as hell, she finished her undergraduate studies at the University of Michigan in three years. Broker attended her graduation. Nobody was surprised when she squared away the huge chip on her shoulder and enlisted in the army. The new volunteer army required some of the old action and needed a certain kind of young person to stiffen its ranks. The kind of kid who'll walk out there and stick her finger in some roadkill. Nina had been like that at twenty-one.

Cards came at Christmas and always on his birthday. And he'd read about her and seen her on the network news after Desert Storm.

Then, last January, she flipped out again and emerged like a Valkyrie, riding a blizzard that roared in from Wisconsin.

Unable to locate him, she had pestered J.T., who, in an uncharacteristic lapse, gave in and passed on Broker's Stillwater number—a mistake—because he was using the house to set up a ring of outlaw bikers. So he met her in a restaurant in Hudson, Wisconsin, a little to the south and across the St. Croix River. She had driven straight through the storm, rounding Chicago from Ann Arbor, where she was going to graduate school.

She was an obsessed, compulsive mess.

She'd had two severe blows in two years. Her unpleasant exit from the army, then her mother's death. Leukemia.

She didn't talk about that. Instead, she was back in the past, fixated on her father. She talked about "the cover-up."

And Broker explained patiently; he'd been there when it happened and at the classified hearings afterwards. He was no fan of any organization, certainly not the U.S. Army, but the investigation had been thorough. He couldn't get through to her. From the time that she was a little girl, Nina believed fanatically that the army had it wrong. Now she added a new twist. She believed her dad had been scapegoated by Cyrus LaPorte.

It was a hard sell. In Broker's book, Caesar's wife was more reproachable than Cyrus LaPorte.

But Nina had made contact with Jimmy Tuna, who had failed big time as a civilian and had killed a guard and wounded several bystanders during a bungled bank robbery in New York in 1976. He was tried and sentenced to twenty to thirty in the Milan Federal Penitentiary in Michigan. He'd been there nineteen years. Last January Nina had "discovered" him.

She had expected Broker to drop everything and come to Michigan—he could get an interview with Tuna, she said. She had this deranged notion that Tuna would only talk to him, Broker, his former comrade in arms.

And him thinking. Twenty years, Nina. Twenty goddamn years ago. In plain language, Broker had told her to grow up. She called him a "chickenshit bastard" and stormed off. Watching her leave he had to admit that she had grown up. He also discovered that she had an effect on him. She had this way of getting under his skin.

Broker sat up in bed and groaned, and not because of his aching thumb. He definitely didn't want to deal with it. He had other problems. It had levels. It involved his core beliefs. No fucking way.

*   *   *

Morning was a renewal of small engines. Lawnmowers and a chain-saw growled somewhere—the first green, gasoline, and grass-scented blast of summer. A rectangle of sunlight fell through the open hospital room window and rapped him on the forehead. He opened his fogged eyes and smelled coffee. Nina held the cup to him. She had changed out of her trashy outfit and had washed her face. Now she wore faded tomboy jeans, a washed-out green cotton blouse with ruffles, and beat-up tennis shoes. A storm of tired freckles prickled her obvious hangover. He looked at her and some perverse part of his brain that lacked common sense was hearing "Greensleeves."

"How do you feel?" she asked.

"All right." Broker's wooden tongue batted furball words. He took the cup in his right hand.

"Good," said Nina as she looked him over like a piece of busted equipment, estimating its longevity.

Then she had to be questioned by ATF while Broker debriefed with Ed Ryan. When Ed left, they cleaned and splinted and rebandaged the thumb. He received a prescription for an antibiotic the doctor affectionately called "gorrillacilian." The doctor told him he could ease the pain by putting his hand on his head. The stitches could come out in two weeks. He should have full use of the thumb in two months. The knuckle joint and tendons were basically intact. The problem was infection.

They released Broker from the hospital at nine A.M. An unmarked squad car drove them to a pharmacy, where he filled his prescription, then to the sheriff's office in the new brick county government complex. They brought him in through the garage and up a back stairwell so that no one would see him.

10

WHEN BROKER STARTED AS A ST. PAUL COP, HIS MOTHER, Irene, had expressed disapproval that he'd misconstrued all the lore she'd fed him with her mother's milk. "Just . . . contrary," she said sadly. "You go to Vietnam when everybody else is leaving and now this." His dad, Mike, had scratched his cheek and said, "I think she wanted you to be a college professor. Something like that."

Broker hadn't worn a uniform for almost twelve years. From the beginning he'd excelled at working alone. His flair for one-man undercover investigations resulted in invidious Serpico jokes and a detective's badge and eventually a unique job offer and promotion to detective lieutenant from the Minnesota Bureau of Criminal Apprehension.

He targeted drugs and illegal weapons. A free agent, he putted through Minnesota counties in his handyman's truck. He coordinated with sheriff's departments, county task forces, the attorney general's office and the feds, usually DEA and ATF.

Automatic military assault weapons were showing up on the street in Minnesota. Broker had been using Washington County, east of the Twin Cities on the Wisconsin border, as a base because Rodney lived there. On this case, he reported to the Washington County sheriff.

As he climbed the stairs he took a deep breath. He hadn't been in the BCA office in St. Paul for two years. He had never set foot in this county building beyond the garage, where he kept his personal vehicle. He had an unreasonable reaction to offices that bordered on claustrophobia.

It was worse now that the jargon and techniques of corporate voodoo had crept into police work. Now they had "solvability tables" to evaluate cases. His dad, who had been driven out of law enforcement by paperwork, called it flatassitis. Male Brokers were genetically resistant to it.

He averted his face from the security camera mounted in the corridor and went through the locked door into the squadroom. The tightness hairballed in his stomach. His ex, Kimberly, had wanted him to be a clotheshorse cop and play department politics. Wanted him to work in an office. Deputy chief maybe. Then run for politics.

He glanced around nervously. *Here come the Lilliputians with a million yards of thread. And the mimeo paper. Death by paper cut. Don't bunch up, boys—they'll get you all with one memo.*

J.T. Merryweather and Ryan were going over paperwork with a couple of Washington County detectives in a makeshift command post in a corner of the investigative unit. They'd nailed Rodney's cohorts and the lab in Pine County at the same time that Earl and company went down. They looked like they'd slept in their shirts.

"In case you're confused at your surroundings, this is a police station," joked J.T. with his sharp features shuffled in a touchy mix of Caribbean and Saracen razor blades. "You notice the modular office spacers designed to promote efficiency, the tidy stacks of paperwork, the new computer system with which we try to keep cowboys in the field legal."

Broker's slightly feverish eyes roamed over the off-white computer plastic that packed the room. The stuff reminded him of the armor worn by the Imperial storm troopers in *Star Wars*. Now the fuckers had occupied every office in America.

He thrust his bandage, big thumbs up. "Two months medical leave. Without me out there, you guys will be breaking down the wrong doors. I can see it in the papers—Waco North." A chorus of groans came from the tired cops.

J.T. rose to his feet and shook Nina's hand. "Been a while, Captain Pryce."

"Ten years, J.T., and it's just plain Nina."

"I was rooting for you when you were on TV. Other than having super bad timing yesterday, how'd you turn out?"

"Broker thinks I'm crazy."

"Uh-huh. How's that man going to know from crazy. C'mon, I'll get your things from the property room."

John Eisenhower appeared in the hall and motioned to Broker to join him in his office. The sheriff's gun belt lay on a chair under a

Norman Rockwell print of a Depression-era cop and a runaway kid sharing adjoining stools at a soda fountain. John had affected a folksy touch now that he was out in the eastern burbs. But Broker knew him from St. Paul, a cop right down to his depleted uranium heart. Broker sat down. This little color-coded laminated card with a fingerprint lay on the desk facing the visitor's chair. *Test your stress level*.

They talked shop for a few minutes. Would Rodney handle in a continuing sting? Ryan wanted to use him to check out the gang-bangers over north in Minneapolis. Broker was unsympathetic to the notion. Rodney was an infant monster. He should be chained up in a damp, leaky basement in Stillwater Prison and bricked over until he resembled a cavefish. Eisenhower's china-blue eyes circled above the fruitless conversation, watching Broker. He ended by saying, "Sorry about the thumb, but you need some time off . . ." He paused, eyes probing.

Broker deflected the close attention to detail in the sheriff's eyes. It was a game they had played off and on for more than a decade of working together. Eisenhower was an excellent administrator who'd never lost the touch of a field man. And he had the confidence to tolerate the idiosyncrasies of a brilliant subordinate, which he knew Broker to be. He'd brought Broker in as a deep undercover, unknown, in the beginning, even to his own investigative unit, answerable only to himself. But he didn't *understand* Broker.

John had done his time working undercover. A good undercover man should be able to fool the assholes, who were not thinking too clearly to begin with. But Broker could fool anybody, even very smart people. And he did it by boldly being himself, which is to say, by being blunt as a locked safe. Sometimes John thought Broker was really presenting his true undercover act when he was in an office, like now. And this disquieted John.

Not even scary J.T. Merryweather, who had partnered with Broker in St. Paul, who was as remote and hostile as a man could be, and who was the only human that Broker minimally confided in, knew the whole story behind Phil Broker.

Several years back, in St. Paul, John had asked a sharp, no-nonsense, female FBI psychologist, who had dated Broker, why she thought he was a cop and where he got his style. The woman, who profiled criminal pathology for a living, had obviously thought about this before and took her time responding.

John Eisenhower, who had graduate degrees in criminology and sociology hanging on his wall, was still disturbed and intrigued by her answer, which he remembered almost verbatim: "Broker got stung somewhere in his background and will not discuss it. Period. As to why he's a cop—that's easy. Phil's a fugitive from modern psychology. He's a romantic primitive who loves to hunt monsters. He expects them. Monsters were in the fairy tales he'd been taught as a child. Grendel in *Beowulf* was not a victim of domestic abuse or faulty nurturing. He's a cautionary totemic being, representing evil, greed, violence, and excess. He believes in monsters because only heroes can stop them. So he can't conceive of living without a weapon and pair of handcuffs in case he encounters one in the checkout line at the grocery.

She'd thrown in a bittersweet spark of intuition: "In a world of monsters, boys can climb the beanstalk and sail for Treasure Island and contend for the hand of a princess. And what are monsters anyway . . . except adults as seen through the brave eyes of a child."

The moment passed. Eisenhower resumed his practical gaze and said: "We pulled a background check on the girl. She won a Silver Star and a Purple Heart in the Gulf. So that's Nina Pryce."

Broker nodded. "I was in the army with her father."

Conversation paused a beat. The only thing Eisenhower knew about Broker's army time was typed in impressive blank verse on his DD214. "Just bad timing, the way she turned up, huh?" he asked, but his eyes said, *Broker, you've been out there too long running your lone wolf number. The girl was a slip.*

He rose to his feet and clapped Broker on the shoulder. "The girl and the thumb threw a funny bounce into things. Your act is blown."

Broker shrugged. "We'll see."

Eisenhower nodded. Decided not to push it. "Get lost, heal up. You going up north?"

"Yeah."

"How's your dad doing?"

"Okay."

"I'll tell BCA to send your checks to Devil's Rock. Rodney and his crew were good for thirty machine guns statewide. A new record for you. Good job, Broker."

Nina and J.T. were waiting in the hall outside the office. Merryweather's droll sneer approximated a smile. "Day is getting closer. Somebody like John's going to put you in one of these office chairs, put you back in uniform, put you through die-versity training and get you trampled by the poe-litically correct pygmy armies like the rest of us."

"I love you too," said Broker.

"Don't forget to write." J.T. blew a kiss. He shook Nina's hand and strolled back into the office.

Without comment, Broker walked directly to the police garage. Nina quick-stepped to keep up, dragging her luggage. He pulled a tarp from his Lincoln Green '94 Cherokee Sport. In contrast to the house on the north end, the car was scrupulously clean.

"Are you in trouble?" she asked.

Broker shrugged and grumbled, "They all think I've been under too long, want to bring me in. Probably figure I'm suffering from Stockholm Syndrome. Starting to identify with the assholes."

"So what do we do now?" she asked.

"We?" said Broker dubiously.

"Somebody followed me from New Orleans. Remember."

"Okay . . . and what were you doing in New Orleans?" Broker recited in a tired voice, remembering the green nose of the Saturn peeking around the corner and its stealthy withdrawal, knowing full well that her personal devil, Cyrus LaPorte, lived in New Orleans.

"I guess Jimmy Tuna sent me."

"Oh yeah?" Broker felt a sinking sensation that it wasn't going away this time.

"We're buds now that he's dying of cancer."

Broker raised an eyebrow. The Tuna he remembered had the constitution of an Italian mule.

"Bone cancer. Came on real quick. Real nasty. He, ah, sold me something, you could say." She reached in her portfolio and withdrew a wrinkled printed page and handed it to Broker.

He unfolded a page from an April copy of *Newsweek*, a page of news briefs. Two pictures were circled in black magic marker. One showed the spare, distinguished features of Gen. Cyrus LaPorte, U.S. Army, Ret. The other was of a sleek, white, unusually outfitted ocean-going vessel. The headline said: COLD WARRIOR MAKES AMENDS.

Broker read the lead, "Gen. Cyrus LaPorte of Vietnam fame and scion of a wealthy New Orleans family has been playing Cousteau. His latest project has him loaning his personal oceanographic vessel, the *Lola*, to Greenpeace to conduct pollution surveys off the coast of Vietnam in the wake of stories of unrestricted oil drilling . . ."

"He *sold* you?" Broker narrowed his eyes as he scanned the rest of the article.

"That's right. That page, for five grand. And this note was in the envelope he left me." She handed Broker a folded sheet of notebook paper. It contained three stark sentences scrawled in a shaky hand: "Find Broker." Under it. "Have Broker find Trin. All arranged." Numbers. And one more word, underlined, like a punch in the nose: "Hue."

Trin. Jesus Christ. Broker staggered back a step, blinking.

"So here I am," said Nina with a shrug. "I found you but I just lost him."

"Tuna?"

"He skipped town on me. He's out, early medical release because of the cancer. He disappeared with five thousand bucks of my money."

"You got robbed by a guy dying of cancer in prison. Wonderful."

"I wrote him a check. For his funeral expenses, I thought. He switched release dates on me. When he didn't show up I thought he might be in New Orleans . . ."

He stared at her. She wasn't dumb. Yesterday people could have been hurt, maybe killed, as a result of her cavalier walk-on appearance. No. It's just that her wild fantasy was more important.

She went to the back of the truck and tried to open the hatchback door.

"What are you doing?" Broker demanded.

"Loading my stuff."

"Uh-uh. Not this time. Look. My dad's . . . busted up. He and Irene are in a real financial jam. I need to spend some time alone with them—"

"You're alone with everybody always!" She stepped forward and lifted her chin aggressively. "I talked to J.T. while you were in the office. He says you're so far out there they're thinking of sending you to a shrink. You haven't had a performance review in two years because you refuse to show up at your supervisor's office. I wonder? Could it have something to do with what happened twenty years ago? That you refuse to deal with. You could be anything, but you make a career of hiding out and setting people up, gaining their trust and then busting them."

Unconsciously, Broker patted his chest pocket for a cigarette. Nina reached in her purse and passed him the crumpled Gauloises. *Hennessey cognac and the French fags*—Broker had a precise memory of the last time he'd seen Ray Pryce take a Gauloises from the gold cigarette case that his wife, Marian, had given him. They were standing on the rolling deck of a Vietnamese minesweep that lay off the coast of Vietnam; it was April 29, 1975.

Just like Ray used to do, Broker tapped the short, fat French cigarette on his thumbnail and put it to his lips. Nina clicked the lighter and stated, "Dammit, don't you get it. General LaPorte's been over there posing as an environmentalist taking pictures of the bottom of the South China Sea."

Broker inhaled the strong tobacco and tightened the bolts on his masking smile to ward off Nina's raving attempt to raise the dead. More than that, he resented her confident quick-study routine. Her zeal. Her confidence. She was starting to have that *effect* on him. The urge to prove her wrong was almost a sneer behind his lips.

"He found it, that's what Tuna's getting at," she asserted. "I have a map with a coordinate. I have a sonar image of a wrecked U.S. Army Chinook helicopter, laying in one hundred feet of water off the coast of central Vietnam. I snuck it from LaPorte's office last night in New Orleans. That's why he's after me. The genie is out of the bottle, Broker."

"The Hue gold," said Broker in a hollow voice.

"The Hue gold. Ten tons of it. Which my father *did not* steal."

11

FOR ALL HE KNEW, THE HUE GOLD REALLY WAS A MYTH. HE had, after all, never actually seen it. No one had. But that one elongated syllable—gold—got stuck in his ears and reverberated in the drafty acoustics of the underground garage.

And, damn, the confident look on her face pissed him off. Watching him nibble around the hook. Finally he put the note in his pocket and grumbled, "You better come with me."

She nodded, loaded her bags, and hopped into the Jeep.

Broker pulled into a FINA station, filled the Cherokee with super unleaded and continued through town without speaking. Tuna alone he could discount. But Tuna *and* Trin ... He stopped at a tobacco shop and bought a carton of cigarettes, American Spirits.

"Starting smoking again, huh? You nervous?" said Nina.

"They don't have chemical additives. They're good for you."

"I get it. Health food cigarettes—"

"Shut up," said Broker.

At his place, he ignored several neighbors who came out to stare at him. Stepping around smashed furniture, Nina heated water and made instant coffee. They took the coffee into his backyard and gazed down the river valley.

"Aren't you going to clean up?" she asked.

"Up north."

"What about breakfast?"

"We'll stop on the road. Right now I just want to get out of town."

"Oh. Look."

Five carnival-striped hot air balloons, which had launched out of

Lakeland, south of town, sailed low up the river. Absurd embellishments presented on the day, Broker thought that they should trail "Monty Python Flying Circus" captions. Like the number five written in the sky . . .

There had been five of them. Ray was dead. Tuna was dying. That left three . . . What it would be like, seeing LaPorte after all these years?

He had glimpsed him occasionally on television. Usually on MacNeil-Lehrer, brought on as a military expert during Grenada, Beirut, Panama, the Gulf War. He had a reputation as a frosty critic of the overreliance on technology in the touchy-feely volunteer army.

Slowly Broker withdrew the folded piece of notebook paper from his pocket and smoothed it on his thigh.

Find Trin.

He looked up. Nina watched him carefully fold the note and tuck it in his chest pocket. "Well, *I'm* going to take a shower, after I pour some Spic 'n' Span in the tub," she said.

Alone in the backyard, he lit a Spirit and sipped his coffee and watched the airships trail over him like gaudy pageantry. Their shadows billowed over his shrubbery and one shadow swallowed him briefly before it passed on.

Broker had accustomed himself to pulling the blinds of his life to ply his trade in darkness. Now, with Nina's sudden intrusion in his life, he was confronted with the naggingly obvious thought he always avoided: The darkness might just be a shadow cast by an object, in this case, an unresolved event.

Even calloused by almost two decades of police work, he had never made peace with Ray Pryce's desertion. He had come to view this as an emotional difficulty that flew in the face of evidence. It was probably the motive behind his continued association with the dead man's crazy daughter. Now maybe he had a chance to lay it to rest. Remove the object. The thought was too big. Magical in its simplicity.

But Nina's assertion that LaPorte was somehow to blame was sheer fantasy. Broker had seen LaPorte literally sacrifice his career at the inquest in an attempt to salvage Pryce's reputation.

Even Jimmy Tuna, who had joked about growing up in a New York Mafia family, and whom LaPorte had expertly kept on a leash, never struck Broker as being capable of deserting a buddy in wartime.

Trin . . .

On the night of April 29, 1975, Broker had gone into Hue City to rescue the always mysterious Colonel Trin . . . or so he thought at the time.

Gold. There was that syllable again. What if LaPorte *was* on a treasure hunt.

Maybe I could cut myself in. He had Nina's paranoia as an entry. Somebody had to return LaPorte's maps . . .

He shook his head, annoyed at the way his imagination broke into a canter. And he was suddenly angry that these men, living, dying, and dead, whom he had known on two brief occasions, were still the planets exerting an influence on his life.

He took out the note again, got up, went into the destroyed kitchen, and stared at the telephone. He cocked an ear and determined that the shower was running upstairs. His hand shook as he picked up the phone and punched information and worked through the voice tapes until he had an overseas operator.

"What country?"

"Vietnam, Hue City," said Broker in a dry voice.

"You can dial direct."

The parts of Broker that lived in the present collided with the parts he kept ice cold on meathooks. He lit another Spirit off the half-burned stub of the one he had going. A film of sweat formed on his palms as he found the international code in the phone book. Just written right there. Vietnam: 11. What do you know. He punched in the number.

Seconds later a Vietnamese voice said hello on the other side of the world. Some hotel, "Hue," he recognized.

He slammed the phone into the cradle as though it was hot.

Crazy.

But he copied the number onto several cards in his wallet for safe-keeping. Broker stored his passport in the freezer of his refrigerator as a precaution against losing it. He opened the icebox and retrieved the frozen document and weighed it in his palm. Then he slid it into the back pocket of his jeans. Now what? He seesawed back and forth. Planets in a tug of war.

It was too much. Twenty years of habit squirmed at this budding heresy and he retreated into the comfort of denial.

She was nuts. Probably still bent out of shape from the army thing.

On the second day of Desert Storm, Capt. Nina Pryce, in charge of a military police company trailing the advance of the 24th Mech. across the Iraqi desert, strayed in a sandstorm, got separated from her troops, and had driven her humvee into a nasty situation that had developed between a lost company of the 24th and a bypassed Republican Guard battalion.

It was an unusual, low-tech close-quarters fight for that "clean" desert cakewalk. A meeting engagement in the blinding sand. Nina arrived to find the company commander and his lieutenants down. A lucky shot had taken out the command vehicle. Communications were snarled. The Iraqis were encircling.

As ranking officer, and by force of example, she took command and proved to be utterly ruthless in action. Instinctively, she led the company in a charge through the encirclement, and reversed the tactical situation and attacked the Iraqis in the rear. The Iraqis, surprised when their pincers closed on empty desert, disintegrated. It took less than an hour. When communications were restored, Nina's M-16 was smoking hot, she had wounds in her left hip and over one hundred Republican Guards were dead and three hundred were prisoners. She lost five men, and took twenty-three wounded, six of whom she had personally dragged out of the line of fire.

Word got out and CNN found her in an unpleasant mood at an aid station after she'd been chewed out for exceeding her authority by a colonel who didn't have the full picture. Nina, always more salty than demure when her ire was stirred up, made a crack, not realizing that the video was rolling. A reporter asked what had happened out there. Nina replied, "Not much, except that if I had a dick I'd probably be a major."

The remark wouldn't die and was rebroadcast endlessly in the media. Sometimes bleeped, sometimes not. It hounded her, but she kept her professional cool, refused to comment, just doing her job. The real firestorm torched off months later. A ranking congresswoman joined forces with some retired generals and used Nina as a stalking horse to pose an inevitable question.

Nina had brilliantly commanded infantry in close-quarters ground combat, even after sustaining wounds. She had personally killed some of the bad guys and had saved some of the good guys and she had won.

They recommended that she be awarded the Combat Infantry Badge for her actions in the Gulf. Fed by rhetorical gasoline from army hard-liners on the one side and Tailhook-impassioned feminists on the other, the dispute rocketed onto national television. More than one TV commentator remarked about Nina's "star quality."

The U.S. Army wasn't impressed. It closed ranks. Someone in the Pentagon took the low road and fed the media a murky snippet about how her father died in the process of deserting his comrades under fire.

The high-road resistance simply stated that a woman had never been awarded the CIB. Technically, Nina wasn't eligible. The award was reserved for infantry and women weren't allowed in the infantry. She could have her Silver Star and her Purple Heart but the CIB was high sacrilege. It would crack open the combat arms to the libbers. Two hundred years of tradition fell on Nina Pryce.

Approached by the press, she coolly pointed out that there was a lot of medal inflation in the Gulf ground war, which had lasted all of four days against human sea attacks of surrendering Iraqis. Her dad, she said, had spent six months under fire against a real army to earn his CIB in Europe. Her response prompted questions about her father and rumors of secret hearings. Her father, she charged, had been falsely convicted in absentia. After laying down that challenge to the army she quietly resigned her commission.

Broker wanted to believe that the combined effect of her resignation and her mother's passing had snapped her. He shook his head. He didn't really know her.

He did know that when she arrived she set up dominion. She was *somebody*. And she had something that was taking on an irresistible momentum.

Find Broker. Have Broker find Trin. All arranged. Written in a dead man's hand.

12

BROKER CALLED HIS FOLKS AND TOLD THEM HE WAS COMING up, and that he had Nina Pryce with him. Then he loaded a quick travel bag and slapped his cell phone into the Jeep glove compartment. As they pulled out of the drive he glowered at Nina as she warily swiveled her head, scouting the street. "You have your gun, right?" she said.

"Don't start. Not yet," said Broker.

He drove downtown to the business district, pulled in back of a row of brick storefronts and took his Thermos into a coffee shop and had it filled with strong French roast. Nina stayed at his side. Getting back into the car, she lightened up a tad. She laughed when she saw a riverboat churn through the old railroad lift bridge that crossed the St. Croix, and the tourists wandering the waterfront pavilions of an art fair and the church steeples that dotted the bluff. "Jeez, Broker, you wound up in a Grandma Moses painting. This isn't you. Uh-uh."

He wanted to strangle her. He wanted his quiet underground life back.

She poured coffee in the Thermos cup and held it for him so he could drive one-and-a-half-handed. He hotfooted it up Highway 95 through the river valley and turned east twenty minutes later, crossing the St. Croix River at Osceola, Wisconsin. Now he took less traveled State 35 up the Wisconsin side. He liked driving this particular road, finding comfort in the way the fields, forest, farms, and small towns stayed frozen in time.

He rolled down the window and felt summer heat crowd in the new foliage along the tree lines and smelled it trickle in damp waves across the new-plowed fields. He'd always had too much imagination and that complicated a cop's instinctive aversion to hot summer nights and full moons. He glanced over at Nina, who had finally yielded to fatigue and yesterday's whiskey and had fallen asleep in the warm sunlight. No, it started before he was a cop. It was his experience that murderous folly flocked in the tropical heat.

The red Georgia dirt was ninety-eight degrees in the shade on the day that Broker went to visit Nina Pryce, in July 1975, on officer's row at Fort Benning. Vietnam was finally done and the flags sagged on the lanyards across the base in the heavy doldrums of defeat.

They were bleak, the houses where the army boards its majors, especially when all the furniture has been removed and the family of a man who will not return from war stands in the empty rooms for the last time.

And the empty rooms were worse when the army moved you out with the cold, efficient energy of censure.

She was nine years old, carrot-topped, with big knees and big gray eyes and braces on her teeth. Her mother's face conveyed a look of absent practicality that wondered: How can I afford the braces now? Her brother sat outside in the car, his head buried in a comic book. Nina stood fiercely at her mother's side.

Marian Pryce was alone. No neighbors had come with casseroles and no children played in the street. The moving van sat in the driveway like the bogeyman.

The officer who faced Marian and her daughter was not a chaplain, but was instead a sassy second lieutenant from the base coordinator's office turned out in glossy leather, starched fatigues, and a laminated helmet liner. Instead of solace, he held a clipboard in his hand. He toured the quarters entering checkmarks on his clipboard, making sure Marian and her two children had not "stolen" anything from the federal government.

The investigation was over and now Ray Pryce's family was being escorted off the base and out of the army.

The little girl had stood up to the starched martinet and stated in a steady, precocious voice: "If my dad is dead in the war he should have a flag even if you can't find his body."

The second lieutenant was a real prick who did not do her the courtesy of meeting her eyes. His pencil scratched on the clipboard and his voice was another cruel dismissal in official language: "Your father is not authorized a flag because his service wasn't honorable."

Perhaps Nina's personality was formed at that moment. She kicked the lieutenant in the shin, carefully hitting him above his boot leather so it'd hurt.

And 1st Lt. Phillip Broker, twenty-three years old, a lean, scorched splinter thrown off from the recent catastrophe in Southeast Asia, who was almost senseless from a week of testifying and being questioned by army lawyers, and whose angry confused attempts to defend Nina's absent father only stacked the evidence against him, Phillip Broker said good-bye to the army.

The method he chose was to take the lieutenant and throw him bodily through the front door and send him sprawling on the sidewalk. Then he stomped his Corcoran jump boot down on the clipboard and smashed it to smithereens. The lieutenant opted for a retrograde maneuver, ass backward through the nearest shrubbery.

Marian Pryce, sensing that Broker was necessary to her daughter at this moment, signaled with her dry eyes and took a last cardboard box from the kitchen counter and carried it out the door. The moving van pulled away. Marian waited in her car.

Nina stood her ground, defiantly alone in the empty house. Broker, knowing nothing of children, knelt and said to her, "I want you to walk out of here like you own the place."

To underscore the point, Broker had escorted her down the rows of houses to a playground. They sat in the swings and their heels made swirls in the hot, chalky-red dust. Nina said nothing. Her large eyes roved the base, vacuuming in detail.

And then Broker had said the words that he'd come to regret: "If you ever need anything, you know, help, come find me."

She'd nodded solemnly. Down the block, her mother blew the horn. Nina's eyes were fixed in a stare across an empty parade field, on a limp American flag hanging in the dripping heat.

13

LIKE THE DOCTOR SAID, BROKER'S HAND DID NOT THROB SO badly when he put it on top of his head. It was awkward driving this way and for the moment, with Nina asleep, he didn't feel so foolish, but the posture suggested the gesture of a slow-witted man pondering an enormous dilemma.

Which wasn't that far off, the dilemma part. Easiest thing would be to reject her story wholesale. Just not think about it.

Drawing strength from the premise of leaving the past undisturbed, he sketched out what he would do: first off, *not get mad* at her. How was she to know he'd be working. Talk to her, humor her and then, at the right time, gently hand her off to a professional. He knew people. It would have to be a woman, but it was a stretch finding a woman therapist qualified to appreciate the lonely piece of ground that Nina had staked out for herself.

Problem being, what *she* needed for a shrink was a bare-ass Celtic warrior-priestess with her nipples dunked in blue woad.

She was like him. Therapy was for other people, people who worked in offices. Got a personal problem? Tell it to the chaplain. In other words: tough shit. His eyes darted to the rearview mirror. He had seen the Saturn yesterday. Damn if he hadn't caught some of her contagious paranoia.

He was well beyond the city traffic now and the limboland where tract houses chewed into tree lines. He smelled fresh manure and the contours of freshly plowed fields eased his eyes. A tiny green John Deere tractor dragged a mustard sail across the horizon.

Gripping the wheel with his knees, he used his good hand to

adjust the rearview mirror, glanced at Nina, and shook his head. Gingerly he poured some more coffee.

She just had to learn.

That was easy for him to say. She'd watched her mother struggle raising her and her brother, working as a legal secretary in the Detroit suburbs. Before her looks went, Marian Pryce married a lawyer in the office. A practical marriage. So her kids could live in a better neighborhood and attend college. Nina had hated the work-obsessed man, who drank too much and was never home. Her mother pretended not to notice the drinking and started to lose her grip thread by thread. Nina blamed the army lynch mob for that too.

Broker had met the guy at Nina's graduation party and couldn't remember his name. He'd done his family the courtesy of making full partner at the firm before he dropped dead of a massive coronary on the ninth hole of the Bloomfield Hills Country Club.

Broker had played at every kind of jive imaginable in his line of work, but underneath, he'd inherited an eccentric, but rock-solid, conservative foundation. He'd been an only kid raised strict on the hardscrabble glory of the Superior Shore.

Growing up he'd learned that some problems didn't come with answers. No amount of talk would fix the hurt. It just hurt and you lived with the hurt and after a while it became part of you, like a line in your face. When her dad had left him hanging, at first, he refused to believe it. And finally, when there seemed to be no other explanation, he had to stick it in that black hole where there were no answers.

Being in law enforcement, he should have learned. People were capable of anything.

The main trick was not to do anything dumb to make it worse. He repeated this last thought for his own benefit because she had stirred him up. Got him thinking about that mess so long ago. So, fix her with straight talk. Finding her a shrink was just a cop-out. Just have it out with her and bang some sense into her head. He'd had that talk with her years ago when she'd run away from home. It was time for another one.

But Broker couldn't resist reaching over and plucking the *Newsweek* page from her fingers and smoothing it between the seats and reading it again.

Sonofabitch. What if LaPorte *had* found it?

He'd inherited a granite foundation all right, but he hadn't built anything on it. He'd backed into it like a bunker. Now here was this really big idea inviting him to come out and play.

Damn her.

Broker woke Nina in the parking lot of a roadside bar and grill outside Superior, Wisconsin, and said: "Breakfast." Inside, he wanted a table in the rear, behind a partition if possible, where he could rest his bandaged hand on top of his head. He ordered pancakes, eggs, sausage, and a large orange juice.

Nina had a vegetarian omelet and black coffee. She ate quickly, efficiently, taking on fuel as her alert eyes scanned the eatery. When Broker had trouble getting his pancakes into bite-sized hunks with only his fork, she leaned over with her knife and fork and cut his food for him.

"Broker, I feel awful. Walking into . . ."

No she didn't. In a high-stakes game, she'd go for mission over men every time. She was a Pryce. He was her expendable commodity. "Forget it. Probably would have gone down the same anyway. Guy like Earl."

Nina sipped her coffee and her eyes tracked the other diners, came back, and rested on Broker's face. "So what happened to Mike?"

Broker lowered his hand from his head and carefully draped it on the back of a chair. "He took a calculated risk. Then he had an accident and some real bad weather."

He explained the fix they were in. How gradually, working summers, they'd converted their lakeshore into a cabin resort. Built eight cabins. Mike Broker had quit laying stone and went into the resort business full time at the end of the eighties. Built up a pretty good business, too. Then he got the bug and decided to upgrade everything. He figured if he could put in some improvements he could go highball on a mortgage and use the loan to build a snazzy lodge.

"Last year he got an interim construction loan from the bank. Between ice out and fishing opener he planned to reroof all the cabins and put in new plumbing, Jacuzzis, new wood stoves, some ambitious stonework for a new lodge. Once the improvements were in he'd get a better assessment for a mortgage and use the mortgage money to pay off the construction loan and complete the lodge.

"We had a mild winter so in March he hired a big crew, thinking he could gang up all the work. He was supervising a cement pour

and it got away from him. He ruptured himself. And then everything went wrong. When the work crew took him to the hospital a
freak straight-line storm tore in and—well, the cabins were exposed,
most of the roofs were torn off, and the interiors got clobbered by
water damage. The trenching for the plumbing weakened some of
the foundations and they washed out.

"He was laid up in the hospital for three months with complica-
tions. The guy he hired to help Irene salvage the construction got
overextended and the interim loan money ran out. The place was in
shambles and Mike lost the whole season. Bills piled up and now the
bank's breathing down his neck. He started out owning a million
dollars plus a slice of prime shoreline free and clear and now he
could lose it all."

"I have some money," she said.

"Do you have a quarter of a million bucks?"

"No," she said and lowered her eyes for a heartbeat of polite
compassion. She came up iron gray and prima facie. He had given
her more ammunition. He had a need. She had a plan. It could be
desirable. "But I know who does. There should be enough to go
around. Smart guy like you could figure out a way to get a little for
your bother."

Broker lost his appetite and tossed his napkin on his unfinished
breakfast. She was right behind him, reminding him to take two
more antibiotics and some Tylenol, insisting on paying the tab. As
they approached the truck she asked for the keys.

"Nah," said Broker, but then he staggered and his knees misfired
and he stood fighting for balance and blinking in the warming sun.

"It's all hitting you. You'll put us in a ditch." She took the keys,
opened the rear hatch and arranged his bag and her suitcase and
made a pillow of some blankets that were there and ordered him to
take a break.

She was right. Broker crawled into the back and stretched out
and she helped him get comfortable with his bad hand propped up
behind his head on the blankets. Then she leaned over the seat with
a road map and said, "It's been a while."

"Cross through Duluth, then follow North Sixty-one up the
shore." He stabbed at the map with his good hand. "If I'm not up,
wake me before we get to Devil's Rock."

The Tylenol filed down the sharp edge of the pain and the sunlight coming through the windows, combined with the pancakes,
pulled a drowsy shade down on his fatigue. His eyelids fluttered. The

whir of the tires on the road lulled him. Broker was a sound sleeper and never dreamed, so the image he carried into sleep was not manufactured by his unconscious. It was his last thought before he dropped off. Ray Pryce's square, freckled face. "Don't sweat it, Phil; I'll get you out, you can take that to the bank."

Man, if ever there was a poor choice of words.

Broker lurched awake and bumped his hand as he sat up and saw a familiar line divide sky and water and felt the brisk tonic of lake air coming through the open windows. Superior. They were past Duluth, into the Minnesota Arrowhead. But something was wrong. He immediately put his good hand to the small of his back. Uh-huh. He looked over the seat.

Nina hunched forward slightly, tense behind the wheel with her eyes riveted to the rearview mirror. The Beretta was tucked under her right thigh, the handle angled back where she could grab it easily.

"Not funny," said Broker.

"I can shoot this thing better than you can. When's the last time you qualified?"

That pissed him off. *"Pull over."*

"The green Saturn, rental plates, staying way back. Been following us since we left Stillwater."

"Nina."

Reluctantly, she jerked onto the shoulder in a hail of gravel. She got out and opened the rear hatch. Broker stood up, stretched and looked back down the two-lane highway. A truck with a boat whooshed by. A camper. No green Saturn.

He glared at her, not quite awake. With difficulty, he reholstered his pistol with one hand and got behind the wheel.

"You're mad at me, huh?" she said.

Broker grimaced in pain when, out of habit, he put his left hand on the wheel as he shifted through the gears. "Why should I be mad at you? You sail into my life and practically get my thumb chewed off. Hell no, I'm not mad at you," he muttered. Despite the sleep, he still nodded behind the wheel.

She folded her arms across her chest and stared out at Lake Superior. They rode in an intricate silence. He could feel her will tearing laps around him. He recalled that when she was at the University of Michigan she just missed the cut for the women's Olympic swim team. Free style. Where she developed that great butt and the strong arms. Now he wished she had put all that energy into swimming; put it anywhere except aimed at him.

So he concentrated on the road that curled through rocky bluffs dressed with clinging white cedar and pine. Cresting a broad turn around a rock face, Broker glanced into the rearview and saw the green dot make a turn about a mile back. He stared at Nina. For the third time in ten minutes the right front tire drifted into the shoulder, and the Jeep wrenched as Broker shakily over-corrected.

"You're a mess," said Nina.

"I don't bounce back quite as quick as I used to," he admitted.

"You need a bath, a meal, and a good night's sleep. It'll keep till then but you have to listen to me and not cut me off like you did before." She glanced over her shoulder. "We don't have a whole lot of time."

14

BROKER CONFIRMED, AS THEY DROVE INTO DEVIL'S ROCK, that a green Saturn with tinted windows and rental plates was trailing them into town. He groaned to himself and remembered something that his mom, the astrology nut, always said about Saturn being the Teacher.

He turned abruptly, wheeled a fast U-turn through the parking lot of Fatty Naslund's bank, and got behind the Saturn long enough to make sure of the plates. The Saturn ran Devil's Rock's one stoplight, accelerated, and disappeared along the waterfront.

"Glove compartment. Cell phone. Gimme," said Broker.

Nina opened the phone and Broker took it in his good hand. He punched in the number with his thumb.

"Devil's Rock Public Safety."

"Give me Tom Jeffords. It's Phil Broker."

"Hey, Broker, Merryweather told Tom some guy ate your thumb. That true?"

"Yeah, yeah, Tom there?"

"I'll patch you through."

"Chief Jeffords."

"Tom, it's Broker."

"No shit, we heard—"

"Later. Look, I just drove into town and I got some citizen in a green Saturn, plates lima lima gulf six two niner, been on my ass since I left Stillwater. I'm heading for Dad's place. Can you have somebody check him out and call me?"

"You think somebody wants your other thumb?"

"You tell me. I'm off the clock."

Broker handed the phone back to Nina. "Could be Earl has a friend looking for some payback," he said.

Nina shook her head. "Guy followed me from New Orleans. Same flight."

"We'll see."

"Yes we will."

North of town Broker turned off on a gravel road and stopped in front of a billboard that advertised the Broker's Beach Resort. A dusty closed sign now bannered it. Broker got out and lowered a chain that closed off the access road. As he returned to his truck, he noticed the green car pulled onto the shoulder, about two hundred yards up the road.

It was getting harder now to dismiss Nina as a paranoid; even more difficult to banish the ten-ton shadow beginning to lurk just below his thoughts. We'll see, he soundlessly challenged the blip of green up the highway.

Nina's view in the passenger seat was blocked by brush and Broker said nothing to disturb her. Assuming he was in someone's binoculars, he took his time. He mused at the cascading irony coming off Jimmy Tuna's cryptic note. He had learned the basic premise of undercover life from Nguyen Van Trin during the one, and only, and unusually, candid private conversation he'd ever had with the man. *Go solitary. Even the most trusted comrade will telegraph. Trust no one.*

He got back in and drove down toward the shore. They broke through the pines and he mused how other people said their childhood environs looked smaller when they revisited them as adults.

No way Lake Superior was ever going to shrink.

The Brokers owned two thousand feet of wild lake frontage, arced in a cove and spectacularly fanged with granite. Tall old red and white pines, which had been preserved from the clear-cut at the end of the last century, cloaked the cabins from the highway. Broker's personal cabin, sometimes rented as overflow, clung to a rock promontory to the side of the resort behind a privacy screen of gnarled white birch, balsam, alder, and mountain ash.

What he really wanted to do was pull the Jeep into the drive, walk down to the beach, strip off his clothes, and dive off his favorite rock into the icy clean water. Then fire up the sauna and do it again. He turned off the key and sagged over the steering wheel.

"Still magic," said Nina.

"Yeah," he nodded.

"Oh oh," said Nina. "Something new."

A seriously large, hundred-fifty-pound silver, black, and tan shepherd bounded from the brush and planted his square paws on the side of the Jeep. His nails drew screeches on the paint and a tongue the size of a size sixteen red lumberjack sock hung between his big pointy teeth. "Hey, get down, Tank." Broker yelled as he got out and tussled with the dog. Nina cautiously got from the passenger side and kept the briefcase that contained her map tight against her side.

"Is he . . . safe?"

"Hell no," said Broker, shaking the ruff of fur around the dog's neck. "He was too aggressive for St. Paul K-nine so I brought him up here. Mike and Irene squared him away, didn't they, Tank." Tank cocked his huge head and his yellow eyes tracked Nina's every move.

Nina squinted at the dog and then at Broker's eyebrows. "There's a family resemblance. And like . . . human intelligence behind those eyes."

"Yeah, retarded human intelligence," said Broker, cuffing the dog playfully. "Come on, let's go see the folks."

Halfway down a trail paved with split granite Tank stood alert, growled deep in his chest, and swung his head toward the road. Broker gripped his choke chain and brought him to heel.

"Do we have company?" Nina asked.

"Maybe," said Broker and they kept walking down into a natural amphitheater cragged with immense bedrock terraces, some the size of three-story buildings. As a boy, Broker thought it looked like a huge, wrinkled pile of gray elephants.

Then he hit the eyesore on the mild late afternoon; the shells of twelve spacious cabins were tucked into the shelves of stone. The oldest ones marked the summers of Broker's college years. He and his dad built one a year from the thick stone foundations to the cedar shake shingles that had plated the roofs. Dawn to dusk, six days a week. The main house was marked by an "Office" sign and sat back from the cabins in a sheltered cranny. In a small bedroom on the second floor his mother still kept his high school and University of Minnesota–Duluth hockey varsity letters tacked to the wall—one of her few touches of conventionality.

When Broker got to the first grade he discovered that other kids went to church on Sunday. He learned he had been raised by North Shore pagans, small p.

His dad kept faith with the primacy of earth, sky, water, and fire. His hands had hauled on the rosary of artisan labor every day of his life as he connected heavy beads of wood, steel, and stone with bullets of sweat. He had rejected the concept of babying teenagers. He believed in preparation. Broker grew up hard.

The odd thing was that his rough, tough dad was a dutiful teddy bear who had read to him the off-the-shelf stories about mice and cuddly rabbits and all of Dr. Seuss.

Quiet, slender Irene sat her baby boy down on the wrinkled elephants during fierce dawns and sunsets, or pulled him through the deep snow in a sled under Orion and the Borealis.

Only half in jest, she told him of the race of Nordic gods who had battled the ice monsters and created the first man from an ash and an alder tree. Their names were still preserved in the days of the week. Tuesday for Odin's son Tyr, Wednesday for Woton, which was another name for Odin himself, Thursday for Thor and Friday for Freya, the goddess of love.

Hail was the foam dropping from the jaws of the Valkyries' horses and the Northern Lights were the flash of their armor as they rode across the sky.

And, of course, she told him about the tree the Christians stole for Christmas.

Broker clicked his teeth. Now the cabins, with makeshift plywood roofing, looked like a refugee village. Some of the sheets had pulled free of their nails, testifying to the cruel whimsy of the lake winds. Weeds already had taken sturdy root and choked the caved-in construction where plumbing had been halted. The downhill end of the foundation for the new lodge had washed out, one-ton granite blocks strewn like a child's wooden playthings. At the edge of the grounds a wheel barrel was imbedded in a shower of cement like a grave marker, one rusty handle twisted to the sky. A winding split granite staircase was locked stillborn in the spill.

Now Mike was under a doctor's orders not to lift anything heavier than a ballpeen hammer.

Irene Broker sat on the deck of the old central lodge arranging Devil's Paintbrush in a vase. When she saw them coming she stood up, lean in faded Levi's and a pigment-smeared blue smock. Her long hippie hair was still crow-dark in her sixties and her eyes, like her son's, were quiet, watchful green, the color of an approaching winter storm. A painting easel was set up behind her. So she was still painting loons for the tourist trade, a hobby that now brought in grocery money. She raised her hand to shade the sun. Broker released Tank who trotted to Irene's side.

"Still painting loons, Irene?" sang out Broker.

She smiled wryly as they came up the steps. The smile broadened into a grin. "Hey, Nina Pryce. You're all grown up. I saw you on TV."

"Hi, Irene."

"Talk to my childless son. *He* never grew up . . ."

Broker hugged her. "Irene believes our only purpose on earth is to replace ourselves."

Irene grinned at Nina. "A fat little grandbaby would be nice, but for that you'd need a woman. What happened to your hand?"

"Guy bit me."

"Don't tell me." Irene walked up to Nina and hugged her. "Speaking of women, you look way too fresh and on the intelligent side for Phil."

Nina said, "That's for sure. He's a piece of work."

"Yeah, yeah. Where's the old man?" asked Broker.

Irene smiled tightly and nodded down toward the shore. "Counting rocks."

Broker called Tank to his side and started down toward the water. Rock was what they had. Rock had been his cradle and his playpen. Like bedrock, Brokers were heavily connected by gravity to the earth. They were difficult to move and hard to the touch. This Broker learned in the silence, working beside his father.

He learned that anger and gentleness should be seldom shown so they were never squandered, so their emphasis was clear.

Now the clan was winnowed by death and geography. Now the developers and bankers laid their plans and waited for the tick of the clock.

He'd assumed the land would always be here, to come back to. He bowed his head and, with the dog at his left heel, went down the stone terraces toward his father.

Mike Broker, despite his injury, was still muscled like a troll at seventy-three. He sat on a throne of granite, facing out toward the horizon, sucking on an unlit pipe. Broker could almost see his father's broad back smile, sensing his son's approach. He turned slowly, a pug-nosed man with a beard and thick longish unruly gray hair over a mat of bushy black eyebrows.

He'd been to Omaha Beach and Korea and had ridden with the wild biker-vets on the West Coast. Then he'd married Irene and stripped off his leathers and made his way laying stone and as a part-time high school teacher. History, civics, and hockey coach in the winter, before he went full time into the resort business. He'd served one term as the local police chief, then refused to run again because of the office work and politics. Broker's first memory of his father was the smell of sweat. It was his favorite memory after his mother's voice.

Broker had his mother's eyes, her patience for fine detail, and, for better or worse, a large dose of her imagination. Misused, thus far, inside him he knew he had an unsmithed vein of German ore that was his father's will.

When Broker was still several feet away, Mike asked casually, "What do you get when you cross a draft dodger and a crooked lawyer?"

"I give."

"Chelsea."

"Hi, Mike," said Broker who had punished Bush for letting the Republican Guard get away into the Iraqi desert and put a check next to Clinton's name.

"Hiya, kid," said Mike, the diehard, Libertarian Perotista.

Broker sat down and pulled out his Spirits. Tank arranged his large body at Mike's feet.

"Bad for you, the cigarettes, you know."

"I know."

"What happened to your hand?"

"Guy bit me."

"What's Nina Pryce doing with you?"

"Long story."

Mike mulled this over and looked out over the water. "Do you ever think about death, capital D?" he asked.

After work came questions. Broker had sat on the rocks and been quizzed by his father and had been made to think. Later Broker came to understand the resemblance of this tutor-pupil relationship to the Socratic method. He was not surprised, when, in high school, he happened on the historical statue that reputed to be Socrates, and which bore a likeness to Mike Broker. Socrates was a stonemason.

"Not every day."

"That'll change when you turn fifty, then it'll be every day. Now, when you turn *sixty*, you start *seeing* it, like a person, a new neighbor, say, who you pick out at a distance but you haven't met. Then comes *seventy* and he starts getting closer and pretty soon you get to know his warts and he waves every once in a while. A nosy kind of neighbor. Before long he's going to be over to borrow a screwdriver. I think, because this is my favorite place to sit, he'll show up in a boat, probably with a fishing rod, in the late spring I think, just after the last ice is out."

"You think, huh?"

"Yeah. I think he comes up and thumps on you like you're a watermelon and then he listens to see if you're ripe."

"Break a knuckle on you," said Broker. "Besides, you always said dying is one of the big whens, not an if."

"Did I say that?"

"Yeah. One of your cautions against wishful thinking."

Mike tapped his pipe against the stone, a sound that Broker associated with this spot and the watery heartbeat of the lake. He took a nail from his pocket and began to scrape the pipe bowl in a slow, regular motion.

"You get tired of police work yet?" he asked.

"Actually, Mike, I'm thinking of making a move."

"Well, you gotta choose carefully. Rough economy out there. Downsizing you know."

"I'll keep that in mind."

Mike turned and faced his son. And Broker could see the complicated truss strapped under his overalls. "Phil," he said, "I know you've been working with Fatty Naslund down at the bank to buy us some time, but I think we're at the end of the rope."

"So what are your plans?" asked Broker.

Mike averted his eyes and adopted a practical and it seemed practiced tone of uncharacteristic reasonableness. "Fatty's lined up a developer who'll give us a decent price for most of the place. We could pay off the bank and save one lot and build a house on it. Have a decent nest egg left over."

Broker gazed across the beach at a particular curved plinth of granite that leaned out toward the water like the bowsprit of a dragon ship. It was called Abner's Rock. Abner Broker had claimed the rock as his own in 1861, before he embarked downcountry to join the First Minnesota Regiment. In 1861 the Broker clan had comprised one fifth of the population of Cook County, Minnesota.

"And do what? Collect Social Security? Watch them build some tourist whorehouse next door? You'll heal, you know. Maybe not like before but well enough to handle this place. We still have thirty days."

"Hell, Phil, we've run down every option short of robbing a bank . . ."

Broker stared out over the water. As a boy, Irene had trained his imagination by coaxing him to read shapes in the endless play of light and shadow in the clouds, to decipher faces in the wind moving through the leaves on trees, to understand motion in the wrestle of the waves.

Forty-three years old and hard as a rake handle left out all winter, he could just make out a galleon, packaged in cumulus, on the horizon.

Which was probably why Nina had come for him.

"Let's make a fire tonight. Down where we used to," he said.

15

He REJOINED IRENE AND NINA BY HIS CABIN AND CALLED Nina aside. They walked off into the trees out of earshot and Broker told her simply: "Put it in one sentence and no bullshit."

She stood very erect and looked him in the eye. "Tuna strongly suggested that a case can be made against LaPorte about what happened to my dad."

"I need proof."

She glanced around. "Maybe we'll get some tonight."

As they walked back to his cabin their hands grazed accidentally on purpose and Broker decided to take a calculated risk with the green Saturn. The local coppers were there as backup. He'd just lay back and let it unfold.

He got out his keys, went up the redwood porch, which was cluttered with flowerpots, and opened the door. Nina carried their bags in from the Jeep and squinted as she passed through the narrow doorway.

Inside, light came mainly from skylights. The windows, like the doors, were built excessively narrow. The interior consisted of a long main room with a small kitchen at one end, a large wood stove, comfortable couches and chairs, and a big kitchen table. A doorway, again too narrow, opened on the left to a bedroom and off the bedroom another door opened on a sauna with its own woodstove. Another doorway beside the kitchen led to a deck that overlooked the shore.

Irene gave the short tour. "Notice how the furniture and appliances don't fit through the doors or windows. He built the entry and windows after he moved everything in, too small for the stuff to fit through." She smiled. "My son the cop."

A wood box and chopping block sat next to the Fisher wood-stove. Broker picked up a short splitting ax in his good hand and stared at the woodbox. Nina quickly stepped in, took the ax, and efficiently knocked several pieces of oak into kindling.

"For the sauna, and the stove. It'll be cold out tonight," said Broker.

"Gotcha. You take a break, I'll get it going." She went into the sauna with her kindling and some newspaper. A few minutes later the smell of smoke and a rusty groan of heating steel permeated the cabin.

"The damper, you gotta—" he yelled.

"I can *do it*," she yelled back. She reappeared and inspected the kitchen cabinets, turned on the faucet, heard the well kick in, tested the gas burners on the stove, and then went outside.

Broker sat in a chair and stared at his throbbing, bandaged left hand. Nina and Irene returned with a handful of . . . weeds.

"What?" he asked.

Irene held three big dandelions, roots and all, under the sink faucet, washing them. She laid them aside and then lifted a large stained kettle. She respected her son's privacy and now, in among his belongings, she had the curiosity of a woman in the men's lavatory. "When's the last time this was clean?" she asked.

Broker shook his head as she filled the kettle with water and threw in the dandelions and set the burner under it. Nina checked the fire in the sauna and then said she was going to look over the beach.

"Keep the dog with you," admonished Broker.

The next thing he knew the phone was ringing. He had crashed again. He smelled the soupy acid simmer of the kettle, saw by the long slanting shadows that the sunlight was going. He went to the phone. Jeffords.

"Your green Saturn is checked into the Best Western. Minneapolis Airport rental to a guy named Bevode Fret who signed in with a Louisiana license, New Orleans address. He followed you out of town and made Mike's place. He took the room for two nights. What do you think?"

"Tom, I got a bad feeling—" But it really was a curious feeling. A kind of litmus test.

"What?"

"Somebody might do a house invasion on me."

"Lyle Torgeson's got patrol tonight. I'll tell him to keep an extra sharp eye up your way. And I'll pull a couple of the boys from Grand Marais down to lend a hand. You want state patrol?"

"Nix on them. Keep it local. And tell Lyle I'm leaving the dog out."

"You really think that's a good idea?" Nina said when Broker insisted on a sauna. Her eyes scanned the treeline.

"Relax. Every copper in the county is watching this place and your green Saturn. Let's see what happens."

"So, now I'm bait," she said.

"You got it. You scared?" he taunted. She reached over and squeezed his injured thumb. "Ow, damn."

Grumbling, he cut off the bandage and stared at the taped splint against his puffy thumb. He'd been wearing the same clothing for forty-eight hours and after one try it was clear that he couldn't get his boots off. A nurse had helped him back into them at the hospital.

"Hey," he protested as she started to undress him.

She shrugged elaborately, a casual gesture that involved a subtle flourish of her eyes and a slow pony toss of her short hair. Femininity. A weapon held in reserve. "I've never thought of you that way. You never let me . . ." She lowered her eyes for a heart-beat. Then she spoke briskly. "Besides, in the army I trained my ovaries not to advance unless they get a direct order."

Bullshit. She was working on him. She was a regular arsenal. If the steel trap didn't take the hill, send in the tender trap.

When she got to his undershorts he warded her off and stepped into the sauna chamber, pulled off his shorts, and sat with a towel around his waist. She came through the door stripped down to nothing but her pale swimsuit stripes, the small skull-and-crossbones tattoo stamped on her shoulder, and two scarlet dimples in her left hip and buttocks where she'd taken the two Iraqi Kalishnikov rounds.

"Put on a towel," he said, clearing his throat but looking. It had been a long time since Broker had seen a naked woman—except when he was working and they didn't count.

She smiled with satisfaction, seeing how Broker had to tear his eyes away. "It's a sauna," she said.

"Towel."

Nina returned wrapped in a towel and filled a bucket. Broker tossed a couple of ladles of water on the stones on top of the stove and the first rush of steam rose. He repeated the process until the moist steam cut back and the searing dry heat came on. Trying to ignore the backbeat throbbing in his thumb, he soaped his face and picked up a razor.

She was beside him. "Here. Lie down and put your hand up." He let her ease him down on the bench and situate his hand. Then she took a can of lather from a shelf, the razor, and shaved him. After she rinsed off the soap, she started in with a big-toothed plastic comb, taking the tangles from his thick dark hair. In the close confines, their skin touched, slick with sweat. Little discoveries.

"I'll get it cut tomorrow," he said.

Nina shook her head. "Keep it. With short hair you almost look like a nice guy."

Broker studied the shiny expression on her face. The way her skin glowed against the redwood. Under her tomboy scruff she was—well, hell, he figured it was time to get out of here. He lurched upright. She raised her eyebrows.

"I'm going to jump in the lake. It's traditional," he muttered.

"Never happen."

He handed her a terrycloth robe, put on his own, and slipped his feet into a busted out pair of running shoes. Unsteadily, he negotiated the front porch stairs and walked down the path to his small beach. The wind had swung to the south and the clouds fluffed up in a South Pacific haze of magenta, pink, and purple. He shivered in the soft breeze. She was right. No way he was going to jump into anything. He dropped his robe and kicked off his shoes and started to wade into the chilly water. His bare feet rebelled at the stony bottom, feeling fragile and vulnerable. He backtracked, put the shoes back on and went back in. Shuddering, he ducked under the water and quenched his flaming thumb in Lake Superior.

He surfaced and his chest heaved, sucking in huge drafts of air, and he felt better. Back on the beach, he stood for a few moments letting the warm southerly breeze chase the water droplets from his body. Then he rubbed vigorously with a scratchy towel.

He watched enviously as Nina nimbly scaled a big hunk of Gabbro—his rock—and peered into the boulder-hemmed pool. "Can I dive here?" she asked.

"Just don't go too deep. It's cold."

She dropped the robe and stood in the first purple flush of twilight. Broker usually referenced attractive women to the movie stars they resembled. His ex-wife Kim had reminded him of Faye Dunaway. Too late he realized she was the Faye Dunaway of *Network*.

There was no precedent for Nina. She meant to set it. One of a

kind, she sprang, a supple mercury-and-orchid jackknife in the mag-
nificent light, and cleanly pierced the water with hardly a splash.
Luminescent pools of bubbles marked the brisk sequence of her
strokes. She swam out a hundred yards, turned, and swam back to
the beach and strode from the surf. Broker took a second look.
Water rolled off her skin like icy marbles.

He retrieved her robe from the rock and handed it to her. She
dried her short hair with an end of the robe, tilting her head in a
girlish pose and, at that moment, bright with cold lake water and
with slippers of wet sand on her feet, she looked normal, a good-
looking, very healthy young woman with her life ahead of her.

Then she said, "C'mon, I want you to try something."

Tank stepped from the shadows and squired them up the path. A
pitcher of liquid sat on the porch steps cooling.

"What's that?" he asked.

"Mom's home remedy and Roto Rooter. I'll show you."

She picked up the pitcher and led him inside and held up the
kettle the dandelions had boiled in. Broker could see his face
reflected in the gleaming bottom of the pot.

"Huh?"

She poured a glass of murky liquid from the pitcher and handed
it to him. "Your mom showed me. If it cleans that pot just think
what it'll do for you."

Broker shook his head. Irene had a new hippie trick. He drained
the concoction. Woody, like boiled toothpicks.

Through a break in the trees, he marked the blue and green of a
patrol car trolling along the highway. He nudged Nina and pointed.
She nodded. Okay.

Mike and Irene had potatoes in tin foil on the grill on the front
porch. Slipping easily into tandem, Nina teamed with Mike. He
pointed and she dragged. A heap of driftwood collected on the
beach below the cabin. Then Mike threw on some venison steaks—
just three. Irene, the vegetarian, sniffed her nose and tossed a salad.
Talk was literally about the weather which was not idle talk next to
the big water. Nina spoke little, carefully watching Broker. Tank lay
at her feet on his back like a giant, hairy, dead cockroach with his
legs sprawled out. Nina slowly petted him and picked wood ticks
from his fur, split them on her thumbnail and tossed them into the
coals. Their ears adjusted to the night sounds and the sunset flamed
out and the air transformed itself into squadrons of fierce tiger mosquitoes that came straight in and stuck like darts.

Time to go inside for repellent.

Broker took Nina into his bedroom and, as he smeared on Muskol, told her to keep Irene in the cabin and to keep Tank with them. He unlocked his gun cabinet and quietly showed her where he kept the double-ought for the twelve-gauge. Then he removed his military issue Colt .45 from a drawer.

He disliked handguns. If it came to a real fight, give him a shotgun or a rifle. But the Colt was a heavy reliable chunk of American history, good for hitting, which was more his style. He cleared it, checked it, and loaded it, easing the slide forward. He tucked it into his waistband and pulled a hooded sweatshirt on to conceal it.

He figured this way: Cops were on the road and he'd only be seconds away down on the beach and the dog would alert him. In the dark, Broker trusted Tank's instincts and speed more than two trained men. Nina queried him with her eyes, turning them toward his folks on the porch. Broker raised a hand in a calming gesture. She nodded and leaned the shotgun in the bedroom corner behind the door.

They had started standing closer together. "You sure about this?" he asked. For the first time in his life he wasn't aware of their age difference.

"Don't fight it," she replied in a steady voice that matched her steady grave eyes. The sound of her voice tingled in his chest like danger.

Back in the kitchen he took out a glass, opened the icebox, fumbled with an ice tray, threw a couple cubes into the glass, dug a bottle of Cutty Sark from a cabinet and poured in a finger of scotch. On second thought, Broker, usually a temperate man, poured in another three fingers. He'd need it to loosen his tongue.

Irene smiled a prescient smile as he came out on to the porch. She and Mike always sensed the difference in their son when he put on his gun. The big German shepherd sensed it too with the peculiar clairvoyance of his breed. He moved protectively to Irene's side and nuzzled her thigh.

"Cops on the road. Something's up," said Mike casually.

"Uh huh," said Broker. "In a little while I want you to take Irene into town, have a few drinks, and check into a motel on me." Broker handed his father a fifty-dollar bill.

"Dirty movies on cable TV," said Irene. Mike wiggled his shaggy eyebrows.

"Keep Tank close while we're down on the beach," Broker cautioned his mother. To Nina he said, "Don't get carried away, it's still early." Then he and Mike took their beverages down the path to the water's edge.

With his Spirits and his drink, Broker sat in an armchair of granite and listened to the murmur of the lake. Mike lit the firewood and removed his pipe from his chest pocket. Out on the water, a loon cried and Broker shivered, shriven by the haunting wilderness a cappella.

The bite of the scotch and a smoke did not wash away the taste of the dandelion tea that curled under his tongue like an old root system. He raised his eyes up the column of flames and followed the stream of sparks up to the star-crazy sky and picked out the Big and Little Bear and the Pole Star and Arcturus and Vega—and right now it looked like a black target shot through with a million bullet holes.

16

"DAD, THERE'S ONE THING I WANT YOU TO KNOW. I NEVER took, all these years. And my kind of work, I had chances."

Mike sucked on his empty pipe and placed a stick on the fire. "Yeeaah," he said slowly. "So?"

"I'm thinking of taking something."

"You talking about straight-out stealing?" asked Mike.

"I don't think so. See, the fact is . . ." Broker laughed and threw out his arms in an absurd posture. "I'm the only cop in Minnesota who's blown up a jail to break the inmates out and who's been investigated for robbing a bank of ten tons of gold bullion."

"Ah," Mike exclaimed softly like a man who had just been handed a key.

"Vietnam. I was the last swinging dick out. April 30, 1975."

"This gold . . . ?"

"National Bank in Hue City."

"And you robbed this bank for the army?"

"No, I went in to break a Vietnamese guy out of jail. I was the diversion for robbing the bank, but, see, I didn't *know* about the bank. I was the fall guy."

"Ha . . ." Mike exhaled.

Broker took a stiff pull on his scotch. "All these years I thought that girl's father had set me up. I trusted him. You might say it soured me on people. Now I'm not so sure I got it right."

Mike carefully placed one knee on the other and grasped the top knee in both hands. "We always thought you had something big in you, Phil. Irene is of the opinion that you were born in the wrong century. Me, I worried you had one of those . . . syndromes."

Broker leaned back and savored another mouthful of scotch, letting it roll medicinally from one side of his mouth to the other. How to communicate the mood that had gripped Vietnam at the end?

"There were five of us, four Americans, one Vietnamese, the same guys who came back for me at Quang Tri City."

"I remember," said Mike.

"Her dad yanked me back over to Nam to work with them again in a Special Intelligence unit. When the bottom fell out in April of seventy-five, we became part of the evacuation effort . . ."

Broker stared at the swirling pattern of the fire. What people had before electric lights and television. Where they saw their hopes and dreams and fears. He became lost in the flicker the flames painted on the lapping water and his voice sounded far away.

LaPorte was a colonel by then, Pryce still a major, Tarantuna a master sergeant. For a month they flew around the collapsing Republic of South Vietnam trying to salvage Vietnamese agents who had worked for American programs—an alphabet soup of acronyms—CORDS and Phoenix and PRUs. It was like running into a burning house to find scattered pictures from a family album.

Pryce had been closest to Trin, knew the language and the culture, they had worked some deep clandestine games over the years. The rumor was that Pryce had talked Trin into leaving the Viet Cong after Tet of '68. LaPorte had the rank but Pryce was the ramrod.

"We grabbed whatever was around, helicopters, boats, sometimes we based in Laos, other times off ships in the South China Sea. We snuck into collection points in the central provinces. Trin did the dangerous work, working behind the lines, lining up evacuees. The command structure was disintegrating, we glommed on to whatever was around."

Down in Saigon, the lemming rush to the sea was over and the last chopper had taken off from the embassy roof. They were winding down, calling it quits, afloat on the departing fleet off the coast.

"We were waiting for Trin to bring out one last group to the coast. Then Pryce learned from a holdout radio site that Trin had been nabbed on the street in Hue City. Trin was being held in the old MACV advisors compound with a group of high-ranking officers and politicals."

A crazed huddle on the deck of a decrepit minesweeper LaPorte had commandeered for them. Cognac and the Gauloises and a slow voltage electrocution of adrenaline on empty. The insane notion was put forth by Pryce and seconded by Tuna—they didn't leave Trin in 1972, so why should they leave him now. LaPorte wasn't even there, he was stuck pulling refugees out of the sea around the port city of Danang. They had to expedite the raid on the radio.

"We decided to go in and get Trin out. Real nuts. But that's what we decided to do. LaPorte got us a helicopter."

They sat down over a street map of Hue City with one of Pryce's agents who'd made it out with a floor plan of the prison. Hopefully, the victory-drunk North Vietnamese might be literally drunk, celebrating on this particular night.

Broker, with Quang Tri City on his mind, volunteered to lead the ground component of the operation.

The last time Broker saw Ray Pryce he was on the deck of the minesweep that had crept in close to the mouth of the Perfume River. Hue City was sixteen kilometers upstream. A Chinook helicopter sat ready on the deck. Broker would go in early, by boat, set some diversions and then blow the jail. The Chinook would rendezvous with them and pull them out. Broker had barely met the pilots. It was all—hey hubba-hubba—let's get this fucker over with.

Before midnight, Broker, with six of Trin's South Vietnamese commandos, slipped up the Perfume River in a fishing boat under the cover of a rain squall. After they set their diversions, the plan was to crack the jail at 3 A.M., free as many prisoners as possible, and get them to the broad lawn on the riverfront where the old province helicopter pad had been. Pryce and Tuna would come in with the Chinook, barrel down the river, land, and pluck them out.

Broker had walked the streets of Hue back in '72 and '73. Now the streets were strewn with flags and clutter from a victory march. That night he crept through garbage in the back alleys, clad in black fatigues with greasepaint on his face and a black watch cap pulled down tight. He was not particularly thrilled or frightened. He was too preoccupied with not screwing up. But it was a mind bender—everyone was leaving and he was going back in.

They set their diversions at a radio tower, a barracks, and the city hall. Just before they blew the plastique, he remembered hearing a dull rumble in the humid rain. Unafraid of the American Air Force, an unbroken convoy of trucks crossed the Perfume River bridge with their lights on, ferrying reinforcements and supplies down National Route 1 to the south.

Then life accelerated and time slowed amid the confused stutter of one last fire fight in the shadows of the blown building. The durable smile of Colonel Trin appeared in the doorway of a cell and Broker made his radio call. They ran for the riverfront and waited for the Chinook.

He remembered hearing the rotors and seeing the shadow of the big chopper flit through the flames from the diversion fires. But it swooped down two blocks away from their location. Frantic, he'd called on his radio. No reply. The helicopter struggled back aloft with a heavily laden cargo net. Wands of sparking groundfire batted around the chopper as it disappeared into the gloom.

They'd been abandoned in the hostile city. North Vietnamese soldiers—angry at the rude nightcap to their victory celebration—boiled out of buildings and swarmed the streets. Broker and his team and the freed prisoners split into small groups and it was every man for himself. A steady cacophony of small arms fire stalked them.

Trin made Broker hide his radio and survival kit, then doff his weapons and remaining gear. They dove into the river and swam to the lower story of a restaurant built over the water. Trin left Broker in the care of the proprietor, a Frenchman, who hid him in his cellar.

The next night Trin returned with a small motorized pirogue and Broker's radio and the survival kit. They paddled through lotus-choked canals and then side channels, then started the motor and went down the Perfume River to the sea. Off the coast, at dawn, Broker raised a Navy rescue channel and a Sea Stallion chopper homed in on his beacon. Trin declined the offer to escape. They exchanged gifts. Broker traded his Zippo lighter for a tiger tooth set in gold on a neck chain. Then Trin turned his small craft back to the misty shore.

17

"THEN ALL HELL BROKE LOOSE," SAID BROKER. HE DOWNED the scotch and let the liquor talk.

On the deck of a navy carrier he learned that he was the sole survivor of the ground team. Only Tuna had survived of the Chinook crew that had gone in with Pryce.

Dumbfounded, he was interrogated by tense, exhausted intelligence types who wanted to know why Pryce had used him as a diversion while he took the Chinook in to rob the National Bank of Hue.

Broker and Tuna were placed in separate detention and didn't get the whole picture until the preliminary investigation for their classified inquiry convened in Fort Benning.

He was saved by the radio communications from the helicopter, which had been monitored by the fleet. And by Tuna who testified that Pryce had switched the plan after the chopper took off.

According to Tuna, Broker's raid was a decoy, to draw attention away from the real mission. Pryce had discovered that the Communists had amassed a huge cache of gold for shipment to Hanoi. Pryce intended to sling the booty and drop it in the Laotian jungle to finance continued resistance. He said it was a high-priority mission, denying assets to the Communists.

And Pryce had it planned to the last minute. Two Vietnamese operatives were positioned inside the bank and had eliminated the guards. They rolled the crated gold ingots out on a forklift and dumped them into the cargo net that was lowered from the chopper. The inside men scrambled up the net and they left.

Tuna had specifically stated under oath that he had queried Pryce about the ground diversion: Shouldn't they pick them up.

According to Tuna, Pryce replied that they were "expendable." The gold came first.

Tuna then described how the chopper was hit by ground fire, how Pryce was seriously wounded and their radio was damaged.

Two radio messages figured prominently in the testimony. The first was a call from the pilot requesting clarification from someone in authority because the mission had been changed in mid-flight. The second was a mayday call. The pilot was about to send a coordinate when the radio stopped transmitting.

The next day, as Broker hid in the restaurant cellar, Tuna was picked up on the South China Sea in a survival raft. He said they had looked for a place to put the bird down after the radio went out and decided against it. With Pryce wounded and the copter damaged, the pilot decided he'd never get back up if he set down. He opted to stay in the air and try to make it back to the fleet. But with the load in the net, he miscalculated. The damaged helicopter went down in the sea and only Tuna came out alive. Ray Pryce, the bird, the alleged gold, and the crew went to the bottom of the South China Sea.

Colonel LaPorte had testified how he had signed for the bird and authorized Pryce's plan for the prisoner extraction. But he'd handled it verbally on the radios and nothing was in writing. When he learned what had happened he burned up the radio channels trying to send in another helicopter to get Broker out. The command had vetoed the project. Radio logs were introduced to verify his testimony.

Tuna and Broker's appointed JAG attorneys presented the "good German" defense. They were cleared of charges when the inquiry board found that they believed they were following different versions of lawful orders. The blame for the renegade operation was conveniently placed on Ray Pryce, who was listed as dead, body unrecoverable. Inexplicably, no evidence was brought in the investigation that the gold really existed. The new Communist rulers of Vietnam never formally registered a complaint. The Hue gold became a mythic story.

The incident was a final ripple in the sewage of defeat and was buried deep. But the stench attached itself to Colonel LaPorte, who never commanded troops again. Doggedly he stayed in the army and got his Brigadier's star before retiring. The dishonor also fell heavily on the Pryce family. Broker had assumed that the weight of it had twisted Nina Pryce into the obsessed young woman she was today.

Broker stared at his empty glass and looked up. Mike said, "Ah, Phil, Nina's up there sitting on the porch with your twelve-gauge."

"She's cool, Mike." He paused. "Actually, she's not. *She's* got the syndrome now," Broker laughed.

He could appreciate the irony. The psychological antics associated with returning veterans were for other people. Hell, that was for the Oliver Stone war. His war was different. Four divisions of NVA— hundreds of tanks—coming at him across the old DMZ and batting him down the length of Quang Tri Province. No time to roll a joint.

Now here he was, saddled with a fucked-up Desert Storm vet. Size six, female type.

"So," said Mike, "why are you telling me this now, tonight?"

"Because Nina says she can get proof that Gen. Cyrus LaPorte set me *and* her dad up. But his gold heist went funny and the gold wound up in the ocean. Now apparently he has a boat over off the coast of Vietnam and he's found the stuff. But the fact that he may have found it doesn't prove he masterminded stealing it."

Mike exhaled. "Ten tons of gold . . . Back up. How's she know this—"

"Because last night she stole a map with the location of the god-damn helicopter wreck off LaPorte's desk in New Orleans. Somebody's after her. She says."

"Oh," said Mike, looking around mildly. "That why you're pack-ing the Colt? Are we expecting bad company?"

"Well, let's put it this way. If we aren't, I tend to disbelieve her story."

Mike puffed on his pipe. "I pity any fool who meets Tank in the woods at night."

Broker nodded. "I already put Tom onto a guy who may have followed us. He's got Lyle Torgeson and some Grand Marais cops keeping an eye on us. We'll be covered. But I still want you and Irene to spend the rest of the night in town."

"So . . ." Mike finally lit his pipe and drew on it, creating a cyclops ember in the dense shadow of his head.

"So," said Broker.

"A map that marks a . . . treasure." Mike Broker chuckled and slapped his knee. "Kinda like when you were a kid and we'd come down here and read—"

"This ain't no story book," said Broker.

"So who's this alleged gold belong to?" asked Mike.

Broker shrugged. "Right now I'm thinking that it got lost in a gray area between two chapters in the history book."

Broker stood up and placed his hands on his hips and watched the firelight bend over the waves that lapped on the rocks. "Maybe it belongs to the people who stole it. Maybe I'm one of them," he said.

Mike joined him on the water's edge. "This LaPorte character, what's he like?"

"Tough, smart, rich, connected."

"And you're going after him?"

"Depends. If she's right. If the gold is real—I'm going after *something*."

"With just that girl?"

Broker laughed. "The other survivor of the raid sent Nina to find me. He's been sitting on something for twenty years in federal prison. Now he's out, he's dying of cancer, and he's disappeared."

"Sounds pretty thin, Phil."

"Right now ten tons of gold sounds pretty heavy to me."

"You're going back to Vietnam?"

"I'm not going *back* anywhere. I might be going *to* someplace. Except this time, I'm going on my own. And I plan to pay myself damn well for my trouble. If all that gold's really there—"

"Can you do that?"

"Watch me," said Broker. He swung his eyes down the dark beach. "We're going to hold on to these rocks."

Mike left Tank on Broker's porch. Then he drove into town with Irene. Nina came from the shadows with the shotgun balanced on her shoulder. "You have a nice talk?"

"Real good one."

"I feel left out."

"No. I'm thinking you're definitely in."

He patted Tank on the head and then told Nina to give it a rest and get some sleep. He'd be sitting up just a few feet away in the bedroom. She said he looked tired. He said that if he nodded off and anything happened the dog would rouse half the goddamn county. He reminded her to be careful with the shotgun, anything she heard moving out in the dark could be cops watching the place. Or the dog.

As he brushed his teeth, a scotch-inspired thought caricatured his lean face in the mirror. He recalled a question on the Minnesota Multiphasic Personality Inventory test, one that had recurred in his imagination while working undercover, a personal joke that John Eisenhower would not approve of: *I am a special agent of God.* Answer yes or no.

18

THE ANGRY SCREAM WAS NINA. THE GRUNT OF PAIN belonged to someone else. Dammit! Broker shot upright on the bed and grabbed for the Colt. *Must have fallen asleep and . . .*

Broker grimaced as he rolled off the bed, at half-speed, because of the thumb, and charged the doorway to the living room. Bodies crashed against furniture, the screen door buckled.

Three figures thrashed on the back porch, breaking his terra cotta pots. A shotgun was somewhere in the middle. In the porch light, a patch of Nina's ribcage showed where her T-shirt was ripped. This tall dude with long, blond hair askew was trying to bear-hug her. Burly Lyle Torgeson's light blue uniform was in there too, trying to lever between them.

The intruder was making the fatal mistake that Earl had made, trying to contain a hysterical woman. Nina darted inside his long reach and butt-stroked viciously with the shotgun stock.

"She's with me," Broker yelled, gingerly looking for a way into the tussle.

"Then tell her to stop hitting *me*," yelled Lyle.

Broker found an opening and clubbed the blond dude in the head with the pistol butt. He slung his good arm around Nina's waist and lifted her free, grunting with the effort because she was compact as a puma and hissing and spitting and she still had a hold on the shotgun.

Lyle had his service pistol out now and jammed the muzzle two inches into the blond guy's cheek. "Don't. Fucking. Move."

"Hey, man, mind the threads, I ain't resisting," said the guy in a ropey drawl. An echo of Earl lay thick on the chilly predawn and

Broker, breathing hard, hurting, shaking, became incensed. He hadn't been in two tussles in two days in a row since he'd been a rookie working patrol.

Urgent footfalls sounded in the brush on the path from the lake. Broker snatched the shotgun from Nina, stuck the Colt in his waistband, and swung the shotgun toward the sound. "It's Mark Halme, from Grand Marias," shouted Lyle. Broker lowered the long gun. "We got this under control," said Lyle to the swift-moving shadow. "Keep an eye on the road." The other cop jogged back on toward the road.

Broker saw the map, mashed flat by a dirty shoeprint, on the redwood planks among the dry potting soil, dead roots, and broken crockery. He snatched it up and set it aside. Then he turned to this new redneck.

Lyle had him face down and was trying to cuff him, but the guy was making it hard so Broker stepped in and gave him a kick. He quieted and Lyle, who had holstered his piece, grabbed a handful of the guy's hair and slammed his head down onto the redwood.

"I got no problem cuffing you unconscious," said Lyle.

"Awright, man, cut the shit, I'm lettin' you do this, you understand," said the guy. A streak of blood on his chin made an oily slick in the yard light. Lyle snapped the shackle.

"Okay, you have the right—"

"Wallet," said the guy.

"Shut your hole," said Lyle.

"Badge in my wallet," said the guy.

Broker glanced over at Nina who sat in a crouch, sweating and gasping for breath, eyes bright. "The green Saturn?"

"Now you believe me? He was on the plane. His name is Fret," she nodded.

"He left the Saturn up on the road," said Lyle. He had the wallet out and squinted at it in the yard light. He handed it to Broker. The blond guy rolled over and came to a sitting position, his back against a bench. He was wearing a charcoal jacket, matching trousers, a black stretchy muscle shirt, and soft, worn black crosstrainers.

The laminated picture ID matched the guy, a pretty boy, cruel face ruined by a bottom-heavy long jaw. Carefully combed blond hair. A silver badge was pinned next to the ID. Det. Sgt. Bevode M. Fret, Orleans Parish, New Orleans Police Department.

"He's no cop. He works for Cyrus LaPorte," said Nina.

"Shut up," said Broker. He turned to Fret. "What're you doing breaking into my house?"

"Recovering stolen property," said Fret confidently.

Broker motioned to Lyle who told Fret to stay put. Then they walked down the steps into the backyard. Lyle said, "Had the car on my sheet, Tom said to keep an eye out, watched him pull out from the motel parking lot at 3 A.M. We had Mark already up here, backed off the road, so I radioed him to look sharp. Asshole there pulled over about a hundred yards from your turnoff. Came in through the woods . . ."

Broker's skin prickled suddenly, his eyes swung from side to side, reaching out into the dark. Then he whistled. The high-pitched whistle echoed through the silent pines. Then he called, "Tank."

Lyle bit his lip and shook his head. "Lured him up onto the road. We found a canine handler's whistle up there. He hit your dog with a Tazer." Lyle paused and toed the dirt. "Then musta snapped his neck."

"Shit."

"He's tricky, we lost him in the trees. Mark swung down to the shore in case he was coming up from the beach. Then I saw him creeping toward your place. He went in and I came running and he comes flying out the screen door with the banshee. She a new love interest?"

"That would be too simple." Broker shivered, barechested in jeans and tennis shoes.

"This some kind of snaky UC shit that followed you up from the Cities?"

Broker shook his head. "This is personal. Can you take him down and put him on ice, no rights, no phone call, nothing. I'll get dressed and meet you at the station. We'll have a talk with him."

"Okay, but I'll have to wake up Tom. This guy's really a cop. He's in our jurisdiction without bonifides."

"This has nothing to do with police work."

"I gotta take the stuff he was bringing out of your house."

Broker nodded. "Just keep it quiet."

"Gotcha." Lyle went back up the steps. "On your feet," he ordered.

"How 'bout you take off the cuffs, huh?" said Fret. "Seeing's I'm a brother officer—"

"You ain't shit," said Lyle. "I saw on 'Sixty Minutes' last week about the NOPD. Feds busted twenty of you guys and the crime rate in New Orleans went down eighteen percent."

"Listen, dickhead, I realize you got it rough up here in the woods going round scooping bear shit off the roads—"

"Move," said Lyle Torgeson. With a menacing glance, Broker warned Nina to stay clear as he handed the map over to Lyle. Coated with goosebumps, he walked Lyle and his prisoner up the drive to Lyle's cruiser. Mark Halme shined his flashlight and led Broker into the thick brush on the shoulder of the highway. They stopped and Broker knelt and put his hand on the still warm mound of dark fur.

Halme shined his light on the silver whistle and the electric stun gun that lay next to the dog's body. He speculated, "That guy had a lot of balls letting *that* dog in close enough to zap him with the Tazer."

"Real good or real desperate," said Broker.

"I already took some pictures. I'll be at the cabin the rest of the night in case there's more of them," said Halme. He gingerly folded the Tazer and the whistle in plastic evidence bags and backed away, giving Broker some room.

Broker jerked nervously. Mosquitoes starting to flock. He fished a crumpled pack of cigarettes and matches from his pocket, lit up, and blew smoke at the insects. It was quiet now except for the waves breaking on the shore. Hyper alert, he could hear his sweat dry, feel the salt crack on his skin.

He took his vows seriously. He'd upheld the ones he'd sworn to the U.S. Constitution and to the people of Minnesota. His failed marriage he still wore like crippling chains.

The Cyrus LaPorte he had known wouldn't use the likes of Bevode Fret. For the first time he formed the thought that maybe it was LaPorte who had not minded his vows. But it was wrapped in hot angry instinct.

For the dog alone I'll hurt you bad, General.

Back off. Think. Cool gears of reason shifted through the wrath. Sorting it. Delaying it. He lifted the huge shepherd in his arms and plodded back to the cabin. Nina confronted him, shaking in her torn shirt. There were purple claw marks down her shoulder and on both arms. She had trouble breathing.

"Now you believe me," she insisted and her voice rasped, barely under control. Then she saw the dead animal. "Aw, God."

Broker nodded and laid Tank down. Then he noticed the blood oozing from her bruised throat in the porch light. The dark shape of Fret's thumb prints. "Your neck?"

"Bastard tried to choke me."

"I'll take you to the hospital—"

"I don't need a fucking hospital. I need some fucking *help*."

Broker patiently hoarded his anger, pushing it into his heart like icy bullets into a spring-loaded magazine. "Get cleaned up, make some coffee. There's a cop named Mark Halme staying close. I'll be back after I talk to this Fret."

"He won't tell you anything."

Broker squinted in the harsh light at the damage on her throat. *Sonofabitch, she'd been fighting for her life.*

"He'll tell me a lot," he said slowly. "But I'll tell him more and then he'll tell LaPorte . . ."

Nina shook her head in a quandary of pain and anger. Broker clamped a hand on her shivering shoulder. "You're not alone anymore, okay?"

She set her lips to keep them from quivering. "We're going to take LaPorte down," she said.

Broker narrowed his eyes. "We'll see. I'm on my way to lay the opening move on Fret."

Nina collapsed into his arms in a tremendous release of anxiety and laughed. Quickly she sobered. "Where do you keep a pick and shovel?" she asked, squaring her shoulders. "You can't dig with that hand and your dad can't and I sure as hell won't let Irene do it."

Broker knelt and patted the stiffening fur. "Wait for Mike. He'll want to pick the spot."

19

THE NORTH SHORE DAWN ROLLED THE FOG IN OFF THE BIG
water and glossed the black granite boulders with glacier sweat and
it was the first day of June. Broker stood on the waterfront across
from the police station and sipped coffee and waited for Tom
Jeffords. Lyle was inside the cop shop running Fret on the computer.

Jeffords showed up in sweats, running shoes, and a light wind-
breaker. Unshaven, he nodded as he eased from his Chevy pickup.
He reached out his hand for Broker's coffee cup and took a sip. "Lyle
says we got big city bullshit before breakfast?"

"Tucker killed Mike's dog."

"Lyle told me. Why, Phil?"

"Remember that kid who stayed with Kim and I? Nina Pryce."

"Sure. Your army brat surrogate kid sister, the celebrity."

"She grew up," Broker said laconically. "This guy says he's a cop
followed her up here from New Orleans. Played real rough with her."

"Lyle's got him for burglarizing your house and assault. The dog
will be impossible to prove. He could claim self-defense. You want to
press the breaking and entering?"

"Not yet. Want to talk to him first."

"This headed in the direction of me doing you a favor?"

"I'd appreciate it."

Jeffords turned Broker's injured hand in his fingers, winced and
said mildly, "You started smoking again."

They went into the station and Lyle handed them a sheet of fax
paper. "He's dirty. Administrative leave from NOPD, implicated in
narcotics and two homicides. Case dropped. Circumstantial. No witnesses. Sound familiar?" Lyle handed over a plastic card. "He also

had this in his wallet. Registered PI with New Orleans."

"Big deal," said Jeffords, "you can send away to a magazine and get one of those."

Lyle held up the map. "All this trouble over a piece of paper."

Jeffords unrolled the map. "Hmmm. This is the coast of . . . Vietnam." He took out a sheet of paper that had been rolled inside the map. The murky graphic could have been a close-up of a rock formation in a lunar crater. "What's this?"

Broker had avoided taking a good look at the contents of Nina's briefcase up until now. He shrugged, but he felt his stomach tighten and the part of his mind that was an intricate museum of facts drew a connection to a picture he'd seen in a *National Geographic* article. *Sidescan sonar.* A shape emerged in the wavy gray lines. The unmistakable rotor masts of a Chinook cargo helicopter. Not on the moon, on the ocean bottom. He looked at Tom and shrugged. "I don't know. Yet." Then he said, "Is there a Xerox in town big enough to copy the map and this thing, good copy?"

"Maybe at the hospital," said Jeffords.

"Could Lyle run copies on the QT while we talk to this guy?"

"I can do that," said Lyle. "One other thing. I had Gloria at the motel pull his phone bill. He made two calls to New Orleans and received one back. All the same number. Listed to a Cyrus LaPorte."

Broker instinctively disliked former New Orleans detective sergeant Bevode Fret. Not just because he wore a men's cologne that had little girls in its ads. Or because he oozed casual superhero violence out of a Nietzschean comic book. When Broker walked into the detention room where they were holding Fret, the southern cop nodded and smiled at him in sinister welcome.

Like he was proud of the brawny backwoods mojo that enabled him to lure a big dangerous animal into killing range. Like he was in control.

The Louisianan sat at a small table under bright electric lights. His lanky frame was relaxed on a folding chair as, tentatively, he sipped from a Styrofoam cup of coffee. He had a bandage on his big jaw and a puffy bruise down his left cheek. He had meticulously combed his duck-butt hair. The charcoal gray, athletic-cut tropical suit he wore must have cost eight hundred bucks. With a twinge of disgust, Broker noticed the prominent day-old suck mark on his neck under his left ear. *Vain Elvis boy has a hickey.*

"You gonna charge me?" he asked as Broker and Jeffords entered the interrogation room.

"How's B&E and felony assault sound?" said Jeffords.

"Where's the felony? She had the shotgun, bro, not me. I ain't carrying. Got no permit up here."

Broker did not mention the marks on Nina's throat or the dog. That would be a personal discussion he'd have later. He said, "You came through my door at four A.M. You didn't knock."

"Door was open."

"Door was locked," said Broker.

Fret shrugged. "Opened for me. I just walked in. Was going to collect some things that didn't belong to her and quietly be on my way. She jumped me."

Jeffords folded his arms and leaned against the wall. Broker sat down in the other chair, facing Fret.

Fret grinned. "Give me my rights and my phone call. I ain't saying do-do."

Broker and Jeffords stared at him. His muddy hazel eyes did not waver. His grin broadened. "Didn't think so. This ain't the kind of situation we want getting more complicated than it already is for you guys or my client."

"Tom, could Sergeant Fret and I could talk privately?" asked Broker.

"Sure, just keep the door open."

Fret grinned again, showing alligator rows of teeth. "You the local badass? Going to trip me down some stairs?"

"Talk," repeated Broker. Jeffords nodded and left them alone. "I'm a cop," said Broker.

"Yeah, so I gathered when I saw the army bust into your house in Stillwater. Checked you out . . ." A little honey humor ran with the mud in Fret's eyes and he let Broker fill in the blanks. Fret knew he had history with LaPorte and Nina and they were talking between the lines. "You're the kind of cop who don't wear a uniform. So if you're a cop why you been driving that cunt around?"

"Her name's Nina Pryce," said Broker.

"Yeah, the nasty little cunt who wormed her way into my client's social circle and then robbed some items."

"What're you getting at?" asked Broker.

"She took some stuff. I take it back. Everything's copacetic. Oh yeah," Fret loosened his features and like some lightbulb coming on in the dungeon of his mind, he recollected, "my client has a soft spot for the . . . girl. That's why he didn't charge her down home. Yet."

"We checked your phone calls. You work for Cyrus LaPorte."

"*General* Cyrus LaPorte."

"And he has a soft spot for Miss Pryce?"

Fret smiled and shifted into a lazy intimate tone of voice, a personal touch that southerners seemed to own as a birthright and that Broker resented because it was absent in himself. "It's like this," said Fret reasonably. "Mr. LaPorte and the girl's daddy were in the army together. Some fuckin' thing way back. She blames General LaPorte for her daddy's shortcomings, you could say. She's messed up her life behind this shit and the general don't necessarily want to lean on her. He'd be willing to let it go if he gets his stuff back and some kind of understanding she leaves him alone." Fret knit his thick blond eyebrows in a convincing display of concern.

"What's the big deal about this map?" asked Broker.

"Not real sure on that, bro," said Fret, smiling broadly and winking. "Not my area of expertise. Something to do with illegal oil drilling General LaPorte detected over in Asia. General LaPorte has these do-good projects, sorta like Jimmy Carter, you understand. Some deal with the Vietnamese government. If it gets in the wrong hands, it could create a problem. But it ain't the paper. It's her intent. General LaPorte is a prominent member of the community. Don't need extra hassle from a nutcase."

"So you're up here on a good will mission?"

"Yeah," said Fret. "Just my nature, I guess." He paused and massaged his hands together and a lazy, bullying contempt surfaced in his swampy eyes. "You could say all my life big dogs been lickin' my hand."

The ugly challenge hung like smoke between them. The barest of smiles drew down Broker's lips. This new ogre was intentionally goading him.

Fret, enjoying himself, asked, "You her boyfriend, huh?"

"Friend of the family," Broker said.

"Oh yeah?" said Fret. They were playing a game. Broker didn't mind games.

"Yeah," said Broker. "She's been . . . upset. Since her mother died. She doesn't need any more crap in her life."

Fret became absorbed in dusting at a dirt smudge on his trousers with his big hands. And Broker chastised himself for being so cavalier about security last night. Fret had contempt for them, and he was vain. *Mind the threads.* He had worn a suit. He didn't expect to get dirty. He had *planned* to get caught. *I'm letting you do this, you understand.* Just a sadistic sonofabitch who couldn't resist killing something. Casually, Fret looked up. "She don't count, bro. Turns out now it's *you* the general wants to talk to."

Broker stood up. "I'll be in touch."

"Do that," said Fret. As Broker left the room he sang out, "Hey, sun's coming up. Can a guy get some breakfast?"

Jeffords pushed off the wall when Broker came into the hall. "How long can you hold him?" Broker asked.

"Thirty-six-hour rule," said Jeffords. "Which doesn't include weekends. So it's Saturday. So I can run him up to county and lock him up and the clock will start as of midnight on Sunday. We don't have to charge him till noon on Tuesday. That give you enough time?"

"That'll do just fine."

"What are we doing here?" said Jeffords.

Broker nodded at the door. They took their coffee to the waterfront. Sunlight steamed the dew on the boulders.

"I was eavesdropping in the hall," said Jeffords. "So, is she really a nutcase?"

"I suppose she is, the way Joan of Arc was a nutcase."

"What? She hears voices?"

"She has a fixed idea that drives her life. Maybe Fret has a point. LaPorte was her dad's commanding officer in the army. He pressed charges against her dad for stealing. She's really twisted about it. Maybe it's time she faced up to the truth." Broker spoke easily, playing into the scenario that Fret had sketched. Dissembling, something he'd watched Trin do effortlessly to Americans in Vietnam, that he had perfected when he first started working undercover with J.T. Merryweather: *Let 'em see the black man and they can't see the person. Gives me extra room to maneuver on their ass.* Stillwater prison was full of people who suspected everybody in the state, except Phil Broker, of turning them. They saw a limited, dangerous blue-collar mensch who worked with his hands when they looked at Broker, and he flowed naturally into their expectations. Talking to Fret he did it innately. Now he was doing it with a friend.

Tom exhaled. "So now what?"

"I'll have a heart to heart with her and then I'll talk to this LaPorte. Arrange to get him his stuff back. If he'll drop charges on her, then we let the redneck go. A trade."

"Tuesday noon. And I keep the Tazer."

"Let Fret know I'm trying to work something out. Then let him use the phone."

"What about Mike's dog?"

"That'll be between him and me when he gets out. You all right
with that?"

"You want to get your butt sued, fine. Just don't get my butt
sued," said Tom Jeffords.

Walking heavily, Broker was on his way to find his folks and tell
them about Tank when he spotted Fatty Naslund wheel his tomato-
red, perfectly restored '51 Thunderbird up to the bank. Broker
stepped off the street into a space between two stores until the
banker was out of his car and inside. He didn't want to see Fatty
now. He'd see him later.

Because Broker had decided he was going to New Orleans to see
a man whom he had idolized in his youth. To see for himself if that
man was who Nina Pryce said he was.

20

THE NORTHEASTERN SKY WAS A PILE OF CUMULONIMBUS, THE color of spoiled mushrooms. Superior coiled flat and green in eerie anticipation. The air hung in sticky olive sheets.

After telling his folks about their dog, Broker followed Mike's station wagon home.

Okay. It was personal now and it was starting to look very tricky. LaPorte wanted to see him? These folks sure had a strange way of sending an invitation.

It was always a good idea to follow the money. In this case, ten tons of gold. Jimmy Tuna was the only living person who had been near that gold. Maybe everybody wanted to locate old Jimmy. Because maybe Jimmy was the only person who knew exactly where it was.

A lot of maybes. But there was the pure adolescent thrill . . .

Arrgh. What might yer name be, matey?

Why, Jim Hawkins, sir.

A sunken treasure. Yesterday the voice had been tiny inside him. Today it had grown to small. Small like Mighty Mouse. *I'm gonna do this.*

More soberly, he caught a spark from Nina's long, patient fury.

They killed my dad.

After meeting Fret, Broker no longer ruled that out. And if that was true, then they'd used him to do it.

His folks turned off and drove toward the main house and a tarp that made a blue lump over Tank on the lawn by the porch. Mike and Irene got out of the car and stood by the tarp.

Nina waited on Broker's porch, sipping coffee. They went inside and Broker slapped the Xeroxed copies of the map and the sonar picture on the table. She poured a cup of coffee and handed it to him. Then she sat down and smoothed out the map. She'd put on sweat pants and a fresh T-shirt. The shirt didn't hide the scarlet and purple bruises that raked her bare forearms. A red bandanna around her neck hid the bruising there. If she hurt, she didn't show it.

The bruises were a reminder. Fret could have killed her if he'd wanted to. Broker paced with his coffee cup and reconsidered Nina Pryce.

His method was to start reading a person with their body, to observe how they occupied their space. Some people were barely connected, flophouse tenants in their own flesh; some were entombed or asleep. Others were conflicted.

Nina wore herself like a veteran, not an ounce more than was necessary. She'd shaken off the attack of this morning and now she sat alert, crackling with energy, keyed on him.

Maybe seeing her as obsessed in a crazy way had been his easy way out. And it had been easy to see her overachiever performance in academics, athletics, and the military as a warped proof that she could outrun her father's shame.

People had said, Broker had said: Something is wrong with her.

Broker took a deep breath and considered the possibility that it was the other way around: Something is wrong with people who choose to live with a criminal lie.

He was still pondering his mea culpas when Nina asked, "What did Fret say?"

"He said LaPorte wants to see me."

"Oh."

"Fret gave me the scenario. I work out a deal; we drop charges on him if LaPorte doesn't charge you in Louisiana. I guarantee that you leave LaPorte alone."

"Really?"

"Yeah. I'll go to New Orleans and personally return the map. Except what I give LaPorte will be a copy. We'll keep the original to mess with his mind."

"And?"

"I'll find out what's going on."

"How?"

"I don't know yet." He paused and said, "I never gave you a fair shake. It was easier to see you as a kind of victim."

"There's a lot of that going around," said Nina. "Back during the army flap, this chichi feminist reporter had trouble seeing me as a soldier. She felt obligated to ask me if my *father* ever abused me. I told her I thought abuse was a sexual option you had when you were alone."

They both laughed a little. Like a good officer, she told an off-color joke to ease the tension of a new relationship. Nina tapped the sonar graphic on the table and raised her eyebrows.

"It's a sonar image of a Chinook," said Broker.

"Laying in one hundred feet of water off the coast of central Vietnam."

"We have to be sure."

"The guy LaPorte hired to take the picture told me."

"No bullshit?"

"No bullshit," she said evenly.

She was Ray Pryce's kid. She had that offhand charisma: *How about you and me go out today and see if we can get ourselves killed in a good cause.*

Nina Pryce grinned. It was the most dangerous kind of grin; it had youth and moral courage and principle and affection in it, and revenge and a crisp-honed edge of duty. But Broker saw a cold flicker of something else there. Something really scary. Ambition.

"I need all the background," said Broker. "Facts, not theories."

She nodded. "I'm out of the army, back at the U of M. You know how I did a search on Tuna and found out he was in Milan. And he wouldn't see me. There was a state highway patrolman in one of my classes, Danny Larkins, and we went out a few times. I mentioned this prisoner in Milan I wanted to talk to and how he wouldn't return my letters or calls. This cop made an inquiry and came up with this interesting *fact*.

"In July 1980 Tuna got in a brawl in the visitor's room with Gen. Cyrus LaPorte—"

Broker cocked his head. "That police report you have—"

"Right," said Nina. "What was LaPorte doing in some medium security federal prison in Michigan in 1980? He was working in the Pentagon in Washington, trying to resurrect his career with the Reagan crowd. LaPorte tried to get the beef put on Tuna, but the guards witnessed it and they all agreed. The guy from Washington in the Armani suit attacked the convict. Not just attacked him but totally lost his cool, raving and throwing things. It was investigated by the FBI. LaPorte wound up paying a fine for misdemeanor assault."

"Did Tuna tell you what it was about?"

"Jimmy Tuna was a very messed-up guy by the time he agreed to see me. I figured—the way his mind was working—he probably forgot it even happened."

"This is looking more and more like Tuna's show. Assume everything he did was for a reason."

She nodded. "It placed the two of them together and it got me thinking."

Broker sat back abruptly. "Nineteen-eighty," he muttered, stabbing the air with his index finger. The shadow of an idea nibbled, tantalizing, but refused to take shape. Gone.

He clicked his teeth together. "So then you got into your scene with Tuna."

"Suddenly he puts me on his visitors list. The first visitor he'd had since LaPorte in 1980. He never mentioned Nam or the gold or my dad. All he'd talk about was funerals. And how much they cost. The advantages and disadvantages of cremation. Whatever. We talked for hours about funerals. He was worried he couldn't pay for it. So I gave him five grand for his alleged funeral expenses."

Broker held up his good hand. "Okay, here's the thing. If we're going to work together we have to understand each other."

"Sure," she said, not quite following.

"You've got this overall picture and you jam in the pieces. I have to work with pieces and see how they fit into patterns . . ."

Nina shook her head.

"Look," said Broker. "Tuna's a retired master sergeant. He had more than twenty years in. They don't stop your pension because you're in jail. He's been collecting a pile of bread for nearly twenty years. He didn't need your money."

Nina slumped back, chastised. "I totally missed it."

"Not your fault," said Broker, starting to warm to it. "You follow Mars, the god of the overworld. I follow Pluto, I turn over rocks in the underworld."

"Christ, you sound like your mother," Nina quipped and sagged in her chair, brows knit, reappraising. "When you were talking to Mike last night she was quizzing me on astrology. My birth time. She said you had this heavy influence, a Mars-Pluto conjunction." She studied Broker's face and said slowly, "Unlimited potential for good or evil . . ."

Broker grinned. "Irene's brain is stuck back in the McGovern campaign."

Nina worried her lower lip between her teeth. "Okay, so Tuna . . . I played along. I figured he'd talk eventually. The day he was supposed to get out I made him an appointment at a mortuary in Ann Arbor. He said he wanted to see the coffin. He wanted to know who did the actual digging. What were the exact dimensions of the grave. Gruesome stuff like that."

"But he got out early."

"Left me standing at the prison gate in a tastefully cut black dress. When I got home a package was waiting with my apartment caretaker, with the *Newsweek* page and the note about you."

"When did he get out?"

"Ten days ago. I walked a circle in my carpet and got completely wired into this thing. I wondered if LaPorte had nabbed him so I flew to New Orleans, rented a car, and hung around LaPorte's house."

"How are you paying for this?"

"Mom's insurance, her savings, and money from the sale of her house."

"How much?"

"Enough for anything we might need to do. Within reason." She paused. "And going to Vietnam is definitely within reason. Which reminds me, I have visa forms."

"Confident, aren't you."

She adjusted the scarf on her neck. "Tuna wasn't there, but a lot of other people were. I followed some of them to a restaurant in the French Quarter."

"People like Fret?"

"No. Oceanographers. Greenpeace guys. They were all staying in the Quarter. And they hung out in this restaurant on Decatur Street. They were throwing around *a lot* of money, so I did a little makeover and got next to one of them."

"The tattoo, the girly outfit?"

Nina nodded. "This nice young guy named Toby was smitten with my tattoo and impressed me with tales of taking pictures of the bottom of the South China Sea."

"He took the picture?"

"Correct, he was just back from a month on the *Lola*. They were documenting illegal oil drilling, taking water samples, stuff like that. He said they had way more high-tech stuff than they needed: a diving sphere, submersibles. But then he said something weird, the crew didn't get to do a dive. They were flown out—bang—just like

that, immediately after they located the wreck. Some rough-looking
Cajuns came in, salvage guys from Louisiana."

"Divers," said Broker.

She nodded. "So I encouraged Toby to think he could get lucky if
he took me back to LaPorte's house to a going-away pool party.
That's where I met Fret. He hit on me. But I snuck into the house
and rifled the office. I found the maps and the pictures under his
blotter on the desk. There's a safe in his office and I wish I could
have got a look into it. Fret must have spotted me coming out."

Broker leaned back thoughtfully. "Think about that," he said.

She met his gaze. After a moment she said, "It was too easy."

Broker nodded. "Remember last winter. The snowstorm. That
restaurant in Wisconsin where we met?"

"Sure."

"I bet LaPorte had someone following you, probably sitting in the
next booth. He's probably had you watched ever since Tuna agreed
to meet with you."

She eyed him, looking a little uneasy after his last remarks.
"Okay. Then it really got weird. I called back to Ann Arbor to check
my voice mail and there's this creepy voice on my machine. You
know, 'Hi, Nina, looking forward to seeing you.' So, being very paranoid at this point, I wisely deduced I was in over my head and took
Tuna's advice to find you. Somehow Fret tailed me." She looked
frankly into Broker's eyes. "What's your take on it?"

"They're after Jimmy. You were his only contact. Now I'm a loose
end connected to you. And Jimmy Tuna always was a cagey fella.
They were watching you and I bet that's how Jimmy slipped by
them," said Broker.

"He convinced me his brain had turned to oatmeal. I keep going
over our talks. We'd sit in this room at Milan."

"Describe it."

"Wooden tables, chairs, plastic ashtrays. A lot of black guys and
their families and—"

"C'mon—"

"The black guys, the young ones bothered him. Not that he said
it but I could see it. And then . . . he'd talk about the building, the
prison itself. How he'd miss the walls, the walls protected him. You
could trust the walls. He said that a lot the last time I saw him and
he'd smile at me."

"Did he ask for anything else besides the money?"

"A picture of me. But that isn't it. It's the other reference, to the walls." Her voice accelerated. "Yesterday morning, at the hospital, I checked voice mail again. Same creepy voice, but . . ."

She picked up Broker's phone off the table and punched in a number, waited, punched in another number, and handed the receiver to him.

A computer voice said, *You have one new message. To listen to your messages, press one.*

Broker pressed one.

First message, left Thursday, May — at 11:03 A.M.: A slow rasping voice. Aldo Ray on downers crawling over broken glass and enjoying it. "Yeah, ah, Miss Pryce. My name's Waldo and you don't know me but I know what you look like and I, ah, put you on my list if you know what I mean." Broker replayed the message and then erased it. He stared at Nina.

"Walls could be Waldo?" she wondered aloud.

"You know," said Broker. "I can go into a prison and talk to a convict in total confidence, you can't. You always have guards around. And LaPorte can afford to buy a few prison guards. Maybe that's why Tuna wanted you to get me. To have a secure conversation. That's why he talked in circles to you . . . dropping bread crumbs—"

"Clues?" said Nina.

"Could be." Broker rubbed his palms together, carefully, because of the thumb. "Let's shake the system and see if anything falls out." He picked up the phone and punched in the number for ATF in St. Paul.

"Is Ryan there, this is Phil Broker. Yeah, yeah, I know it's Saturday. Yeah, it looks like a burnt bratwurst." Broker whistled soundlessly, stared at his swollen thumb. "Hey, Ryan, how do you like Rodney? He's a real sweetheart, isn't he. Sure. Look, I need a favor. There's a federal prisoner who just got out of Milan. Bank robber named James Tarantuna, goes by Jimmy Tuna. Could you find out if he hung with a guy named Waldo in the joint? Another thing. Back in 1980 Tuna got in a beef in the visitors room with a Cyrus LaPorte. Could you check with the FBI and get me all the paper on that. Fax it to Tom Jeffords at the Devil's Rock cop shop. Right. I'm up north at my cabin resting the thumb." Broker gave Ryan his number. Said thanks and hung up.

"So," said Nina, "Tuna never had a visitor between the time he had the fight with LaPorte and the moment he contacted me."

Broker nodded. "Could be he had a buddy inside he confided in and might use as a mailbox. Let's see what Ryan comes up with in federal corrections." He stood up.

"There's more, he gave me—" she said.

"Not now. Watch the phone. I need to take a walk."

Storm shadows seeped up from the rock crevasses and ran inky between the smooth lakeshore cobbles. Boulders wore an ebony sheen. Broker had to force the charged air into his lungs and then wring it out.

He walked up the driveway and turned north onto Highway 61. He liked to jog along the shore road, but he usually took Tank on those runs.

Today he changed his pattern and crossed the highway and took an overgrown gravel lane inland until he came to a buckled, tar, two-lane road that ran parallel to the highway. The creepy old road had grass marching across the washouts and the rickety skeletons of wood-frame houses dotted the brush. It was a depressing place that he usually avoided.

Nineteen-eighty was stuck in his memory. Don't try to figure it head on. Unfocus. Trick it out. Think normal thoughts. He turned right on the road and followed it north. Two hundred yards away, screened by dense poplar and birch, he heard the traffic race toward Grand Portage and the casino up there, toward the Canadian border, toward the millennium. The year 2000.

The smart thing would be to just move up here, run the lodge, live out the century in a landscape that was familiar . . . But his thoughts turned back to Jimmy Tuna and his fascination with funerals.

Tuna had not been a normal NCO. A lot of high-ranking officers are abetted by Machiavellian senior sergeants. Tuna was in that mold, with the appearance and the wile of a Renaissance condottieri. Why would he beg for money and fixate on his own last rites over and over with Nina? Funerals. Burial. Graves.

Another thing about Tuna. Always the joker.

He stopped in mid-thought. The unmistakable stench of decaying flesh clotted the heavy air. Fifty yards ahead, a black shiny shape spilled from the brush into the road.

He padded forward, instinctively checking the surrounding forest. Alone with the sweaty zing of cicadas, he closed the distance to the feeding frenzy of the flies.

A heavy-duty, black plastic garbage bag was dumped in the

weeds. Under the fat swarming deer flies, Broker saw the boned-out ribcage of a deer and the maggots that foamed on the shreds of sun-spoiled meat. His gag reflex cocked.

Another argument for winter.

Broker stepped back and grabbed for a cigarette. Why he'd started smoking in Vietnam—it put a lid on that particular odor. He thought of Bevode Fret sitting in jail and mused that New Orleans might smell a little bit like the deer carcass, slick with gamey sweat on the edge of the Tropic of Cancer.

Then the shadow flitted in his memory and he clearly recalled the Chinook struggling up over the flare-lit tile rooftops of Hue, straining with the dangling cargo net while tracer rounds stitched the rainy night.

Broker grinned. *Jimmy, you sneaky old fucker, what are you up to?* He turned and ran back toward the cabin.

21

NINA JUMPED UP FROM A BENCH ON THE BACK PORCH AND waved him in. "He called, the ATF guy."

Broker breathing hard, his thumb banging, "What did he say?"

"Wouldn't talk to me, said for you to call him back."

Broker punched in Ryan's number. Nina plucked the cordless phone from the bedroom.

Ryan said, "Your guy's cell mate is a lifer who's never getting out. Name is Waldo Jenke. He's a real yard bull. I mean big. Name he goes by in the joint is Walls. Whiskey alpha lima lima sierra."

"What's he in for?" But Broker was thinking. Jimmy needed someone to watch his back if Cyrus was after him.

"Creepy shit. He kidnapped children and their pets in Michigan and Illinois in the late seventies. When he was through with them he buried them together on his farm. He was back before video. He took Polaroids."

"Any notes on him?"

"Ah, he fixated on pictures of his victims. That's what caught him. They found a picture of a Rottweiler named Heidi in his truck during a routine traffic stop. They let him out of maximum security five years ago and put him out to pasture in Milan. The bureau hasn't been forthcoming on the paperwork thing."

"Keep trying. Thanks, Ryan."

Nina came into the main room and gave Broker a thumbs-up sign. He went to the fridge, took out a bottle of Grain Belt and popped it open on the opener screwed to the counter. Grinning, he kicked open the screen door and went out through the front porch, down the stairs and the path, and out to his favorite rock. Nina followed him.

He sat down and watched the storm marshal its artillery.

"Nineteen-eighty." Broker savored a swig of beer and poked the bottle at Nina. "In July 1980 the gold market peaked. That's why LaPorte lost his cookies with Tuna."

"All that gold appreciating like hell and it's rusting at the bottom of the ocean and only Tuna knows where it went down."

"Gold doesn't rust," said Broker.

"LaPorte found a helicopter wreck," Nina speculated. "But maybe it's the wrong wreck—"

"Could be. And if Jimmy knows where it is, he's willing to tell us *something*. He sure isn't making himself available to LaPorte." Broker pulled Tuna's crumpled note from his pocket, smoothed it out and pointed to Trin's name.

Nina cocked her head. "Trin and my dad were friends. But I don't see how he fits."

"It could mean that Tuna, in prison, somehow located Trin in Vietnam after twenty years." The idea excited Broker. "If Trin's in our future he'd work better with somebody he knows. And the trail Tuna is setting up probably needs an investigator to follow." Broker paused. "The thing about Jimmy Tuna, he loved pulling practical jokes. And setting booby traps. Fall asleep on ambush, Jimmy would tie your bootlaces together."

"So it could be a trap for us too?"

"That's the fun, isn't it?" said Broker with a tight smile.

"What about Trin? The phone number?" Nina asked. "You want to give it a try?"

"Let's wait. I don't want to bump into Trin blind after twenty years."

"He helped save your neck in Quang Tri City. You saved his. I thought he was a buddy?"

"Nguyen Van Trin was a strange guy. He fought for the Commies and for us and was disgusted with both sides. He even designed his own flag. A white lotus in a sea of fire." Broker shook his head. "The only person Trin is buddies with is the ghosts of his ancestors. We'll wait."

Their voices had dropped a register and their heads had drawn close. Nina's eyes were slits. "Now that you're hooked on gold fever, let me explain where my interest lies. He knows how to get LaPorte. Jimmy does."

"Wishful thinking."

"No. He knows. He showed me. But it was like the pension. I

didn't see it." Her voice trailed off and her eyes conjured.

Her enthusiasm was going to be a definite obstacle. But he needed her. How much he wasn't sure. At least to talk to this Jenke character and hopefully pick up Tuna's trail. As an excuse to see LaPorte.

"How about we find Jimmy Tuna and ask him," Broker said with a gentle hint of rebuff. "And let's spend some of your money. Grab a charter to Ann Arbor and talk to Waldo Jenke. Then I'll need a day in New Orleans to see LaPorte before Bevode Fret gets out of jail."

"There's fifty thousand in the bank in Ann Arbor. I'll spend it all to clear Dad's name and to see LaPorte stand trial."

Broker cautioned her again. "None of this is proof. The fact LaPorte may have found gold in the ocean doesn't connect him with the alleged robbery or your dad's death."

"But he was in command," said Nina.

"True," said Broker patiently. "But he wasn't there. And Tuna would have to change his story and impeach his earlier testimony, which means he's a liar. And he's dying. LaPorte has the right to cross-examine his accuser. And there's no court with the jurisdiction to charge LaPorte for a criminal act during an undeclared war twenty years ago in a country that doesn't even exist anymore."

Nina stood up and put her hands on her hips. "Wrong. When you take that oath to the U.S. Constitution, it's forever, mister. I told you. Tuna knows a way." She spun and tramped up the path to the cabin. A minute later she came back down the path and tossed a thick oxblood-covered text book into his lap. Broker read the cover: United States Code Annotated, Title 10, Armed Forces, 1 to 835.

Broker clicked his teeth. The UCMJ. The Uniform Code of Military Justice. A Post-it note marked the pages. He opened to it and struggled through a paragraph underlined in yellow marker: "803. Article 3. Jurisdiction to try certain personnel: (a) Subject to section 843 of this title (article 43), a person who is in a status in which the person is subject to this chapter and who committed an offense against this chapter while formally in a status in which the person was subject to this chapter is not relieved from amenability to the jurisdiction of this chapter for that offense by reason of a termination of that person's former status."

"Define 'certain personnel,'" said Broker.

"Once you're in, and you're an officer type and you're eligible for a pension, you're never really out. There's precedent. I ran it kind of obliquely by a JAG guy I know. They reactivated a retired colonel in the seventies and tried him for misappropriating canteen funds in Vietnam in nineteen sixty-six."

"Where'd you get this?"

"That's my point. *I* didn't underline that. Jimmy Tuna did. It was in the package he left the day he stood me up at prison. That note and the *Newsweek* page were folded, marking the section."

Broker was impressed. It suggested another level to the thing.

Her eyes sharpened to pencil points. "So you're a cop. Solve me a bank robbery."

She was working on a full body flush of anticipation. Broker leaned away from her infectious excitement. "You got stars in your eyes. We need evidence," he cautioned.

"Why would Jimmy give me the UCMJ unless he had evidence? But I need *you* to find *him*."

"Before God does," said Broker. "And we could still come up empty. And if you really want to nail LaPorte, it may not happen in the strict legal sense."

"No. You can get the pieces any way you want, but I do it by the book. He gets tried. It gets on the record. My dad gets his name cleared." Very serious, she planted her knuckles on her hips.

He reappraised Nina Pryce again. This time with pure intuition. She thought LaPorte's head on a platter could pave her way back into the army. So she had a little Pluto in her too. And stars in her eyes. Two, at least. One for each shoulder. He said, "I'm going to get some of it—"

"That's your business." She looked away. "I won't help you steal. But what I don't see, I don't know."

"This will go down in Vietnam. No sense letting the Communists have it."

"It," said Nina coolly.

He gazed across the turbulent plain of Lake Superior. There were three of them now. The third being a tangible presence that neither he nor Nina would invite out of the silence. The faint, dry rustle crept down the centuries, twisted serpentine through the bones of Cortés and Pizarro and Sir Francis Drake, and whispered in his ear.

22

NINA WENT INTO THE CABIN AND CAME OUT STRIPPED DOWN to a pair of shorts, a running bra, and an old pair of Reeboks. She tied the red bandanna around her forehead and collected a pick and shovel and walked toward the lodge. Broker could see his dad sitting at the kitchen table, in a rectangle of yellow light that was framed in the shadow of the house under the darkening sky. Mike cupped his chin in his hands and stared out over the lake.

Broker climbed to the end of his promontory and watched while Irene and Mike showed Nina where they wanted the hole dug, in a rocky cleft overlooking the shore. Nina spread her feet and hefted the pick in her hands. Then she set to work with a slow, powerful rhythm. Fifty yards away and above her, Broker watched the flat muscles of her back and shoulders swing smoothly and oil with sweat.

She put down the pick and started with the shovel, difficult going because she lacked the proper footwear, but she didn't flinch and soon a dark ring of sweat soaked into her shorts. Then she went back to the pick and swung it to the fitful smash of waves breaking against the tiers of stone. Last night the Big Water lay placid under a "Bali H'ai" sunset. Today whitecaps rode the north wind and it looked like *Victory at Sea* out there.

Broker was not prone to admitting it, but he added up to more than just a set of balls and fast-twitch muscles. Once, back when he still showed up for evaluations at the BCA, he'd taken a routine MMPI psychological profile. He was graded by an uptight office guy who told Broker he tested out with a deviant male identity.

Broker took the test results to a lady he was dating who did profiles for the FBI. After much teasing she interpreted the grade and, that night, staring at her bedroom ceiling, she told him that the MMPI was culture-bound and dated. "Your sensitivity range graphs out within normal parameters for a woman. Off the charts for a male. That must have freaked out the guy who graded it."

Broker had intuition.

With his eyes he saw a young woman digging on the rocky beach; bandanna fluttering in a rising wind, she looked like a slender buccaneer. But his intuition was starting to fathom that she was a new kind of woman for a new century. And she had the spirit to march into the spooky old woods with the U.S Code and drag LaPorte out like a gutted deer and face down the U.S. Army. She would use her dad, who was dead, and Broker, who was living right now, to do it. Goddamn. She probably *would* be the first woman to get the CIB.

He visualized the crossed bones below the skull tattoo on her glistening shoulder. She'd want to get her way. So did he . . .

He'd known ambitious women. But Nina was the first one who came utterly without insecurity. She didn't crave power. She had it already, inside her. Call it charisma. Leadership. It was power. He sure felt it start to pop when their fingers touched. But she was young and she hadn't mastered the voltage. He could wind up electrocuted if he got too close.

And gold didn't tempt her. She demanded justice, but she also figured she was owed advancement and silver. She would trade a treasure for vindication, for LaPorte's scalp, for reinstatement in the army, and eventually for a tiny drop of silver, fashioned in the shape of the five-pointed star that brigadier generals wear on their shoulders.

And he reflected that the search for Jimmy Tuna would be fraught with puzzles and traps and it was poetic justice that the game might end in Vietnam where the ambush was invented.

Down on the beach the hole was chest deep. Nina climbed out and lowered in the lump of tarp, and, without pausing, hurrying now, with sidelong glances at the roiling sky, she filled in the grave.

Then, as it began to sprinkle, she patted the mounded dirt and laid down the shovel and carried a towel and soap down the granite polyps to the water's edge. She stripped off her work-fouled clothes and waded up to her thighs in the crashing surf and scrubbed as lightning scurried across the horizon. Thunder banged the bedrock and the first fat raindrops sizzled around her. It was magic light. The sun hid. Storm charge and ozone shook the air like a shaman's rattle. Untextured by shadow, every surface—the rocks, her skin, the heaving water—shone with its own luminous electricity.

She rinsed her hard arms and reached up to embrace the furious sky and the gray wall of rain that dashed across Superior, like the hooves of running ponies, straight for her.

Broker didn't know if Amazon hoplites really fought on the plains of Troy, and he didn't know if America was ready for them now. He knew he wasn't. But goddamn, man . . .

There it is.

23

BROKER WAS HAPPY. IT WAS STORMING. HE HAD A BUILDING crisis on his hands. He got on the phone and enlisted Tom Jeffords to expedite a charter flight to Ann Arbor while he called the warden's office at Milan Federal Prison. He introduced himself as Det. Lt. Phillip Broker of the Minnesota BCA and set up an interview with Waldo Jenke for late afternoon.

Tuna had made a point of soliciting money he didn't need. So follow the money Jimmy did have. It took longer to find out how Tuna handled his finances. His case manager was off for the weekend. After hopping around the prison switchboard Broker finally schmoozed a supervisor, who checked the computer. Tuna had given power of attorney to a banker in Ann Arbor. The Liberty State Bank on Michigan Street.

"I know where that is," said Nina.

"We have a problem, there's this thing called the Right to Financial Privacy Act. We'd need a subpoena, a search warrant. I could start that rolling if I had an open case going . . ."

He reached for the phone again and called a college friend in Stillwater who ran a travel agency and who owed him a few favors. Broker explained to Don Larson at Larson's Travel that he might be needing some tap-dancing on the scheduling computer.

Larson asked was it national or international.

Broker winked at Nina and pulled his passport from his back jeans pocket and slapped it down on the table. Casually he told Don to check on two round trips to the Socialist Republic of Vietnam. Nina laughed and held up her palm for a high five.

Larson reminded him to make sure that his passport was current, to contact the Vietnamese embassy for visas, and to check with the travel clinic at Ramsey Hospital in St. Paul for recommended shots.

Then Broker had him book a Northwest flight to New Orleans from Detroit early tomorrow morning and a return trip to Minneapolis the following morning. He left it to Don to find him a room. And another flight from Detroit back to the Twin Cities for Nina. She could grab a room at the airport Holiday Inn and wait until he returned from New Orleans. Then he asked Larson to expedite two visas. They'd mail the applications to his office. Larson groaned.

Nina checked the slim local yellow pages and found a photo shop that took passport photos. They needed two each for the visa forms. They both sat down and filled out the paperwork.

"Port of entry?" asked Nina.

"Hanoi. Never been there."

"Purpose of visit?" asked Nina straight-faced.

"Vacation," said Broker, just as straight-faced.

He winced at his thumb, which ached, and went back to the phone and checked with Tom again. Two more calls had come into the switchboard at the Best Western for Bevode Fret from LaPorte's number in New Orleans. And Fret had used a police phone to call LaPorte before they took him to the county jail.

Then Broker dug in his closet and dressed casually in a light sports coat, jeans, loafers, and a summer shirt. He tossed an extra shirt, a change of underwear, and a travel kit in his overnight bag and retaped his thumb. He changed from his hideout holster to a break-away shoulder rig that fit neatly under his left armpit and stuffed in the Colt .45.

Nina watched him pack in silence. He set his bag aside and rummaged in his dresser drawers and became agitated. Christ. *Did I lose it?* Ha. He took out a pendant on a fine yellow chain. She held out her hand to inspect it.

The tiger tooth was tipped and mounted in yellow metal and discolored from years in the drawer. She pressed her thumbnail into the metal and made a slight dent.

"What's that for?" she asked.

"Luck." Broker hung it around his neck and tucked it into his shirt. Then he took out his wallet and unfolded the note with Tuna's scrawled handwriting. He pointed to Trin's name. "He gave it to me."

On the way to the airstrip, they stopped at the photo shop, had pictures made, checked in with Jeffords, and left Tuna's note and

LaPorte's original map and sonar graphic in his safe in a plain envelope. Next they stopped at the post office, where they express mailed the visa forms with their passports to the Vietnamese Embassy in Washington, D.C. Broker wanted to stop for a quick haircut but Nina counseled against it. Keep the ponytail. It would fit in better with the New Orleans's scene. An hour later they were winging east, skirting the storm over Superior in a Cessna.

It was raining when they landed in Ann Arbor and continued to rain as they cabbed into town. From Nina's cramped student apartment, Broker reconfirmed his appointment with the warden's office at Milan. Nina drove her Volkswagen Horizon over the familiar route to the prison. Broker toyed with the tiger tooth through his shirt.

Milan was a three-story brick structure and could have been a big trade school except for the apron of concertina gleaming in the rain on the chain link outer fence and the rifle towers dotting the inner walls.

They signed in at the bubble, a guard station walled by thick bullet-proof glass. Broker showed his badge and checked his weapon. Access into the visitors' area was regulated from the bubble through a heavy-barred electrically controlled door. Waldo would be escorted through this sally port and patted down by the guards. After the interview he would be strip searched.

Beyond the sally port, Broker detected the low grumble of institutional uneasiness. He believed that a prison was a thousand-eyed animal that could intuit a cop through steel walls. He imagined the malice beading and starting to drip.

Broker had requested extra privacy, so they were led down a corridor past the regular visitors' rooms. The guard walked them through another locked door and out onto a patio that was like an aviary, surrounded on three sides and partially roofed beyond the overhang with chain link fencing.

The guard jerked his head. "How's this for out of earshot?"

Broker nodded. The guard pointed to a small table with several chairs in a dry spot out of the rain under an overhang. They walked to the table and waited. Out in the mist, cars with their low beams on slowly traveled a slick black road in the emerald gloom of the Michigan countryside.

24

WALDO JENKE'S STIFF WHITE BRUSHCUT SCRAPED THE TOP of the door frame and he oozed toward them with the Silly Putty gait of a Don Martin cartoon from old *Mad* magazine in size-sixteen tennis shoes. Somewhere around 350 pounds, Broker's head would just reach and fit into the hollow of the convict's massive armpit. He wore a freshly laundered baby blue sweatsuit. He had showered recently and Broker could clearly smell corn starch on his skin in the damp air.

He had mild pink eyes and very white skin, a killer albino rabbit who could bench press six hundred pounds. His doughy face was blank. "What's this about?" he rasped.

Then he saw Nina and his eyes eloquently explored her face and roved her body. She had put on khaki slacks, a Madras blouse, sandals, and a scarf that matched the blouse to conceal the bruises on her throat. Jenke's eyes stopped on the bruises on her forearms, then they slid down her body and fixed on the hard flesh of her bare ankles. He motioned to the guard watching through the window in the door. The guard entered. Jenke whispered to him. The guard turned to Broker.

"He's got a book in his cell he wants to give the girl. What do you think?"

"Fine," said Broker.

The guard nodded. "Take a few minutes to fetch it." He went to the door. They heard him speak to someone in the hall.

Jenke's watery eyes finished their rove over Nina and then fixed on Broker and stopped at his taped thumb. He studied the discolored, stitched flesh with interest. His blunt rabbit nose nuzzled the scent of the wound.

He smiled slightly. His yellow baby teeth were imbedded in massive gums, like a crooked kernels of new corn stuck in a cob of bubble gum.

"You know what this is about," stated Broker.

"I ain't *saying* shit," Jenke replied with great deliberation. Then, in a display of elaborately guarded reflexes, he removed a single cigarette from the pack in the kangaroo pocket of his sweats and lit it with a plain matchbook. His big white fingers fluttered. Elegantly long, the fingernails were manicured and dusted with talc.

Minutes passed. Nina untied the scarf and retied it. Jenke showed two inches of gum in a horrible grin when he saw the bruises on her throat.

Then he crushed out his smoke and lit another and leaned back, a torpid mountain of flesh. His lips puckered and his chest jerked. Wreaths of smoke rings floated on the damp air and softly tore apart in front of Nina's face.

"You notice how I talk funny?" he asked her.

"I noticed," she said evenly.

"Reason is, when I was a kid Andy Devine was my favorite actor. He talked like that because when *he* was a kid he got stabbed in the throat with a fork." He grinned. "So I stabbed myself in the throat with a fork."

The door opened and the guard came through. He had a battered, water-damaged, blue softcover book in his hand. Broker saw the embossed crucifix on the cover and recognized it as an old Armed Forces New Testament. Jenke took the book and said to Broker in a gravel whisper, "Get the screw out of here."

Broker jerked his head at the guard, who nodded and went through the door and watched through a heavy glass window reinforced with mesh. They were alone on the patio.

As if conveying an object of ceremony, Jenke placed the Bible in the middle of the table. He opened it and pointed to the faded name written on the flyleaf: *S. Sgt. James Tarantuna.* Again the inquisitive gaze, prompting. Broker nodded.

Jenke opened the Bible to the place marked with the photograph of Nina. Her college graduation picture. He removed the picture and held it face up in his palm. Then he leaned forward.

Jenke smiled and flicked the picture in his long fingers, turning it over with almost magical speed. They both read the note printed on the back in blocky ballpoint pen: *If he stole it, why's he buried with it?*

Nina drew in a deep, shuddering breath. Porcupine sweat stabbed the muscles of Broker's chest where the cool, gold-tipped arc lay, prodding his banging heart.

Buried implied dig as in dry land. That's what Tuna's grave-digger fixation was about.

He glanced at Nina and saw the same thought ignite in her eyes. They both crouched forward, ready to race from the prison like it had just caught on fire.

"We're cool," said Broker, dry-mouthed.

"Absolutely," said Nina in a steady voice.

Jenke watched their reaction, not particularly impressed, and then prompted with his eyes. *You got it.* Broker nodded. *Yes.* Jenke withdrew the picture and artfully, beyond the guard's line of sight, tore it into quarters, which he hid in his spacious palm as he raised his cigarette to his lips. Quick as a snake he fingered the pieces into his mouth and methodically chewed and then swallowed. Then he nodded a final time. Their business was concluded. His favor to Jimmy Tuna was discharged. Broker didn't care to think about how it had been incurred.

Abruptly Jenke got up, turned and lumbered to the door. He nodded to the guard and never looked back. The door opened and Waldo Jenke disappeared.

The guard came to the table and pointed to the Bible. "He told me that's for the lady. Because she used to visit Jimmy. No good to Walls. He's terminally dyslexic. He can't read word one. All TV, that guy." The guard paused. "Ah, you all right, miss?"

"Oh yes," said Nina. Her eyes glistened. "Just fine."

25

THEY SAT ON THE FLOOR IN NINA'S APARTMENT HALFWAY through a deluxe Domino's pizza with excitement smearing their eyes as hot as the grease on their fingers. Broker took in the reins on his runaway imagination. When you're charged up, you overlook things.

"Wait a minute," he said. "Where's that Bible?" He got up and washed and dried his hands. When he picked up the Bible, Nina squirreled in close and recited, "Everything Jimmy Tuna does is for a reason."

"Need a sharp knife," said Broker.

With a small paring knife he slit the plump water-swollen back cover and peeled away the mildewed cardboard. He removed a square of folded paper.

"Bingo," said Broker.

"What is it?"

"Follow the money." He unfolded the paper and held it up for her to see. "It's a customer consent form from the goddamn bank allowing Nina Pryce to see his records."

"He's playing games with us," mused Nina. "Poor Jimmy, sitting on a fortune, then—do not pass go, do not collect ten tons of gold, go directly to jail and get cancer."

Abruptly Broker looked her in the eye. Their visit with Waldo had nudged him toward her conspiracy theory. "Nina, this 'poor' guy might have killed your father."

Nina went out on her small balcony and stood in the light rain for a few minutes. She returned more sober and said, "During the inquiry, it came out. The radio call. They were damaged and setting down for repairs. Remember?"

Broker remembered. "Tuna testified they didn't land."

"They made an emergency landing."

"Maybe," said Broker.

"They did, and they dumped my dad with it." On their knees, bumping foreheads, they unrolled LaPorte's Xeroxed nautical map. Broker studied the familiar coast of central Vietnam—Quang Tri Province below the old DMZ. Where he'd been. LaPorte had marked the wreck off the coast of the next province to the south, Thua Thien, where Hue City was located.

Broker shook his head. "That's for a boat. We need a one to fifty thousand grid, a tactical map. Then what have we got? We could draw an arc around Hue based on a loaded Chinook's probable flight time. And it was rainy, humid; that affects a chopper's lift. To handle a ten-ton load they probably cut back on fuel. And it was hit by ground fire. So how do we estimate the air speed or even if they were flying in a straight line? It could be anywhere, north into Quang Tri Province, south. Hell, they could get to Laos. Even if we find him, if he doesn't have a precise location we're screwed."

But they were getting close.

Nina's brow bunched in concentration. "So how do we find him?"

"It has to be in his banking records. That's your job." Broker waved his pizza slice at the consent form on the coffee table. "I go to New Orleans and get reacquainted with Cyrus LaPorte."

"I don't like splitting up," she said.

"It'll save time."

Nina studied him carefully and backed off before it became a test of wills. "Okay," she said.

Broker nodded. "Up till now it's been mostly talk. Once I call LaPorte the thing's in motion."

"How are you going to play it?" she asked.

Broker shrugged. "Burned-out cop starts doing an old war buddy's daughter a favor and sniffs a stash of found money to which he has a peculiar link. He has a map with a location. He sees a once in a lifetime blackmail angle to parley that map into an early retirement bonus." Which wasn't that far from the truth.

"And me?"

Broker grinned. "I think you're the nutcase albatross hanging around everybody's neck. LaPorte's playing philanthropist. I'll appeal to his charitable side to get you some help. Expensive long-term therapy. How's that sound?"

"Kiss my rock-hard buns."

"I thought you'd like it."

Nina reached for the phone and handed it to Broker. "Let's do it."

Broker nodded and punched in the New Orleans number. LaPorte's screening machine was purely utilitarian. "You have reached . . . leave a message."

After the beep Broker said in his best judgmental cop voice: "This is Det. Lt. Phillip Broker from the Minnesota Bureau of Criminal Apprehension. We're old asshole army buddies. Right now I have a fugitive from an Elvis lookalike contest named Bevode Fret cooling it in a jail cell. He keeps getting calls at his hotel room from this number. I also have Ray Pryce's daughter, who can charge Fret with felonious assault. Let's talk." He left Nina's number.

The call from New Orleans came back in ten minutes. A callow young voice, "So why should General LaPorte talk to some Yankee copper?"

"Ask him what doesn't fly anymore and sits in a hundred feet of water. I'll be on LaPorte's doorstep tomorrow at three P.M. Put me first on his schedule."

There was a pause. Then, "I'll pass it on."

"Three o'clock in the afternoon, cornpone." Broker hung up and smiled.

"You're having a good time."

"Absolutely." Then Broker pawed in his wallet for the flight numbers and times he'd gotten from Larson. He called J.T.'s home in St. Paul and left a message on his machine. "Calling in a chit. Nina is arriving at Minneapolis–St. Paul on Northwest 97 from Detroit at five-thirty P.M. on Monday. Need you to meet her at the airport. Appreciate it if you could keep an eye on her till I get back in town."

"I can take care of myself," Nina reminded him.

"I know. I'm just old fashioned."

The phone calls completed, Broker leaned back and sighed.

"Good. What else?"

"We're set," said Nina.

"My flight leaves Detroit at nine-thirty in the morning."

Nina nodded. "I should get you to the gate by nine A.M."

"By eight. I need to play credentials with airport security about that." Broker pointed to the .45 laying in its holster on a chair. "Enough. We need some sleep."

26

BROKER TOOK A SHOWER, CHANGED THE DRESSING ON HIS thumb, and swallowed two Tylenol. Leery of using too many antibiotics, he'd left them behind in Minnesota.

The rain had stopped and now a sweet, warm June breeze teased in through the open windows and balcony door. Nina'd laid out sheets for him on the couch so he draped a sheet toga-fashion around his waist and shoulders and scanned her one-bedroom digs.

The refrigerator held a barky-looking bottle of V-8 juice, some yogurt with expired labels, and three cans of Vernor's ginger ale. He opened one of the cans and roamed her space. The books on her desk had titles that suggested she had been taking graduate studies in business administration. No television set. No stereo. No magazines and no houseplants. Like she hung herself in the closet like a bat.

A scalloped, varnished wooden edge that protruded from between two textbooks caught his eye. He pulled it out. A plaque. A trophy statuette holding a pistol was affixed in gilt relief. And the inscription:

Captain Nina Pryce, U.S. Army
.45 Caliber Pistol, Second Place, 50 Yard Slow Fire
National Inter-Service Match
1992. Camp Perry, Ohio.

Reverently, Broker, who barely kept his police qualification at twenty-five yards with his Beretta, tucked the award back between the books. Outshoot her with a rifle, he told himself.

The only personal touch on her desk were two framed photos. One was of her mother, father, and herself standing in what looked like Georgia pines when she was about seven. The other showed

Ray Pryce and Broker himself, sitting on some baked paddy dike wearing olive drab that was busted out with sweat fade. And that foreign red dirt.

Broker picked up the picture and scanned the husky freckled man with the bluff features and sandy red hair. The guy who did everything by the book—*I put twenty years of insulation between us, Ray.* He lit a cigarette and studied Ray Pryce's face through what seemed like twenty feet of plate glass.

They had not been friends in the strict sense. Too much of an age difference.

Nina came out of her bedroom in an extra-large olive drab T-shirt with black jump wings stenciled on it. The hem swept her thighs like a Spartan chiton. She opened the windows wider and turned on a fan. "The smoke, sorry."

"What happened to your brother?" he asked, returning the picture to the desk.

"Yuppie puke lawyer in Atlanta."

Broker hitched up his sheet and took the rest of his butt out on the small balcony. Nina fished another Vernor's from the icebox and joined him.

The wind combed through her short hair as she pushed off the railing and turned to him. "Can I ask you a personal question?"

"Shoot."

"You have any gremlins that will make going back to Vietnam a problem?"

Broker laughed. But he lit another cigarette off the smoldering butt of the one he had going. "You see *Platoon*?"

"Everybody did, and *Apocalypse Now* and *Full Metal Jacket*."

"You see me in any of them?"

"What's your point?"

"Your ideas about Nam come from Hollywood. Hell, my ideas about Desert Storm come from CNN. Anyway, I missed the rock-and-roll drug opera. I had pure Greek tragedy at the end."

"Let me put it another way. You thought pretty highly of LaPorte once; and my dad, Tuna, Trin. The way you talked about them, that summer I stayed with you . . . it's like you still couldn't believe what happened."

"No hang-ups, Nina. Nothing that will get in the way," Broker said emphatically.

Tenacity and tact debated in her eyes and she proposed carefully, "Maybe we should both go to New Orleans."

Broker shook his head. "We have too much ground to cover."

Seeing that he was adamant, she switched the subject. "What about the gold maybe buried out in the jungle? You get any interesting vibes off that? Like it coming between us and you maybe slitting my throat?"

"Do you?"

She hugged herself. "Scares me. Excites me. But I don't think so."

"What about 'Tempts you'?" he asked.

"Not my style, Broker. And I never figured you for the money type."

"Oh?"

"That's right." She touched his cheek lightly. "And we're not the stay at home, cozy type either. The soaps weren't invented for us. Or diapers. No patience for the little things. Sound familiar . . ." Her voice trailed a hint of sadness.

She moved behind him and the immediate silence balanced precariously and became charged. Through the budding trees Broker watched traffic curl on a freeway. Her fingers trolled his bare shoulders. Gently kneaded the muscle.

"We're fixers," she said. "We sit around waiting for something bad to happen so we can jump in." Her warm breath was scented with Colgate and trailed softly across his neck. "Doesn't mean we don't get lonely."

The moment reared, strong enough to topple them off the balcony and into each other's arms.

"Nina, when I met you, you were wearing braces."

"I'm not your little sister. I'm probably the only woman who could put up with you. Better than that bitch you married."

Broker stood up and propped himself against the railing a safe distance away. He looked up. Ann Arbor made a glitter dome of freeway traffic. Rows of fast food signs stole the heavens.

He changed the subject. "LaPorte was one of the great ones out there, like John Vann and Tim Randall."

In a flat voice, she said, "People change."

"And you're right. I still have trouble believing he made a wrong turn. Or your dad."

She turned away. "Their whole generation did, yours too." She faced him and stood up straight and her voice chiseled away her fugue of hormones. "Now it's up to my generation to square it."

She wasn't talking about generations. She was talking about herself. Broker flipped his cigarette past her in an arc of sparks that briefly scouted her profile. Was it a warrior-virgin he saw in those taut, pure features? Could that be the source of her strength?

An hour later he was asleep on the couch and awoke suddenly to find her sitting over him, watching him. She turned on the lamp and he saw a stealthy shadow of intimacy peek from behind her crinkled eyes.

She leaned over and kissed him on the lips, a chaste kiss on the surface, but a little way down he felt the jolt of quiet longing.

"You're not like a lot of guys, but you really don't know anything about women, do you?" She winced fondly and rose and went away without finishing the thought.

27

BROKER HAS STEPPED ACROSS THE ORIGIN OF MISSISSIPPI WHERE it trickles out of Lake Itaska and now, from five thousand feet, he sees the other end of the river drape a sluggish coil around Lake Ponchartrain. New Orleans squeezes between the lake and the river like a dark sponge soaking up the downhill poison of a continent. Farther out, the Gulf horizon stews in a muddy ultramarine haze that nurses the energy of sharks and hurricanes.

A place where it never freezes can never be clean.

The Northwest flight bumped down its flaps and the wheels jerked for terra firma. Broker sat back and gripped the armrests. Getting older, he had discovered, meant worrying that the Rodneys of the world were overrepresented in the machinist union that serviced jet engines.

While the other passengers deplaned he took some Tylenol. The infection in his thumb smacked festered lips, anticipating the heat and a bumper crop of germs.

He had a thousand dollars in his pocket, room reservations for the night in a French Quarter hotel, and a gold tiger tooth combing the sweat worming through his chest. He felt naked in his muggy clothes. As per airline regulations, his weapon resided in the baggage compartment, unloaded; the ammunition packed separately in a shaving kit bag under the eye of the Detroit Airport Police.

A few minutes later, slick with sweat, he stood at the baggage conveyer and grimaced when he spotted his AWOL bag trundle down the line, shaving kit attached. The floppy, blaze orange, steal-me tag brayed: FIREARM ENCLOSED.

In a men's room, past the metal detectors, he slipped in a toilet stall, unpacked the bag, and put on the shoulder rig. With the .45 slung like an overdeveloped steel muscle in leather tendons under his left armpit, he felt better.

He smiled, despite his thumb and the close heat, and savored his independence as he strolled through baggage into the southern afternoon. The Louisiana air was wet gauze tented on spiked palms. In three seconds he was mummy-wrapped in the temperature of jaded blood. The barrier of his skin dissolved in a bath of sweat, and Broker, a lonely white corpuscle, floated into the gaudy fever stream of New Orleans.

On the street travelers cued up for cabs and a black woman in an airport uniform directed him to the next available car. The driver was a black man in his sixties with a neck and shoulders like a pliant fireplug. He turned in his seat with tourist maps in his hand and a relaxed smile on his broad lips.

His eyes assumed a familiarity, warm and alive and immediate, that would shock people up north. They sized up Broker's shoulders, the ponytail, the bandaged hand. They noted the sag under the lapel of his light sports coat. The cabby laughed. A patois of gristly inflection that rode a high-pitched chuckle. "Po-leese. Where from?"

"Minnesota."

"Get you a baggy shirt to cover all that iron. You gonna die wearing that jacket down here."

Beads dangled from the rear-view mirror, family pictures and some pendants of suspicious origin twined with a cameo of the Virgin Mary.

Broker laughed and gave the cabby LaPorte's address.

"Uh-huh. Gen. Cyrus LaPorte lives in that big house on St. Charles in the Garden District. The Tourrine Mansion. Now that belonged originally to a Confederate general. The LaPorte family acquired it back in 1909. He pretty big too, get his picture in the paper a lot. "

Broker rolled down the window and lit a cigarette. "It always this hot?"

"Ain't hot. Hot come out at night."

They rode a freeway, turned off and passed acres of white ramshackle tombs. "Cemetery," said the cabby. "Above ground. This whole fallin'-down motherfucker built in a swamp."

Broker, from bedrock country, nodded. It was a pushed-around moraine and delta city built on debris the glaciers had kicked down the length of North America. Then they were on St. Charles, and there were mule-drawn carriages and a green street car. But Broker noticed the fences. Friendly people but lots of tall iron fences.

"You going to the wedding?" asked the cabby.

"What?"

"You my second airport ride to the Tourrine. Wedding this afternoon. They rent it out for weddings."

"Why's a rich guy like LaPorte rent his house out for weddings?"

"Rich man never quit findin' ways to make money. Why he rich," said the cabby. "That's it, that white monster on the right, takes most of the block."

The three-story house wore a crisp petticoat of new white paint, but it was Mansard-gabled, gargoyled and turreted with enough sinister energy to inspire Edgar Allan Poe. The seven-foot fence that surrounded the grounds was stylized black wrought iron. Curved spears articulated as thickly clustered blooming lilacs.

A uniformed New Orleans cop lounged at the entrance. Banquet tables were being set up on the broad lawn by black men in short-waisted white coats and dark slacks who sleepwalked in the drowsy heat.

"Drive around the block and up the alley," said Broker.

The cabby chuckled. "You planning to rob the place, huh, you casing it now."

Absolutely, thought Broker. The back of the house was walled off from the rest of the lawn and the alley by thick hedges. A second-story balcony ran the length of the back of the house and was supported by grillwork and hung with showers of geraniums and impatiens. An oak tree, draped in Spanish moss, grew conveniently close to a corner.

"What's behind the hedges?" asked Broker.

"Swimming pool."

"Okay. Now take me here." He handed the cabby the address of the hotel Larson had squeezed him into.

The cabby nodded. "Doniat. On Charters. That's a nice place, too."

Broker missed the romance of the French Quarter. He keyed on the cramped passageways gated with more spear-tipped wrought iron. The iron was topped with tangles of barbed wire. The wire was pulled serpentine in a tangle-foot pattern that he associated with Developing World wars. A billboard poster emblazoned with the astronomical New Orleans homicide statistics shouted on a store window. "MORE THAN BOSTON, MORE THAN DETROIT." Letters large enough for Broker to read from a passing car.

The cabby demanded his attention. "Now listen up, Minnesota. This here's Rampart Street we crossin' now, just don't be wandering round north of here drunk with money hanging out of your pocket and you just might make it."

Broker thanked him, tipped him generously with Nina's money and checked into the Doniat. He took a bottle of mineral water from the honor bar and let a young porter carry his small athletic bag up the stairs and to a room at the end of the hall with windows that opened on a gallery that overlooked the street.

After tipping the kid for his exertion he called Nina's.

"I'm two hours from meeting the great man. How's your end?"

"I'll be at the bank tomorrow morning as soon as it opens. Watch yourself, Broker."

"You too."

Broker tucked the Xerox copy of LaPorte's map and the sonar graphic in the inner lapel pocket of his jacket, called a cab, and went to the Civic Center to visit the main library. He spent an hour and a half skimming every reference to the LaPorte family that a harried librarian could locate. Then he grabbed another cab and headed for the Garden District. This time he drew a short, bald white firecracker for a driver.

"Guadalcanal, Saipan, Okinawa, and Iwo. I made all those goddamn landings. And now I'm seventy-two years old and I have to take shit from these fucking trash-talking jungle bunnies in my own hometown. Threw three of the shitbirds out of my cab just the other day."

The man's neck was the color of angina, veins ridged his cranium.

"Damn niggers are taking over the goddamn streets. Hell if I'm going to ride any more those sonsabitches—"

"Hey, man, just drive the fuckin' car, okay?"

Finally the apoplectic cabby dropped him off. He didn't get a tip. Broker stood on the street and watched men in suits and women in formal dresses roam the lawn with plastic glasses of champagne. Maybe no one could afford to live in a house like this anymore, even in Louisiana, where you didn't have to foot the heating bill. So even Cyrus LaPorte had to accommodate and peddle his living space.

Broker went through the stockade of iron lilacs and the uniform was alert enough in the heat to come out of his lounging posture in the shade and challenge the tall, serious-moving man in the ponytail. Broker flashed his badge. The cop nodded and stepped back. Broker went in.

The lower level was a gleam of varnished wood floors and intricately carved antebellum woodwork. Servants glided with silver trays or arranged platters of finger food. The gay mountains of floral arrangements smelled damp . . . like funerals. He asked one of the waiters where to find Mr. LaPorte.

The waiter rolled his eyes to a spiral oak staircase. At the top a snake-boned young man with strawberry hair, who nobody would want at their wedding, leaned against a railing. His feral handsome face and hot hazel eyes suggested that he and Bevode Fret had hatched out of the same stagnant malarial pool and had grown up fighting the gators for their supper. But his anemic complexion and the sniffles suggested that he was on a Colombian diet. Broker mounted the stairs and said, "Phillip Broker. I have a three o'clock appointment with LaPorte."

"That's General LaPorte. What you got under the coat?" The punk assumed a blocking stance. Broker showed his badge again. "Give me the badge, your ID, and the piece," said the guy.

"Fuck you," said Broker. He eyed the cocaine pathology squirming in the punk's sinuses and in his dilated pupils. The current American nightmare—armed, popcorn tough, ready to blow at a moment's notice, and not much underneath to back it up after he'd touched off a magazine of nine millimeter. "Go announce me."

He stared the punk down. The punk went.

Broker looked around. He didn't know much about real money. So he didn't really register the magnitude of the furnishings and art objects and the Persian carpets strewn all around him. He knew that the air became smoother, taking a subtle bounce along the pigment of paintings and the scarred volcanic faces of pre-Columbian art. He rubbed the sweaty stubble on his chin and felt like a Goth who'd slipped into Rome. And planned to be back with a lot of his pals.

The punk returned wearing an obsequious sneer and yanked his head for Broker to follow him. He was admitted to a spacious room with high ceilings and walls festooned with trophies and mementos. The room took up the right rear corner of the house. The foliage from the oak tree on the lawn shaded the windows that overlooked the wedding party.

The general would be with him in a moment and would he like a refreshment.

Broker ran his eyes over the decor and said, "Rum." Then he

eased into an upholstered leather chair that faced a heavy carved teak desk elevated on a two-step dais so that the man sitting behind the desk could look down on his visitors.

An elderly black man in a shiny black suitcoat and trousers, with a bulbous hearing aid growing in his left ear and his back bent by scoliosis, or the pressure of place, shuffled in. Eyes downcast, he carried a tray on which sat a bottle of rum, a glass, and a decanter of ice cubes. His tempo was geared to the listlessly turning ceiling fans, which slowly stirred the languid air. Time definitely slowed down here. Broker wondered if there was a plan to turn it back.

He poured a shot of rum and lit a Spirit and squirmed slightly in the studded leather upholstery. His thumb throbbed and sweat itched on his chin. The room made his bones glow like an X-ray machine.

It had never occurred to him that he could *have* things. He'd accepted the fact that the most he could hope for was to *do* things.

Three of the walls held the bric-a-brac of the stillborn greatness of LaPorte's life. Broker perused the athletic, academic, and military mementos. There was the glass case with eight rows of combat decorations, including two Distinguished Service Crosses and five Silver Stars. There were pictures of LaPorte with William Westmoreland and Creighton Abrams.

Another wall was an abattoir of trophy antlers and skulls mounted in the European style. The configuration of the horns was exotic to Broker's Northwoods eyes. Things that died in Africa and Asia.

The last wall was a true museum, hung with plantation implements arranged in an almost votive pattern around an imposing, larger-than-life, full-length portrait.

Broker recognized the set of that intense furrowed brow and gimlet eyes staring down from the oil. The thin slash mouth and the stingy lips projected a cold Creole profile of power.

Royale LaPorte, a hero of the Battle of New Orleans, was portrayed in a gentleman's ruffled shirt and a brocaded greatcoat. His left sleeve was empty and pinned to the shoulder. His right hand was inserted in his lapel, Napoleon fashion, and the buckled shoe on his stockinged right foot rested on a globe of the world.

Broker raised his glass to the painting and drank his shot of rum. He set the glass aside and continued his inspection. Directly underneath the painting a shiny braided bullwhip coiled on a wooden peg. Below the whip, its filigree all but melted by time from the steel, squatted a square antique safe. The safe took a key. The keyhole was nicked and bright from use.

French doors made up the fourth wall and opened out onto the gallery that overlooked the swimming pool. Broker's eyes drifted back to the desk. Not one cubic inch of off-white computer plastic in the whole damn place. The phone was a 1940s ashtray style, obstinate black ceramic and heavy enough to crack a coconut. So LaPorte, like Broker, was still a wood and steel kind of guy.

An energetic beam of minty aftershave cut the bouillabaisse air.

"Broker. It's been a long time, son."

The voice was a generous muddy baritone, vigorous and amused. Broker turned his head and his skin prickled. Gen. Cyrus LaPorte ambled into the room with the alien grace and vigor of a six-foot-tall, two-legged spider.

28

LAPORTE WORE SNOWY TOPSIDERS, A TAN SHORT-SLEEVED shirt, and casual pleated trousers. His bare, corded arms had shriveled but not weakened, and his neck compressed toward his shoulders, which added to the sidling insect gait. His eyes were pale blue, pitted and shiny as two musket balls, but seemed darker because of the pressure ridge of his brow. Salt-and-pepper short-cropped hair capped his bony head and the hand he extended was hard as tanned hide.

LaPorte pointed to the bandaged thumb. Broker did not respond. LaPorte's smile effortlessly glossed over twenty years. "Appreciate you taking the time to come."

He motioned for Broker to resume his seat, mounted the steps and sat, elevated behind his wide desk. The platform bothered Broker. It was a conceit that the LaPorte of twenty years ago would have had contempt for. He flipped open a manila folder and shot his lead eyes at Broker. "You were a lieutenant during that shitstorm back in seventy-five." LaPorte let the folder fall shut. "Still a lieutenant, I see. Does policework agree with you, Phil?"

It was the first time that LaPorte had ever called him by his given name. Even prepared to discover that this man had arranged to leave him to die in Hue City, the small gesture affected Broker. He graced LaPorte with the most exhausted of cynical smiles.

"So," said LaPorte, "you're still mixed up with the Pryce family."

"And now I'm mixed up with you."

"You'll recall, when we were at Benning for that witch hunt, I cautioned you to walk away. But you had to go over and help Marian move off the base."

"Marian died and Nina doesn't need any extra hassle. She has enough hassle inside her own head."

"I hear you." LaPorte squinted philosophically.

Broker withdrew the folded map from his inside jacket pocket and tossed it on LaPorte's desk, knocking over a collection of terra cotta figurines. LaPorte pursed his lips and set the bundle aside.

"There's your maps and sonar pictures. And I'll let your friend Bevode go . . ." Broker pronounced Fret's name Bee-voo-dee.

LaPorte corrected, with a dry smile, "Bevode. Rhymes with commode."

"Whatever. I want your word that he leaves Nina Pryce alone."

LaPorte grinned, revealing a half-inch of root on his molars. "My word."

"I was thinking more along the lines that if you break it you and me will have a personal problem."

LaPorte responded with a pompous tic, shooting the nonexistent cuffs on his thick wrists. "I can understand how you'd be upset. This came on sort of sudden."

Broker rose slowly from his chair, letting his coat fall open to reveal the holster and his voice growled, intimate with menace. "Don't think so. It's been coming on for twenty years. And if you and I don't reach an agreement, financial and otherwise, in the next few minutes I'm going to flat kick the slats out of your whole corn-crib. I already stove in that pussy you sent up north."

LaPorte shrugged his shoulders. "Bevode tends to be . . . overzealous."

"He's a punk. He had a fucking hickey on his neck." Broker made a face and resumed his seat.

LaPorte leaned back and massaged a liver spot on his hand. "Would it surprise you to know that Bevode Fret was once a very dedicated cop, lavishly commended, and known throughout the parish as a man who couldn't be bought?"

"Point being?"

LaPorte shrugged. The lead eyes probed. "Perhaps the work got to him. Does the work ever get to you?"

"You mean protecting the rich rats from the poor rats?"

"I mean too many rats in the cage. A man can start looking for options."

Broker exhaled and inspected his hands. "Yeah, right. Crime's supposed to be deviant behavior. Now there's nothing to deviate from. Folks are choosing up sides. Some kind of cultural street challenge that's going on."

LaPorte smiled faintly. "Down here the rabble associate that dilemma with skin pigmentation."

Broker flicked ashes into his turned-up Levi's cuff. "It's the climate. Encourages one-crop agriculture and simple-mindedness."

LaPorte laughed and opened a drawer and stood up. He came around the desk and handed an ashtray to Broker. "Mind the ashes, Phil; that rug cost more than you earned last year."

Broker took the ashtray and slowly rolled the ash into it. LaPorte leaned back on the desk and smiled. "Now, if we can get past the macho tantrums, I have a proposition for you."

"Just like that," said Broker. "After all this time. And your goon kicks down my door . . ."

LaPorte clasped his hands behind his back and walked to the window that overlooked the wedding party. He squinted down at the lawn then turned and picked up a pair of binoculars from a shelf on the wall. He bent, focused the glasses, then shook his head. He came back to his desk and pressed a button. He grinned at Broker and chuckled. "The minimum wage. They just can't get it right."

The elderly black man who had brought Broker his drink crab-walked into the room. LaPorte spoke with elaborate politeness.

"Hiram, get on Artis down there to tell the guests not to put the knives, forks, and spoons into the trash containers. Keep it separate. And the glasses."

"Okay, Mr. Cyrus," the servant replied and shuffled off.

LaPorte sighed. "I've been telling that man for ten years to drop the 'Mister.' Old habits."

"You were saying?" said Broker.

A puff of wind stirred the long curtains and LaPorte said, "Maybe we'll get an afternoon breeze. Let's go out on the balcony."

They sat in wrought-iron chairs as a tremble of impending rain ruffled the cascading impatiens. Beyond the hedges, the wedding party buzzed in pre-event conversation.

LaPorte looked up and found the sun in a hazy hole in the clouds. He stared directly at it unblinking and stated, "The fact is, I'm in a ticklish spot."

Broker hawked, leaned forward, and spit over the balcony. "You don't strike me as the ticklish kind. You're more the agony of psoriasis."

LaPorte cleared his throat. "Who else knows about the map?"

Broker answered offhand. "I called Mel Fisher for an opinion—"

"That's not funny," said LaPorte. "The Hue gold is a remote legend. I'd like to keep it that way. When the war ended the Communists didn't register a complaint that it had been stolen. Which is part of the mystery. It crops up from time to time as a low-key buzz in the international treasure hunting community. But, with Clinton getting ready to normalize relations with Vietnam, and with Nina Pryce waving around the Freedom of Information Act, I suspect interest will start picking up."

"So?"

"So answer the question."

"Nina Pryce. Me."

"Let's cut the bullshit. It's Jimmy Tuna I care about. If you can't see that, we're both wasting our time."

"Okay," said Broker. "He disappeared without a trace from Milan."

"Did you talk to the prison doctor?" asked LaPorte. Broker shook his head. "I did," said LaPorte. "Tuna has weeks left. Maybe days. He always was a hard luck guy . . ." LaPorte's eyes cruised the far wall where he kept his war mementos. "He married this foxy German girl in sixty-six. She gets over here, gets her citizenship, buys everything in sight, and then sends Tuna this tape of her screwing a guy as a Dear John." LaPorte shook his head. "He played it over and over. Her screaming with bedsprings in the background." LaPorte lapsed into a guttural German accent: "'Fok me, hunny,' Christmas Eve, 1970. Rainy night in the team house on the Laotian border." He sighed and shook his head. "Went off the deep end. Tried to rob a bank . . . prison all these years. Now cancer."

"Maybe robbing banks was habit forming," said Broker. The words hung in the heavy air with his cigarette smoke.

LaPorte leaned back in his chair, squinted into the sun, and shook his head. "It was the fucking war. We all went wrong." He turned to Broker. "Bound to happen when you lose human scale." He laughed cynically and slid in and out of past and present tense: "We let them bring in the gadgets. You know, like, they used to pollinate the jungle with these dealy bobs—body heat sniffers. So a monkey comes along and trips one. And it's B-52 time and it starts raining dead monkeys. Not to mention blowing a lot of fine hardwoods to bits . . ."

His leaden eyes drooped, too heavy for his face and his voice lowered, speaking to himself. "The hill tribesmen told me that the tigers were growing up without learning how to hunt. They just fed on all the dead monkey meat laying around. So they grow up and don't know how to teach *their* young to hunt . . ."

Cyrus LaPorte caught himself and laughed. "Do you know that they give recruits these stress cards now in Marine boot camp? If they're feeling *abused* they hold them up to the drill instructor. God in heaven; the new gadgeted-up American tiger that never learned how to hunt."

LaPorte became aware that Broker was staring at him and asked softly, "Does it really matter what happened that night?"

"It matters to Nina Pryce."

LaPorte grimaced and exhaled slowly. "Phil, she really doesn't want to know."

"Try me."

"Okay." LaPorte brought his palms down on the wire arms of the chair as if to rise. But it was meant as an emphatic gesture. "I'll fucking tell you then. Our former worthy foes are less worthy since they opened the door to the west. I'm doing some business over there, building a hotel in Hoi An; great site, virtually untouched. Which means I've had to spread the dash around. Take a few ranking party members out to dinner. Some long cruises on my boat.

"So I asked one of these gentlemen to do a little digging for me and it turns out we didn't know half of what was going on that night."

"Like what?"

LaPorte pointed his finger. "Who was the key to pulling former assets out of the central provinces?"

"Trin."

"Correct. And what was Trin's first rule?"

"Trust no one." Broker felt his shoulders curl forward, body-armoring against the tug of LaPorte's will.

"And who did Trin trust?"

"Pryce."

"Now, back to my Commie bureaucrat, who was panting like a bitch in heat for the new Land Rover I was going to buy him. He checked around. Didn't take much. A number of people made their reputations capturing Trin. According to this guy, Trin was grabbed in a secure house in Hue because the North Vietnamese were tipped by an American . . ."

LaPorte paused. "This alleged American arranged a clandestine meet, through a double agent. On the coast. To give up Trin. And hear this. My informant said it was written right in the report: The American was described as having a gold cigarette case."

"What did this guy get in return for handing over Trin?" asked Broker.

LaPorte smiled thinly. "Bastard wouldn't tell me. That'd probably cost another Land Rover."

"Hearsay," said Broker.

"My ass. It was planned in depth. First position Trin as the bait. Then send you in as the decoy. And I tried to defend that son-ofabitch . . ." His eyes scanned the rustling foliage and he said softly, "For which I paid a very steep price." LaPorte stood up abruptly and seized the railing until his knuckles turned white. "Give me a cigarette, please," he asked softly.

There was a time when Broker could not imagine Cyrus LaPorte losing control. He shrugged and held out his pack. LaPorte took one and a light from Broker's lighter.

LaPorte inhaled, blew a stream of smoke and immediately rested two fingers on his left wrist to test his pulse. Broker remembered what his dad had said and he wondered if LaPorte, who was in his early sixties, had glimpsed death creeping the iron lilacs, staking out squatter's rights on his estate. LaPorte tossed the smoke away and made a face. "I haven't had one of those in eight years." He spun on Broker. "So you can see why I'm not crazy about Nina Pryce nosing around in my affairs."

"What do you care. You've found your helicopter."

"Goddammit, man, we've gridded the bottom and sonar mapped the whole area. We've been all over that wreck and we've got bones and coral-wrapped hand grenades, but we've only brought up *seven* bars of gold," said LaPorte. "It's not there."

"And you think Tuna knows where it is?"

With a glare like point-blank muskets, LaPorte fumed, "Of course I do. Don't fuck around. So do you!"

29

THE WOMAN WALKED OUT FROM BENEATH THE BALCONY, staying to the dappled shadows along the right side of the pool deck. Divots of sunlight peeked through the hedge and caught in her dark hair and flowed in snakeskin patterns on her olive arms and legs. She wore a high-necked T-shirt and light shorts like a coat of black cotton paint and she carried a faded blue rubber mat under her arm. She used absolutely every muscle in her body in the simple act of walking.

Broker's eyes stayed fixed on the woman as she knelt and smoothed out her mat.

"I don't know about Minnesota, but down here it's not considered polite to stare at a man's wife," said LaPorte.

"Very attractive," said Broker.

"Really? All you can see is her back."

"And young."

LaPorte snorted. "No, Lola's merely well preserved."

Impolitely, Broker continued to stare at Lola LaPorte as she swung her body through a continuous series of postures. Her limbs swung light as balsa, but they were anchored in the tension of driven pilings.

Yoga. Irene Broker studied it to file down the teeth of aging. But Mom did it on rocks.

LaPorte leaned over the balcony and called out, irritably, "Lola, cut that shit out and come over here."

Lightly she unwound from a pose and stood, staring up at them. Her large eyes, wide cheeks, full lips, and perfect shoulder-length hair communicated a certain taboo physical range: rich guy's wife. As cool in the tropical heat as a pristine winter shadow Lola LaPorte walked halfway to the balcony and put her hands on her hips. "What?" she said, annoyed, not turning her face up.

LaPorte rose and leaned over the balcony. "Mr. Phillip Broker is up here, he's the detective from Minnesota we discussed last night. I get the impression he's embarking on a new career as a blackmailer."

"Is he here to study or to practice?" said Lola in a bored voice. Broker appreciated that the LaPortes, in conversation, volleyed a siege energy of contempt.

LaPorte made a face and lowered his voice. "You married, Broker?"

"Divorced."

"Kids?"

Broker shook his head.

"I wanted kids," said LaPorte in a sour tone. Then he called to his wife. "I was thinking of inviting Mr. Broker to supper."

"Sorry, I have plans," said Broker who didn't want to seem too eager to curry LaPorte's favor.

"So does Cyrus," said Lola sweetly. She waved her wrist idly in parting and returned to her exercise.

LaPorte grimaced and then inclined his palm back toward his office and they went inside and sat in the chairs in front of the desk. This time their eyes were on the same level. "Let's get down to it, Phil. I'll tell you what I want. You tell me what you want."

Broker waited, expressionless.

"I need Nina Pryce contained," said LaPorte. "Bought off, diverted, made happy, whatever it takes. Things are too delicate right now to have a loose cannon on deck. Second, I have to locate Tuna." He held up his hand. "Let me enlarge a bit: I've had Tuna watched for years. Every approach I've made to him he turned down. When Nina started visiting him I had *her* watched. So, after she went to see you last January, I've had you checked out in detail.

"Bevode can do more than drag his knuckles. He ran a credit profile on you. We know you've been trying to arrange large loans through your employees' credit union. We've been in contact with Neil Naslund, the banker in Devil's Rock. We know about your problem." LaPorte steepled his fingers. "If we can find a way to cooperate, I can make that problem go away."

Broker's turn. He ad-libbed easily.

"The map I gave you is a Xerox. The original shows a grid coordinate circled in grease pencil that pinpoints a location well within the coastal waters of the Socialist Republic of Vietnam. And I have the original chopper graphic. And a transcript of an FBI inquiry into a ruckus in the Milan Pen visitor's room between you and Tuna in 1980."

LaPorte stroked his chin ruefully. "Now there's a hitch that Robert Louis Stevenson didn't have to deal with. Xerox machines."

Broker paused to let it sink in. "I left them in a sealed envelope in my lawyer's files in St. Paul. And I wrote a speculative letter that mentions your name frequently. If anything unusual happens to me or Nina Pryce the envelope gets delivered to the United States Attorney. Another copy goes to the Vietnamese Embassy."

LaPorte glanced at his watch, then smiled. "Maybe you and Bevode Fret are more kin than you think. Have you put a figure on it?"

"First let's get Nina off the table."

LaPorte leaned forward. "Is she really . . . unbalanced?"

"She's just extreme."

"Okay, okay . . . What do you think would solve her problem?"

Broker smiled. "To see you hang for killing her father."

LaPorte chuckled. "Does she have a fallback position?"

"I could suggest one," said Broker.

LaPorte opened his hands in an entreating gesture. Broker continued. "You pay for a year of discreet counseling. I mean serious stuff, a psychiatrist. Then you make a good faith effort to help her get reinstated in the army."

LaPorte sputtered and smiled at the same time, instantly grasping the symmetry in the solution. "Getting back in would make her well, huh?"

"Just my opinion."

LaPorte shook his head. "God, I'd lose my pension. The good old boys in the army think she's a libber fanatic bitch. She was all over the TV."

"You could do it," Broker said mildly.

"Jesus Christ, I don't know. Maybe with the Bush crowd but these Arkansas hippies—"

"Easier with the hippies. You could do it," repeated Broker. "For Ray."

"Fuck Ray Pryce, the horse he rode in on, and the colonel who sent him." LaPorte thumped his chest. "I signed for that fucking helicopter *he* lost. They made me *pay* for it. You know how much a Chinook costs. I was pay-deducted through Ford and Carter and finally Reagan got me off the hook and got me my money back."

Broker found the outburst curious. In the public library he'd read that the LaPorte family was worth $70 million. His eyes strayed to the tall portrait of the pirate on the wall. "You're not in this strictly for the money, are you?" he asked.

"We're not talking about money. Money just sits in a bank and accrues. This is . . . treasure. I'm sixty-one years old. This is probably the last exciting thing I'll do in my life." LaPorte shook his head impatiently. "The Pryce kid? Will she shut up?"

"Can you grease the skids to get her back in?"

"That would take an absurd, and not entirely legal, contribution to a presidential campaign." He grimaced. "It might be done."

"I'll take that as a yes. Now for Jimmy Tuna—"

LaPorte raised a hand. His eyes glowed faintly and Broker had conflicting impressions. Sensuality. And molten lead being poured.

"Are you sure you want to mix in our dirty business, Phil?"

Broker looked directly into LaPorte's metallic eyes. "The Hue gold is . . . morally ambiguous."

"The Eagle Scout I knew twenty years ago wouldn't have said that."

"People change."

Something merry danced in LaPorte's eyes and Broker thought it might be the old male slow dance; LaPorte wanted him to admit he was rolling over and baring his throat to the stronger alpha wolf. "Please continue, Phil," said LaPorte.

"I don't want Tuna hurt."

"The man is dying," LaPorte said impatiently. "Do you know where he is?"

"Not yet."

The heat left LaPorte's eyes and they froze with a subtle click of calculation above his smile. Broker had ceased to be important.

And Broker's own false smile masked the ice pick that suddenly pinned his heart. He'd made a fatal mistake. A number of them. LaPorte had probably shut his eyes and drawn a circle on that map. The treasure map had no leverage power because it was a phony. Easy bait for an eager Nina. And he knew Fret wasn't alone. His whole act was designed to siphon Broker off to New Orleans. *And if I could figure out that the trail to Tuna led through his banking records, so could Cyrus LaPorte.* They were still following her. And if they grabbed her coming out of the bank in Ann Arbor . . .

"How much?" said LaPorte with a convincing pained expression.

Broker was treading water. LaPorte was comfortably standing on the bottom.

"Five hundred thousand. For Nina, for my silence, and for Tuna. Half now. Half when it's done. And do it some way it can't be traced."

"I'm willing to pick up the note on your dad's white elephant and hold it. If everything works out, you'll get a another hundred thousand."

"That's a hundred and fifty thousand shy of the figure I had in mind."

"Let's think about it." LaPorte stood up briskly and pressed the button on his desk. "When are you leaving New Orleans?" he asked.

"Ten tomorrow morning."

"Where are you staying?"

"The Doniat. On Chartiers."

"I'll pick you up at eight and drive you to the airport. We'll see where we're at then." They shook hands.

The old black guy in the shiny trousers appeared at the door and LaPorte said cordially, "Hiram, show Mr. Broker out. I'm leaving through the garage. I'd drop you but I'm going in the other direction. Hiram can call you a cab, but you should really take the streetcar." LaPorte smiled and walked energetically down the hall and through a doorway.

"I need to use a phone," Broker immediately said to Hiram.

"Uh-huh, but you wait a second." Hiram cocked his ear out the open balcony doors. Seconds slid by like abacus beads on a wire of sweat. Broker heard the faint squeal of tires on hot cement down near the pool apron.

"Okay. Now you use that phone right there," said Hiram, pointing to the raised desk. Then he turned and shuffled into the hall.

Broker stabbed in Nina's number. On the third ring a rough male voice answered, "Hello," and Broker hammered the desk with his fist. Then the voice said, "I say, Merry. What do you say?"

Broker shook his head, blinked and then almost shouted, "Weather."

"Hi there," said Nina in a bright voice.

"Who—"

She cut him off. "I told you we shouldn't split up. The only guy who was good at that was Robert E. Lee."

"Nina?"

"Relax. I'm playing Scrabble with Sgt. Danny Larkins of the

Michigan Highway Patrol. We took a grad course together, remember."

In the background the deep voice said, "Sociology of deviance. It was *boring*."

Nina continued. "For an outrageous amount of cash Danny has taken two personal leave days to squire me around and tuck me on an airplane. And he's got this great big gun."

"She's just dying to touch it," yodeled Danny Larkins. They both laughed.

Broker, glad that someone was having fun, sagged on LaPorte's desk. "I screwed up."

"That's okay. I didn't. How's it going?"

"You're it. They got me down here on a draw play. The map's all bullshit. Watch yourself." He wondered if the call could be monitored. "Especially tomorrow."

"About what I figured. No sweat. We're having a poker party tonight. Six cops. I'm buying the beer."

"Strip poker. And all of us are these *huge* motherfuckers," crowed Larkins.

"I gotta go, I'm using LaPorte's phone," said Broker.

"I'm covered. You take care," said Nina. Broker thought he heard her blow a kiss into the receiver. He hung up, dismounted the dais, and started for the door. Hiram appeared in front of him.

"You ain't leaving yet," said the old man.

Broker glowered down at Hiram's mostly bald beige skull. "Say again?"

Hiram shook his head. "Out there on the balcony. Go ahead. Somebody you gotta talk to."

"Who? Why?"

Hiram's voice was eloquent with the absurdity of watching white people. "Cause they in over they head just like you."

Lola LaPorte smoothed her hands through her hair as she walked along the pool deck toward the balcony. When she was within easy speaking range, she looked up. Through a haze of anger and humiliation Broker saw that her features keyed to the way she moved, hard and soft, a mobile pentagram of squares and triangles seamlessly turning inside of circles. He thought that her wide, somber eyes might be light brown.

"He's gone," she called up to him. Nice voice when her husband wasn't around. Full range, like the rest of her. Mature and disciplined. "When policemen visit my husband it usually concerns money. What exactly is Cyrus paying you to do, Mr. Broker?"

With a tight smile Broker grabbed at the only straw in sight. "Get some counseling for a girl named Nina Pryce and let Bevode Fret out of jail in Minnesota."

She put her hands on her hips in a self-consciously mocking feminine pose and pitched her voice to match. "Nina Pryce is hardly a *girl* and I myself, given the opportunity to keep Bevode Fret in a jailhouse, would never consent to letting him go; a sentiment shared, I assure you, by half the sensible people of New Orleans. But then, half the sensible people in New Orleans would be a distinct minority."

"What can I say—"

"Are you corrupt, Mr. Broker?"

"Only in Louisiana, so far."

Broker tried to make out her expression, but she stood in a subtle riot of shadow cast by the hedges and he couldn't tell.

"Relax, we're alone for a while. I'll be right up," she said.

30

HE RETREATED FROM THE BALCONY AND THE HOT SENSATION stoked in his cheeks and in his hands. LaPorte had made a fool of him. The fury banked like coals when he recalled Bevode Fret's assured smile. Broker prayed that Danny Larkins and company knew their stuff better than he did.

The second wave of anger was packed harder and took a direction. *Get even.* No. *Punish . . .*

His eyes tracked the office as his hands burned to seize on something. Something that would make LaPorte feel as foolish as he felt right now. He yanked in frustration on a locked desk drawer. He kicked the desk.

Lola's cool voice reined him in. "Forget it, Broker. Cyrus is crazy as a March hare but he wouldn't leave anything valuable just laying around."

The breeze carried the tangerine scent of sweat from her damp clothing. She'd tied a filmy purple silk scarf around her throat and put on a pearl silk kimono with billowing sleeves. She was around five seven. Hard to estimate the weight she packed in all that velvet muscle. He'd been close on the eyes, brown but lighter, sand-colored. A streak of premature gray twisted above the left side of her widow's peak.

And Broker was suddenly very eager to discover the exact dimensions of the marital tension between Lola and Cyrus LaPorte.

She padded toward him, her bare feet sinking into the Persian carpet, and at twenty feet she engaged the eyes like a translated idea. Like art. At ten feet he could see the tiny suggestion of lines around the corners of her mouth and her eyes. Uh-huh. Surgeons had airbrushed some of that artwork. She had her fingernails dug in to the quick, hanging on to forty. But like LaPorte said, very well preserved. Maybe he saw a wisp of curiosity rise from the bored ashes in her eyes. Her lower lip bunched in a bittersweet smile and that's where some of the lines got their exercise.

She misread his steaming bold stare and mocked him with an adult smile. "Wrong room, Cowboy. I keep the sex drive in the kitchen now, on the Cuisinart, right between chop and puree."

Broker patiently tried to melt his agitation. Not fast enough.

She sighed. "Yes, Mr. Broker, I was a cheerleader and I can still do the splits and I was homecoming queen and I was Miss Baton Rouge and I even was the Sweetheart of Delta Chi. Eye-fucking. That's one of your Vietnam words, isn't it?"

He said, "I was in on the end. I missed the fun cultural nuances."

"Well don't get hot at me. I haven't got it. It's in there." She pointed to the safe. "Seven ingots." She dropped her eyes. "What happened to your hand?"

"Some geek tried to bite my thumb off resisting arrest."

"Sounds like you got too close. Close could be dangerous," she said, and watched his reaction.

Broker was thinking clearer now. Hiram the butler had kept him from leaving. Lola had been waiting for a chance to talk.

About what? He wondered if Lola liked her money cooked in blood like Cyrus and Bevode.

Cooler, he retreated to the safe and squatted and ran his hands over the door. "This is old." He fingered the keyhole in the handle. "Takes a key."

"It was forged in eighteen sixteen. Fourteen-hundred pounds of solid steel. According to the legend, cannon from Royale LaPorte's ship were melted down to make it."

Broker stood up and pointed to the portrait. "The pirate."

Lola sat in the leather chair and crossed her knees in a silken swish.

"I boned up," said Broker. "Royale LaPorte lost an arm fighting under Andy Jackson at the Battle of New Orleans. President Madison pardoned him. The books say he danced with Marie Laveau the voodoo queen and kept his severed left hand pickled in rum in a glass jar. The hand is said to continue with the LaPorte family to this day."

Lola clapped her hands in slow applause. Very deliberately, Broker pointed at the ancient safe and raised his eyebrows.

She nodded. "Probably climbed out of its gory pot and is in there caressing those bars at this very minute."

Broker glanced at the imposing painting on the wall. "Maybe the

Hue gold's the general's way of sailing back into history to commune with his ancestors?"

"What a kind why to put it, Mr. Broker," she said tartly. "The fact is that with the travel time on the boat, paying off the Greenpeace kids, bringing in the diving crew and the new undersea excavation equipment—you can tell Nina Pryce that Cyrus is barely breaking even with his seven bars of gold."

"You know Nina Pryce?"

"I met her at the party the other night when she robbed the place. I remember the tattoo. It was out of place on her."

"Do the Vietnamese have any idea?"

"You and I having a conversation about Cyrus's business is dangerous." It was a frank statement.

"Do they?" Broker repeated.

She folded her hands and raised them just under her chin. "No. This is a case where knowledge really is power. Do you feel powerful? With your treasure map?"

"The map's a phony. I'm down here chasing wild geese."

"Then you should be wondering why Cyrus would purchase your silence when he can *insure* it."

Broker, unfazed, crossed the room and pointed to the whip on the wall. "What's this?"

"Family heirloom. Cyrus's great granddaddy used it to motivate the help." She got up and walked to a closet in the wall of antlers. She opened the door and dug in a drawer and removed a frayed, discolored red silk hooded robe. "That whip was there, along with this, right next to old Bedford Forest when the order was founded." The bittersweet smile crinkled the corners of her mouth. "I'm a little over the hill to be a princess, but I sure as hell married a dragon." She cocked her head and he wondered how she got her hair to move in place all the time. Maybe it was a secret only taught to millionaire's wives. "You always talk like this to strangers?" he asked.

"You know the Tennessee Williams line about us southern girls relying on the kindness of strangers."

"She was a drunk and I ain't Marlon Brando."

"True. Brando has gone to fat. You don't look like you ever will. Does it bother you that so many police officers have Michelin tires around their waists these days?"

Lola got up and mounted the dais and sat behind her husband's desk. She opened the manila folder that LaPorte had referred to earlier and held up a sheet of paper. "On the other hand, Cyrus can't resist a clean cop." She folded her arms on the desk. "Another cop who was too good to be true stood in this office once. Cyrus knew Bevode Fret was so good that he was only one cold-blooded murder away from being very, very bad. You see, my husband has turned into a collector. Before I met him he used to collect medals and honors. But after that incident in seventy-five they were holding him back in the army. He decided he needed a trophy wife to talk up the generals' wives at the club. And there I was, a Tulane graduate with two years of law school up against the financial wall so I was clerking in a firm downtown and he sized me up like a doll on a shelf and said, 'I'll take that one.' He always said when he retired we'd raise a family. I think he started to come apart when the Berlin Wall came down." She smiled bitterly. "That fucking wall was apparently holding up his character . . ."

She placed her palms together. "Well, we didn't have a family. Instead he went through his antler phase. Cyrus has come a long way since he won those medals. Now he has a little bottle where he collects people's souls."

"Sounds like true love."

She frowned. "I've lived with that man so long I'm not sure I'd recognize a good guy when he's standing right in front of me."

Broker shrugged.

"You are one of the good guys, aren't you?" she asked. Broker started to laugh, but, seeing her serious expression, he stopped. She went on. "I mean, you wouldn't really sell Nina out for money, would you?"

Broker shivered a little in the filmy heat. She was utterly unreadable as, he supposed, he was. It gave them an odd intimacy.

She shook her head. "Poor Broker. Standing there thinking you're touching bottom."

"No. I was recently disabused of that illusion," he said.

"Then you know you're standing on a dying man's shoulders."

"Jimmy Tuna," said Broker.

She nodded. "When Jimmy goes, so do you, and so does young Nina Pryce." You could bury empires in Lola's sad, empty eyes.

"You have any suggestions?" asked Broker.

She said, "I've been married to Cyrus LaPorte for fifteen years and this house is full of lies I raised from infancy. I suggest you start telling somebody the truth."

Broker met her gaze. He stood far from home, on alien ground, surrounded by whips, skulls, twisted antlers, and an eight-foot-tall, one-armed pirate.

31

LOLA LEFT THE DESK, TURNED HER BACK ON HIM, AND walked to the window, where she gazed down on the wedding crowd. "I wonder if she has any idea what she's getting into?" she mused.

"You calling me a liar?" Broker enunciated.

She faced about, leaned back on the windowsill, and the gauzy curtains enfolded her like embroidered wings. "Hardly. I'm calling you *honest*."

They stared at each other for a full minute.

She continued. "Honest and I'd say pretty dumb. You're way off your beat. This is New Orleans and you're messing with Cyrus LaPorte. You can disappear like that." She snapped her fingers. "And the sewers wouldn't even belch."

"Oh, I don't know," said Broker. "Looks to me like the palace guard is down to one coked-up kid making sure nobody steals the stairs. And I've got the general's pet creep in a jail up north. Am I missing anything?"

She leaned back. "Ah, you mean the boys. The boys are in sunny Vietnam, diving and watching over the boat."

"That leaves one naked general."

Lola inclined her head. "Really."

Broker stared, pointed at the safe, waited a moment and said, "How's the addition so far?"

She walked in the direction of his eyes, stopped and traced the circle of the bullwhip on the wall. Her finger traveled down the suspended lash and touched the top of the safe. "Are you really that bold, Mr. Broker?"

"How alone are we? What about the punk on the stairs?" he asked.

"Virgil Fret," she said with distaste, "is driving Cyrus across town to commit adultery with some bimbo milkmaid."

"There's lawyers. This thing called divorce."

"Cyrus is old fashioned. You know, 'till death do us part.'"

Broker cocked his head.

Lola's smile was practical. "I haven't wasted a word or a dollar since I turned twenty-one years old. So listen very carefully. That painting up there is not symbolic. You're among pirates, Mr. Broker. Cyrus plans to kill you and Nina as soon as you lead him to that poor dying convict. Which is the risk you run for your high adventure. But I'm not having anything like an adventure and the fact is—he plans to kill me too."

She paused to let Broker evaluate her words, which were veined with intrigue and not necessarily going in the direction of sincerity. Then she caressed the old safe with her palm. "Have you ever seen fifty pounds of pure gold that's been cradled in the salt sea? It's better than diamonds."

She left the safe and walked toward the doorway to the hall. "Now I have to shower and get dressed. That should take about fifteen minutes. I suggest you use the time well. I've told the officers downstairs that you're my guest so they won't interfere." She paused at the door. "There's nothing on the third floor. That's where I live."

Broker stared at the safe. He hadn't stolen anything since he got caught shoplifting comics at Nestor's Drug Store when he was nine.

Best way to hurt a fucking pirate. Take his gold.

It involved getting in. Getting out. And a key. Once he'd established that he was alone on the second floor he peeked into the bedrooms and checked the French doors and windows for evidence of motion detectors. None. He went into the bathroom and urinated. After he washed his hands he eased open the linen closet and saw a 12-gauge shotgun nestled among the towels and sheets. It was loaded with buckshot. Remington, not Westinghouse, was the local security system.

He walked down the stairs, avoided a room full of wedding guests at a wet bar, and went out on the pool deck and continued on past a three-car garage to the side street driveway. His eyes inspected the heavy wrought-iron fence.

A flushed woman in a bale of lavender lace tumbled up to him. "Are you the help for setting up the band?" she asked breathlessly. Her cheeks were rouged with excitement and champagne.

"Take off," growled Broker. The woman flared the whites of her eyes and departed.

He tracked the iron lilacs and his eyes stopped at a thick tangle of vines that engulfed the fence in the corner by the pool. No cameras. No sensors. No dogs. Probably a few armed good ole boys usually hung out here. But more than that. Reputation guarded the place. Nobody in town would be dumb enough to incur LaPorte's disfavor.

Broker, of course, didn't live here.

On the way back in he studied the twisted oak that grew up over the hedge and shaded the house. One of its Spanish moss–draped branches curled next to the gallery off LaPorte's study. A sturdy drainpipe ran down the corner of the house. But would it hold a heavily laden man? Probably not. The tree was more reliable.

He went back inside and walked past an unconcerned uniformed patrolman who leaned against the staircase, lifted a fork from a plate of food, and nodded. Upstairs, he padded the hall for a closer look at LaPorte's bedroom at the end of the hall. Inside he saw a king-sized bed with fresh sheets turned down, a long gun cabinet, and two sets of mounted antelope horns on the wall next to a Frederic Remington cavalry print. Nothing in the room or in the long closet suggested that Lola LaPorte slept there.

He glanced up and down the hall and slipped into the master bedroom. He slid open the drawer on the bedside table and saw the dull gleam of gun metal, a snub .38 Smith. Some change, some business cards. Didn't figure he'd leave the key to the safe just laying around.

Probably kept it with him all the time.

There were three other bedrooms on the second level. In the first one the bed and furniture were stockaded with sheets. When he opened the second door he hesitated on the threshold, stayed by a potent sense of trespass.

The room contained an ornate, white wicker bassinet, a cradle, a changing table, and a baby bed bundled with a gaily colored bumper and matching quilt and pillow. The furniture items and the shelves on the wall were piled with a Noah's Ark of stuffed animals and dolls. A glider rocking chair and ottoman were positioned in the corner by the window. Next to the chair he noticed a basket full of children's books. He could read the title of the top book, "Baby Bug." A little boy and a little girl played with a rabbit on the cover.

Someone used this room. It was spotlessly maintained and the smell of freshly ironed cotton hugged the sunlight filtering through the fluffy curtains. Broker backed into the hall and slowly closed the door. He wondered if he had just stumbled into the dungeon where Lola LaPorte visited her emotions.

Okay. He reminded himself. It's all too easy. They were tricky folks. But so was he.

The third bedroom adjoined LaPorte's and was unvisited by the cleaning staff.

A bench and a set of weights were strewn around the unmade king-size bed and a stipple of suspicious stains stiffened the sheets. Candystripe Calvin Klein briefs and a pile of socks lay in a corner. The dresser drawers were askew and a silk T-shirt draped from one of them. There were a dozen suits cloaked in cellophane from a dry cleaner in the closet, and a dozen pairs of shoes lined up below them. A rainbow of expensive silk ties littered the door. He went in.

The walls were bare except for a yellowed newspaper clipping that had been matted and expensively framed under glass. Broker went closer and read the sentiment that was scrawled on the mat paper. "To Bevode. Happy birthday—Cyrus."

The folio line announced the *Picayune*, an incomplete date, August; it looked like 1880 something.

Fragments of a story about a Cholera epidemic ran off the clipping. The headline read: HOW TO TELL WHETHER A PERSON IS DEAD OR ALIVE.

> Apply the flame of a candle to the tip of one of the great
> toes of the supposed corpse, and a blister will immediately
> rise. If the vitality is gone, this will be full of air, and
> will burst with some noise if the flame be applied to it a
> few seconds longer; if life is not extinct, the blister will
> be full of matter and will not burst.

Broker sniffed. Bevode Fret's room had the polecat funk of marsh grass where a big animal had lain and soaked up a belly full of meat. A keen ray of something Broker hadn't smelled in a long time—fingernail polish—cut across the tiger-house scent. He turned. Lola, silent on barefeet, stood in the doorway wearing a simple, sleeveless white cotton dress. Her wet hair was pulled tight against her skull and she had painted her fingernails a livid funereal purple. "Our child's room," she said with icy contempt.

Lola's fingernails rattled an anxious tattoo on LaPorte's shiny, massive teak desk.

"Cyrus believes that manageable people have handles. The handle allows them to be controlled. You and Nina have handles until Tuna is found. I'm afraid I never grew any. No handles. You get dropped."

Broker's eyes roved the walls and he wondered how many years she'd spent collecting and decorating this house for Cyrus LaPorte's pleasure. What plans she'd made here . . .

When she'd come up from the pool, even a little lathered from exercise, her makeup had still been precisely applied. Now, with her hair limp and wearing nothing on her face except her skin, she looked drawn and vulnerable to the harsh Louisiana light that hunted shadows around her cheeks, the edges of her lips, and the corners of her eyes.

The gruesome painted fingernails continued to chatter on the wood. "Please say something, Mr. Broker," she demanded.

"How do you know he wants to get rid of you?" said Broker.

"Bevode told me." She pushed the button for service. Hiram appeared almost instantly. "Could we have some coffee, Hiram, out on the gallery?" she said.

"Sure, Miss Lola," said the decrepit old man affectionately. "I make it good and thick for you and the genman."

When they were alone again she went out on the gallery and leaned on the railing. When he stood beside her she looked at him from the corner of her eye and chose her words carefully. "Nina is in danger. Cyrus believes the way to Tuna lies through her," she said.

"She's covered," said Broker.

"I hope you're right. But the price Cyrus pays for luring you down here is having Bevode off the field. Perhaps Tennessee Williams is apropos."

"Go on."

She held up her right hand and stared at her palm. "My grandmother read my palm when I was twenty-one. See this line? It's the lifeline. Mine branches, one fork ends, the other continues on into this happy nest of wrinkles." She cocked her head and placed her left index finger on the small juncture of creases in her skin. "I'm right here, right now. With you."

An acoustic flip in the breeze brought a trill of happy laughter from the wedding party up over the hedges. Broker heard it as a crazy jungle sound.

They stayed that way for two minutes, exploring the twists and barbs of a silence as tangled as the iron lilacs that fenced General LaPorte's home. Then a clatter of metal announced Hiram returning with a tray and silver service. After he set it on the table between the chairs, he bent and whispered in Lola's ear. She smiled and turned to Broker. "Hiram is curious about what you wear on the gold chain around your neck."

Broker pulled the tiger tooth out. Hiram executed a delicate hop, ancient and birdlike, and stared at the pendant. "It need cleanin' up," he said. "I got just the thing for it down in the pantry."

Lola nodded indulgent assent, so Broker removed the chain and handed it to the septuagenarian butler, who cradled it in his crevassed palm and withdrew.

Lola held her coffee cup in both hands and blew on the thick liquid. The heat clotted around them and her voice sounded far away, underwater. "It says in your dossier that you work undercover . . ."

Clouds hid the sun and in the diffuse light her skin acquired the parchment softness of a Renaissance Madonna. She had long dark eyelashes. He wondered if they were real.

"But so far you've only played the sticks. How do you think you'd do in the big time?"

He cleared his throat. "Define big time."

"The difference between Minnesota and the big time, Broker, is the difference between the frying pan and the fucking fire."

She was grabbing at straws too.

"I heard your husband's wish list. What's yours?" asked Broker.

"Sometimes I sit up here and I think how nice it would be if I were a widow before I was a corpse."

"A very rich widow," said Broker. The subject was murder.

"Exactly." She inhaled and steepled her fingers. "I am chattel in this house, Mr. Broker—"

"Phillip."

She inclined her head slightly. "I have no money of my own to speak of. But, with Bevode gone, we are quite insecure at the moment. Virgil is hardly reliable." She took a deep breath. "If the gold in that safe disappeared, considering where it came from no one is going to report it missing." She exhaled. "Be discreet and *it* could make your loan problem go away." She continued to gaze at the slowly tossing foliage. "We could call it a good faith down payment. Do we understand each other?"

"So far."

She turned and drew an X with one cool finger at the base of his throat where the tiger tooth chain had hung. "Don't forget, Cyrus has your little pendant," she said.

"I have some questions . . ."

She patted her cheeks lightly with her palms as a flush of color rose from her throat. "In time. Right now there are some words I find difficult to get past my lips."

They stood up together, without a signal. A mutual arising.

"Where are you staying?" she asked.

"The Doniat. On Chartiers," he said for the second time.

"I'll come see you. At nine," she said, still staring into the distance.

Broker smelled the lingering mint of LaPorte's aftershave evaporate like frost in the humid air and he heard the rattle of a streetcar and the hooves of a mule-drawn carriage clip-clop on St. Charles. Below them and through a screen of hedge, the bride and groom assembled in front of a white gazebo where a flutist played a wedding march. A hot gust of Gulf wind grabbed the stately notes and threw them in their faces.

Impulsively, she seized his arm and tugged him off the gallery, into the study, into hiding, in a furl of billowing curtain. She arched up on tiptoe and kissed him on the throat, on an electric spot just under his left ear. Her lips lingered in a wanton squirm of tongue that sent shivers down the inside of his chest and almost pried his stomach muscles inside out.

She stepped back and inspected his reaction, which was biologically predictable. She drew a cool tentative finger down his cheek. "You should really stop at a barber shop, Phillip. That long hair is all wrong for your face."

Lola LaPorte spun away and ran down the hall, as light on her feet as a girl.

32

BROKER PAUSED IN THE HALL IN FRONT OF A GILDED MIRROR and studied the trademark rosette of the hickey stamped on his neck. Now he had one too. Just like Bevode.

A little creative tension maybe. Two widowmakers applying for the same job. Okay. He kept his hands at his sides. He didn't want to touch anything. The walls probably leaked shit. His move. Hiram did it with Trin's tiger tooth in the kitchen.

He pushed through the wedding crowd and spied Hiram stooped over, with a platter of finger food balanced precariously on his shoulder. Gracefully the old man sidled up. "Take one of the crab-meats, they pretty good. When this tray empty you follow me back into the house."

Broker stood like a hard-bitten scarecrow staked to the grass among the whirling finery and bright eyes of the wedding guests. He glowered at a sharp blonde in a black dress with a Nikon who snapped several shots of him. Finally Hiram reappeared with an empty tray and he followed him around the back of the house and through a door into the steaming kitchen.

A young black woman in a drenched white apron and a glaze of sweat stood at a stainless steel sink counter drying and sorting a huge lump of plastic forks, knives, and spoons. Broker tapped Hiram on the shoulder and pointed at the piles of plastic.

Hiram giggled. "Mr. Cyrus use that plastic shit over and over to cut the overhead. Never miss a chance to make a buck. He 'fraid some-body steal his silverware if he put it out there. C'mon, we go in here."

He pushed open a door and they entered a narrow room with folding chairs and a banquet table. Two waiters were sitting down sipping from cups and smoking. When they saw Hiram and Broker they both quickly rose and left. Hiram pointed to a chair. Broker sat. Hiram took a chair across the table.

The old man dug in his pocket and produced the gold chain. "See, all cleaned up." The chain and the tooth sparkled in Broker's hand and he noticed that a narrow sliver of polished bone had been affixed to the chain next to the gold-capped tooth. He raised an eyebrow.

"Maybe that tooth help you up north but down here I give you a little added protection." Hiram smiled, showing even nicotine-stained teeth. "That a piece out of a black cat's tail. Go on, put it on."

Broker slipped the pendant over his head and tucked it in his shirt. He squinted at Hiram and eased back the lapel of his jacket so Hiram could see the Colt .45 slung in the shoulder rig. "You know who I am, old man."

"Hey, be cool, I just the messenger." Hiram winked.

Broker opened his mouth to ask a question but Hiram wagged a wrinkled index finger in his face. "Miss Lola hope you a smart man, so be smart and listen to somebody who been breathing and kicking for seventy-six years. She send you down here to listen not play badass dick." Hiram took the hearing aid from his ear. He grinned. "Yeah, and I still got most all my teeth too."

Hiram leaned back in his chair and slipped a flat half-pint of Old Granddad from his pocket. He raised it to his lips, drank and sighed. He held the flask out to Broker. Broker declined and handed it back. Hiram put it back in his pocket.

"Now," said Hiram, as he fished the stump of a cigar from another pocket and put it in his mouth unlit. "Some things you should know. Mr. Cyrus and Mr. Bevode think they real smart too. Specially Mr. Bevode.

"Man is like a child, swing his skinny ass in the bathroom, sing to the mirror like old Elvis Presley. Ain't hardly a man at all, more like a dog, wish he was a dog too, then he could lick his own balls.

"Mr. Bevode grew up way back in the swamp so he say he can smell things. So right after he come to work here, he always looking for ways to get on Mr. Cyrus's good side. Problem was, that's where Miss Lola always was. Well, he sniffed around Miss Lola and think he smell something and so he go diggin', just like a damn dog.

"He go paw around in this courthouse down in Jack Bayou where she born and he discover that Miss Lola's maternal grand-mother was Octoroon. You know what that mean down here?"

Broker nodded his head.

"Well, Mr. Bevode got out his pencil stub and sat down at the kitchen table and do his multiplying on the back of a grocery bag and come up with Miss Lola having one sixty-fourth Nigra blood. Tongue hanging out he scoot to Mr. Cyrus. And alla sudden Miss Lola look less like some pretty Baton Rouge white trash gal who better herself and she start looking more like Lena Horne. And there go Miss Lola's plans to have a family in this fine big house. Mr. Cyrus been trying to get rid of her ever since. They have separate bedrooms for five years so it don't surprise me she let you know she a bit lonely." Hiram grinned lasciviously.

"Why doesn't he divorce her?" asked Broker.

"What if everybody know Mr. Cyrus a dumb fool marry a nigger gal. And she say half all this hers. They deadlocked. I said she smart. Didn't say she was ever gonna make saint. But you be gentle with her, not force her like Mr. Cyrus used to do."

Broker cocked his head. "Used to do?"

"Uh-huh. She won't let him touch her no more. Not after what happened." Hiram paused and studied Broker's face. "Now this either goin' scare you away or it gonna piss you off. I hope it piss you off."

Broker wiped sweat from his chin and lit a Spirit. The cigarette turned soggy in the humid air.

"You sure sweat a lot," said Hiram. "You gonna carry that piece down here, get you a baggy sports shirt . . ."

Then Hiram's words sliced the steamy air into cold autopsy slices. "Mr. Cyrus got likkered blind drunk one night and beat her with that whip he keep and then he get the urge to fuck her when she bloody . . . push her down the stairs. After that night Miss Lola find out she can't have no baby ever."

"Why does she stay?" asked Broker.

"Man hate hot and forget. Woman hate ice cold forever. She been waiting for Mr. Cyrus want something as much as she want a child. And now that he's found his heart's desire maybe she been waiting for someone to appear who could help her deny it to him." Hiram squinted. "She think that man might be you."

"Why in the hell do *you* stay around here?"

Hiram shrugged and rolled his cigar stub across his broad lips and said frankly, "Mr. Cyrus and I attached, like a cancer. Problem run in both our families."

Broker slipped his hand in his pocket and palmed one of Nina's hundred-dollar bills. He slid it across the table until their fingers touched. Hiram smoothly drew his hand back and dropped it in his lap.

"Royale LaPorte's hand really in the safe in the study?" asked Broker.

Hiram's eyes popped, polished hard as marbles. A gleam of fire deep inside. "Marie Laveau pack that dead hand in a special jar way back. Mr. Cyrus check on it every morning."

"Where's the key?"

"Never leaves his body. Wear it on a cord around his neck."

"He a sound sleeper?"

"Like out cold when he been drinking and lately he been drinking, especially with Mr. Bevode gone."

Another hundred-dollar bill moved swiftly across the table.

"That kid, Virgil, he any good?" Broker asked.

"Little dope fiend. Surprise Mr. Cyrus let him have a loaded gun. His big brother slap him up alongside the head more than once for blowin' that toot."

"So, not real alert."

"Not after midnight."

Broker stood up and walked to the small rectangular louvered window and cranked it open a few inches more and squinted at a patch of fitful sky. "Storm tonight," he said.

Hiram grinned. "Big one. Probably tip over some of them brick and mortar graves around town. Scatter bones. Dogs be busy in the morning."

"What would scare the shit out of Mr. Cyrus?"

Hiram grinned broadly and extended his withered right hand and delicately squeezed the shiny clip of bone on the chain around Broker's neck. He winked elaborately.

Broker tucked the tiger tooth charm into his shirt, buttoned his sports coat, and reached over and shook Hiram's hand.

The old man opened his palm and saw a third folded hundred. He leaned back and grinned. "Be nice if Mr. Cyrus and Mr. Bevode be gone and Miss Lola be in charge in this house. Maybe we chuck that plastic shit and be polishing the silverware again."

Broker was out the door, pushing through the broiling kitchen onto the lawn but there was no fresh air, just a poisonous steam of magnolias and azaleas against the sticky iron lilacs. Head down, he shouldered through the blurred watercolors of the wedding party and out the front gate onto St. Charles and, from the corner of his eye, he caught the arc of a flung bouquet flash against the leafy swaying air and the outstretched hands and then, as he walked away, he laughed hilariously when he heard the happy applause.

33

THERE WAS MUSIC, BUT HE DIDN'T HEAR IT. HE WALKED THE cramped streets of the French Quarter, looking for a barbershop. The grillwork sagged from the galleries like twisted metal guts and the people looked like lost groupie-pilgrims searching for a rock concert. A tattooed man walked by carrying a full-grown python over his arms and shoulders. Broker shook his head. Warm weather all year round was like life support for a lot of people that a good blizzard would weed out.

He grabbed a pay phone in a shopping arcade and dialed Nina's number in Ann Arbor. Busy. Sweat ran in his eyes. He was a boreal hunter in the near tropics and right now he was shedding his winter coat. Melting. He spied a barber pole and recalled that barbers were originally surgeons. The pole stood for bloody ribbons. Bandages.

He told the barber to take it up above the ears. The dark ponytail went in one crisp snip. Not for Lola. He wasn't going to truck all that hair through Vietnam in the summer.

If Nina found the way to Jimmy.

He hoped her copper friend was on the job. It occurred to him that if she were here she'd veto what he was going to do. Nina would put Lola off limits in two seconds flat.

But he needed a backdoor into LaPorte. Even if it swung both ways. He smiled. A handle . . .

The barber sheared off his burrs and Broker emerged like scrubbed bark, clean, eyebrows trimmed, but still rough to the touch. Then came steaming towels. After today, he owed himself a close shave. So he sighed and closed his eyes and enjoyed the taut scrape of the straight razor on his throat.

He allowed himself a minute of enjoyment, thcn he asked the barber for the Yellow Pages. As the barber massaged tonic around his temples Broker called the nearest Hertz rental and arranged for a car.

Then he hailed a cab, went to Hertz, and filled out the paperwork on the vehicle, hit the street, and parked in the nearest mall. He took some of Nina's money shopping.

In a sporting goods store he bought a pair of black Nike crosstrainers, a baggy pair of dark cotton slacks, a loose long-sleeve matching shirt, two pairs of dark cotton gloves, a cheap charcoal gray raincoat, and a pair of thin black rubber galoshes. He searched for a heavy, strong-stitched grip bag. Finally he bought a stout black bowling bag. Then he went to a hardware store and picked up a small Wonder Bar and a sturdy razor-sharp scissors. On the way out he grabbed a couple of souvenir T-shirts for Mike and Irene.

No phone messages back at the hotel. He called Nina's apartment in Ann Arbor. Busy again. He dug the note from his wallet where he'd noted Nina's flight from Detroit to Minneapolis–St.Paul and called J.T.'s machine. He left another message reminding his old partner to meet her.

He took a long cool shower. Then he changed the dressing on his thumb, doused it in hydrogen peroxide, and bandaged it loosely.

He took a Jax beer from the small refrigerator under the TV and lay on the four poster bed and talked for an hour on the phone to Northwest Airlines, rescheduling his departure. During long periods on hold, he watched the fan turn slowly on the high ceiling. Then he called Nina again. Still busy.

He picked up the TV remote and scanned the cable channels and happened on an installment of *Prime Suspect*, the BBC series featuring Helen Mirren as Inspector Jane Tennyson. He opened another beer and watched for a while.

The thing about this British cop show was: *no guns*. Intricate storyline, snappy dialogue you had to pay attention to, and no guns. Broker stretched out, sipped his beer, and wondered what it would be like to catch a bad guy who spoke in complete sentences. And no guns.

He turned off the TV and watched the late afternoon shadows ink in the curlicue grillwork on the balconies across the street. Fireflies of faraway lightning flickered through the tall gallery windows.

Was Lola for real? Did it matter? She was right about one thing: No one would report that gold to the police if it went missing.

He reached for the phone and called Nina in Ann Arbor. This time he got through.

"I miss you," she said with wispy intuition. She sounded like a woman who had been sitting watching a phone, except she'd been on the damn phone for hours.

"Down here everybody's smiling and we're all lying through our teeth. I called but your phone's been busy."

"I called some people."

"What kind of people?" He sat up.

"Some army folks. Don't worry. I'm being cool. Just trying to get a line on the MIA office in Hanoi. I intend to recover Dad's remains."

Jesus, Broker knuckled his forehead. "Is that cop still with you?"

"I'm drowning in testosterone and guns. Tomorrow I'll be knee deep in his pals from the bank all the way to the airport."

"Okay. Call J.T. and confirm your flight and arrival time. He'll go with you to the Holiday Inn. I'll meet you there tomorrow afternoon."

"What are you going to do?"

"LaPorte wants to talk to me in the morning so," he paused to hurtle a canyon of omission, "tonight I'll treat myself to a meal and maybe catch some jazz."

She said circumspectly, "You're not a jazz kind of guy."

"Do what J.T. says. No side trips," Broker said a little hotly. He hung up the phone without saying good-bye. Why wasn't he a jazz kind of guy? Hell, he could be any kind of guy he wanted. And what the hell was she doing calling around to the army . . . He caught himself. He sensed that he and Nina were on the verge of a boy-girl dilemma complicated by who was going to run the show. And right now she was ahead on points. He could feel a fight coming. The kind of fight where you make up in bed.

At 7 P.M. Broker went out and ate frog's legs, a bowl of turtle soup, and an enormous bread pudding. He did not check out the musical fare because Nina was essentially right. He had been kicked out of his high school band—alto sax—no sense of rhythm.

The storm stalked the edge of the city as he took his time walking an elaborate pattern back to the hotel. If anybody was following him they were better than he was. He called room service and ordered a pot of coffee.

Broker took the tray out on the gallery and watched the street lights come on. As he sipped the thick Creole java the first crooked trident of lightning branched and quivered on the rooftops.

He counted, waiting for the punch of thunder.

The sky boomed and the suffocating rain came straight down and brought no relief from the heat.

34

SHE CAME IN A CAB AND SHE WORE A LOOSE GRAY TRENCH-
coat unbuttoned in a furl of triangle lapels and buckles. Her black
dress slung around her hips like a raw silk lariat. Bareheaded, she
walked across Chartiers in two-inch heels that stabbed a reflected
band of neon. The raindrops sizzled at her every step. She looked up
and saw him standing above her.

He left the gallery and waited in the shadowed archway at the
top of the stairs.

"Much better," she said, seeing the haircut.

The dress had a low scoop neck and buttons down the front. Rain
slipped down her throat and trickled from her tanned collarbones.
Her perfume was homicide beaded on a razor's edge and it slit the
air. "You're wet," he said.

"Do we understand each other?" she asked.

"You better dry off," he said.

"Take me to your room."

The gumbo rain beat on the gallery as the curtains billowed
through the open windows and people shouted happily, running, in
the street. Across the way, loud music cranked up louder to compete
with the thunder—Warren Zevon, "Roland, the Headless Thompson
Gunner."

She touched her wet hair, excused herself, and went into the
bathroom. Broker sat down in an armchair and stared at the bathroom door. When it came to women, the last few years, his work
had cast him, at best, in a slick beer commercial.

Lola had the complex fine detail of a David Lean epic, which is to
say, of Broker's fantasies. And he thought how Lean should have

made a film about New Orleans. No need to build a set. The whole place was theater. The air itself was special effects and the brochure on the bedside table said this hotel had been built in 1847. Broker loved a good historical epic and he loved to read history, which he saw as a cold record of solved crimes . . .

The bathroom door opened and Lola stood for a moment fluffing her hair with a towel. She put down the towel and came over and stood in front of him.

She took off her earrings, making that nice female gesture, elbows to the front, head cocked, hands to the side of her face. "You have to tell me . . . what you expect."

"I'd like you to undress," he said.

"Okay." Her hands were in his hair and he could almost believe she'd been five years on the shelf when she kissed him. He did not believe Cyrus LaPorte got kissed like this. She was the original frog-changer kisser. Why settle for being a jazz kind of guy when he could be a prince . . .

She stepped back and held him by his shoulders and stared directly into his eyes. Her hair had artfully tumbled out of place and the gliding rain shadows dabbed film noir war paint on her face. She said, "All I'm saying is, I could be in a position to do you a favor. And not just tonight."

Slowly she stepped out of her shoes and unbuttoned the front of her dress and peeled it back and down over her shoulders. The dress shivered down in a damp little pile around her ankles.

"If I return the favor," he said. Her back was to the mantel of a marble fireplace. There was a mirror over it but he couldn't quite make out her bare shoulders.

She closed her eyes and shuddered when he ran his hands down her neck over her shoulder blades. Her back squirmed and he felt a lattice of raised tissue under the faint patina of perspiration. He turned her around and switched on the floor lamp next to the mantel.

"Please, Phillip . . ." She lurched free and flung an arm at the lamp, knocking it over. It bounced on the bed and crashed to the floor where it continued to throw a cone of light up the side of the wall.

"Show me," said Broker.

Reluctantly she turned and bowed her head. Long raised marks started just above the waistband of her panties. They clawed diagonally from her left buttocks across her back, went under her bra straps and stopped at her right scapula. The dead welted tissue cast a quarter-inch shadow.

The scars were the first real thing he'd seen in New Orleans. Broker shook his head. "Doesn't make sense you'd stick around after a beating like that."

She turned and her eyes glowed under the jungle of her hair. "I intend to outlive the bastard and get his money, his house, and keep his name."

"That simple?"

"It's not simple. He plans to outlive me and replace me with younger suitable breeding material. There have to be more LaPortes to rape and pillage the world."

"And you know this because Bevode told you?"

She smiled ruefully. "We're all going to eventually wind up in Vietnam. Bevode has upstart potential. He strongly hinted at a boating accident. He has gallantly offered his services to come to my rescue and help Cyrus fall in the ocean in my place. The diving crew that runs the boat are his relatives. All I have to do is kneel at his big herpes-infected cock for the rest of my life. But then who would save me from Bevode?"

"You're the one who chose to live with pirates all round," said Broker.

"Not like this." She raised her lips and expected to be kissed.

"Slow down," said Broker.

"This ride don't come with brakes." She breathed in his ear and threw her arms around his neck.

She was beset by problems. And like her town, she was elaborately guarded by gates and fences and levees and potions and masks. But in the end they formed a flimsy tinsel wish against the Bad Thing that comes out in the dark cypress swamps, out of the gulf, out of the damp night air: yellow fever, cholera, flood, fire, hurricane, slave rebellion. But now that he was next to her, compared with Nina, it was like being at the gym and the idea of actually screwing her became about as inviting as being strapped into a motorized Nautilus machine. Pumping iron.

He could see Bevode doing it. Not him.

Broker pushed her onto the bed and didn't join her. She propped herself up on her elbows and gave him a quizzical look.

He shrugged. "If I jump in the sack with you you'll forget me by tomorrow morning. This way you just might remember me the rest of your life."

"Honest and dumb *and* romantic." She shook her head. "Cyrus and the boys will eat you alive."

"Old fashioned," said Broker.

"Get me that shirt," she asked, suddenly modest, holding an arm across her bra. Broker threw her the souvenir T-shirt that was draped across the chair. It was black with a white pattern of alligator skeletons in a chorus line across the front and *NEW ORLEANS,* spidery in bone letters, glittered incandescent in a flash of lightning as she pulled it on.

Her eyes started slowly and then accelerated and flowed over his face like an army of marcher ants testing every crease and plane and pore for a way into his thoughts.

"Just exactly what do you want?" asked Broker.

"I want everyone to get what they deserve." Her brows knit, witchy, and her eyes shot a spark of wrath from way back in the cypress swamps. "You know what I want."

"I won't do that."

"None of us know what we'll do when we finally stare ten tons of gold in the face."

And that was the first truthful statement he'd heard in New Orleans. He said, "I'd say there's a good chance Cyrus and Bevode could wind up in a Communist jail. Will that do?"

"I already know that." She threw up her hands. "Hell, *they* know that. Can you guarantee me he'll go to jail *before* something happens to me?" she demanded.

"I'll give it a hell of a try."

"Phillip, did you really leave a letter implicating Cyrus in a lawyer's office?"

"Nah, why let word get out."

She shook her head. "Are you a cop or a thief? They go together easily enough down here but I don't know about Minnesota."

They listened to the rain as Broker considered her question and lit a cigarette and smoked half of it. He turned to her. "Two questions. Can you help me get into that safe? Second, why would you?"

"Yes," she replied with finality. And, "To hurt him."

He believed the smolder in her eyes. For now.

"What about that zoned-out kid on the stairs?" he asked.

"We'll spike his malt. Hiram and I."

Broker raised his trimmed eyebrows.

She gave him a wry smile. "Cyrus once told me the army is run by clerks in peacetime and radiomen in wartime. Well, down here, homes of a certain station are run by the staff. Hiram gets Virgil a malt and a bucket of fried chicken every night. Don't worry about him." She cocked her head and concern pursed her lips. "I know you need money to help your folks, and that makes sense, but I'll bet you've never stolen anything in your life."

Broker had thought about this a lot. "It's not stealing. It's like . . . capturing the flag."

"Ye God, this is for keeps. Men are such kids."

Broker drew himself up. "Some men," he said stiffly.

She peeled out of the T-shirt, rolled off the bed, and stooped for her dress. "I didn't really want to do it with you anyway," she said as the silk slithered over her tanned arms and fell to her knees. "Nothing personal. I just don't like it anymore."

"I understand."

"Do you?"

"No. Look, how do I get the damn key?"

She spoke matter of factly as she dressed, called for a cab, and brushed her hair. "After midnight no one should be up except Hiram. He'll be down in the den watching TV. Cyrus always locks up before he goes to bed, but I'll leave the French doors to the study open. You can climb a tree, can't you?"

Broker nodded impatiently.

"Okay." Lola put on her coat. "Cyrus sleeps with the key on a thong around his neck. He always keeps his right hand tight in a fist around it. But if he's lying on his back and he snores, poke him firmly in the left side. He'll turn over and let go of the key and stop snoring."

She held out her hand. He took it and she said, "If you find Jimmy Tuna they'll come after you hard. If you can detain Bevode it might help."

"As in 'permanently'?"

"No. Cyrus won't go to Vietnam without him." She slipped a business card from her pocket and handed it to him. The card was for the Century Riverside Hotel, 49 Le Loi Street, Hue, Vietnam. Imperial Room was written in flowing felt tip across the calligraphy-swirl red capital-C logo. "You'll need all the help you can get once you're over there. Till then." She peered at him and was gone. He closed the door behind her.

Broker stared at the card and filled in the silent question that had been in Lola's eyes: If you get over there.

35

BROKER REMOVED THE BOWLING BAG FROM THE CLOSET and changed into his dark outfit while he had a conversation with himself in the bathroom mirror. If she wasn't for real, he was on his way to eat a twelve-gauge. But he had something to prove to himself and he was going to do it.

He'd put LaPorte on a pedestal once. Now that pedestal was a stack of stolen gold.

Cut him off at the knees.

He sat down on the toilet and stared at his injured thumb. Could slow him up. Slowly he unbandaged it and gingerly removed the gauze that stuck to the infected sutures.

First he lightly dabbed some Vaseline on the finger and looped a single layer of gauze around it. The jelly held the gauze in place. He took a deep breath and eyed the roll of adhesive tape on the sink counter.

He started to whistle "Everything's Coming Up Roses." When he wrenched the first turn of tape around the thumb all his saliva poured out at once. He spit it into the sink, took a second tight turn, and all his saliva dried up. When he'd finished, his whistling sounded like a shaky bone xylophone. There. Armored in adhesive. He tested it against the sink. Still painful as hell but less vulnerable.

Then he strapped his .45 on and pulled on the light raincoat and Nikes. He smiled at the black wool watch cap, dropped it in the bag, and padded down the back stairs from his hotel room. *This is how it all started.*

He'd rented a gray V8 Buick, in case he had to drive fast. Now he spread a street map of New Orleans on the seat and studied it by the dome light. He decided on the residential neighborhoods west of LaPorte's place to find what he needed.

Broker drove through the rain for three hours, back and forth, up and down quiet side streets under overarching canopies of old oaks and Spanish moss that shivered in the storm. On his third try he found what he was looking for. When he had it wrapped in his bowling bag he turned the car back toward the LaPorte mansion.

He parked a block away. He quartered toward the house in the cheap gray raincoat and light slip-on rubber boots. The bowling bag was in his right hand, the .45 snug in its harness across his chest. He walked past a flower bed and a damp humus of soil and orchids brought back tatters of Lola's perfume, a scent of murder, chilly bright and sharp as a fishhook. But this was payback for Bevode, moonlight financing, and a personal challenge he meant to slap in Cyrus LaPorte's face.

A trickle of lightning silently spiderwebbed the trees and the creepy turrets and gables jittered against the electric sky.

Like a fucking pirate ship. Then came the boom.

He slipped along the alley fence until he came to the overgrown portion he'd spied early in the afternoon. Then he placed the three trash cans, making sure their covers were secure. One, then two, in a stack. Steps. He climbed the cans and tossed his bag over the fence. Then he gripped the thick vines against the spear tips with his right hand and swung himself up, slid over on the bumpy massed vines, and dropped down on the other side.

As a peel of thunder smacked the blowing trees, Broker slid along the inky hedge. The yard lights were out and the interior to the house was dark except for lights in the kitchen and another room downstairs. Fainter hall and stairway lights upstairs.

He came to the base of the oak tree and squeezed past it and through the hedge and came out on the pool side. A dozen feet away, through the window, he saw Virgil Fret slouched in a chair at the kitchen table, nodding. An empty bucket of fried chicken sat next to a tall milkshake. Grease spots dribbled on his white T-shirt and the static on a TV screen three feet away on the counter monitored his brain waves. A bright, blocky 9mm pistol was stuffed into his waist band. Broker could almost hear him snoring through the steady rain.

Too perfect. Like Lola's hair. *Keep going.*

He crept to the back of the home until he could observe the other light. Hiram sat in a den at the other side of the first floor, watching television. He returned to the dark corner formed by the hedge and the tree.

He separated the looped handles of the bag and inserted his arms, effectively making the bag a backpack. The light cotton gloves had serrated rubber grips. He measured his distance and leaped up, seizing a low branch with his strong right hand, grunting as his knees clamped the slippery bark.

Sweat and rain blurred his vision as he struggled up the trunk, finally gaining the larger branches. With hand-and footholds he gained the branch he wanted. Balancing, he inched over the hedge.

Now the decision. Try to leap for the gallery or take the shorter jump to the drainpipe.

He figured the drainpipe wouldn't hold. He gathered himself and sprung for the railing. He hit it mid-chest level. Locked his good hand over it. Pots of impatiens wobbled in their crockery saucers but the sound was drowned by the wind and rain. Nothing fell to the pool deck.

Out of the rain, under the balcony, he quickly stripped off the raincoat and the boots, furled them, and tucked them aside. He removed the wet gloves and put on a fresh pair. The French doors swung open. No need for the jimmy.

Dry as bone, he entered the sleeping home of Cyrus LaPorte like a bad dream.

He squatted just inside the study until his eyes adjusted. He listened, separating out the sounds of the house from the storm. Television downstairs. Roof timbers creaking. Checked his wristwatch: 2:13 in the morning.

Then he left his bag and crept down the varnished maple hallway to LaPorte's bedroom. His eyes wandered up the stairwell to the third floor. Was she asleep? Or laying in her bed wide-eyed as a girl the night before the prom.

LaPorte curled in the fetal position on the king-sized bed. Aquarium shadows undulated over him, cast by branches dancing in a streetlight and the grid of window sashes. He wore pajama bottoms. No sheet. The grizzled hair on his chest was white as hoarfrost.

His right hand clenched against that silvery hair and slowly, in the weaving shadows, Broker picked out the irregular shape of the thong around LaPorte's neck.

Broker squatted behind the gun cabinet, where a flash of lightning would not delineate him, and waited. After a few minutes he could smell the sleeping man, a halitosis of sour alcohol and digestive juices gusting through raw sirloin. His breathing was deep and regular.

Ten minutes later the sound of the television stopped downstairs. Broker strained his ears, thought he heard faint sounds. Hiram going to bed. Must sleep downstairs. Nothing from the kitchen. He wondered if Virgil made rounds. Used an alarm of some kind to wake up.

His sweat felt like a swarming antbath, his legs started to cramp. He blinked to clear his eyes. His gloved hand checked the scissors tucked into his waistband and then squeezed his own neck pendant to calm himself.

Lola was right. And Nina would second her. A lot of what men did was childish. *Lord of the Flies* childish.

Forty-five tense, cramped minutes passed. Then, after a particularly loud clap of thunder, LaPorte squirmed in a stuttering white flash.

Rolled on his back. Good. His left hand pawed the sheets briefly. Broker held his breath as LaPorte gurgled slightly, then stronger. *C'mon, man, saw some wood.*

And finally, slowly, rhythmically, Cyrus LaPorte began to snore, a deep nasal gurgle, the troughs followed by long wheezes.

Broker gave it ten more minutes. Checked his watch again. It was almost four. Be dawn soon. The storm was lessening.

Gotta do it now. He eased around the side of the bed and leaned his right arm across the sheets. How would a wife poke a sleeping man? He tried to remember. Kim had always jabbed him with her elbow. Would his fist feel like an elbow? Probably not. The angle would be wrong.

Absurdly, Broker carefully crawled into bed with Cyrus LaPorte and lay next to him. What would J.T. say? Fuck that. This was one story he wasn't telling anybody.

Broker inhaled, gathered up his nerve, held it, and jammed his right elbow into LaPorte's side. LaPorte grunted but continued to snore. Broker's hand quivered, about to reach for the Colt. Then he jammed him again, harder, deciding that Lola would not have a light touch faced with this ungodly racket.

LaPorte sighed, the snoring ceased, and he rearranged himself, turning toward Broker who lay wide-eyed as LaPorte threw out a sleep-heavy right arm that landed on Broker's hip. The dense shadow of the key lay on the sheet between them.

Then LaPorte snuggled toward Broker and his right arm found a comfortable perch on Broker's ass.

Broker gasped. He had been holding his breath for almost a minute. Ever so slowly he eased the shears from his waistband and delicately snared the thong in the blades. Snip. He took another breath and gently reeled the leather out from between LaPorte's throat and the pillow.

Getting dizzy, he made himself breathe through his nose to calm down and closed his hand around the key. LaPorte stirred at the sound and moved closer. Like some precoital shimmy from the insect kingdom, LaPorte slowly squirmed his bony hips closer.

Broker sat up, clutching the key, and slid away from LaPorte's hand and pushed the other pillow toward the man. LaPorte grumbled and slowly folded himself around the pillow.

In the hall Broker let out a deep breath and realized he was almost giddy with laughter, this insane helium balloon filling his chest. Taking very disciplined steps, he went back down the hall into the study.

The key did not open the lock easily. It had to be inserted, turn one set of antique tumblers then inserted deeper. His hand was shaking when the lock finally popped.

A corkscrew of excitement cored him and left his toenails tingling. *So this is why the assholes do it.* Broker had never seen bars of gold before. A wet mercury gleam in a flicker of lightning. With raised Chinese characters on them. Gold. Seven ingots. Cleaned up and shiny in the dark. Heavy too. Over five pounds a piece. More where that came from . . .

He opened the bowling bag and removed the bundle of hotel towels. Set it aside and transferred the gold to the bag.

Just crossing *a* line, he told himself. Not *the* line.

He made himself quiet down to listen. Then he tiptoed back down the hall to make sure LaPorte was still out. Like a baby. Okay. Go back for the prize.

The thick antique glass crock was banded and studded with discolored brass ribs. And it was damn near as heavy as three of the gold bars. He held it up and tried to decipher the contents in the weak light. Slosh. Looked like a rotten log in swamp water. Carefully he unwrapped the bundle of towels and swaddled the container. Used more towels to wedge it among the gold.

Okay. Then he took the seriously dead cat that had been wrapped in the towels and placed it in the safe. It wasn't completely black, but close enough. The first two he'd come upon were entirely wrong, a tabby and a spotted gray. Waffled with the tire tread of the vehicle that had flattened it, the cat's viscera and bones curled like Technicolor fettuccine around the squashed fur. *Welcome home to New Orleans, motherfucker.*

Broker left the safe door open.

He left the key in the lock, put on his raincoat and boots, and slipped the bag over his shoulders. As he adjusted to the heft of the weight he looked up in a tremble of lightning. Royale LaPorte's cracked enigmatic smile flickered down from the painting.

Like he approved.

A flash flood of adrenaline compensated for the weight and he made it swiftly down the tree. He opened the bag, took out the glass crock, waited for a lightning-thunder stroke, and smashed the container on the cement walk by the pool.

The smell of history and pirate shanties maybe, briny and gruesome. Worse to touch it. Yuk. But Broker resolutely picked up the squishy, blackened hand and, in another crackle of lightning, saw that the fingernails had grown curled and thick as claws.

Real monsters this time.

He mounted a lawn chair and impaled the hand, wrist-down, with a sickening crunch on a lilac spear on the iron fence. Slippery damn mess. His gloved fingers struggled with it, but when he left, the middle finger was extended skyward and the other digits were folded back.

36

AT 7:55 A.M. BROKER LEANED IN THE SHADOW OF THE gallery at the front door of the Doniat. Waiting on a cab and wondering if Cyrus LaPorte would show. Across the street, black kids in blue jumpers and slacks, white shirts and blouses, were herded by nuns toward the colonial whitewash of an Ursaline mission.

He'd treated himself to an expensive pair of sunglasses and wore them now to disguise his bloodshot, sleepless eyes. The gold bars were tucked into the locked trunk of his rented car. Before dawn, he'd left the vehicle in the airport police garage at the New Orleans airport. He'd cabbed back into the city.

His sports coat was open, the stump of the Colt was loose in the holster, and his airline ticket was tucked into the waistband of his jeans. He wore the black T-shirt with the city's name spelled in dead alligators. He was drinking a Jax beer for breakfast.

The big navy-blue Seville with tinted windows came around the corner so fast and low on its suspension that it raked sparks off the bricks and almost demolished a languidly moving mule-drawn carriage full of tourists. The school kids had excellent drive-by reflexes. They scattered and ran for cover.

Broker smiled and took another sip of beer. He was enjoying himself. His thumb, still wrapped in adhesive, hardly bothered him.

The car doors sprung open. Virgil Fret, his face as chalky as uncut cocaine, hopped out of the driver's side and did a little stationary dance like he had to take a piss. His hand hovered to his baggy shirt. Cyrus LaPorte was entombed in the back seat in burgundy upholstery like an albino in an air-conditioned cave. His color seemed off, but that could have been the tinted glass.

Broker ignored Virgil and pointed his beer bottle at LaPorte. "Get out and stand in the sun," he said in a cordial voice.

"Think you're pretty smart," said LaPorte, pushing up and out of the seat. He was ashen in the thick morning heat. Icy with control.

"Stand back from him, General," said Virgil Fret. Sniffing, hitching up his crotch, opening and closing his spare muscular fingers.

"Leave us be, Virgil," said LaPorte, exasperated.

"Tell him to get back in the car," said Broker.

"Get back in the car," ordered LaPorte. Twisting in a tight flurry of catnip reflexes, Virgil started to protest. "Now, you nitwit," growled LaPorte. The punk dropped his shoulders and got back in the car. LaPorte turned to Broker. "You have something that belongs to me."

"You got a beef? Call the cops."

"You're out of your depth, Broker."

"Don't think so. You're the one coming up empty in a hundred feet of salt water."

LaPorte executed a thin frosty smile. "It's too big for you. I know my way around over there. You don't."

"Watch me."

LaPorte squinted at him and burst into incredulous laughter. "No shit, you waited around just to *taunt* me?"

Across the street the school kids milled in front of the mission, antsy in their uniforms. It was nice out, they were eager for school to end. Through the Caddy's tinted windows Virgil's fitful shadow bounced on the seat.

Broker smiled and wondered how he was doing as a pirate. "No," he said, "to caution you. You saved my life once, so I figure you deserve a warning."

"*You*," sputtered LaPorte, "threatening *me*!"

"That's right. It's you and me now. Winner take all, General, and if you go to Vietnam you'll never come back. Consider yourself warned."

Broker sat the empty beer bottle down on the curb as his cab pulled up. LaPorte couldn't stop himself from seizing at Broker's bag. Broker didn't resist. The weight told LaPorte it contained only clothing. He dropped his arms to his sides in frustration. Broker opened the cab door and tossed in his grip. He turned and smiled. "It's been fun. Anytime you need a hand, just let me know." He left LaPorte looking like he might eat the tires off that Caddy and, hopefully, furious enough to make a mistake.

*   *   *

They followed the cab. They followed him into the airport. LaPorte left Virgil stranded at the metal detector and came down the concourse to check the flight number.

When Broker got to the actual airplane door he flipped his badge and talked to the attendant. When he'd dropped off the rental car he'd made arrangements with the airport police. He explained that he was a Minnesota state investigator and he had to get back into the terminal without going back up the walkway. The attendant nodded and directed him to the maintenance stairway. Broker went down the stairs and rode a baggage cart back to the terminal.

He threaded through a subterranean warren of baggage conveyors and went for a phone.

He dialed Nina's in Ann Arbor. No answer. Damn. He paced in a break area and drank a cup of coffee. An airport cop met him with a concourse buggy and whisked him underground to his car.

An hour later Broker had his baggage checked and was waiting in the underground on another flight to the Twin Cities. He thought of calling Ed Ryan to keep an eye on his aborted Northeast flight into Minneapolis–St. Paul, to see if anybody interesting turned up to meet it. He decided against it. Too many people were already involved.

He had a last cigarette in New Orleans, out of sight, in a baggage handler laughing-place behind a deplaning ramp. Then he tried Nina's again. No answer. He tried J.T.'s home but got the machine. Everybody was stuck in between. Hoping that Danny Larkins was on the job, he boarded his airplane.

37

"SHE DIDN'T CALL YOU?"

"Nah, man, nothing," said J.T. who had gone out to meet Nina's plane and checked the manifest when she wasn't on it. J.T. was working, so Broker had to keep paging him. They were having their sixth phone conversation in five hours. It was 11:45 P.M. Broker leaned, exhausted, over a telephone in the lobby of the Minneapolis Airport Holiday Inn. His arm ached from lugging the heavy bowling bag. He had taken a room when he got in, early afternoon. Nina was nowhere in sight. Had left no messages.

Broker thought about calling the Michigan State Police, but decided to wait and tried her apartment again. Nothing.

He had called the Liberty State Bank in Ann Arbor just before they closed and a tight-ass banker had given him a lecture on the Right to Financial Privacy Act. Broker's name over the phone was not enough to authenticate his identity. The banker would not confirm or deny that Nina Pryce had been in his office. He called J.T. again.

"I need a favor," said Broker.

"I thought I was already doing you a favor," said J.T. in that apprehensive voice.

"Could you get free for a day? I made three reservations for a hop to Duluth. We can rent a car and get to Devil's Rock."

"Uh-huh?"

"Leaves at five—"

"In the morning?"

"Yeah. There's a guy in county up in Lake, he gets out noon tomorrow, thirty-six-hour rule. I'm going to fuck him up and . . . well, if you aren't there I just might overdo it."

"This an open case?"

"This is personal."

"And it's got to do with Nina being missing?"

"Could be. I shouldn't have left her alone."

"You going to tell me about it?"

"Ah, there could be a problem with perjury."

Silence. "Airport Holiday Inn."

"Right."

"Fly to Duluth."

"Yeah, J.T."

"Fuuack. Gimme an hour."

At 2:15 A.M. Broker kneed J.T., who was dozing next to him, and shot out of the couch in the Holiday Inn lobby when Nina Pryce marched through the door in the company of a guy with a handlebar mustache who looked like a side of buffalo squeezed into jeans and cowboy boots. Bobbing in a porcupine quill aura of caffeine and adrenaline, hair frizzed, pupils enlarged; she crowed in hollow-cheeked triumph, "I'm in the wrong business. I should be the freakin' detective."

"Where the hell have you been?" demanded Broker.

"Meet Danny Larkins. Hello, J.T.," said Nina.

"Always a pleasure." J.T. yawned. Broker's hand disappeared into Larkins's giant hoof.

"Two guys," said Larkins. "They picked us up in Ann Arbor and followed us to Lansing."

"Lansing?" mumbled Broker.

"I'll explain," said Nina. She stared quizzically at Broker's lop-sided posture and at the bowling bag grafted to his right hand.

"We lost them at the Lansing airport when we got on the shuttle to Detroit. I was the last guy on the plane and they did not board," said Larkins.

"You get a description?" asked Broker.

"I saw them, Broker, you can ask me," Nina interjected.

Larkins yawned. "One's tall, Caucasian, middle-aged but strong like a carpenter. Looks like a fucking hound dog. Wore sunglasses. The other was ordinary white bread. They stayed in their car, a gray Nova. They must have thought they were the president with a state cruiser in and front and behind."

Nina grinned. "Danny had these guys time their patrols to convoy us. It was great."

Broker handed Larkins the room key. "Go on. Get some sleep."

Larkins grinned. "Don't suppose anybody will tell me—"

"Nope," said Nina. "That wasn't our deal, Danny."

"Okay. Pay me, show me the way to the elevator."

Nina hugged the huge cop. He lolled out his tongue and panted like a horny dog on a cocktail napkin. "One last thing," he leered at Nina. "Promise me you won't abort our love child." Nina rolled her eyes and walked Larkins to the elevator, digging in her purse.

When she came back she stared at Broker and his black bag, blinked, and said, "What happened to you?"

"I got a haircut?"

She frowned. "You have a hickey on your neck."

Broker smiled tightly. "C'mon, let's find someplace to talk."

J.T. sat in the corner of an empty banquet room dubiously drinking room service coffee. Broker slid his bag under a table and paced. The tables had been set. Lights reflected off crystal and hurt his eyes. Folded winged napkins looked like squadrons of origami warming up on aircraft carriers.

Nina marched to a window and opened it to let out Broker's cigarette smoke. The growl of jet engines entered the room on that cool, bluesy, up-all-night, morning air.

"So." She spread open a manila folder full of computer printouts on the table next to Broker. "Tuna came through the bank ten days ago. He withdrew twenty thousand and left the account open. There's another twenty thousand still in it."

"So where is he?"

"I haven't got a clue. He's been sending checks for eighteen years to an address in Italy. Paying the taxes on a farmhouse in Tuscany. The banker showed me the correspondence."

Broker shook his head. "He's too sick to travel to Italy. Where would he get a passport?"

"That's what I thought," said Nina. "There's these canceled checks to someone named Ann Marie Sporta. They start in 1988 and stop in 1993. About fifteen thousand all together. They were stamped at a bank in Madison, Wisconsin. What do you think?"

Broker rubbed his eyes, glanced at the checks. "Don't know. What else?"

"The jackpot," said Nina "It's all in his records at the bank, canceled checks, letters, accounting forms. Since nineteen eighty-nine, when things started loosening up with Vietnam, he's been donating heavily to something called the Southeast Asian Relief."

"Define heavily?" asked Broker.

"Oh, about fifty thousand bucks—"

"To some . . . relief charity?" Broker shook his head.

"The SAR is just a go-between the banker found, you can't just send money to someone in Vietnam. So he used this aid organization headquartered in Lansing, Michigan. Guy named Kevin Eichleay runs it. Nam vet. Was a medic in the Air Cav. He ships over medical supplies. Runs tours of vets who rehab hamlets, hospitals, stuff like that. I called him up and said I wanted to donate some money. Then we drove like hell to Lansing with those two guys following us."

"You should have waited for me," said Broker.

Nina arched an eyebrow and went on. "Poor Kevin," she smiled, "he's a low-key, salt-of-the-earth dude and I came cooking into his office like the Pillsbury bake-off. Larkins freaked him a bit, but he quieted down when I got my checkbook out. For five hundred bucks and a few hugs I got the whole story. Told him Tuna and my dad were in the army together. That I was going to Nam to look for my dad's remains. Man, I threw the book at him."

"What the fuck is this?" grumbled J.T. suspiciously.

Broker held up a hand. Patience.

Nina spread a sheaf of official looking Xeroxes down on the hotel table like four aces. They bore strange stamps in Vietnamese. Stars and sheaves of rice. "Approvals that Kevin negotiated on trips he made. From a local People's Committee all the way up to the Vietnamese General Assembly. Get this: For the last five years Tuna has been sponsoring an old vets' home for Viet Cong amputees. Guess who runs it?"

Broker shook his head. "Oh boy," he said softly.

"You got that right," said Nina. "Nguyen Van Trin manages it. Tuna worked through the banker to bankroll Kevin to go to Nam in eighty-nine to find Trin. I showed Kevin the phone number in Hue and he confirmed it as the number Trin uses."

"Where's this home located?" asked Broker slowly.

"On the beach, in Quang Tri Province, exactly where Tuna wanted it built," said Nina mysteriously. She placed both hands on Broker's shoulders and shook him with infectious excitement. "And, Tuna bought them a serious boat to go fishing with. Kevin said it was way too much boat, big enough to run heavy cargo on the high seas. But Tuna insisted on it. That's what most of the bread went for.

Permits for the boat. The Vietnamese government went through a sensitive period about people with boats."

"God, he had it all planned, for years," said Broker.

"Yep. Put everything in place and then he got cancer," said Nina.

"Trin." Broker said the name like an incantation.

"Yeah," said Nina. "How much does he know?"

"Whoa. Wait. Man, what the fuck is this?" J.T. stood up, raising his hands to dodge the high-energy splinters zipping off Broker and Nina.

"You don't want to know," said Broker.

"I want to know," said J.T.

"Okay." Broker reached down and unzipped his bowling bag. With a flourish he whipped out a glittering bar of gold and tossed it across the room.

J.T. caught it, hefted the surprising weight and groaned, "Oh oh . . ."

"Wow," said Nina. "You got into his safe!"

"Huh?" J.T. blinked.

"There's this guy who thinks he's a pirate and he's looking for a sunken treasure," explained Broker.

"Except it's not sunken, it's buried," added Nina. She startled. "Or is it? Where'd he find the gold?"

"By the chopper. But only seven ingots and they've had a crew over there churning up the bottom."

"I don't get it," said Nina.

Broker shrugged. "Maybe it's in two locations?"

J.T.'s eyes went first to Nina, then to Broker, and back to Nina again. "Right," he said.

"It's all dirty and we're going to bust his ass," explained Broker, throwing his hands in the air.

"A pirate." J.T. glowered at the gold ingot in his hand. "A treasure." He shook his head. "In Duluth?" he asked incredulously.

"In Vietnam. If you can get a week off you can come with us," said Broker.

"Fuck that. Once was enough." J.T. carefully put down the gold bar on the table and said, "You're right, I don't want to know. I'll just help you *talk* to that guy and quietly depart."

"Talk to what guy?" asked Nina.

"Bevode Fret," said Broker, stashing the bar back in the bag.

"Talk?"

"Yeah, the kind of talk that'll keep him in traction for a while," said Broker.

Nina said, "Not a good idea. We lost those guys in Lansing but they *know* where Bevode is. You go after him, they'll pick us up again."

Broker shook his head, he'd been looking forward to this. "Bevode gets his comeuppance. If somebody heavy is tailing us they'll stick out like a sore thumb in Devil's Rock."

"Along with me," said J.T. with a calm demented smile.

Nina folded her arms. "We already screwed up once. If I didn't know Danny, where would we be?"

Broker grimaced and rubbed his eyes. "If LaPorte can buy prison guards he can probably penetrate a commercial airline's scheduling computer. We aren't going to lose whoever's following us for long. And we're all going to the same place."

"We have to ditch them if we find Tuna," said Nina.

"*When* we find Tuna," said Broker. "It's in here." He sat down at the table and spread out the contents of Nina's folder. He pushed the Italian correspondence aside. He wondered if a man dying of cancer would try to make it to Vietnam. Tuna had prepared this for a long time.

An hour of eye-strain went by as Broker scanned through the records looking for incidental payments that could have gone for a forged passport and ID. Nina's Reeboks squeegeed on the glossy floor, pacing behind him. J.T. snored lightly, stretched out on three chairs. Finally Broker turned to the checks issued to Ann Marie Sporta. He looked at his watch, got up, and went looking for a phone, hoping that Ed Ryan had gone to bed early the night before.

In silence, red-eyed and grumpy, they drove north from Duluth in a rental car. They stopped in Two Harbors and Broker called Fatty Naslund. He told Fatty to meet him north of town at William Magny State Park, near a violent waterfall called the Devil's Kettle, where they had played as kids.

Then he called Tom Jeffords at the Devil's Rock police station and made an arrangement concerning Bevode Fret. Then he called Ed Ryan, who had been shaken out of bed by Broker's first call and was now at the ATF office and who was grumbling about Broker having used up all his chits. But he was working the computers and talking to the FBI. Broker hung up the phone and found Nina and J.T. sound asleep in the car. Broker drove to the park on stale adrenaline fumes and black Amoco station coffee.

The Kettle was reputed to be bottomless, and while he waited,

Broker toyed with the concept of throwing Bevode Fret into it. Another reason to have J.T. along.

Fatty Naslund drove up cautiously in his T-Bird, avoiding mud holes. When he got out he grimaced at the mud splatters along the rocker panels.

He arched a disapproving eye at the rented car and the unmoving forms curled on the seats. "That's a black guy and a white woman?"

"They're with me," said Broker.

Fatty straightened his cuffs. Just the reflex motion. He had been working out and wore a ribbed T-shirt ordered out of a Patagonia catalogue. He was a compulsively lean, neat man who kept a rowing machine in his office at the bank so he could work up a sweat while he watched Rush Limbaugh on cable. He had been perversely nick-named Fatty by the other kids because he was the banker's son. Now he lived in fear of excess body weight, had little calipers to pinch and measure his body fat, and went once a month to a clinic in Duluth to submerge in a tank and compute his fat-to-muscle ratio. Fatty was fastidious. He still thought copper pennies counted.

"Little unusual, isn't this?" said Fatty, striding toward the picnic table where Broker sat. He grinned his best chamber of commerce grin. His brilliant white teeth were so healthy they looked like they had definition and veins in them.

Broker unzipped the bowling bag and methodically removed the seven flat ingots of gold and stacked them in a blazing pyramid in the early morning sun. Fatty's eyes went wide then cranked down to suspicious slits.

Then Broker took out the Colt, racked the slide back, and sat it beside the metal bars.

"Holy shit," said Fatty in feigned shock. "This is like payday in basic training. PFC Naslund reports for pay."

"How long you known me, Fatty?"

"Since kindergarten."

"You ever know me to throw you a curve on anything?"

"Where'd the gold come from, Phil?" Fatty fingered an ingot, caressing the Chinese ideograms embossed on its surface.

"From a gray area."

Fatty sat down at the table and carefully prodded the barrel of the .45 with his index finger so the muzzle pointed toward the waterfall upstream. "A gray area like New Orleans?"

"What gives you that idea?"

Fatty pointed at Broker's chest. "The T-shirt. And certain

inquiries from a big property management firm down there. I faxed them Mike's loan history this week."

"You hear about the guy who killed Mike's dog?"

Fatty nodded. "All over town."

"He works for the guy who owns the property outfit in New Orleans."

Fatty stared at the gold with a pained smile. "Ah, look, Phil—"

"Don't worry. It's going to wind up perfectly legal."

"But it isn't right now, is it?"

"Remember how you always ask me about what I do? This fantasy of yours, about being involved in an undercover operation?"

"Yeeaah . . ."

"Well, this is going to be the biggest thing I ever tried."

"But is it legal? You know. Gavels. Juries. Cell doors clanging shut."

"Fatty, this is evidence," said Broker seriously.

"Then why is it sitting on a picnic table in Magny State Park instead of on the attorney general's desk?"

"I'm in the preliminary stage of an investigation."

"Yeaah?"

"In the meantime, I'd like you to secure these items in a safe place and tell absolutely no one."

"That's all?"

"No. Chain up the developer you sicced on my dad. One way or another this gold is going to settle that note."

"You know, Phil, there's enough weight here to take care of the loan. Maybe throw in a new Lexus," estimated Fatty. "Hmmm, and it looks real old. If it's rare it could be worth even more . . ." He reached out and petted a bar like it was a cat.

Broker said, "Forget the inquiry from New Orleans. It never happened."

"Is it legal?" he asked again.

Broker leaned across the table and lowered his voice. "Fatty, it's exciting. Haven't you ever wanted to do something . . . exciting?"

"Jesus, Phil." Fatty swallowed and looked around the deserted camping area again. "How exciting?" he whispered.

"It's *Communist* gold," whispered Broker.

Fatty Naslund straightened up and said, "Well, in that case, fuck 'em if they can't take a joke."

38

BROKER LEFT NINA WITH JEFFORDS AT THE POLICE STATION, then made a quick stop at Mike and Irene's to pick up his truck. Now he whipped the Jeep down gravel back roads, through thick forest. J.T. sat in the passenger seat. "Now I'm going to mess this guy up—" said Broker.

"Like the old days," yawned J.T.

"But not too much."

"You know me, pard, the model of restraint," said J.T. He took out a pair of soft leather gloves and slapped them on his thigh.

The old days.

They had been old-fashioned cops together. Dirty Harry dinosaurs. Back when Broker thought he could make a difference.

He and J.T. worked triage on the streets. They'd developed an eye for who could be saved and who belonged in the toilet. They had agreed on a personal approach. They put the word out that people were accountable to them personally. They told the punks, "If you don't have a father one will be assigned to you. You can have him or me."

They were consequences. They were rough. They played Catcher in the Shit. Some of those kids were now in the service or in college.

Elected officials, human services, neighborhood organizations, and the press had a different description of what they did. They said it verged on police brutality. Broker decided he wanted off the streets. He didn't want to wind up shooting some fifteen-year-old kid. He had moved toward the margins and then the shadows, into undercover work.

Bevode Fret wasn't no kid. He was a cold-blooded, dog-killing swamp animal.

J.T. pulled his gloves tight and glanced at Broker. "Don't know I like you looking so happy."

"Man should be happy when he's killing snakes," said Broker.

"You know, Phil, for years brother cops been coming to me for reassurance you ain't a psycho. Say I'm not a liar."

"Dead cool," said Broker, thinking ahead. *I've been waiting for something like this my whole life.*

39

BEVODE FRET WAS LET OUT OF A POLICE CAR AT THE TOWN limits of Devil's Rock on a dirt road that ended on a deserted cobble beach. Broker waited on the shore. He kept the motor running in his Jeep.

Bevode held up his handcuffed hands to Lyle Torgeson, who sat behind the wheel of the police car. Lyle, his eyes unavailable behind sunglasses, tossed a key to Broker. Then he dropped a manila envelope out the car window and drove away.

"Pick it up," said Broker, nodding to the envelope.

Bevode smiled. "You and Cyrus have a good time down home? Get all reacquainted . . ." He stooped and picked up the envelope that contained the personal possessions he had been carrying in his pockets. When he regained his full stature he stared at Broker. He was an inch taller, maybe five, six; younger. Probably in better shape.

He opened the envelope, reached in and retrieved a pocket comb. Taking a stance with his hips spread and shoulders hunched like a teenager preening in front of a mirror, he ran the comb through his thick blond hair two handed.

He was handsome and he was vain and he was totally self-assured. He was fearless. He couldn't be scared. He could be destroyed or he could be greatly inconvenienced.

A gull flew over and its shadow touched both of them. Bevode smiled.

Bevode put the comb away. In a smooth deceptively fast motion, Broker's right hand came from under his sports coat, brought the big Colt out, and, without pausing, with a twist of his trunk and shoulders, brought the heavy automatic sideways through the air and cracked Bevode across the mouth with the barrel.

, Bevode groaned and staggered to his knees. Blood drops dotted the clean round cobbles. His cuffed hands went to his swelling mouth. Broker saw with satisfaction that one of Fret's front teeth came loose in a gout of red. Bevode tendered it in his slippery fingers and stared at it in disbelieving fury.

"That's for Nina," said Broker. "And to slow you up. I'll bet even an autographed invitation from Mr. Cyrus won't get you back on the street till you get that smile fixed." Broker grinned. "Now get in the car."

He shoved the staggered man into the passenger seat and strapped the seat belt over his arms. Then he drove up the access road, across Highway 61, and followed the gravel road into the woods.

Bevode's muddy eyes were steamy with pain, but also concentration, as they left the gravel and shot down a bumpy logging trail, and the trees grew thicker and the shadows cut off the light. From the corner of his eyes Broker watched Bevode try to keep himself oriented, looking for the sun, but soon the trees and foliage and close green shadows closed off the sky. They came out on a gravel road again and pulled through a gated entrance to an overgrown parking area.

Broker stopped the truck, got out and pulled an old gate across the access. Then he drove into a camping area.

There was a solitary picnic table, a fire ring, a pipe with a faucet, a trash barrel where a convention of flies were feeding, and a sturdy Minnesota Department of National Resources park toilet.

"Get out," said Broker, unclipping the seat belt.

Bevode warily got out and looked around. His eyes were feral, calculating. Unflinching.

And Broker, who wanted to stay reasonably in control about this, found that he couldn't. In a surge he rushed Bevode and knocked him back against the toilet door. "So you're going to save Lola from Cyrus, huh?"

An expression of incredulous enlightenment flickered on Bevode's torn features. "Oh *no*," he groaned. "The bitch tried to get to you too."

Broker stayed his punch in midair and squinted at Bevode, who grinned horribly with his gap-toothed smile and his puffy lips. "That yoga-shit really builds up the old pudenda, don't it. Lola can fire a harpoon out of that jelly roll." He shook his head with great sincerity and laughed bitterly. "Knew I shouldn't've left Cyrus alone with her."

His candor was thoroughly believable and he was still utterly unafraid. "Aw, man," he said. "Lemme guess."

"Shut up." Broker pushed him against the toilet door again.

Bevode chuckled, slobbering blood. He raised his cuffed hands to his neck, to the faded hickey, and then pointed at Broker's neck, at the tell-tale blood bruise coiled under his left ear. "Looks like we been bit by the same snake, bro. That lady is relentless." Despite the damage to his face, Bevode Fret winked.

Broker stepped back and grimaced.

"Hey, I can dig it," said Bevode fraternally. "I started out the same way. Just tryin' to help." He shook his head. "Get wise, you sorry Yankee piece of shit."

Bevode had opened his bloody palms in a reassuring gesture and took a half step toward Broker. "I mean," he said, "she wants it all for herself, you dig? She gets everybody fighting each other. She's down there right now telling Cyrus that I'm ready to back-stab him, don't you get it?"

Bevode took another half step encouraged by the frown on Broker's face. "Hey, don't feel bad," he sympathized. "You ain't the first guy she took in. Hell, look what she did to ole Cyrus. Sold him a load of bullshit about where she came from . . . and he'd've fathered her mulatto child for an heir to the LaPorte fortune if I hadn't sniffed out the nigger in *that* woodpile."

Bevode made his move. His cuffed hands flashed instinctively for Broker's injured thumb, his weak spot. Broker anticipated it and made a fist around the painful digit. Bevode's powerful hands, still slick from his bleeding mouth, slipped off Broker's knuckles and Broker happily kicked him in the balls and sent him back against the toilet.

Bevode came off the door in a crouch, not even breathing hard, still game to try again. A deep, gleeful voice boomed behind him, resonating against the plastic door: *"Fee fie fo fum. I smell the blood of a white motherfucker!"*

"Huh?" ejected Bevode, his jaw going slack.

The black arm that shot out from the ajar door looked like a railroad tie cooked in creosote and the hand at the end of it pawed around until it seized Bevode by his still-in-place ducktail hairdo.

"What the . . ." Bevode was yanked off his feet with the aid of Broker's foot, placed strategically to trip him. J. T. Merryweather emerged from the toilet. Working effortlessly in tandem, they jackhammered Bevode to his knees.

"Broker, my man," exclaimed J.T., "there's no toilet paper in this outhouse." Then he turned his coal-hard eyes to Bevode who was immobilized, stretched out between J.T's hand in his hair yanking his head back and Broker's heel in the small of his back. Bevode was wide-eyed, but not with actual fear. More puzzled and indignant, like a man who had just discovered a garter belt in his underwear drawer.

"What's that you got in your hand, J.T.?" asked Broker.

"Why," J.T. peered into Bevode's wide eyes, "it's Louisiana baby-soft Charmins. I'll bet I can just wipe my ass with this baby soft face and then . . ."

Together they sang happily, spontaneously, "Toss it down the hole with the rest of the shit."

40

"**G**UYS," IMPLORED BEVODE IN A STRANGLED VOICE.

"You hurt Nina, so I hurt you," said Broker. "But you suckered me down to New Orleans, while some of the boys went after Nina—"

J.T. glowered. "And for that we're going to take your southern manhood. Grab your balls for the last time, Fauvus . . . 'cause tomorrow you gonna be a bitch and I wouldn't be surprised somebody makes an anonymous call down to New Orleans and tells the whole fuckin' police department how we put your sorry ass down."

Bevode roared to life and twisted and thrashed like a large carnivore caught in a net and that's why Broker needed J.T. here because he'd never be able to put him down alone and what he had in mind was something that even Lyle Torgeson in Devil's Rock wouldn't countenance. For this, Broker needed a partner.

The plastic shed rocked as they battled him through the doorway. J.T. dragged, one hand in Bevode's hair and the other on the chain between the cuffs. Broker pushed. The main threat came from Bevode's powerfully kicking feet. Broker managed to get his arms over the tops of both of Bevode's knees and, with his knees up under his armpits, they forced him through the door.

Inside, the light was filtered through green and white corrugated plastic. Flies buzzed in a heady, early summer soup of disinfectant and several cubic yards of human feces and urine that percolated up through the stout brown plastic commode bolted to the cement foundation. Broker thanked the DNR for building strong biffies.

They got him to the commode and J.T., groaning with the effort, pulled Bevode's hands down in front of him with one hand and slammed his face on the toilet seat with the other. With the muscles of his arms stacked in ripped cuts, he manhandled Bevode's cuffed hands through the opening and put a knee to his back. Momentarily free, Broker knelt and smiled into Bevode's biblically outraged eyes.

"First the handcuff keys." He dropped the key a few inches past Bevode's nose and crossed eyes, through the hole into the foulness below.

"Aw jeez," lamented Bevode, gritting his teeth.

Broker dug items from the manila envelope and dropped them one by one. "Wallet. Rental car keys. Travelers checks." Gingerly he held up the leather folder that held Bevode's police identification. "One New Orleans police ID and badge, used."

Then they both surged down on him as he put up a mighty struggle to fight away from the oval maw of the toilet. "Gimme some air," gasped Bevode. "I can't breathe."

"What's your deal with Lola?" Broker yelled.

Bevode panted, pinned to the toilet. "No deal. Aw, man, she played prick tease with me to pick my brain like she did you. She don't fuck nobody no more," he gasped.

Broker seized Bevode's long wild hair in his right fist and yanked his head back. "Now listen up. You go back to New Orleans and tell your boss I ain't playing games from now on."

Bevode rolled his eyes at the plastic toilet seat and groaned. "Oh, man, wait a minute here. Just slow down."

It really bothered Broker that Bevode was probably more worried about his suit than his life. "Who else is in this? In Vietnam?" he yelled.

Bevode grinned weakly, surging away from the latrine opening. "Just us, don't cha see. Thing like this, gotta keep it tight. It's a foreign place. Bunch of Godless atheists. Just the salvage crew, general's picked men."

"And you expect me to lead you to it," said Broker flatly.

Bevode smiled painfully. "General decided that there's no way that cu . . . ," he caught himself, eyed the slime waiting below, and his smile stretched a bloody inch, "Miss Nina Pryce could track down that old jailbird herself. He's bettin' on you."

Broker eased up on his hold. J.T.'s corded arms relaxed. Bevode took a breath and some hope. "Be reasonable, man; Nina's a crazy lady. She don't get it. Tuna and her dad were in it *together.* Think about it. The general stuck up for them and it ruined his career. Hell, if the army wasn't in such a bummer about Vietnam, even *they* would've figured that out." Bevode took another breath, his voice getting stronger. "They used you, man. Pryce's kid and Tuna are *still* using you."

Broker balked for a second. *LaPorte, Tuna, and Pryce. Inseparable buddies for years.* Could have been all three of them. He shook his head. What he got for believing in heroes.

J.T. eyed him for a cue. "What?"

Broker peered at Bevode. "Who are the other guys following Nina?"

Bevode ignored the question and smiled. "Look here. Only one way it can end. We got the fuckin' boat. And we got the gear to get it off the bottom. We've bribed the shit out of the whole government. Hell, we can work it out."

Broker decided to keep it simple and said, "You shouldn't have killed Mike's dog." He nodded to J.T. They both surged down on the Cajun.

"Oh oh. This about the fucking *dog?*" Bevode gasped, eyes wide, amazed.

They each grabbed a leg and levered him into the toilet. "He won't fit through," growled J.T. With one hand he reached down and tore at the seat. On the third try it came screeching loose from under Bevode. Then J.T. smashed at the plastic sides of the commode, cracking the plastic, kicking at the springy shards that twanged around Bevode's twitching head.

They jammed one of Bevode's shoulders and his head through the widened hole and his voice continued to bellow, but muffled. J.T. took the yoke of the toilet seat in both hands and began to pound on Bevode's back with the flat. Between blows, Broker stomped.

"Two hundred pounds of crap," *whack*, "won't fit through a ten-pound hole," *whack*. J.T. kept swinging, glistened with sweat. But then the other shoulder did go through and Bevode screamed like a cat nailed to a stump and his hips balanced on the edge of the cracked stool and his feet wildly churned in midair.

"Bevode," yelled Broker, "rhymes with commode."

As Bevode's pant legs and shoes disappeared, Broker and J.T. leaped toward the door in a fit of hysterical laughter and got tangled together trying to fit through, now fighting each other to escape the mighty splash.

Still laughing, they made it outside and slammed the door shut and planted themselves side by side, backs up against it in an effort to suppress the subterranean thrashing howl emanating up from the ground.

"Like a goddamn monster movie," gasped J.T.

"Like *The Creature from the Black Lagoon*," giggled Broker.

They both went to the faucet and scrubbed off furiously. Broker returned to the lavatory and snapped a Yale lock on the door.

As they walked to the Jeep, J.T. mused, "Somebody should call one of those bleeding heart liberal anchor*persons* on TV and report a case of po-leece brutality."

"Should call Paul Wellstone," Broker agreed.

A few minutes later Broker pulled the Jeep to the side of the access road leading into the remote campground. They opened the gate and after Broker drove through, they wrestled the gate shut. Broker turned to J.T. and shook his hand.

"You really going to do it? All the way to Vietnam?" asked J.T.

"I'm going to do it."

"You gonna have backup?"

"I'm working on it," said Broker.

41

BROKER SAT AT THE TABLE IN HIS CABIN AND WAITED FOR ED Ryan to call. He lit a cigarette and made a face. He'd lit the filter end. In a foul mood, he hurled the cigarette across the room.

"What *is* wrong with you?" said Nina, who sat opposite him counting money. She had withdrawn ten thousand dollars from her savings in Ann Arbor. Now she was dividing crisp hundred-dollar bills into two piles. Two rubbery white security belts curled at her elbow. Their flimsy elastic straps reminded Broker of female undergarments.

"Nothing," said Broker. He got up, manhandling his chair out of the way. The clatter echoed in the silence.

A lot was wrong. He was beginning to feel like a kid from a small town who'd gone off to see the world and had been turned around by some big leaguers.

Bevode's warning still echoed in his ears. *They're still using you.*

There was one person who definitely hadn't used him that night, unless he'd masterminded the gold robbery from his cell in a Communist jail.

Broker walked to the table and snatched at the phone.

"I thought we were waiting for Ryan to call," said Nina.

"I'm calling Trin." Broker dug in his wallet for the card with the Vietnam number.

"Isn't that jumping the gun?" said Nina.

Broker took a deep breath to clear away twenty years of cobwebs and punched up an international patch and hit the number. Satellites played tag during an eerie silence. Then, after five rings, a sleepy Vietnamese voice answered.

"English?" asked Broker.

"Okay. Huong Giang Hotel on Le Loi Street."

"I'm trying to locate Nguyen Van Trin. I was given this number," said Broker.

"Sure, Trin," said the voice. "He work this desk sometime."

"I have to talk to him."

Pause. "It's four in the morning here."

Broker had totally overlooked the time zones. "It's urgent."

"I'll have to wake people up," said the clerk. He took Broker's phone number and asked what message he should give to Trin.

"Tell him I'm with Ray Pryce's daughter and I want my cigarette lighter back." Broker repeated the message slowly so the clerk could write it down. Broker hung up the phone.

"Feel better now?" said Nina with a lilt of sarcasm. She stuffed the thick wads of hundreds in the security belts.

Broker looked over his shoulder. He had recurring visions of Bevode Fret howling and bounding through the tamarack like a Shasquatch tarred and feathered in turds and clammy wads of toilet paper.

"Trin's a long shot," said Nina.

"We need someone we can trust over there. An expediter, to finesse the Vietnamese authorities."

"Finesse? You haven't seen this guy in twenty years."

Broker shook his head. "Trin used to be a real sharp individual."

"Used to be won't do it," said Nina in a slightly testy voice. "I'm starting to think we should keep it American right down the line."

"The new world order don't cut shit in the Socialist Republic of Vietnam, goddammit. They belong to a small exclusive modern club, people who have won real wars. The Gulf doesn't count."

"There's the U.S. Liaison Office in Hanoi," she insisted.

"We were both in the army, remember. We both got the royal shaft." He glared across the table. "What did you talk about with your army buddies while I was in New Orleans?"

Nina recrossed her arms. "I was curious to see if anybody I knew was in or had been in Hanoi on the MIA mission."

"Well?"

She shook her head.

"Good," said Broker.

"Why good," she snapped.

"Because the minute we tell anybody else what we're doing the whole thing blows up in our faces. They don't call it 'gold rush' for nothing."

"I presume we're going to let someone in on it who has some authority, to—you know—*arrest them*," said Nina. Anger turned her freckles slightly purple.

"Look," fumed Broker. "What I do isn't a science. It's not enough to know the peasant wants to steal the goat. You have to *catch him* stealing the goddamn goat. We have to catch them digging it up and loading it. In the act."

"Right," she shot back. "If Tuna turns up. If the gold's where he says it is. If LaPorte goes for it after you robbed his house. If Trin's reliable. If we can get the Vietnamese to cooperate . . . if, if."

Broker ground his teeth and rubbed his eyes. He was exhausted. His whole body ached from the tussle with Bevode. They were both beat. Getting snarly.

Striving for control, he said, "I'm thinking, we get there and check out Trin. We locate the stuff. *Then* you approach the MIA mission. I tip LaPorte. The MIA people bring in the Vietnamese and hopefully they don't screw up dropping the net—"

"I don't like it," said Nina.

"What don't you like?"

"Relying so much on Trin."

"I know how to do this," he asserted.

"I'm not so sure."

"Are you on the rag or something?"

"Hey. Fuck you." She balled her fists.

Edgy, he shot back a flash of street. "You fuck me your heart'll give out."

Nina glowered and stamped from the room, slammed the screen door, and stalked off the porch. Outside, she paced back and forth, arms locked across her chest, trampling pine needles. Broker smoothed his fingers through his new short hair. The pressure was definitely starting to get to them.

Then the phone rang. Broker snatched it up. A calm voice on the other side of the planet announced in impeccable English, "I need some flints for the Zippo. They're hard to get over here."

The screen door slammed and Nina stood at his side. "Ryan?"

Broker shook his head and turned to the receiver and wondered aloud, "Trin?"

"It's me."

"I'm coming over there," said Broker.

"I know."

"What do you mean, you know?"

"It's all arranged. Jimmy bought you and Nina Pryce a tour. I'm a tour guide. I have hotels reserved in Hanoi and Hue. We'll take the train from Hanoi. I just need a time and a flight number."

"Where's Jimmy, Trin?"

"Don't you know. He's in jail. In America." Trin's voice sounded confused. The long-distance connection had a delay and a background rush like the inside of an artificial lung. Hard to talk.

"I'll be in touch as soon as I have a flight," said Broker. There was an awkward silence. "Long time, Trin," he said.

"Yes," said Trin. "Long time."

He hung up the phone, crossed his arms heavily on the table and lowered his head. What did he expect. Trin had been an intelligence operative. He'd never discuss business on the phone.

He looked at Nina and said in an amazed voice, "He's *expecting* us."

"Oh boy," she breathed.

Now they paced. They re-aired all their speculations and anxieties. They finished a pot of coffee and made another one. They watched the sun sink lower in the sky. They stared at the phone.

Finally it rang. Broker picked it up and Ed Ryan said, "I don't know why I do this shit for you."

42

"ANN MARIE SPORTA ATTENDED THE UNIVERSITY OF Wisconsin at Madison between 1988 and 1993," said Ryan. "Which is interesting, because her mother was collecting food stamps in Chicago and Ann Marie wasn't on a scholarship. We checked. Her grades weren't that good . . ."

And Broker thought: Jimmy Tuna, *sponsor,* champion of gimpy Viet Cong and underachieving college students.

Ryan paused for tantalizing seconds. "Her father, Anthony Sporta out of Skokie, was a guest of the government at Marion at the time, for transporting a stolen car across state lines." Ryan paused again. "So you probably want to know why your guy in Milan was his daughter's benefactor . . ."

"Ryan?"

"Aw. Take a guess."

Broker batted at the air, too tired for jokes. But he had pulled Ryan out of bed at four A.M.

"Give up?" taunted Ryan. "Okay. Tony Sporta's father married James Tarantuna's aunt. They're *fucking cousins*. And I just happen to know where Tony Sporta is because I thought you might ask."

"Ryan, I love you," shouted Broker. He flipped Nina a bandaged thumbs up.

With mock sobriety, Ryan stated, "We here at ATF have been through diversity, team, and sensitivity training. Doesn't mean you can get near my asshole."

"Where?"

"You ever hear of Loki, Wisconsin?"

"Spell it."

"Lima Oscar kilo India. Sounds Indian . . ." Ryan speculated.

Ryan was Boston. Southie. Irish. Broker shook his head. Not Indian. Norski. In the stories Irene told him as a little boy, Loki ran with Thor and Odin. "Where is it?" he asked.

"Polk County. Near Amery. There's nothing there—literally— except a cheese factory. And a lot of cows standing around."

"Shit, that's right across the river from the Twin Cities. What's Sporta doing in Loki fucking Wisconsin?"

"Runs the cheese factory. According to the bureau, there's certain Italian gentlemen in Chicago who own the Red, White, and Green pizza franchise. It does a good cash business and that's always a great way to launder money. They make lotsa pizza. So they need cheese in bulk. So they bought this factory. I have no idea why they put Tony in there. By the way, you never told me what you're doing."

"Thanks, buddy." Broker slammed down the phone and jumped up from the chair. He pawed at the air. "Wisconsin road map!" Nina dashed out to look in the glove compartment of the Jeep. Broker rifled his kitchen drawers and shelves. Outside, Nina held her hands, palms up.

"Forget it, we'll grab one on the road," he yelled. They went sparky as frayed live wires. The cabin snapped with brown energy as they grabbed up their meager, unpacked travel bags. He had to call Larson and check on flights. The visas. Christ, their passports were with the visa applications. Later.

They had money stuffed in the security belts. Credit cards for backup.

Weapons . . .

He pulled the Colt from his waistband, put it on the table. Went into the bedroom, glanced at the shotgun. Nah, too obvious. He picked up the Beretta, spare magazines for both handguns, and carried it all out. He stopped. Nina was hefting the heavy .45.

"Trust me on this," she said in that heels-dug-in tone.

They stared at each other. She wasn't going to give it up. Deal with it later. She tucked the heavy pistol in her tote bag. Broker kept the Beretta.

It took Broker thirty seconds and two quick hugs to say good-bye to Mike and Irene.

Their concerned faces made brief cameos in his rearview mirror. His tires chewed clods of dirt and splattered the pine trees with gravel shrapnel. Broker and Nina exchanged exhausted demented smiles. Off to see the Wizard.

"Makes sense." Broker pounded the steering wheel with his injured left hand, oblivious to the pain. "He had Waldo Jenke to watch his back in the joint but now he's on the run and he's hurting bad."

"So he can't go far," said Nina.

"Family," Broker grinned. "He's *Italian*." He ran the stop light in Devil's Rock and smoked past the fifty-five mph speed limit sign doing twenty mph over.

"Now we'll get some answers," he said. "The cards are going to fall where they fucking fall."

"Fine with me." Nina grinned wryly.

"What?"

"You're like a kid, we could be charging into an ambush and you're happy," said Nina. "That's why I came to you. No one else would be nuts enough to go for this."

He *was* happy. The doubts and insecurities of an hour ago had evaporated. It was a quest. Now blessed by a strange serendipity.

They gassed up at the Holiday Station in Tofte. As he got back behind the wheel he handed a travel cup of coffee and a Wisconsin road map to Nina and asked, "You know who Loki was?"

"Norse God."

"Yeah." Broker wedged his coffee cup between his thighs and tore the cellophane off a beef jerky with his teeth and spit it out the window. "He liked to play pranks. He made an arrow out of Mistletoe and deceived Odin's blind son into shooting it into his brother Balder. Balder's death set the gods on the path to Ragnarokk."

"Like kaput," said Nina.

"Right. The end." Broker grinned. "So it kind of makes sense that Jimmy Tuna's holed up in a place called Loki, dying and laughing."

"How could you be a cop for all this time and still think like this?" asked Nina.

Broker shrugged it off. But he saw by her watchful eyes that it was meant as a serious question. Well, they had some serious talking to do.

He lit a cigarette and settled behind the wheel. "Besides my dad the four men who shaped my life were LaPorte, *your* dad, Tuna, and Trin. After knowing them, how the hell was I supposed to go back and have an ordinary life?

"It's like a riddle. How could they be so solid and then fly apart in this gold scam?" He eyeballed her. "What if we find out they were all in it together? Except for Trin, who was in jail."

"The army never cared about the bank. They censured Dad for desertion. I'm not saying he wouldn't knock off an enemy bank. I'm saying he wouldn't leave you up shit creek to do it," she stated simply.

"C'mon. You barely knew him. He was always gone."

"He told me once that the most important thing was for kids to grow up in a home where there was nothing to hide. He was there even when he wasn't there. He was an ordinary guy, Broker; being an officer was a big deal for him. It didn't come easy."

"So we both have our myths."

Nina sipped her coffee and stared at the twinkling horizon of Lake Superior. "When I was seven he came back to Georgia on leave and we went to Michigan to visit Mom's relatives. It was deer season and Dad went hunting with two of my uncles. I said I wanted to go along and he agreed to take me.

"We went up north, into a big woods beyond some farms. There wasn't even much snow. I remember that he had this red Elmer Fudd hunting hat with the funny flaps over the ears. He took out a county map and showed me the roads and where we were going. Then he gave me his compass and explained what to do if I got separated and lost. Go west until I came to a road. Then go to a farmhouse and ask to use the telephone.

"But we didn't get separated. We didn't see any deer either. The sky changed and the wind came up and the snow . . . suddenly it got so cold it hurt and we couldn't see."

"Whiteout," said Broker.

Nina nodded. "From nowhere. A real live killer blizzard. We weren't dressed for it. I was too young, I didn't know how bad it was. He gave me a job, which was to read the compass. Then he unzipped his parka and put me inside with my arms and legs around his waist. He belted me in and then zipped the coat over me. Every few minutes he'd unzip and ask me to show him the compass.

"He kept going on a compass heading through that storm. Sometimes he counted to himself, over and over. One, two, three, four." She smiled. "You know, like cadence. Finally he found a fence line and he walked along it for hours, with one hand on the barbed wire. When he found a mailbox and a driveway his glove was torn to bloody shreds. I don't remember the things he said. I remember that he kept me warm and he smelled like sweat inside his coat and he didn't leave me and he didn't quit and he kept his rifle."

She turned to him and spoke with uncomplicated conviction. "I didn't have to spend a lot of time with him to know him."

Broker clicked his teeth. "I believed in LaPorte. I even went down to New Orleans still half believing in him."

"You were blinded. You're about to get your sight back. LaPorte's Darth Vader. And Bevode is his monster and Tuna is a trickster. I have no idea who Trin is." She smiled and spoofed him. "All we need is a princess, huh?"

She unfolded the road map and studied the index. "Loki. Population forty-three." She referenced the locators and put her finger on a spot. "How long will it take us to get there?"

"About three hours once we cross into Wisconsin at Duluth and we're about forty minutes out of Duluth."

She looked at the sky. "Do we want to roll into Loki in the dark? I doubt that Tony Sporta lives in the cheese factory. And we're both shot. We need some sleep."

Broker exhaled. "You have a point."

She raised up in the seat. "What's that up ahead, on the left?"

"Sloden's Resort. A real yuppie tourist trap. They have shops, masseurs, two restaurants. I think they even have baby-sitters for your cat."

Nina drew her fingers through her slack unwashed hair. "If there's a room, let's spend the night. My treat."

43

NINA REMOVED A TUBE OF LIPSTICK FROM HER PURSE, MED-
icated her dry lips, and mugged in the rearview mirror. She ogled
Broker's mild frown and exclaimed, "What?"

They were closer now and Broker pointed to the large road sign
that said: VACANCY and ROOMS STARTING FROM $79.00. The parking lot
was half full, divided with white lines like a shopping center. "No
problem finding a room. Season doesn't really start up here until
June fifteenth," he explained. "School's not out yet." With a touch
or irony he added, "This part of the year is called the 'quiet time' in
resort lingo."

"Just what I had in mind," said Nina.

They parked the Jeep and carried their bags across the parking
lot, past the tennis court and toward a kiosk-looking office that had
a registration sign above the door. On the way, they skirted little
islands of curbed grass with barbecue grills cemented into them.
Seeing the transplanted suburban grills made Broker think that
Sloden's was the kind of place that Fatty Nasland wished someone
would build in Devil's Rock, probably on Mike's land—until Fatty
lifted a bowling bag full of gold.

There was an auditorium, meeting rooms, and a health spa, with
two saunas, an indoor pool, an outdoor pool, a hot tub, and a work-
out room. The units were Cape Cod, cookie-cutter clapboard,
smartly painted Prussian Blue and cream and as monotonous as a
rank of Continental soldiers. Just right for fussy city people who
didn't want to get *too* near the woods.

The young lady at the registration desk showed them a map of
the grounds and explained that the gravel Lakewalk along the shore

led to a mini-mall where they could find an espresso and pastry shop and a boutique.

"Good," said Nina. "I can go shopping."

Broker wasn't listening. He watched traffic on the highway. Since they'd turned into the resort no other car had entered the parking lot. Maybe she *had* lost them in Lansing.

Nina discovered that there was a hair salon in the resort proper, next to the video arcade. She fingered her head of copper straw and issued an appeal that brought a sympathetic response from the receptionist. Broker grinned. Colt .45 in her bag and she was girl-talking. The receptionist quickly dialed a number and cajoled somebody into staying late for an appointment.

Then Nina splurged and took the third most expensive room in the joint, with a king-sized bed, full bath, and a Jacuzzi overlooking Lake Superior. "Spectacular view," said the brochure.

They signed in and got the key and carried their bags up to their room. The king-sized bed looked good. But Nina insisted on going shopping. It was nearly five-thirty, her appointment was at six.

They practically ran the Lakewalk. In the boutique, Broker blundered into a jangling déjà vu ambush when Nina stepped out of a dressing room wearing a snug, dark purple dress with price tags hanging off it. She said, "Do you think this is too tight?"

Little alarms flashed in the back of his mind. Many mornings when he was a married man, Kimberly would come down the stairs and say exactly those words.

"It's fine," said Broker, backpedaling.

"What about the way it fits here?" She ran her fingers along the taut material over her left hip—*where the Iraqis shot her*—and she continued, word for word what his ex-wife used to say: "Give me an honest opinion."

"I think you should get it," said Broker.

"Just tell me how it looks when I walk away, from behind."

"Well, it does kind of show off your . . ." *Oh shit.*

"So it is too tight or . . ."

Broker spun on his heel and went outside before he got pulled into the vortex of the F-word. Not the one that stood for "unlawful carnal knowledge," the one that ended in *at*.

He smoked a cigarette and watched the highway, the resort parking lot, and the Lakewalk. Finally Nina came out of the shop with an armful of bags and immediately set off across the road. He jogged to catch up. She headed for a strip of stores: a grocery, a liquor store, and a sporting goods–bait shop. She headed for the door with the prominent neon sign that blared GUNS.

With the same easy aplomb she'd shown among the dresses and the shoes, she bought two pistol cleaning kits, one for a 9mm and one for the Colt, and a box of Federal .45 caliber, 230 grain ball rounds.

As they left the store and hurried across the highway, Broker asked, "What the hell are you doing?"

"You had hollow points in the Colt," she explained in a professional voice that sounded like, *you dumb shit.*

"Aw, God," groaned Broker.

Then she convinced him that Bevode Fret and company were nowhere in sight and that they certainly weren't going to snatch her from the beauty shop. So Broker carried all the shopping bags up to the room. He stripped and stayed under the shower for twenty minutes and emerged from the bathroom, clean and shaven. He changed the bandage on his thumb. The swelling had gone down. He experimented with making a fist.

He put on his only change of clothes, the light sport jacket he'd worn to New Orleans, cotton slacks, a short-sleeved shirt, and worn loafers. All slightly wrinkled.

He took a Heineken from the small refrigerator and sat out on the balcony to revive himself with the "spectacular view" of a dead flat Lake Superior. A loon motored by, some gulls dived, three ducks landed. He tapped his index finger at the circle Nina had drawn around Loki, Wisconsin, on the map. Then he stared at a castle of clouds and thought about Nguyen Van Trin.

Right after he first arrived in Vietnam. Before the Big Offensive. Before he'd learned to wear his sweat. The older, red-haired major on the team, whom the others called "Mama Pryce," sat him down.

"You notice there's graves all over the place? The Vietnamese have this thing about graves," Pryce said. "And they have these lunar holidays when they go fix up their graves. Well, we are in the middle of one of those lunar holidays and I want you to take the Jeep and drive Colonel Trin, the commander of the regiment, over to the old Dong Ha combat base. There's still some American units stationed there and some of our guys live in the house where he was born. You know, sorta go in and smooth it and help him dress up the family cemetery."

In a more optimistic time the combat base had looked like primitive Rome. A legion of U.S. Marines had built it on seven hills that overlooked a muddy river. Now it had reverted to the South Vietnamese and resembled a military slum transplanted from Mars. Nothing but rusty barbed wire, collapsed barracks, and clouds of gritty red dust blowing over the gummy red hills.

Broker found Colonel Trin to be the most foreign presence he had ever known. With his flat face, his cold, brown wraparound Asian eyes and scars lumped on his high, wide cheeks, he could have been a bronze Sphinx. Broker also noted that he smelled strongly of onions and garlic. And the Sphinx did not speak. And Broker had no Vietnamese language skills. Considering the late hour, the army had canceled the course. So he just drove the Jeep. Trin sat stiffly in the passenger seat and pointed. Two shovels, a mattock, a hoe, and a rake clattered in the back.

Trin directed Broker down a maze of dusty roads until they came to a very old and roomy country home of masonry and tile that was misplaced in the military debris. Garden terraces were choked with weeds and blurred out in the adobe-colored dirt. An outbuilding had taken a direct artillery hit. A dusty Jeep and a three-quarter-ton truck were parked haphazardly on the patio.

Trin jerked his hand toward the house. Broker picked his way up the path, past boles of orange, rust-fused barbed wire, soggy heaps of C-ration cardboard and an ornate, stone-carved griffin that was toppled on its side. As he neared the door he had to detour around an upright, ornamental stone slab that barred direct entrance.

Broker stepped around the screen and yelled, "Anybody home?" No answer. He went in. The damp walls dripped with marijuana fatigue and, in the central room, he found three U.S. army enlisted men sprawled on cots. Their gear lay heaped in mildewed piles, their rifles were dirty. Pin-ups from *Playboy* and *Cavalier* made a solid tit-heavy collage of the walls. A can of C-Ration ham and mother fuckers—lima beans—heated on a small kerosene stove. The smell of bubbling beans mingled with the albumin stench of urine. Somebody was taking a piss in the next room.

It was 1972. Nobody saluted second lieutenants. "What?" said one of the GIs. Two others ignored Broker. A fourth came through the door buttoning his fatigue trousers.

Base rats. Attached to some signal outfit.

Broker had been taught in officer candidate school never to lay a hand on an enlisted man. So he turned to the one who had spoken and booted him to the floor, overturning his cot.

"Outside," said Broker.

They formed a huddle. "What's going on?" demanded the black one. Broker squinted at them. They thought it was a democracy. They were like the kids back home, sucking down dope, going to concerts, and thinking life was supposed to be fair. Broker, young and dumb, still thought it was the army at war.

But in deference to the times, which were bad, he didn't push it. They measured him and saw that he was made out of piano wire and ax handles and that he wore the flap to his holstered .45 unsnapped. And that was enough. They whispered among themselves. One of them offered a sloppy salute.

Broker ignored the salute and explained. "A Vietnamese colonel, whose house you're pissing in, wants to look after some things. So take your asses down the road for a few hours."

As they filed out, one of them said, "Fuckin' gooks."

When they were gone, Colonel Trin walked stiffly into the building carrying a small green canvas satchel. His face remained a graven image as he visited each room. Then he went out the back door and through the brush toward a gentle, overgrown hillock that the GIs used for their garbage dump. Broker went back to the Jeep and grabbed the tools.

When he returned, Colonel Trin had stripped off his tunic and had stooped to work, graceful with muscle and scar tissue. He kicked at rusty cans and cardboard and worse, he yanked handfuls of tall weeds. A pendant swinging from a chain around his neck caught a flash of sun. It got in the way and Trin snatched it off and put it in his pocket. He looked up and saw that Broker was staring at the thick raised scars on his back and chest. Broker lowered his eyes and pulled off his fatigue shirt and stood, barechested, hefting the mattock, looking for a way into the job.

Trin narrowed his hooded eyes for a brief second and then took Broker by the arm and put him to work clearing brush away from a low, round cement wall that surrounded a weed-choked earthen mound. The round wall did not go full circle. There was an entrance and it was ceremonially blocked by an upright cement slab that was smaller than but similar to the one in front of the main house's front door. Another dozen mounds were spread through the brush.

Broker swung the mattock. He hoped to make up for his goof-off countrymen tossing their garbage on other people's graves.

They worked side by side through the siesta hour as the red earth fought them like a bed of coals. Broker was getting a sense of the Vietnamese colonel: He was a worker. And he hardly sweated drop one. Broker put out fluids like a hunk of fatback pork in a skillet, but he was determined to keep up. Soon he became dizzy in the heat and had to go to the Jeep for the water can. He brought the container back with him and offered a canteen cup to the short, indefatigable Asian.

Trin straightened up, took one sip, and returned the cup. When their shadows were longer than they were tall, they'd cleared the hill of brush and weeds. Broker had raked the garbage into a pile closer to the house. As Trin expertly used a shovel and a hoe to shape the grave mounds, Broker smoothed the ground between them.

Then the warlike colonel kneeled and took a fistful of incense from his small satchel. He lit the joss sticks and jammed them in the soft dirt of the nearest grave mound.

Buddha stuff. Broker looked around the barbed-wire skirted hills. He saw piles of tin and plywood, the collapsed housing of departed Americans. And then he began picking out the subtle, neglected earthen mounds. Ancestor worship. They were everywhere and some of them were probably there and looking old when Jesus Christ was just learning to swing a hammer.

And Broker, who had an *N,* for "none," stamped on his dog tags in the space reserved for a religious affiliation, was stumped at what do next. So he gathered up the tools and walked back to the Jeep.

Colonel Trin returned with his tunic buttoned and his stern eyes shaded by the brim of his military cap. He pointed the way back to Dong Ha. Except he had Broker turn off short of the compound and down a side street dense with twittering, smiling people. Trin pointed one last time. A restaurant.

When they were seated, Trin removed his cap and ran his hand through his thick black hair. His smile came sudden and disarming and warm, like his previous face had been a mask that had dropped off. He withdrew a pack of cigarettes from his pocket and offered one to Broker.

Broker declined. He didn't smoke—yet. He was two weeks away from laying on the ground all night next to dead bodies that had swelled all day in the sun.

Trin tapped the pack. "Bastos," he said. "Algerian. The French paratroopers used to smoke them." He spoke impeccable English in a deep voice.

And he talked like a storybook. "Now we will have a real Vietnamese meal and I'll explain why foreign garbage has an affinity for Vietnamese graves. I will tell you the history of my country. You will learn about sorrow."

They talked all night.

He jerked alert and checked his watch. She'd been gone for almost an hour. He was starting to worry when there was a knock on the door.

The face of Mama Pryce's daughter was distorted in the fish-eye security peephole. He opened the door and she came in and . . . Hmmm. She'd had her hair fixed—no longer a wash-and-wear mop, now it was swept around in a subtle way that showcased the sparse lines of her neck and chin and cheeks. Her eyes were bigger, grayer. And she wore earrings. Long silver jobs with dangling jade half moons.

"Give me an hour," she said. "Now beat it. I'll meet you in the bar by the restaurant."

44

HE WAS NURSING THE DREGS OF A BEER WHEN NINA CAME
through the bar room door like a panther crashing a poodle show.

High heels realigned her posture and catapulted her from the girl
next door. And the hair and the simple, elegant black dress.
Especially the dress that, through some sorcery of design, spring-
loaded the tilt of her hips and made them very emphatic. The crisp
black skull-and-crossbones tattoo popped on her bare left shoulder
as cautionary in its own right as a Harley logo stamped on a muscular forearm.

The silver and jade earrings played to a touch of carotene eyeshadow. Lipstick made rose petals of her lips. And the perfume—
Lola LaPorte's perfume had smelled like danger and loneliness.
Nina's was an alchemy of mother's milk and happy sex and Broker,
with his Achilles' groin, smelled the danger of the kitchen. Of fixing
screen doors. A dumb, happy danger.

"Well?" she asked casually.

"Impressive," said Broker, blindsided.

"You didn't really think I was a lifer dike, did you?"

"I said I was impressed."

She fingered the cheap rumpled material of his summer jacket.
"You look like a mechanic."

"A squeaky clean mechanic," said Broker. He stood up and gallantly walked her into the restaurant feeling like a rough trade date
whom a model had rented for the night.

Why not? They had a rendezvous in Loki, Wisconsin, where
uncomfortable truths might wait. Tomorrow could be bullet time.
And she looked great.

Nina ordered a vodka martini and specified three olives. Broker, trying hard to relax with the Beretta jamming his kidneys and scanning the restaurant doorway, decided to go nonalcoholic and ordered a Sharp's.

The drinks arrived and she fished an olive out with a toothpick and held it between her teeth for a moment before chewing it. Broker sipped his weak beer. Their eyes met and they both asked questions at the same time. Hers: "Why didn't you remarry?" His: "Why in the hell did you join the army?" His came out a little bit first.

She speared the second olive and shrugged and asked another question. "Why did you?"

"I didn't join. I had a high lottery number."

"But you went Airborne and Ranger and OCS."

"What's your point?"

Nina went after the third olive. "We're old-fashioned cannon fodder, you and I. Squares. I'll bet when you hear the national anthem you put your hand over your heart."

The waiter returned and Nina ordered a New York strip, medium rare, a baked potato, no sour cream, and a salad with vinaigrette dressing. Broker went for the lake trout. He was watching her almost exclusively now and hardly cased the doorway.

"What you're really asking is did I go into the army because of my father."

"Okay. Did you?"

"Partly. The other reason is a corny vow that a certain group of young women can never admit that they've taken. But one of us is going to *really* command soldiers someday. It's the last hurdle."

"You did."

"I only did what I was trained to do. Make decisions in a crisis."

"Modest."

She lowered her eyes. "We have to be. Sojer men don't like them pushy broads." She smiled wryly. "*You* don't like pushy broads."

He stared hard at her.

"Okay," she shrugged. "I'd like to be the first, but I don't have any illusions. Basically I'm just the little Dutch girl's thumb. I'll probably end up jumping in to plug a gap somewhere. That's the life I opted for."

He continued to stare at her. "What I don't like is the way you jump to conclusions about Ray being all good and LaPorte being all bad."

Their food arrived and when she cut into her steak, for the first time, he noticed her fingers. And he remembered Lola and her lacquered nails. Nina kept her fingernails trimmed almost fanatically close to the cuticle. He reached over, took her right hand, and turned it over. Then her left. Scallops of scar tissue patterned the pads of her palms.

She shrugged. "That night in the desert. Coming down from the fight, I wouldn't leave until all the wounded were out. I sat with some of the dying. Figured it came with the territory. Everyone was watching my face. I guess I clawed hunks out of my hands. Didn't even know it. My nails were too long." She picked up her knife and resumed cutting her steak. "Won't happen next time."

Broker thoughtfully chewed a mouthful of trout and almonds in silence. Then he asked, "What about the other part of joining the army, about your father?"

Nina looked up with a practical expression. "That's where the people who know Dad and LaPorte were. Some of them are generals now. Most of them refused to talk to me. But some did and they all said the same thing." She pointed her fork across the table. "Dad had a reason for being there at the end in Vietnam. He was deeply committed to evacuating people who'd worked for our side. But they all said that LaPorte stayed one tour too long. Not smart for a guy who'd been fast tracking for a first star, hanging on to a lost cause that way. They even used the same words to describe it. Like he was literally trying to find something." She paused. "I didn't get here by myself, Broker. A couple of those foxy old warriors pointed me in a direction."

"Maybe we'll find out tomorrow," he said.

"I think we will find out tomorrow," she said.

They finished their meal in silence. Beyond the windows, Lake Superior dimmed down to an empty ebony ballroom and a soft-shoe of moonlight. They paid the check and walked into the lobby.

"C'mon, Broker," she said. "Spin me down the beach."

45

THE SUPERIOR SURF COULD NEVER REALLY MURMUR. IT WAS for rolling rocks. Broker smiled at the insight and wondered if he'd just described himself.

Leaving the restaurant, because of the eyeshadow, he noticed that her iris had flecks of green and that her eyelashes were golden; because of the lipstick, he noticed the curve of her upper lip. As they walked the gravel path along the shore he was very aware of the temperature of her leg when it swept against his. And the rustle of her dress, the click of her heels, and the swing of her hips.

She turned and cuddled against his chest and smoothed a hand down his lapel. The languid motion stopped abruptly. "What's this?"

He tapped the folded files in his inside jacket pocket. "The banking records. Just a precaution."

Her eyes soaked up the moonlight. "You have any idea what this dress cost? Do me a favor. Stop working for the rest of tonight." She stepped out, holding his hand high, and twirled back under it into him.

She grinned. "See how easy it is?" She had wrapped his arm around her shoulders and looked up. "Do me another favor," she said.

"Sure."

"For one night stop thinking of me as a nine-year-old in braces."

Actually, Broker was thinking she was more like ice cream in a black dress. "How come *you* never got married?" he asked, stealing her question to him.

A lake breeze moved across the material of her dress and he felt the motion, warm, inside the skin of his hands. "I don't need a husband. I need a fucking wife," she observed frankly.

He took her hand and his fingers grazed the ridges of scars in her palm. "Okay. You're all grown up."

"This could be our last night ashore. Know what I mean?"

He nodded. "It could get rough."

They stopped walking and stood close. A couple in shorts, with wires distorting the silhouettes of their heads, speed-walked by wearing Walkmans in the dark. Like blinders. Another time, Broker might have pushed them into the lake.

"So . . . maybe there will never be another night quite like this. Why don't we just appreciate it," she said. Slowly she raised her arms and put them, no longer hard but soft and willowy, around his neck. As her energy circled him, her hipbones pressed, definite and hard, and it was very warm down there between them.

His capillaries stood up like happy red wires and he lived through a perfect kiss.

"Don't worry, tomorrow I'll turn back into a tomboy with a dead frog in my pocket," she whispered and punctuated it with a hot lick to his earlobe.

"No you won't."

"Yes, I will. That's the problem."

First they did it with their eyes in the moonlight.

Eloquent with the eyes. The body can only try to take the shape. The body is awkward, it sweats, and fumbles and that is why, even in the dark, you look into each other's eyes when you make love, to pretend you are not just an animal, to pray that there really is a soul.

Then, like all the best moments of his life, the details were lost in the absence of the ordinary and, like always when he rediscovered this place, he wondered why he couldn't live here all the time.

For a while they continued to float in each other's arms soaking up the last tremblers. Then it was eyes again. And breathing returning to normal and the tickle of drying sweat.

Very slowly they found their way back into their own skins and, after an interval, she rolled to the side, removed one of his cigarettes from the pack on the nightstand, lit it, and passed it to him. Now they'd have to talk. Talk ruined the world. What the world needed was a government of eyes.

"What are you thinking?" she asked.

Broker exhaled a stream of smoke at the ceiling. "I never thought this would ever happen again."

"What?"

"Lay in bed with a woman and look at the ceiling and share a cigarette. It's not allowed in Minnesota."

They both laughed and Broker knew that when this was over, he would be old. He just knew. Days like this would never never come his way again.

He watched her roll off the bed and go to the refrigerator and open a mineral water. Then she crossed the deep pile carpet in a glide against the triangles of Scandinavian maple that framed the windows. Broker sighed with happy fatalism. The arena was full of pirates. Now he had opened the last two remaining doors and admitted the lady *and* the tiger.

But for now the night air came tactile through the screens, still special to the moment and they nudged it with their eyes, back and forth across the room, against each other's skin.

She sat on the window ledge tipped in quicksilver against the night and stars. The cool, beaded bottle rested on her thigh. She drew one knee up and stretched her left arm over it.

He tried to picture her with long hair. A few more pounds.

He tried to picture her . . . cooking.

Making love with her had been an outrageous clean, free place. And now a long moment of calm.

But nothing was free, was it?

And they had made love in the eye of the storm.

Broker saw the problem. The castle walls in her eyes had been kicked down in the rumpus on the bed. She had been generous. She could play at surrender and back and forth. Now she had to rebuild her fort and stamp out the seeds of romantic entanglement that could sprout like weeds from every drop of her sweat.

With a mischievous salty grin she ambled to the bed. "The trouble with guys," she said, "is once they find a great piece of ass," she took a swig of water, "they don't know what to do with it."

"Some guys," said Broker, pushing up on his elbows. So much for the warrior-virgin theory. "I guess we're used to it being quieter . . . after."

"Sorry," she said. "I know, I should be spacey and postcoital gooey. Was Kimberly, the space alien, like that in the dark?" Tough talk, but her eyes were still big and grave. "All the guys I've been with said the same thing: 'Let's get married after you quit the army.'"

"Well, you quit the army."

"I didn't jump. I was pushed. And not because of the Gulf stink. It was later. Because of a little scrap of tin that costs a dollar in the PX." She laughed and extended her finger. "You got one and I don't." She pointed at his penis, but she was talking about the Combat Infantry Badge. She started stacking up the rocks in her eyes.

"Never happen," said Broker. "They give it to you, they have to open the combat arms to women."

"I did the work. I should get paid like everybody else." She pointed to the two scars in her hip. "What'd I do here, knick myself baking cookies?"

"You're right," sighed Broker. "Definitely not postcoital gooey."

Nina put on a freckled roughneck grin. "I have to mind my stereotypes if I'm going to gatecrash their party and nail LaPorte's scalp to the clubhouse wall."

"You really think that'll work?"

"So I've been led to believe." She set the bottle down on the night table. "The same senior officers who put the bug in my ear about LaPorte think it's inevitable. A woman is going to cross the line in the next five years—the army just needs a push. The kind of push that comes from a big splash. If LaPorte drops from a great height, I'll get my splash."

"Ambitious," said Broker. More comfortable now that it was out in the open.

She jerked her lips in a bawdy grin. "Somebody has to be the first swinging vagina to command a rifle company." She climbed on the bed and straddled his hips. "You secure enough to handle that kind of ambition?"

"Sounds fine to me." He reached up for her.

"Uh-uh. This time I get to be on top."

"Okay."

"Can you handle that?"

"Like I said, some men—"

"Confident, aren't you?"

"Too much talk."

"One last thought before the next round of killing starts. Could you handle being a general's wife?"

"What?"

Nina looked down with a warm smile and said, "See." Broker threw the pillow at her. She threw it back.

More serious now, she lay down beside him. A prolonged silence buried the banter and she said, "Tell me about my dad, Broker."

Broker adjusted a pillow under his head. "His left foot was a cornerstone. Guys like him hold institutions together."

Nina flicked a curl of lint from a tidy breast and knit her brows. "Had he lived and stayed in the army he'd never have made it past colonel. You know what I mean?"

"Uh-huh. He lived by the book but he wasn't an ass kisser. He told me once he'd grown up in the shadow of giants. He was talking about men like Ridgway, Bradley, Patton. He had a little of that aura."

"All gone now."

"Yeah."

Nina tossed her head and aimed a puff of breath at her mussed hair. "Oh I don't know, I just got rolled around by a little of that aura." She grinned.

Broker slowly clipped her chin with affectionate knuckles. Nina took his cigarette and rolled over and dragged experimentally, holding the smoke between her thumb and index finger.

"In a funny way it's guys like my dad who held me up in the army. The dinosaurs," she said, handing back the smoke. "Just a bunch of old white men bitching about upper-body strength."

"Powell wasn't an old white man, he didn't want you guys in the foxholes."

"He's wrong. Hell, I'm not a fanatic. I know that most women can't handle it. But what pisses me off is that they won't admit that most men can't handle it either." She laughed. "John Wayne is still the macho symbol of the soldier. Did you ever see John Wayne *run* in a movie. No. He always walked."

"I kinda liked the way he walked." Broker grinned.

"He was tippy and overweight. He would have dropped dead on a PT test." She turned to him frankly. "Look at me, what do you see?"

"A damn good-looking female human," said Broker playfully.

"Right. A female human who weighs about the same as Audie fucking Murphy." She set her jaw. "Maybe I'll make it, maybe I won't. Whoever makes it, she won't be off the PC funny farm that took over after Tailhook . . .

"In the end we'll do it the old-fashioned way." She sat up and linked her arms around her knees. "It's just arithmetic. More and more of us are in forward positions. And we'll be in some dead-end posting and there'll be a total clusterfuck—like the Rangers in

Somalia. When the body parts stop dripping from the trees, the pile of dead ovaries will be bigger than the pile of dead testicles. That's how you get a soldier's attention. With a bucket of blood. We know about blood. Hell, we should all be awarded Purple Hearts when we get our first period."

Broker chose his words carefully. "I think it's older. We decided we can get dirty in wars and we always lie about how fucked up it really is. If women start getting dirty the same way, who's going to raise the kids?"

She licked her index finger and chalked a number one in the dark. Her lips curved down. "So how was I? Dirty?"

"Nina . . ."

Her lips formed a smile but she wasn't smiling. "I shot two Republican Guards no farther away than it is to that doorway. They came around a burning track. They hesitated. I didn't. I've never felt bad about those two guys in the moral sense. But sometimes I wish I'd had a kid before I killed my first man in combat."

The Jericho eyes were back and the pliant lover of twenty minutes ago departed her like vapor. She stood up and walked to a chair where she'd thrown her luscious black dress. She picked it up and held it for a moment and rocked it against her cheek. Then she dropped it to the floor and when she turned to him again she wore her nakedness like a tailored Class-A uniform. She planted her knuckles on her hips again and teased, "So, now are you going to tell me where you got the hickey on your neck?"

46

BROKER WOKE UP AND STRETCHED. FOR A WONDERFUL HALF second he drowsed with an adolescent languor until an odor smacked him that was about as far from the memory of lovemaking as you can get: Hoppe's gun-cleaning solvent.

A shower had knocked the quaff from Nina's hair and her face was bare of makeup. She wore baggy jeans, a pebble-gray T-shirt, and busted tennis shoes. He sat up and squinted. Probably changed to the bigger jeans because he'd said that dress was too tight at the store . . .

Her pant legs were drenched almost to the knees. Cockleburs stuck to them. Wet grass and bits of brush were pasted to her rubber soles. He reached for his car keys on the bedside table. Gone.

"What the hell?"

"I took the Jeep up into the hills. Ran a few rounds through the .45 to see where it shoots," she said mildly as she held up the pistol. "A foot off to the left at eight o'clock over approximately fifty yards . . ."

Broker rubbed his eyes. "Let me have that cannon. Take the Beretta, it's lighter."

Nina hefted the Colt's weight and said fondly, "Uh-uh, this lump of iron is the longest continuing in-service military handgun in the world for a reason."

She sat at the table by the kitchenette surrounded by bore brushes, patches and plastic bottles, little wire brushes, cleaning rods, and a box of pistol ammunition. His Beretta lay to one side, obviously oiled. Her fingers flew, reassembling the Colt. The slide ratcheted forward with a springing snap. She fixed him with a direct, scrubbed morning stare. "Last night doesn't mean I'm your squaw, you got that?"

"C'mon—" said Broker.

"It could complicate taking care of business, agreed?"

"Just a weak moment," said Broker.

"A choice I made. Nothing weak about it," she said with finality.

Broker made a face and needed to brush his teeth. Grumbling, he headed to the bathroom.

At the sink he wondered how he would get his Colt back. Should have brought the shotgun. Maybe they should stop on the road and buy one. He'd never relied on handguns, which he considered wildly inaccurate in the hands of normal people—he recalled the army pistol-shooting trophy in Nina's apartment in Ann Arbor—unless you were an obsessive-compulsive nut who spent thousands of hours at the range. Which she could very well be.

Broker continued to grumble through a shower and a shave. When he came out, he dressed quickly. They packed their bags, clipped on their security belts, jammed guns in their waistbands, left their T-shirts untucked to cover them, and walked from the fancy room without looking back.

Broker jump-started his heart with three thimbles of espresso on the deck of the fern-elegant pastry shop next to the resort. As Nina had a vegetable omelet he watched the pewter sky heat up over the lake. With uncharacteristic ennui he wondered if he'd ever see snow again. Then they hit the road. Nobody tailed them as far as he could determine.

Nina read aloud from Tuna's prison jacket while Broker monitored the rearview. "Graduate degree in business administration from the University of Michigan extension service. Two years of Vietnamese. Graduate courses in international investment. Tuna and I were going to school together."

"Biding his time, getting ready for something. He always was a tricky guy but—"

"But what?"

"He always had bad luck."

"No shit."

In an hour they had crossed through Duluth and Superior, Wisconsin, and were speeding south on the road they'd originally taken up to Mike and Irene's. The early morning haze burned off and humidity hugged the fields and tree lines like a lazy bejeweled python. Barefoot, early summer day, when the yellowjacket stings you in the soft flesh under your instep in the tall wet grass.

They didn't talk much. The map lay open on Nina's lap. Twenty years telescoped for Broker. Twenty years in which he had failed at a marriage and put a lot of guys and two or three women in jail. Not much to show. He glanced at Nina, who stared straight ahead. He wondered if some of her concentration was morning-after blues. Passion and spontaneity had overruled precaution last night.

He smiled tightly, remembering his mother's maxim: *Our only real job here on earth is to replace ourselves.*

But the fact was, when you're driving toward who knows what with loaded guns in your pants, you're a long way from workaday hedges against reality like condoms and diaphragms. Seeming to sense his thoughts she turned and asked, "How are you doing, Broker?"

"We'll do just fine," he said.

"I think so too." For a few moments she held his hand. Broker leaned forward and stepped on the gas.

They turned east on Highway 8 at St. Croix Falls, and then south on County 65. They consulted the map and made a turn on County F and raced down the winding tar two-lane that was hemmed in by hilly fields and a lot of swamp and small woods. They found Loki near a place called Wanderoos.

Like Ryan said. There was nothing there except a decaying A&W Root Beer stand with weeds growing in the parking lot and a two-story cinderblock building with four pickups parked behind the loading dock.

The peeling white paint on the building's side had sprouted quaint Burma Shave whiskers and failed to blot out huge faded letters that spelled out a previous owner: CAMP'S EXTRA MILD CHEESE. 1926. A newer sign was bolted to a pillar on the loading dock and bore an Italian flag–colored cockade logo and the business name: RED, WHITE, AND GREEN, INC. Cracked cement steps rose to the dock and a sign jutted at one end. Office.

The sun was high and cropped their shadows short as they crossed the gravel lot and mounted the steps. A bell jingled as they entered.

A plaque on the desk announced ANTHONY SPORTA, MGR. The man behind the nameplate filled a red T-shirt and bib overalls with the swollen dignity of a Sumo wrestler. Beneath ringlets of black hair, his beady eyes peered from a face the texture of Italian sausage. The real hard kind. A twist of flypaper hung directly above his head coated with a jam of dead insects. He squinted at them. His right index finger described a dainty curlicue in the air that signaled, "Hello, come in. I know who you are."

A muted sound of machinery carried through the walls. Lactose mist seeped in the air. Not looking real happy, Tony Sporta opened a drawer, pulled something out, and tossed it on the desk. It was a picture, twenty years old, that had been taken in a waterfront restaurant in Hue City. LaPorte, Pryce, Tuna, and Broker sat behind a forest of beer cans. An arrow drawn in marker indicated Broker's head. Younger, but the eyebrows. Sporta's practiced gaze settled on Broker.

"Now why does a guy who's in shape wear his shirt out?" he said.

"Is that a bathroom?" asked Nina, pointing to an open door next to some file cabinets.

"Just stay put a second." Sporta glowered.

Nina offered him a pained smile. "I have a female situation I have to attend to."

Sporta grumbled, "Leave the purse." Feigning indignance, Nina put her purse on the desk and pulled out a travel pack of super maxipads. Sporta jerked his thumb at the door and perused Broker as Nina locked the door behind her. "He says you're a cop, but I shouldn't let that bother me."

"How is he?" asked Broker.

"Real fucked up. He wants you and the girl in quick, out quick, and he's got rules." The toilet flushed behind the bathroom door. Water pipes rattled.

"Okay," said Broker.

"Nothin's okay. He should see a doctor." Sporta cleared his throat and stood up, light-footed for a big man. "He should see a priest." The bathroom door opened and Nina came out holding up her wet hands. She was walking a little funny, but you had to have been in bed with her to tell.

"You're out of towels," she said.

"Sorry," said Sporta. He turned back to Broker. "You leave your vehicle here. I drive you partway. You walk the rest."

Broker nodded.

"You take nothing in there. No cameras, no tape recorders, no bags or purses, and *no guns*. So I gotta pat you down. Both of you. Empty your pockets. Put it on the desk." Change and keys and spare folding cash made two little piles on Sporta's dirty desk blotter. Then he motioned to Broker, who reluctantly lifted his arms. Sporta's hand went right to the Beretta jammed in his waistband in the middle of his back. Broker watched Nina's eyes, which had gone very quiet and neutral. Sporta placed the pistol on his desk.

"What's this?" asked Sporta, patting just below Broker's belt loops.

"Security belt."

"What's in it?"

Broker pulled the elastic folder out and zipped it open. "Money, ID."

"Okay. Keep that. Lift up your pant legs so I can see your socks." Broker did. Sporta turned to Nina. "Now you."

His thick fingers quickly circled her waist, went lower, and hit the security belt. She pulled it out and opened it. He nodded and went through the socks routine with her. As he straightened up from inspecting her ankles he grimaced slightly. "Sorry, miss, but you got a little bulge there, front and back."

Nina reddened and handed Sporta the maxipads. "Go ahead," she said grimly. "You're the one out of towels . . ."

Sporta delicately scratched his chin and decided to pass. He told them to retrieve their pocket items, took her purse, collected the Beretta, and put them in the desk drawer, which he then locked. "You'll get them back."

He bent and picked up a Coleman cooler that sat next to the desk. "You can take him some lunch. C'mon," he said.

When Nina was sandwiched in the front seat of a huge red truck between Sporta's girth and Broker riding shotgun, Sporta paused before he twisted the ignition. "Won't do you any good to ask me because he didn't tell me anything. He just gave me the picture and said bring you the minute you showed up."

"You brought him over from Milan?" asked Broker.

"Yeah. I did do that. My mother's his aunt. He made me promise not to even tell her he was here."

As they drove away from the Red, White, and Green cheese factory a black Subaru station wagon overtook them and passed at high speed on the hilly, curving road. Broker felt a hitch in his stomach when he saw the tinted windows zip past. Bevode Fret had driven a green Saturn with smoked glass. Sweat trickled down the small of his back where the Beretta had been.

Sporta puffed on a Camel straight. His forearms, draped on the wheel, looked like tattooed Easter hams. "Now this place we're going to is on a thousand acres my employers bought to go deer hunting. So they only use it in November."

"How bad is he?" asked Nina.

Sporta shook his head. "Last week I'd get four shopping bags of food at the grocery. Now I get a bag at a time."

They came over a hill and Broker saw the black station wagon, going slower now, keeping pace in front of them. "You recognize that car?" he asked.

"Lotta lake homes around here. There's all kinds of cars." Sporta shrugged. "Relax. There's only one way in and I'll be blocking it. I got some firepower in the back." Sporta grinned. "Don't tell my parole officer."

They turned off on a gravel road and Sporta pointed to a high stand of pines and oak about a mile away. "Cabin's up there. Swamp runs all around that hill. The water's been high so the road don't go through. You have to get your feet wet and walk the last three hundred yards." He stopped the truck at a padlocked steel gate. The posts were festooned with No Trespassing and Armed Response signs.

When Sporta got out to unlock the gate, Broker turned to Nina. "Where'n the hell did you put the Colt?"

She batted her eyes. Sporta got back in and they drove through shadowy screens of young alders that grew dense as bamboo. Sporta said, "This is second growth. It opens up ahead. Fields we put in the land bank." They bounced down the rutted road and the tires began to churn through mud wallows. The thick jackpine, poplar, and alders ended abruptly and the gravel road bed disappeared into a glue of trampled cattails. A leafy grove of old oak trees stood cross the swamp. Access to the other side was over a causeway of crushed rock and railroad ties. Now the roadbed was scattered and submerged. A rut of suction holes marked where someone had tramped back and forth.

Tony slumped behind the wheel. "He's got money saved. He could'a gone to the Mayo." They got out of the truck and Sporta pointed. A child's blue plastic sled, with a length of yellow plastic clothesline attached, lay in the brush at the edge of the swamp. "Put the cooler in there and drag it." Broker wondered if that's how Sporta had ferried Jimmy Tuna across.

"The road picks up again after fifty yards, goes through a little oak woods and then there's a field that leads up to the cabin. When you come out of that woods he might be watching you through a rifle scope so don't move sudden." Sporta grumbled, "If he's awake. Sometimes he messes his pants. It ain't pretty up there."

Broker and Nina waited beside the cooler while Sporta took a gun case from the back of his truck, pulled out a 12-gauge pump, and loaded it. "I'll be down a little ways back from the gate. I'll come back in two hours and meet you here." He climbed into his truck, leaned the shotgun out the passenger side window, and studied them. "I hope this is worth it. For him and for you." Shaking his head, Tony Sporta backed down the road. They waited until the sound of his engine had receded in the distance.

"Turn around," Nina said crisply, unsnapping her jeans' button and starting the zipper.

Broker faced away with a smile, listened to a rustle of denim. A huge, snow white sanitary napkin bounced off his leg and tumbled into the water. "Christ, that looks like a diaper," he quipped.

"Very funny," said Nina. "You can turn around now."

He did. With a broad grin he stared at the large pistol in her hand. "I gotta ask? Did it involve penetration?"

"No. It's all angles and knowing how to take advantage of the terrain. Forget it. The Freudian implications will just screw up your mind." Nina possessively jammed the Colt into her waist band and pulled down her shirt. They placed the cooler in the sled and waded into the swamp.

Knee-deep in the gluey sediment and halfway across, they heard a sharp slapping report. They both ducked. Jumpy. And then Broker pointed to a channel of moving water and a broad pool ahead of them. A whiskery, beady-eyed knob cruised like a U-boat. "Beaver alerting," he said.

They continued to slog. He blinked away sweat, more dripped from his fingers. The beaver had plugged him into the humid bog, sensitive to every soft buzz and chirr, to the ticking eyes of insects. He studied the shadow fan of spring ferns along the far bank, the tremble of pitcher plants that strained like flat green elephant ears from a punky log, the dry rattle of reeds. A slick orange blight of mushrooms pushed through the limp bark of a white birch and he thought: cancer.

Broker lifted one foot from the warm, soaking tickle of the mud and heard the suction pop and echo through the reeds. A brood of black ducks squirted from some bulrushes and the mama duck's doting quacks sounded suddenly foreboding. He scanned the grove of red oaks beyond the swamp grass where the road emerged from the water. The beaver was closer to the far shore than to them.

"I think you'd better give me the pistol," he said to Nina.

"No fucking way," she said.

Broker clicked his teeth and wondered if someone could have gotten in ahead of them. And if so, how? They climbed back on dry land and left the sunlight. He lifted the cooler from the plastic sled and carried it in front of his chest and winced at the slosh of ice cubes on glass at his every step. Nina fell in close behind him. Halfway through the oak trees he heard the musty crunch of a boot come down on dry acorn shells.

The laconic southern voice called out, "Hi there."

47

TWO OF THEM. THEY STEPPED FROM THE COVER OF THE trees about sixty yards ahead, camouflaged in the shadows at the edge of the grove. Through the foliage, Broker could see an open field dance in the breeze, purple with wild alfalfa and red clover and a spray of wildflowers. The corner and the shingled roof of a cedar plank cabin at the top of the hill was just visible.

The one who had called to them resembled Danny Larkins's description from Ann Arbor: lean, weathered, sunglasses. He stood casually in a faded blue workshirt and jeans, with his hands on his hips, next to the trunk of a thick oak tree. A pack frame leaned against the tree. A pair of binoculars dangled from a low branch.

The other one did not fit Larkins's description as ordinary. He was skinny as the rickets and wore a gray T-shirt and a tractor cap. He covered them offhand with a Mini-14 from which curved a thirty-round magazine.

It was turning into a regular plague of rednecks.

"Stay behind me," said Broker to Nina, who had embraced his back in feigned terror.

"I need five more yards," she whispered and nudged him. Awkwardly, he held the cooler in his raised hands and stumbled forward. *Please, God, don't let her try something stupid with the handgun.* In this bad light. At extreme range. In a semi-automatic rifle's sights. Sweat electrified his eyes and the alfalfa and sweet clover beckoned, ravishing, normal, in the sun. Their hot perfume struck him dizzy. He heard the crickets, bees. They were so damn close.

"Put the cooler down to the side and stay in front of me," she whispered in a husky high-diver's voice.

Very slowly Broker set down the plastic box. Then he took another uncertain step forward and raised his hands.

"That's good. Relax. We ain't going to hurt you," called out Sunglasses. "If you're carrying anything under those shirts, now'd be the time to drop it. Real slow."

Broker shook his head. Raised his hands higher. Hoping that his hands going up would distract the rifleman from the way his knees trembled in a tense crouch.

"It's like this," called Sunglasses. "We know he's up there and we been waiting for you to show. We got a feeling he won't talk to us."

"How'd you find us?" Broker called back. He looked around, shook his head.

"We hired one of those electronic nerd guys. We tapped your telephone, you dumb shit. Then we went to the cheese factory and followed the fat man in last night. We camped out with the fuckin' bugs so we ain't real cordial. Now, listen up. What I got in mind is the girl stays with us and you go up and talk. You know what the general wants."

"How's Bevode doing?" yelled Broker. Talking to buy some time. Sporta said that Tuna had a rifle. These guys didn't seem to know. If he could get up there . . .

"Cousin Bevode's looking forward to seeing you, that's for sure. He wanted to be here but he had to go to the dentist."

"You! Don't move there," yelled the one with the rifle.

"*Nina,*" whispered Broker, sensitive to the faint rustle behind him.

"Get clear," said Nina in a cold, determined voice.

"Honey," yelled Tractor Hat in an amused drawl as he brought his rifle up, "put that popgun down. You can't hit shit at this distance and I can pick your titties off."

"Move fast," shouted Nina and he knew she was going to do it and all he could do was follow the play. Broker dived. From the corner of his eye he caught a flash of her coming to a point, hair spilling forward, tongue stuck in the right corner of her mouth, as she took a basic bull's-eye shooter's stance: body turned forty-five degrees away from her target, right hand sweeping the big Colt up. Extending. Steadying. . . . Before he hit the dirt he cringed when he heard the two shots: a close-by whap from the Colt and the crack and simultaneous, air-tunneling shock wave of a rifle bullet . . .

Passing above them, snapping branches through the overhead.

Sunglasses yelped in a thoroughly amazed voice, "Holy Shit!"

Broker rolled. Processed. Tractor Hat was down. Sunglasses was backpedaling, reaching under his shirt. Broker was on his feet in a sprint. Nina swung the pistol to the second man, who was bringing out a long-barreled heavy revolver, but still moving backward, chastised now, seeking cover on the sunny side of the big oak tree, with his back to the field.

Broker covered ground. Charging a .44 magnum as the Colt cracked bark off the oak tree. Good. Keep his head down. But Sunglasses had that big revolver leveled and was flattened in good cover and was drawing a bead on Nina, who stood in the open.

"*Run*," screamed Broker. Ten yards out and closing. Sunglasses had to make a decision. His mournful leather-strap features shook into a wrinkled toothy grin. Keeping the tree between himself and Nina, he swung his arm, taking his time, as Broker hurtled in his sights.

Broker closed his eyes when he heard the shot. Diving in blackness, maybe toward the constellation Orion, he tackled the man. When he opened his eyes, aside from a sharp pain in his bruised right shoulder where he and the gunman had smashed into a sharp gnarl of oak root, he determined he was unhit.

Sunglasses had lost his sunglasses and now his sad brown eyes opened wide, leaving shock, going for the mystery dropoff. He twitched once on the fragrant mattress of alfalfa. A tiny storm of striped bees rose from the clover as if exiting the body and a dark stain drenched the left armpit of his blue denim Oshkosh shirt.

"Nina," Broker yelled. Shaken. Hyperventilating. She stood calmly with the pistol dangling from her hand. "You hit?"

She shook her head and walked slowly toward the unmoving, face-down shape of the man with the rifle. The Colt slug had knocked him back and over a full turn.

Broker ran toward her, grabbed her, and checked her for wounds. She put her hand on his shoulder, briefly touched the back of his neck and then wormed from his embrace and hooked her muddy tennis shoe under the body and rolled it over. The man who inhabited the now-still flesh had worn a gray T-shirt with a Rebel battleflag across the chest. A ragged blood-ringed hole was punched two inches to the left of the crossed Stars and Bars.

Broker started to say lucky shot, but then he remembered how he'd scoffed at her trophy in Ann Arbor. He kept his mouth shut, stooped, and picked up the rifle.

They walked without speaking from the swaying shadows of the trees to the other body in the sunny field. Out of habit Broker knelt and checked for the carotid pulse. Nothing. He retrieved the Magnum and stuffed it in his belt.

They started to shiver in the bright sun, up to their knees in a gorgeous quilt of orange and Canada hawk weed, the red clover, ox-eyed daisies. Amid the wind-ruffled flowers, they swatted with exaggerated reflexes at flies that blundered into their bare arms. One fly, gross as a gumdrop, wallowed, buzzing, in a pool of blood trapped in the left corner of Sunglasses's mouth. Their eyes met over the corpse and acknowledged that it just got big-time real.

With an exaggerated roughness to glove her bare hands, Nina rolled over the corpse and squatted gingerly, avoiding the mess in the grass. She felt for his wallet, found it, opened it, and said, "We just killed a Fret."

Broker read the name on the Louisiana driver's license: William Bedford Fret. It was a day of cousins. He dropped the wallet and looked up the hill. A deck extended off the side of the cabin on stilts and someone was moving up there.

"You think there's more of them?" Nina asked as she pulled a cell phone from the back pocket of Sunglasses's jeans. Her voice was too calm, strait-jacketed.

"I don't know!" His fingers clenched on the rifle and his shout sounded like nerve bundles tearing.

His raw tone tripped Nina into a shudder of delayed shock. He watched her blunt the tremor of mortal fear with a spasm as old as warfare. She dropped the cell phone and kicked the body viciously. A reflex he'd seen many times in combat. "Piece of shit," she muttered and stepped back and hugged herself, prickly with the frostbite of sudden death at high noon. "How'd you get him?" she asked quietly. "You were behind the tree."

Broker glanced up the slope. "I didn't."

About a hundred and eighty yards up through the wildflowers and alfalfa, glass twinkled. He walked a few steps, unhooked the binoculars from the oak branch, and focused up the hill.

On the deck of the cabin, the vague shape materialized into a stick figure slumped in a chair. It was pitched forward, emaciated elbows planted on the railing with forearms twisted in bondage to a sniper-sling on a scoped rifle. Broker sharpened the focus on the man's hollow face.

Jimmy Tuna was smiling.

48

"MANNLICHER-CARCANO," RASPED JIMMY TUNA BY WAY OF greeting, thrusting the old-bolt action rifle in his wasted arms as they trudged up the steps to the porch. "Found it inside. Tony's bosses must keep it here as a kind of joke. Same rifle Oswald got Kennedy with." He flipped up the bolt and yanked it back and sent a twinkling yellow cartridge casing somersaulting into the sunlight. As the brass skittered on the cedar planks, he shot the bolt forward and carefully leaned the weapon against the deck railing. "Who says the Italians don't make good stuff?" He grinned and sagged back into his chair, exhausted.

Jimmy Tuna, fifty-eight going on Lazarus, was a husk—his two hundred pounds of twenty years ago had wilted to a hundred twenty. His large nose had once trumpeted abundant appetites. Now it protruded, a bone beak stuck in carrion. The concentration required to shoot Sunglasses looked like it had gobbled up a big hunk of his remaining life.

A faded army-issue baseball cap shaded his eyes and his roadmap-veined arms poked like sticks from a sagging black T-shirt that bore the exuberant motto: "GO FOR THE GUSTO!"

"Gusto" was crusted with dried vomit. Baggy khaki trousers, also fouled, enveloped his legs. Like a tree boil, his left hip made a grotesque angle, pushed out against the pants. The toenails on his bare feet had a mucus-colored curl of accelerated growth and, piled there, in the old redwood lawn chair in the sun, his face was a chiaroscuro going to black and he smelled like the first hour of death.

He pitched back in the chair and removed his cap and his head

was more skull than face: a cadaverous jack-o-lantern with eyes that
burned like brown coals. Nothing was left inside the loose sack of his
skin but the galloping disease.

And a secret.

Broker placed the cooler on the deck and yanked the .44 Mag
from his belt and placed it on the railing along with the cell phone.
Nina leaned the Mini-14 alongside. They just stared at him, panting,
catching their breath, and recovering from the last ten minutes. Face
to face. Finally.

Tuna grinned. "Sorry I didn't put out party favors for old home
week." He extended a clawlike right hand. "How you doing, Phil?"

Broker took the hand. Tuna tried to generate some of his old
strength and his old grin. He was drenched in sweat and his grip felt
like slimy cold pasta. "Think there's any more of them?"

Broker shook his head, "Just the two, I think." He pointed to the
portable telephone. "One of them had that."

Tuna shook his head. "Won't work out here. I've been watching
them all morning, but they stayed in the trees. I couldn't get a shot.
I even thought they might be with you."

"They're LaPorte's boys. They were overconfident. They told us."

"How'd you get the other one?"

"Nina got him. She snuck a .45 past Sporta."

Tuna nodded. "Tony'll have to dump them in the swamp. He
won't like that, but he's done it before. Guys he works for use this
place for more than deer hunting." He brightened. "You get ahold of
Trin?"

Broker nodded. Tuna leaned back and glided behind his eyes. His
vision focused and he asked, "You figure it out yet?"

Broker chewed his lip. "Cyrus found some gold next to the chopper wreck. Your note said—"

Tuna cackled and held up a shaky hand. "Be patient. Let me tell
it my way." He coughed and looked around. "Well, shit. You turned
into a fuckin' cop. Which don't surprise me, you always had that
Boy Scout look in your eyes. And you found me but this ain't 'NYPD
Blue' you're messin' in, kid. Uh-uh." He coughed again and glanced
down into the oak grove.

Broker looked around and said, "Will the shots bring cops?"

"Hell no, way out here? And I been plunking away from this
deck for a week with this old piece to kill time." Tuna's sunken eyes
fixed in space. "Now that's an odd phrase, don't you think? Kill
time."

He held up a withered hand and turned his attention to Nina. "Forgetting my manners. Hello there, Miss Pryce."

"Hello, Jimmy," said Nina evenly. "So this is where you got to with your 'funeral' money."

With difficulty he put his hand in his trouser pocket and withdrew a folded bank check. He handed it to her. "Didn't need your money, but I had to bait the hook. Sorry about the puzzle palace you had to go through to find me. Cyrus has been on me for years. Guards. Other inmates coming at me. Thank God for conservative Republican bankers. Cyrus couldn't get into those records."

"How the hell did you find Trin?" asked Broker.

"That was hard. But I had a lot of time. You talked to the bank in Ann Arbor, right?"

"I did," said Nina. "And Kevin Eichleay."

Tuna nodded. "Kevin told the banker, said Trin looked like hell. The Commies must have worked him over good. Reeducated him. But he's there. And he's Trin. Was going to be my ace in the hole." Tuna gritted his teeth at a stab of real or psychological pain. "Yours now."

"What does he know?"

"He knows I'm his padrone. I'm a fuckin' one-man charity. Set up his vet's home for wayward Viet Cong. Helped him get started in the tour business. I was coming as a tourist. Now you and Nina are going in my place. I paid him to set up a tour. Hanoi to Hue. Reserved rooms both places for two weeks. Didn't know when you'd show up. What'd he say to you?"

"He thinks you're still in the joint."

"I used Tony's phone. Called him up a week ago. Told him I was detained. That I was sending you instead."

"He wanted to know when our plane arrived, pretty straightforward stuff."

"The revolution musta gone to hell, huh? They're all nuts to make a buck off tourists over there now. Trin too, I guess." He fell back heavily into the chair, spent.

"All these years. You were planning to go back for it . . ." said Broker.

"Yeah. I was dumb back in seventy-six. Thought I could bankroll the trip with that bank job. Not dumb anymore . . . aw, shit." He feebly waved his hand. "Take a break." He pointed to the Coleman cooler and his hollow eyes took on a keen luster of anticipation. "What's for lunch?"

Nina took out eight cold bottles of San Miguel beer and some ham and cheese sandwiches. There was a Tupperware container in the bottom. It contained a neatly folded white cloth napkin. Tuna held out his hand, fingers fluttering in a gimme gesture. She handed over the cloth, which he unfolded with great ceremony. A plastic packet full of white powder lay in the center.

He flipped up a corner of a towel that covered a low redwood table next to his chair and revealed a syringe, a spoon, and a length of rubber tubing. Methodically he tied off his frail arm and pumped his fist. Then he pushed some of the powder into the spoon with his little finger. He thumbed a plastic lighter and cooked up. When the chemical bubbled and cooled to liquid, he inserted the syringe and drew down a shot. Then he pumped his hand again.

"Never used smack, not even in the joint. I even joined AA once. Now it's the only medicine that works," he said cheerfully, and his hand floated out and touched the plump vein on the hollow of Broker's right elbow. "Man, what I wouldn't give for that storm sewer you got in your arm."

In the short noon shadows they watched Tuna fix. Watched him tremble and nod back in his chair until spittle dribbled from his caked lips and his eyes turned up into his head like a shark before it bites. His voice surged. "So," he said, grinning directly into the sun. "What took you guys so long?" Then he vomited at a leisurely pace, fouling the emaciated wattles at his throat and his shirt with a mealy steam of dog food that reeked of stomach acid. His bowels released and his upper lip curled up to reveal bloody gums and long, yellowed teeth. Sightless eyes wide open, Jimmy Tuna glared at them like a raging Jolly Roger.

49

"NOW WHAT? HE'S OUT COLD. WHAT IF HE DIES ON US?" NINA muttered. Had to be ninety in the shade. Her arms still bubbled with goosebumps. One hand hugged the small grinning skull and crossbones on her shoulder.

"He'll come around. We're what's keeping him alive," said Broker. Suddenly he was very thirsty. He saw the powerline running into the cabin. "Let me get this beer out of the sun." He went into the cool interior. The kitchen was right inside the door. He tried a light switch, saw that the electric worked and spied the icebox. He put the beer inside, found an opener in a drawer next to the sink, and opened two bottles. San Miguel. Tuna's old favorite.

Nina entered the kitchen, paused for a moment, got her bearings and disappeared into a back room. She returned with towels and clean folded clothing. Then she filled a basin with water and went back out to the deck.

Broker followed her outside and stood in a patch of shade and sipped his beer. Nina bent over Tuna and methodically removed his fouled trousers, bundled them, and tossed them aside.

Broker averted his eyes from Tuna's emaciation and the tumor that torqued out of his left hip. The Tuna he remembered from twenty years ago had been muscled like a Greco-Roman wrestler. "Do you have to do that right now?"

"Not the first time I've seen a man mess his pants," she muttered and cast a dirtied towel aside and rinsed a fresh one. She tossed the dirty water over the patio, slapped the messy trousers in the empty basin, and handed it to Broker. "Lend a hand, this old jailbird just saved our lives." Broker set down his beer and went for more water.

Tuna lolled in their hands as they washed his white loose flesh and then pulled on new underwear, a pair of baggy cotton trousers, and a clean T-shirt. Washing their hands in the kitchen they heard someone moving on the stairs . . .

Tony Sporta stuck his curly head into the kitchen. Sweat dripped from his nose. "He shit his pants again," he said. "And there's two dead guys in the woods." He frowned like he wasn't sure which of his observations vexed him most.

"Jimmy says you should put the dead guys in the swamp," said Broker.

"Are you sure you're a cop?"

"Way down in the swamp," said Broker.

Sporta threw his hands in the air. He paused long enough to stick the .44 revolver in his pocket and then marched down the stairs, cursing. His voice carried all the way down the field to the trees.

Nina came out of the cabin and stood next to him. "What will Cyrus do now?"

"Keep after us until he knows where it is . . ." Some wooden wind chimes rattled in the breeze. Tuna's paper lungs made a shallow rustle. Cicadas buzzed in the brush. "Should have told you before. We may have an ally inside LaPorte's bunch. We're supposed to think so, anyway," he said.

"Who?"

"Someone who hates LaPorte."

"Broker!"

Broker grinned. "His wife."

Nina laughed sarcastically. "Wonderful. It's Terry and the Pirates. And now we got Lola the freaking Dragon Lady." She rolled her eyes. "All I need. Some glamorous facelift bitch who has a boat named after her." She squinted. "You slept with her, didn't you—"

"No I didn't," said Broker frankly. "She says we have . . . mutual interests."

"I'll bet."

"We needed an in with them. Well, I'm in," Broker patiently explained. "LaPorte has a roving eye for younger women for breeding purposes." He wiped a handful of sweat from his brow. "Lola thinks she may get to Vietnam and get pushed off that boat that's named after her and accidentally drown. So turnabout is fair play."

Nina reached up and clipped his chin. "I knew I shouldn't have let you go to New Orleans alone. You don't know anything about women. I tried to tell you in Ann Arbor. They," she paused, "we, are your weak spot."

Broker cleared his throat. It was different, explaining this to the woman you slept with the previous night and who turned out to be, in addition to Audie fucking Murphy, Annie fucking Oakley. "She wants someone to, ah, sort of disappear her husband in the course of events. She gets to wear black for a while and haul in the family estate."

"Someone, Broker? When did you develop this subtle speech impediment?"

"Okay. Me."

Nina frowned. "I thought we agreed. I don't want LaPorte *murdered*. I want him *tried*."

Broker stood up, irritated. "Nina, goddammit! There's no way in hell that can happen."

"Sonofabitch, I *hate* this soap opera shit! She bought you off. That's how you got that gold."

"She helped me take it, that's true—"

"*Fuck* you. You got what you want and now you're getting cold feet." She scowled. "I got in bed with you . . ."

And saved my life. Broker tried to placate her. "We can still nail him. Not exactly the way you want, but maybe we can get him busted by the Vietnamese as a thief. You'll have to settle for that."

Jimmy Tuna stirred and opened one cadaverous eye. Then he smiled so slowly that his teeth appeared one by one like corroded yellow bullets in the wrinkled maw of his lips. He croaked emphatically, "Wrong."

50

"THIRSTY," SAID TUNA. HE FANNED HIS MOUTH. PARCHED. Nina darted into the cabin and returned with two open bottles of iced beer. He nodded and asked very politely, "Tony brought me some cherries last night, in a bowl in the icebox?" Nina turned promptly and returned with the large bowl of cherries. She placed them on the table next to Tuna's chair and handed him one of the chilled bottles. She tucked the extra between his legs in the baggy folds of his trousers.

Tuna drank one beer in a long dreamy gurgle. He set the empty aside and picked up the fresh bottle. He held the ice-sweating glass to the inside of his papery left forearm and sighed. Then his other hand fumbled on the table for a pack of Pall Malls. In slow motion he lit one and inhaled. Exhaled and coughed violently

"Shit's probably in my lungs," he said as heroin merriness flooded his sunken cheeks and twinkled in his cratered eyes. Seeing the corpselike figure animate with the strange current of energy and thinking about the rednecks laying stiff in the shade of an oak tree had the perverse effect of making Broker hungry. He chewed one of the ham and cheese sandwiches and washed it down with San Miguel.

Tuna began to eat the cherries, ferrying them one by one in his taloned hand, savoring them with a gluttonous sucking of lips and tongue. He spit the pits onto the deck where they collected like tiny red bodies. Ants formed industrious columns, going after the shreds of pulp.

Nina smiled tightly. "I wish there was some way we could record this."

The stoned laughter that gushed from Tuna's cherry-stained lips sounded like a flock of insane birds. There was some of the muscular oily humor of the old Tuna in that laugh. "How many words you think I got left? A thousand? Five hundred? I'll do my talking to people, not a goddamned machine."

"Okay," said Nina, crossing her arms and waiting patiently.

Tuna cackled and his eyes and voice went into a glide. "Paget's disease," he whispered. "Four Purple Hearts and I walked away from each of them. Fucking Indians have casinos. Nigger kids got high-top tennis shoes, nine millimeters, and crack franchises. I got a fortune in gold and I get cancer. In prison . . ."

He smiled luridly. "The medical book says, get this," he quoted: "'The dread complication of Paget's disease is osteosarcoma, which *fortunately* occurs in fewer than one percent of the patients.'" He sucked on his Pall Mall. "That's quite a word—*dread*."

He bit his cracked lips. "It's in my rectum now. And my bladder. And my kidneys. When it gets to my lungs . . . hat roi."

Hat roi was the Vietnamese phrase for "all gone."

"Like taking a crap through a turnstile." Tuna tried to laugh and began coughing again.

His eyes moistened. "We had some great days, Phil. Quang Tri City. That was like a chapter out of the fucking Bible. Nobody even knew. Remember?"

"Yeah, Jimmy."

Tuna took a deep breath. "Okay. I'll give it to you straight. We left you and Trin . . ." He spun out the Vietnamese name and the sound twisted on the hot afternoon like a cool shadow. "Hell, we did more than that. We gave them Trin. We knew Pryce was crazy enough to go try to get him out."

"Pryce didn't know?" demanded Broker.

"Mama Pryce. You kidding? Him and Trin didn't know shit." Tuna chortled. "Trin's gonna freak . . ."

Broker couldn't imagine anything more distant from an angel than this talking corpse. But he'd just sprung Broker from Purgatory and put an avenging sword in his hand. Broker took a clean breath of fire.

Now Tuna looked Nina straight in the eye. "I killed your father. The plan was Cyrus's. But I pulled the trigger. He was dead before we got to Hue."

Nina stared at him, stone cold. Her voice buckled down tight. "And the pilots went along with this?"

"They were Air America, Cyrus's cronies from Laos. Hell, by then they'd flown more dope than the Medellin cartel."

"Go on," said Nina. Tip of the iceberg.

"After we hit the bank I changed the plan a little," said Tuna. He hefted the empty beer bottle and smiled helplessly. Nina averted her face. Broker went into the house and returned with two more bottles. When Tuna had taken a drink, Broker asked his main question: "Why'd you do it, Jimmy?"

Tuna squinted. "Cyrus don't like losing. Guess I don't either. It was plunder. We were soldiers. We wanted it, so we took it, goddammit."

Broker shook his head slowly. So under the pomp and medals, LaPorte was just another asshole. A desire to crank the bracelets down on a retired general took precedence over dreams of gold. Automatically, he started asking questions like a cop.

"So how did you do it physically? Move all that gold out of the bank without drawing attention? There wasn't time that night."

Tuna cackled. "Haven't you figured it out? Wasn't *in* the fuckin' bank. It was crated up on a pallet in ammo boxes in back of the bank. The Commies *didn't even know it was there*. That's why they didn't raise hell about it. That was the beauty of the thing. Nobody knew it existed."

"Ammo boxes?" Broker was stymied.

"Look," said Tuna. "We had it disguised as a pallet of *artillery rounds*. We'd managed to get it as far as the courtyard of the bank. Then the Commies took Hue in March, remember? It just sat there for a month. All the gear the ARVNs left laying around when they split—who'd notice another pallet of ammo?"

"Where'd it come from?"

"Ask Cyrus, he got onto it. We didn't steal it. We *found* it. Spent two years looking for that stuff. He was like a crazy man. That's how it all started."

Broker shook his head. "Ten tons of gold just *sat* there for over a month?"

"It ain't *just* gold . . ."

"What do you mean?"

"You'll see," said Tuna. A spark of dark humor ignited in his tortured eyes.

"What about my dad, Jimmy?" Nina said in a level voice.

Tuna looked at her frankly. "You know about the original mission? How we were going in to bust Trin out of jail?"

Nina nodded.

"After Phil went in by boat, Cyrus personally changed the plan."

"But he was down the coast off Danang," said Broker slowly.

"He was, huh. Did you see him there?"

"I heard him on the radio . . ."

"He was on the radio, all right. In a light observation chopper about a mile from our boat. Cyrus could fly helicopters, you recall. He was gone from the fleet off Danang for a little over an hour, long enough to land and talk to Pryce. Then he popped back. Our guys off Danang thought he was out trying to spot refugees in the water." Tuna cocked his head. "You remember anything about that minesweep? Like how the only Americans on it were you, me, Pryce, and the helicopter pilots? Like, no other witnesses."

Quietly Nina said, "How'd it happen?"

"Simple. Cyrus gave Ray new orders. Made it sound like it came down from on high. First go in and sling out the pallet and bring it back to the boat, *then* pick up Phil and Trin."

"New orders," said Nina.

"Yeah, except we never meant to go back." He paused, trying to wet his parched lips, staring at Nina. "Out of spit," he said.

"What about the radio call that was in the inquest record? Someone made a net call saying my dad had changed the orders and requesting clarification," said Nina.

"He was already dead. I made the call to shift the blame on him. It was planned that way. When we got to the bank, in the confusion, he got dumped out the door."

"At the bank?" asked Broker, leaning forward.

"Yeah. We had two guys on the ground with a big forklift. They maneuvered the pallet in the net, scrambled up, and we boogied. Except the bird was shot up and the pilots were sweating it. Didn't think they could fly with the weight. I made a mayday call, said we were hit and we had to set down." Tuna smiled triumphantly. "Then it came to me. All those years I always did what Cyrus wanted. Suddenly I was in a position to do what *I* wanted. We were so damn close anyway and I had the place all picked out. Just like that."

"The place?" asked Broker.

"Perfect place," said Tuna, grinning. "You'll see."

Broker studied the relish on Tuna's face. Going out on one last joke.

"Wasn't hard to convince the pilots to dump the stuff. So I showed them where. There was this ravine. We dropped the sling into it, cast it off, and then we landed. We set some charges and blew this slope down over the gully."

Nina was bursting with her question. Broker stayed her with his hand. Tuna spoke rapidly now. "It was getting light. Without the load we could fly, they thought . . ."

Tuna sucked at the bottle and slowly lit another Pall Mall. He blew a stream of smoke and inspected his curled fingernails. "We didn't fly far. I saw to that."

"You sabotaged the chopper?" asked Nina.

"Part of the plan. We were going to drop the pallet on the boat and then deep-six the chopper and the pilots and Ray's body in the sea. So I put a whole magazine in the controls. Auto rotation time," said Tuna, his voice softened, musing. "Funny thing about gold, Phil. It's just a word until you actually see it, touch it. There's nothing like it, even in the dark of the moon, in the rain . . ."

Nina took a sharp breath and held it.

"Let him finish," said Broker.

"They were like kids, those other guys. They couldn't help grabbing at some ingots and stuffing them into their flak jackets before we covered it." Tuna cackled. "I'd tossed out the life jackets, except for one. Gold has a lot of magical properties but flotation isn't one of them. Saved me the trouble of shooting from a tippy raft."

Broker shook his head. "That's why LaPorte found ingots with the chopper wreck."

Tuna grinned. "When we went in the water I stuffed *this* in my jacket." He reached under the towel on the crate and threw a folded, worn piece of laminated paper at Broker. A tactical map of Quang Tri Province. Grid squares. One-to-fifty-thousand scale. "So simple. A piece of paper. An X that marks the spot," he said.

"Jimmy," said Broker patiently. "There's no X on this map."

"Not yet. Saved the best for last." He took another sip of beer. "Everyone was gone. Drowned by their gold. I sat on that raft all day memorizing that grid coordinate. I was the only person in the world who knew where it was. So I just played along with Cyrus's cover story. Said it all went into the drink. Last person I wanted on my case was fuckin' Cyrus."

"Dammit, Tuna." The fire and ice in Nina's eyes was starting to melt. "That creep Walls gave us this note that said my dad—"

"Walls is something, isn't he? I befriended him just by reading to him. No one bothered me in there after Walls and me were buddies."

"Yeah, buddies are nice," said Broker softly.

Tuna's chest heaved and he looked away. "We saved your young ass in Quang Tri City. Maybe you belonged to us after that. Maybe you were ours to spend." His eyelids drooped and Broker thought he might be getting ready to go. He gripped the map in both hands.

"Jimmy, for Christ sake," said Nina.

Tuna's eyes rolled dreamily. "I had plans, man. You know, I educated myself in prison. I figured I had time. Be more mature. No more nutty stuff like that bank mess in New York. Be easier now, going back, because we were normalizing relations . . . Set up the whole operation with Trin."

"How much does Trin know about this?" Broker shook Tuna by the collar. "It's important."

Tuna grinned. "Remember how Trin used to know everything. Not this time, baby." His eyes turned dreamy again. "I was going to go back to this village in Italy where my family were dirt poor peasants and live like a prince . . ."

Heroin tears dripped down Tuna's sunken cheeks. For the first time he seemed to become aware of his physical condition. With a look of horror he touched his hands, his bony knees jutting through the trousers. Something snapped in his eyes. A malevolent grin twisted his festered lips. "Now to get the rest you gotta forgive me," he croaked. "Both of you. For my act of contrition."

"Man, I've done some hard shit in my life . . ." Nina breathed out, breathed in and said, "Fuck you, Jimmy. And damn you to Hell."

Tuna fell back in his chair and laughed. "Didn't hurt to try," he said. "Aw, shit. I don't care who gets it now, long as Cyrus doesn't. You guys take it. Give it to the gooks. Theirs anyway . . ." His voice tailed off and a whitewater of foul-smelling perspiration poured from the cancer rapids. They were losing him. Helplessly, they listened to his shallow breathing. The only living thing left in his body were his eyes, two bright Christmas ornaments sinking in decayed flesh.

"Ray," said Tuna very distinctly in a chilling voice, as if he were greeting a fourth person on the porch. "Gold," he muttered and then he slurred a word that sounded like "disgrace."

They stooped forward. Nina held a bottle up and dribbled beer on his caked lips. He coughed and pronounced with deliberation, "Cigarette case." His hand fumbled toward his bloody works that lay on the towel, then suddenly dropped still. The bowl of cherries spilled over and cracked apart on the deck and the fruit bounced in a frenzy around their feet.

51

BROKER NODDED. "RAY'S CIGARETTE CASE."

Nina's eyes narrowed. "Mom gave it to him for Christmas."

They leaned close, undeterred by Tuna's putrid breath. He arched as if electrocuted and fell back and groped feebly and muttered, "Big one . . ."

Nina's fingers flew over the towel on the crate. "Hold this." She slapped the cooking spoon in Broker's hand like a scalpel.

"That's too much," said Broker as she shook the heroin into the spoon and thumbed the plastic lighter. They watched the powder turn gummy in the heat, bubble.

"Sorry about the dirty needle, Jimmy," Nina said under her breath as she inserted the syringe and drew back the plunger. "Okay." She took a breath.

Broker fastened the rubber tie around Tuna's left arm. Last time he'd shot in the right. Then he held the arm straight down and with both hands tried to duplicate the motions of clenching Tuna's fist.

"Not much of a vein," said Nina, judging her target.

"Hit him," said Broker.

The needle punched into the flour-colored parchment of Tuna's arm. She pulled back the plunger and got a watery blossom of blood in the clear liquid. She shoved the shot home. Total concentration. Nothing but steady. She was field-grade material, all right. She could send men to their deaths. No problem.

Tuna's jaw unhinged and fell slack. His tongue got stuck in the dry rot of his cheeks. Nina reached for a napkin next to the food plates and wet it with San Miguel and swabbed his lips. "C'mon, Jimmy," she crooned. She could have been coaxing an infant.

This time Tuna didn't vomit. Broker imagined the cancer chasing down the jet of heroin like a sparkle of tracers in the dark cavern of Tuna's brain.

"Joke," gasped Tuna. "Joke's on Cyrus."

"We got him back," said Nina.

Tuna blinked and then smiled with immense calm. "Man, she's something, ain't she," he said and stared at the bloody needle in Nina's hand. "They teach you that at OCS?"

"What about Ray's gold cigarette case?" asked Broker.

"Evidence," said Tuna and nodded out. They shook him.

One eye rolled open. "That night . . . morning really . . . when Cyrus showed up, Ray wouldn't do it. You know Ray. By the book. Insisted on getting the orders in writing. Made Cyrus write it down, sign it. Op order to go for the gold . . . get it?"

Broker and Nina locked eyes.

Tuna giggled. "Saw him fold it in a piece of radio battery plastic, tuck it in his cigarette case, and button it into his chest pocket. All comes down to me fucking up. I was supposed to take it off him . . . forgot when the shooting started."

Nina made a face but did not look away.

"He rolled out. But he fell into the *cargo net*. Snake city, fire coming in. The guys on the ground had the gold on the forklift, tipped it into the net on top of Ray. Get it?"

"If he stole it why's he buried with it," recited Nina.

"You got it, he's on the beach under the gold, order's should be there with his . . . remains. Evidence," he pronounced, again. Then he surged up toward Nina. "You still got that copy of the UCMJ, the article I underlined?"

"Yes I do," said Nina.

"Figuring that out kept me going after I got the cancer. Now go out there and burn Cyrus at the fucking stake for everybody to see. That's my act of contrition. My gift to you . . ." said Tuna. He turned to Broker. "You keep her on track over there. Do this right and you and Trin can get moderately rich. But to nail Cyrus the gooks have to catch him digging it up. So promise me, they get most of it."

Broker nodded.

Tuna croaked again. "Map."

Broker held up the map. Tuna blinked. "There's this gook graveyard, on a hill over the dunes. And this little cove—here." He stabbed the map. "It's about four klics north of Trin's vet's home." Tuna cackled. "Jimmy Tuna's Memorial Home for Crippled Viet

Cong. I love it. See the cemetery symbols?" Broker saw them. "Three of those old graves, with the big round walls . . . hope they're still there."

Broker nodded. "Get me something to write with," he said urgently.

Tuna shook his head. "Don't mark the map." He grinned. "Trin's rules, remember. Memorize the location. Center grave. Fix on the grave to your right, shoot an azimuth, one hundred and sixty-three degrees. Walk eighty-two steps. I paced it off. And dig."

"You getting this?" said Broker, looking up.

"Got it," said Nina.

There was an interval of silence while Tuna rested. All things revolved unsaid. Just eyes.

"That's it. Now go," Tuna blurted. He reached up and pulled Broker close by the arm. For a second his old strength flowed with the heroin. "Wait. Tell Tony not to bury them. And gimme the Colt. When the time comes I'll have Tony leave me down there with the rifle and the pistol. Send for the sheriff so none of this rubs off on you."

Nina nodded and handed Jimmy the .45. He squinted. "When push comes to shove, go with Trin, you understand?"

"I understand," said Broker.

"Now you better split," said Tuna. "Tony and me will fix it all here. Don't worry, they won't get to me. Be nice, though, if a few more of them would come through the woods into that field." He lurched in his chair, fumbled at the rifle leaning against the rail, picked it up, and locked his eye to the scope. He scanned the trees. "Coming. Hear 'em in the grass. Black maggot sonsabitches."

Broker stood up and tucked the map under his shirt. He hefted the Mini-14 and turned to Tuna. "Does this square it for killing Ray?"

"Fuck you, Broker." He grinned and brandished the rifle. "Get outta here and let me die in peace."

"That's it, let's go," Broker yelled to Nina.

They ran.

Halfway across the field she stopped and held him by the arm. "What did he mean? Trin's rules?"

"Trin's first rule: Trust no one," said Broker. "Now run."

They jogged down through the springy alfalfa and into the oak grove. Jimmy Tuna's raucous stoned laughter and the crack of the Carcano echoed through the trees, over the roar of the cicadas. Crazy. Shooting at sunspots.

A beleaguered Tony Sporta, breathing heavily, his overalls smeared with mud, waved to them from across the swamp. They plowed into the deep drag trail that now furrowed the sunken causeway, sinking past their knees. The two bodies lay in the muck just ahead.

"C'mon, c'mon. Leave 'em be," yelled Sporta, waving them on. "I gotta go get some logging chains for weight."

"There's been a change," yelled Broker. "No logging chains." Sporta held his cupped hands to his ears and then stomped in a circle, swearing.

As they dragged their feet through the mire and struggled, half stepping, half slithering, over the corpses, Nina panted, "Remind you of anything?"

Broker frowned and she started chanting something under her breath, upbeat and vaguely familiar.

"Country Joe and the Fish," said Broker. He scanned the trees. The Mini-14 floated in one hand, the other touched the tiger tooth under his shirt for luck. The mud sucked at his feet.

Next stop, Vietnam.

52

THEY HAD A MAP. THE MAP WOULD DRAW CYRUS LIKE HONEY. Broker popped the clutch. Rubber scorched. Tony Sporta had thrown them the Beretta and Nina's purse and shooed them from his office. Now he ducked a volley of gravel and, still swearing mightily, waved them on with a final gesture of good riddance.

They were wearing slimy hip waders of mud. Broker's tennis shoe slipped off the accelerator.

Nina yelled over the grinding engine, "We *have* to run this by the U.S. Mission in Hanoi. Catch him red-handed. Arrange to get him . . . extradited."

Broker rolled his eyes and yelled back, "The United States doesn't have an extradition treaty with the Vietnamese government, god-dammit. They haven't even *set up* an embassy yet. I want Cyrus, Nina; I want him bad. But it has to go down right or he'll weasel away. We have to check out Tuna's story first. Locate the stuff. See if the orders are with . . . the remains." He swiveled his head to see the road behind. "Is there anybody following us?"

"No. I've been watching," she went on without missing a beat. "There's an advance team in Hanoi. There's the U.S. liaison office. I have a number—"

"Slow down."

Nina grabbed the wheel as Broker overdrove the shoulder and swiped ten yards of weeds growing at the lip of a ditch. "You slow down." She glanced in the backseat where the Mini-14 lay, locked and loaded, in plain view. "Isn't it against the law to drive around with that rifle uncased?"

Broker ignored her and reached across her knees and clawed his cell phone from the glove compartment. The battery was dead. And no spare. They'd left the other one with Tuna. He slowed down to seventy-five when he saw an Amoco station up ahead at a cross-roads. He braked precipitously, leaving another smoking swatch of Goodyear products in Wisconsin.

"Jesus," muttered Nina, bracing.

"Phone," said Broker.

"What?"

"Tickets. Visas. Phone." He left the motor running and the door open as he ran for the pay phone. After he picked up the receiver he realized it was a toll call. He still had a wad of hundreds in his pocket from New Orleans. Two dimes and six pennies.

He ran back to the Jeep. "I need quarters." Nina dug in her purse, handed him two coins. He used one of the quarters to call an opera-tor and place a collect person-to-person call to Don Larson's office in Stillwater.

A woman answered and told the operator that Don Larson wasn't in the office, he had taken his daughter to the dentist. Broker ran back for the car, jumped behind the wheel, and suddenly just sat there.

"Now what?" asked Nina, who still bounced with forward momentum.

"What are we doing?" Broker proposed calmly.

"It looks to me like we were running for our lives," she said.

Broker shook his head. "If there were more of them they would have stormed the cabin. Short of that, they wouldn't have let Tony come up there after the shooting."

Nina thought about it.

Broker continued. "LaPorte can't afford to let anybody in on this. Bevode told me. It's a small, hand-picked group. The Fret family. Which is now diminished by two."

"Maybe they don't care about us. They know where Tuna is."

"Tuna's beyond intimidation. No." Broker shook his head. "If I was LaPorte I'd put my money where it buys more, like in Vietnam. He's probably paid so much in bribes over there that he's a majority stockholder in the Communist party."

"Very funny."

"I'm serious. He'll just hook into their diplomatic service and get our visa forms. Air Vietnam is a state-run company, so he'll probably connect with them too. When we get tickets, he'll have his hands on a manifest." Broker leaned back and slid his wallet from his pocket.

He dug around, handed Nina a card and then shut his eyes. "He knows where I'm going, anyway."

"The Century Hotel, Hue City. Who wrote this room information?" she asked.

"Lola LaPorte. Can you decipher psychological traits in handwriting?"

"No."

"Neither can I. I used to know this very serious FBI lady who could, but she transferred to San Francisco." Broker grinned. "She told me I was a fugitive from modern psychology."

Nina sunk deeper in her seat and extended her hand. "Give me one of those health food cigarettes."

Broker opened one eye.

She explained. "I only smoke when I drink too much, which is usually once a year on my birthday. And in special circumstances." She grimaced.

"Like when you shoot somebody." Broker handed over his cigarettes and said, "I'm thirsty, what about you?" Nina agreed so he tracked mud into the station and bought a cold six-pack of Mountain Dew. When he came out, Nina said, "Yuk, I never drink that stuff."

"We're nodding out. It's loaded with caffeine and it's cold."

They slouched down in the seats like two teenagers sneaking cigarettes and sipped from the green cans.

Broker suggested, "We finish our pop, try to clean up, drive leisurely to Hudson, Wisconsin, and check into a motel—just in case I'm wrong and LaPorte has someone watching my house. Don should be back by then. We find out about our travel plans, go shopping—"

Nina sat up. "You have the map."

Broker tapped his pocket. "I have the map."

"Then let's get going before we fall asleep."

Broker started the Jeep and pulled back on the road. He was silent for a few minutes and then, keeping his eyes straight ahead, he said, "That was some shooting . . ."

Her voice came back, a flat conditioned response, "Guys are always surprised. It's because we don't bring bad habits or macho posturing to the firing line. And we're good at taking instruction."

Broker said it again, "That was some shooting, *Pryce*."

"Thank you."

*   *   *

Broker parked in a secluded rest area and they changed out of their
sopping clothes. After cat-washing in the men's lavatory, he dug in
his travel bag and emerged barefoot in his loafers, wearing rumpled
cotton slacks and a fresh T-shirt. Nina waited by the Jeep in clean
jeans, the ruffled, faded green blouse she'd worn that morning in
the hospital, and sandals. They stripped the muddy seat covers and
Broker unloaded the rifle, folded down the backseat, and stuck the
weapon under it.

When they were back on the road, Nina leaned over and dabbed
at a smudge of swamp on Broker's cheek with her red bandanna.
"So you really think LaPorte will be waiting for us at the airport in
Hanoi?"

Broker nodded. "Close. I picked up a Vietnam tourist book in
New Orleans and read it on the way back. The Hanoi terminal is
tiny, on a military airstrip an hour's drive outside of the city. So it's
probably a pretty secure area. Lots of customs cops for sure. He'll
probably spot us there and follow us. That's why we need an expediter like Trin. We'll have to go to ground, fast. We can't do that on
our own. We don't even speak the language."

Nina stared out the window. Holstein dairy cows, large and stupid as black and white spotted balloons, bobbled in a pasture. "And
you're definitely against contacting any Americans."

"We tell nobody nothing until we get a feel for what it's like over
there—"

"Okay, then you better tell me everything you know about
Nguyen Van Trin."

Broker tried to visualize Trin as the green Wisconsin dairy land
zipped by. "He's a guy who always went his own way. He comes
from Mandarins. His family owned a cement factory near Hue City.
A rich kid. He spent four years at Georgetown getting a degree in
business and English lit. So he speaks better English than both of us
put together.

"He went home and freaked out his parents by becoming an
apprentice monk. In 1966 he was real involved in the Buddhist
Uprising in Hue. The Buddhists were crushed. Trin said what the
Buddhists needed was more guns. So he joined the Viet Cong.

"He switched sides after the Tet Offensive. That's when he got
involved with your dad. They had this notion they could split the
Viet Cong away from Hanoi. It was pretty esoteric stuff. He was a
pretty disillusioned guy by the time I met him."

Nina squinted. "Can we *trust* him?"

Broker smiled. "He told me something once. 'When you share an idea it grows another brain and a set of hands and a pair of feet to walk around on. It can get away from you.'"

"That's what Jimmy meant when he said 'Trin's rules,' huh? Sounds like another disillusioned young man took them to heart," said Nina, poking him in the arm.

Broker shrugged. "Trin said it was a dilemma. To work a good plan you can't trust anyone. But what can you accomplish all alone? He said he wouldn't be a robot or a puppet. That's what he called the Communists, robots. Just disciplined hands and feet, no brains. He saw the Saigon government as puppets of the West. So, he was screwed in the middle."

"Sounds like a real upbeat guy."

"Yeah, but Cyrus LaPorte, standing on Jimmy Tuna's shoulders, wouldn't come up to Trin, and he's about five four." Broker turned to her. "Your dad said Trin could run an army or a government."

"Dad trusted him?"

"You got it. That's all we've really got to go on. Their friendship. Twenty years ago. Nina, I didn't know these guys. Not even your dad. Not really. I was a young dumb stud. I risked my neck just to get a nod from them. LaPorte, Ray, Trin, even Tuna—they were— are, well, smarter than I am."

"I don't know about that," said Nina. "I *do* know that when it really mattered you ran right at a forty-four mag to draw fire away from me."

Broker clicked his teeth. "Not real smart."

Nina perused him. "Dad had rules too; he used to say: 'The map is not the terrain.' There are all these brilliant people and they think up these boffo schemes and when the plans all fall apart—because they always do—someone like you holds things together."

"So fuck a bunch of office guys," said Broker with a broad grin.

"Absolutely."

Broker stepped on the gas and whisked down a ramp onto Interstate 94 and exceeded the speed limit to Hudson, Wisconsin.

"Where the hell have you been?" said Don Larson on the phone.

"Shopping," said Broker, looking at a plastic bag from an outdoor store they'd found in a mall near the Best Western motel in Hudson. Nina stood in the bathroom doorway, sleek and bright in a towel and a wreath of steam.

"I've got your visas and your passports. I expedited them so it costs extra. But to schedule a flight it would help if I *knew when you want to leave*."

"How about tonight? It's real urgent, Don." They read him the number off Nina's credit card.

Larson groaned. "So I eat at my desk tonight. Okay. Twin Cities to Seattle . . ." Broker heard the patter of a computer keyboard as Larson talked. "Connect to . . . Hong Kong or Bangkok?" he asked.

"Whatever opens up first."

"Then Air Vietnam to Hanoi. Give me a number where I can reach you and stay close to the phone. If something pops up you'll have to jump on it." He paused. "You get your shots?"

"No."

"Take two hours, go to Ramsey. It's serious malaria country where you're going. Then stay at a number where I can reach you."

Broker gave him the room extension and hung up the phone.

"So?" asked Nina, fluffing her hair with a towel.

"So," said Broker, "tell me, when's the last time you wore your hair long?"

"Don't do this to me, Broker." But he caught an edge of a smile as she spun away.

Four hours passed in a whirlwind. They'd used his badge to speed getting a full round of inoculations for Vietnam at the Ramsey Travel Clinic in St. Paul. Nina submitted to the shots and filed the prescriptions reluctantly, explaining how she had refused to take the experimental biological and nerve agent antidotes in the Gulf. She'd put her faith in her gas mask. "See," she said, "no rashes or night sweats—"

"Just a three-foot-wide stripe of purple ambition down your back," Broker commented.

They went back to the motel and called Larson. He had them on an evening flight to Seattle but was having trouble with the Hong Kong connection. They ate take-out and watched the phone and packed. They were traveling light, one carry-on apiece. Broker studied himself in a mirror in his baggy new tropical shirt with lots of pockets and armpit vents. He cut the brand name off it with fingernail clippers and had just pried the piece of bone off the tiger tooth when Larson called. They were through to Hong Kong after a six-hour layover in Seattle. They'd have to scramble from there but it shouldn't be a problem if their paperwork was in order. Air Vietnam's line in Hong Kong was down but Northwest reservations told him that the airline always had empty seats.

They left the motor running at the travel agency, thanked Don Larson profusely, grabbed their passports and visas and tickets and drove like hell.

Two hours later the Jeep was tucked away in the long-term parking ramp at Minneapolis-St. Paul International. Broker felt the empty place in the small of his back where his Beretta used to live. They'd left the guns in the car.

They buckled their seatbelts. Broker glanced around and maybe it was fatigue-induced hallucinations or maybe it was clarity but it looked like the 747 was crammed with all of Rodney the arms dealer's rude, overweight dumbed-down extended American family off on a mission to sink Seattle with cellulite.

After takeoff, Broker unfolded himself from the cramped economy seat and got up. "My feet hurt," he explained to Nina. Which was true. From kicking Bevode and swamp walking. But he also wanted to check out the passengers to see if anyone resembling the Fret family was onboard. He saw a lot of physiognomy that suggested latent serial killers and depressed gene pools but none of them with the long jackass bone structure of the Frets.

He returned, restacked himself in the Procrustean seat and fell asleep and didn't wake up until the flaps cranked down as the jet made its landing approach. Nina, still fast asleep, snuggled on his shoulder with her hand warm where her fingers curled around a dead tiger's gold-tipped fang against his chest.

After they landed in Seattle they took a bus into town and ate at a restaurant with so many ferns that it felt like jungle survival training in Panama all over again. At four in the morning, Seattle time, so slap-happy they were making stale Dorothy and Toto jokes, they remembered that they hadn't called Trin. They left their incomplete flight information with the hotel desk clerk at the number in Hue. They'd arrive in Hanoi on the first open flight from Hong Kong. Trin would have to fill in the Air Vietnam blanks. In the background, Broker could hear the alien bells and growls of Vietnamese afternoon traffic. Then they showed their passports and boarded their flight.

53

THE PLANE IS FULL OF PEOPLE WITH BLACK HAIR AND THOSE wraparound brown eyes. No idea what they're talking about. Everything is backward and upside down. Sleep has slipped between the cracks of a dozen time zones. Nina is coping better. She snoozes on his shoulder. No-smoking flight. His mouth and his nerves ache for a cigarette.

He stares at the Northwest Far East magazine he finds in the seat pocket. The centerfold is a brightly colored map of the world. Like a Rorschach. The Asian continent is a spotted beast rearing out of the crouched leg of Africa with Europe in its hip pocket. North America is an afterthought cropped and running off the page left and right.

Marginal.

No calling 911 where he's going.

The flaps jerked, their ears swelled and popped, and Hong Kong emerged from a layer of dirty clouds. Cement high-rises streaked by like smoke, window lights for sparks. They banked sharply and the pilot kicked the big 747 through a fighter-jet turn, passing—it seemed to Broker—right between the tall buildings.

Cramped and numb they lumbered out the door and the clouds were burning tires and the air was rancid dishwater that stuck to Broker's cheeks. China was a fractured sensation. His first steamy look at the oldest engine in the world.

Customs queues, immigration, and a six-hour wait for the Air Vietnam desk to open for business. The terminal was a racket of Chinese. They hired a cab and escaped into the neon constellations of Kowloon and Mercedes gridlock on the streets. The working-class sections zipped by like the sets for *Bladerunner*. Across the bay, Hong

Kong nestled against the mountains like a silver money clip. They found a glittering glass and chrome restaurant. Outside the air smelled like a vat of stewing sweat and dirt and blood. Like money. Inside, they found the cleanest, most well-dressed people in the world. Hydroponics mannequins. Scientifically bred in posh display windows until they'd grown into their perfect tailoring.

After the most expensive meal of their lives they took another cab back to the airport. Beyond conversation, too nerved up to sleep, they paced and drank coffee and smoked cigarettes and waited.

A smiling young woman in a blue blazer happily took their money and stamped their tickets for Hanoi. After another round of customs and immigration, an airport bus ferried them out to a smaller white jet with a blue flying crane logo on the tail section.

A slender Air Vietnam hostess in a flowing blue au dai and filmy white trousers checked their boarding passes. Broker remembered the subtle magic of the garment that covered and revealed. He marked the panty line on her flank, the slip of bare midriff. They boarded the plane.

Vietnamese voices flowed like forgotten poems. The plane became a miniature time machine and it wasn't just in his imagination. He cocked his head and heard—impossibly—an Elvis Presley tune from the sixties piped in on the intercom. He couldn't stop his youth from shinnying up and peeking from the corners of his eyes.

Doing it on purpose. Like they know.

Gritty, exhausted, Nina hugged his arm and laughed.

The exuberance didn't last long. A hulking Caucasian giant barred their path. Six four, dressed in flip flops, and an ensemble of blue shorts and a T-shirt that looked like underwear or pajamas. He exhaled a nightmare breath of booze.

The upright pig-giant had twinkling gimlet eyes and spoke an accented dialect of the English language known only to his drunken tribe of one. He could have been Bevode Fret's libido unchained and walking around . . .

But he was an Aussie, stoned on nitrous oxide maybe.

He chirped, leering at Nina.

"Fuck off, mate." Broker stabbed a sharp finger into his bloated midsection. The pig-giant fluttered his left hand in an inebriated incantation and backed off and rolled deeper into the plane, a blue hazard that the Vietnamese hostesses steered adroitly to a berth.

Nina and Broker flopped to their seats. The frantic tempo of Hong Kong dissipated on Air Vietnam. Only half the seats were filled. A hostess handed Broker a steamed perfumed towel with a forceps.

He wiped the grime from his face and felt time slow down. *It's going to be different now . . .*

Australian voices, Broker glanced back and saw them crowd the aisle. A tour. He gathered that the snoring pig-giant was one of their number. He dozed for a while. Woke with a start and wondered if he had dreamed the episode with Jimmy Tuna. They were served a meal. Broker drank a cup of coffee and studied a map of Vietnam in a glossy Air Vietnam magazine.

The country was shaped like an S hook hanging off the belly of China, wrapped around Laos and Kampuchea: fat on the ends, thin in the middle. They'd land in Hanoi, near the top of the S and then head for the skinny panhandle in the center. To Hue City on the Perfume River. And in Hue there would be a police station.

He'd only accepted one cliché in his life: that cops were cops the world over. They understood each other. But they were *Communist cops* where he was going. And they worked for the only government in the world that had whipped the United States of America in open warfare.

He tried to put himself in the place of a Vietnamese cop listening to a wild story coming from the lips of an American tourist. They probably would have an office guy assigned to hearing complaints from the tourist trade. An office guy would phone his boss. And on up the line until someone who had LaPorte's money in his pocket would hear the story.

It was like everything else. Cops were cops. Except when they weren't.

So it all depended on Trin. And the minute they opened their mouths their *lives* would be in his hands. With this disconcerting thought for a lullaby, Broker dozed.

And then. Not that long. The now familiar sensation and pressure in the ears. The jet grumbled in the air and slowed for descent. Looking down from an aircraft together with the word Vietnam had always meant an aerial view of a smashed landscape. Lunar craters. Broker took a look. Just green fields, treelines. Not one crater. Rustic farmland.

"Any advice?" asked Nina.

"Don't touch the kids on the head, don't wave at people, don't put your feet on the table."

"How's it feel coming back?"

"Not coming back. Going to," said Broker.

Nina poked his shoulder and then pointed out the window. Three stubby MiG 21s lined up on a black cement apron. Green rice fields and red dirt stretched on either side. Broker saw the tiny conical straw hats, the women stooped in shiny black pantaloons. Then, reality tapped his eyes. A Communist flag fluttered over a tiny mustard-walled colonial-style terminal.

Hong Kong was a movie he'd watched. Just colored lights. Down there it was going to be sweat, orange-brown *bazen* dirt, and buffalo shit. Hard core. Third World. Real.

Nina leaned back in her seat and stared straight ahead. Getting ready. Broker supplied the word like he was lighting a fuse.

"Trin."

54

A RED FLAG WITH A YELLOW STAR FLUTTERED UNDER A DIRTY brass sun.

Broker stepped into the climate with one hand clenched on Jimmy Tuna's map inside his security belt. The paradoxical heat and humidity wilted right through him like radiation and made him feel *young*. Excited, he took in the iron land that monsoon rains had turned to rust. The airport was in the middle of nowhere. Just fields, bicycles, and water buffalo.

Two buses pulled toward the aircraft. As they turned and opened their doors to admit the arriving passengers, Nina leaned against his shoulder and laughed. Absurdly, garish blue Pepsi logos adorned their sides.

The bus drove them across the runway and, slow motion, in the heat, they entered the terminal. On scuffed tile floors, they queued up for the customs station and the ragtag X-ray machines beyond. Weary officers wore brown uniforms that were too tight or too loose. They stood behind antique wooden counters and shuffled papers and stared mainly at their hands. Broker didn't see a single gun being worn in the building.

A crowd of Vietnamese taxi drivers pressed against the doors and windows. Broker searched for the face of a man he hadn't seen in twenty years.

Nina pulled him by the arm toward a hand-held sign floating above the crowd. *Phillip Broker/Nina Pryce. Vietnam Hue Tours greets you!*

"Huh?" said Broker.

Nguyen Van Trin, at five feet four inches, needed the sign. He came up to the top of Nina's ears but his grin was six feet tall. Trim down the nose, slant the eyes and Trin could have posed for one of the stone faces on Easter Island. He'd picked up a few more scars on his drum-tight kisser since the last time Broker had seen him.

"Trin, you sonofabitch." Awkwardly, they clasped arms.

"It's me," said Trin and his easy English came through the foreignness of the place like hope. But his voice had lost its deep resonance. Now sardonic, cautious. The old military fire had long extinguished.

"How are you?"

"Ah, well . . ." He affected a Gallic shrug. His once intense brown eyes now reminded Broker of tired wood, still hard, but flat and brittle. His body was husky and durable, round with muscle and deeply tanned, like he'd been working outside. He wore baggy cotton slacks, loafers, and a black T-shirt; his black hair was a little shaggy. Unmasked in this intimate moment, he was frail around the eyes. Studying the ashes of Trin's smile, Broker gauged: *They broke him.*

"Jimmy Tuna sends his regards," said Broker.

"How is he?" asked Trin, confused but smiling.

"Dying."

Trin nodded politely, then, sensing Nina's scrutiny, he turned to her, touched his cheek, and pointed. "Freckles," he said. "Like Ray."

Nina pursed her lips. She accepted Trin's solemn handshake.

"We have to talk about my dad," she said frankly.

"Yes," said Trin casually, "but not here. Do you have other bags?"

"Just what we're carrying," said Broker.

"The car's over here," said Trin, making a display of taking Nina's shoulder bag and leading them to a gray tourist van with Vietnam Hue Tours, stenciled on the side. The driver was a lean, waspish northerner in a dark shirt and slacks who nodded enthusiastically. "This is Mr. Hai, our driver for Hanoi," explained Trin. "Mr. Hai speaks English; he used to listen to Americans talk on the radio all the time, right, Mr. Hai?"

Hai nodded and declaimed, "Alpha Bravo Charley." He held the door open for Broker and Nina. "Uniform Victor Whiskey."

"So how was your flight?" asked Trin.

"Quiet," said Nina. "The plane was only half full."

"Yes and no. Air Vietnam makes room for ghosts," said Trin.

A man in NVA green and a pith helmet came straight at Broker on a bicycle. His stomach tightened. The man smiled broadly and rode by and Broker's eyes began to absorb the visual judo chops. Red flags draped like bullfighter capes from the front of the dusty hooch-shacks that lined the road. Wicker walls. Banana thatch roofs. Fields of rice. Women in straw hats bent to the grain. In the fields, surrounded by ancestral grave mounds, a crude billboard displayed a syringe and warned against AIDS in *English* and Vietnamese.

"I don't see men in the fields," said Nina.

"Men prepare the land, women handle the rice," said Trin. He gazed at the stooped laborers and said quietly, "Heart to earth, back to sky."

Mr. Hai drove with his horn, brushing off clouds of bicyclists. They passed a putting motorscooter with wicker cylinders of live pigs trussed on the back, behind the driver.

Broker read aloud a sign in English. "'Tourist information. Souvenirs'?" He shook his head, then a billboard announcing a new luxury hotel. "English? In Hanoi?"

"The language of commerce," said Trin philosophically. Nina leaned forward. Trin lowered his hand over the seat, below the driver's line of sight in the rearview and stayed her question with firm pressure on her forearm. His eyes wandered toward the driver. Nina understood, leaned back. "What is the population of Hanoi?" she asked.

Trin replied in his best tour guide voice, "Three million, about two and a half million more than it can handle." He smiled. "Curtis LeMay said he was going to bomb Hanoi back to the stone age. He failed. But Hanoi has put itself in the stone age with overdevelopment."

Nina nodded politely.

The van beeped monotonously as it entered swarms of scooters and bikes and the rickshaws known locally as cyclos. No rules governed the swelling human cataract; everybody preferred the middle of the road, both directions. The open fields disappeared and they were in narrow streets among two-story tenements.

Broker continued to process. He saw his third Marlboro billboard in twenty-four hours: the first had been in English, which is to say American, in Seattle; the second was in Hong Kong, a hundred feet high and splashed with Chinese calligraphy. The one he saw now had the same hard-riding lung cancer cowboy but was in the Romanized Vietnamese alphabet. The letters were familiar, the sounds they made utterly alien. Like anagram puzzles.

Then they plunged into a sea of people on wheels who moved less like traffic than like blood through arteries and capillaries and, sealed in their air-conditioned bubble, they shouldered into the heartbeat of Hanoi.

The hotel was a white stucco jukebox with a spitting lime neon band wrapping its marquee. A grinning youth in a long blue coat and a captain's hat rushed to open the plate glass door. "Three star, joint venture. The plumbing works. CNN on satellite dish," recited Trin as they got out of the van.

Hanoi was bells, horns, raw sewage, fish sauce that smelled like bad feminine hygiene, a million charcoal fires, Samsung and Soni signs, and Socialist Realist hammers and sickles bursting in Peter Max colors on billboards. Flimsy new construction competed with rundown French Colonial and sooty aging brick with twist-up pagoda tile roofs. Down the alleys: Confucian shadows.

Too much for jet-lagged senses.

Trin chatted briefly with the driver. The van pulled away. Broker and Nina clung to the reception desk in the hotel lobby. Another slender life raft of English. They handed over their passports. Europeans jammed the lobby; French and German languages predominated. Trin joined them at the desk.

"The driver will pick us up in the morning. We'll see some sights before we catch the train to Hue," he said.

"Train?" asked Broker.

"Yes, it'll give us time to get reacquainted," said Trin. He advised them to change some dollars for dong, which they did. Broker put a wad of currency in his pocket the size of a small roll of toilet paper.

"Will you join us for a drink, Mister Trin?" he asked formally for the benefit of the hotel staff behind the counter.

"Thank you," said Trin, bowing slightly.

A grinning bellhop escorted them up the elevator and to adjoining rooms on the third floor. Nina turned pointedly to Broker. "You going to tell him?"

"I'm going to tell him," said Broker.

Trin listened with a bland smile. His smile was echoed by the hovering bellhop.

She turned to Trin. "You two have some catching up to do. I'm going to take a shower." She took her bag from the bellhop and entered her room. Broker and Trin went next door to Broker's room.

They waited while the bellhop opened the drapes and turned on the air conditioner. Broker tipped him with a dollar bill and closed the door behind him.

Trin, watchful, keyed up, hid behind a shrug. "Sorry, Phil, caution is an old habit. Tour guide is my main income when I can get away with it. Explain to Nina that a good guide must be friendly with Americans. But it's not a good idea to be familiar with them the minute they get off the plane."

Broker opened the mini icebox and tossed Trin a chilled green can of Tiger beer, then opened one for himself. They sat in chairs across a low table in front of the window. Below them the Kamikaze traffic coursed through an intersection. Children kicked a soccer ball in a park across the street.

For a full minute there was silence as he debated how to start. How to span two decades. Outside, cloud cover cut the sun and the window oscillated between transparent and opaque. Their reflections flirted, barely visible in the glass. Then disappeared.

"So, how is it hearing Vietnamese being spoken again, Phil?" Trin asked slowly.

Broker stared at the trees around the park. They looked like massive Bonsai, foreign and tortured, like they'd been traumatized by bombs. "Not sure yet. Everybody's so . . . friendly. All the signs in English. I'd think they'd hate our guts here."

"Things changed," said Trin with shrill gunshot abruptness. Then his demeanor softened. "Actually, Americans are new to them here in Hanoi. The only personal contact they had with you—besides the bombs—were the Senator John McCains falling by parachute into the local lakes, and Jane Fonda. Down south it will be different, where the Lieutenant Calleys left their mark." He offered a cigarette and as Broker accepted it he saw that they had a ritual to perform. He drew the chain from around his neck and handed Trin the tiger tooth.

Trin cradled it in his hand. "Thank you. This has been in my family for over four hundred years." Broker thought, but could not say: *Well, it's been laying in my underwear drawer for almost twenty . . .*

Broker's old Zippo appeared in Trin's hand. Broker took the lighter, turned it to read the sentiment engraved on the side and winced.

Lt. Phil Broker. Quang Tri City. 1972.

When I die reincarnate me as a 2,000-pound bomb.

"You were young," said Trin. He looked out the window. "I had to bury that for fourteen years." He smiled bitterly. "I dug it up in eighty-nine when the door opened to the West."

Broker tapped the Zippo on the table. "How are you doing, Trin?"

Shadows gathered in the lumped scar tissue on Trin's left cheekbone. "What did the girl mean—you have something to tell me? What am I mixed up in, Phil?" he asked softly.

The Zippo clicked nervously on the table. "You have a family? Kids?" asked Broker.

"My wife formalized our divorce in seventy-five, after Liberation. She stayed with the winning side. She has never let me forget I didn't. My son and daughter grew up with her, here in Hanoi. Now they're both in school, in France." Trin narrowed his eyes. "No family. No kids. Would it make a difference?"

Broker clicked his teeth. "Sorry, but I have to ask . . ."

Trin smiled sadly. "You're evaluating me, Phil."

"Yeah, sorry," sighed Broker.

"The student has become the teacher?"

"I said I was sorry."

"What do you do for a living, Phil?"

"I'm a policeman."

"Really? You hated the army. I'd have thought you were too independent to put up with . . . structure."

"An undercover policeman."

Trin took a long meditative drag on his cigarette. "I see. Are you here working on a case?"

"You could say that."

Trin exhaled and his eyes wandered out the window. "Pieces come back. Ever since Jimmy found me. It's like a bad dream. Cyrus is here . . ."

Broker nodded. "In Hue, checked into the Century Riverside Hotel, The Imperial Suite."

Trin sagged. "He has a big boat off the coast. I read it in the newspaper. It's been on the state TV."

"You're getting warm."

"Jimmy," said Trin. He bit his lip.

"Too bad Jimmy can't make it to the reunion," said Broker.

Trin stared at his hands. "The last time we were together we almost got killed. When Jimmy called he told me Ray did get killed. I saw that helicopter fly off with a heavy load in its sling. There are . . . crazy rumors."

"Not rumors," said Broker.

Trin looked up and perspiration beaded on his forehead. He spoke very slowly as his eyes scoured Broker's face. "A convict in an American prison sends an intermediary to find me six years ago. He sets me up running a convalescent home for disabled Front veterans. He specifies exactly where he wants the home built on a deserted strip of coast in Quang Tri Province. He has me buy a boat. A fairly large boat. Because I am helping disabled Liberation Front fighters I am allowed to do all these things. To spend money. Otherwise, because I fought for the South, I can be a hotel clerk, a waiter, or a cyclo-boy. Or, because I went through the camps, there's a program for former southern officers. I can immigrate to America if I have a sponsor.

"And then, when Jimmy is ready to come himself, he develops a fatal disease." Trin's eyes were getting hotter. "And a secret police-man comes in his place with the daughter of a dead friend. Is the girl supposed to make it all palatable?"

They stared across the table.

Trin took another drag on his cigarette and his wooden eyes kin-dled. "Once you asked me why my men burned slips of paper before going into battle. I never answered you." He paused and picked up a sheet off the hotel notepad on the table and took a pen from his pocket. He slapped the pen down on the sheet. "They were writing prayers. Write a prayer for me that tells me why you're here."

Broker squinted, saw that he was serious. "Okay," he said. He picked up the pen and printed: We *know where Ray is buried under ten tons of gold. Cyrus doesn't.*

Trin sat transfixed, driven into the carpet. Then he inhaled sharply and muttered, "Choi Oui." He exhaled, grabbed the pen from Broker and wrote furiously on the note: *Rumors.* He looked up; his eyes lost all caution. Broker took the pen back and wrote: *Fact.*

Trin laughed nervously. He picked up the lighter and ignited the note. A tongue of flame and smoke curled from his fingers. Delicately he carried the burning slip to the window, opened the latch, and tossed it out. He pointed to the smoke detector on the ceiling. Then he sat back down and said slowly, "Buddhists write prayers to their ancestors and then burn them because the dead can only read smoke. Like incense." His voice trembled but his eyes were an inferno. "No bullshit?" he gasped.

"No bullshit. That famous night? Cyrus used us as a decoy and had Ray murdered to steal that gold from the bank of Hue. Jimmy helped do it, except Jimmy changed the plan. He ditched the gold on the coast. Everybody, including Cyrus, thought it went down at sea. Now Cyrus thinks the gold is in the ocean near a wrecked helicopter. But it isn't. It's buried. On the beach." Broker grinned.

Trin groped, dizzy. He blurted, "And you plan to do *what*?"

"Couple of things. How good's that boat you got?"

"Oh God." Trin explored his burning face with his fingers as though he was establishing his own reality. He swallowed. "It's a fishing boat, forty feet long, inboard engine. But it's not covered. Actually, it's falling apart. They wouldn't let me get a real oceangoing boat. A lot of people have left . . ." He shook his head. "I don't know anything about boats. We never use it."

"But it would handle a couple tons, say. We could remove some of the stuff before—"

"Before what!" Trin sat bolt upright. He scanned the walls. "What?" he repeated.

"Before I lure Cyrus in and arrest the sonofabitch when he digs it up!"

"*Here?*" Trin whispered. His eyes swelled.

"Nina wants to work through the American Mission. I'd prefer to coordinate with the police in Hue. You can help me line up the local cops and—"

"No. Don't go to the police . . . no." Trin's palm squashed lumps of sweat on his forehead. "Excuse me." He got up, moved in jerky steps to the bar set up over the pint-sized icebox, and picked up a tiny airplane bottle of scotch. He broke the foil seal, opened it, and drank it. He coughed, came back, and resumed his seat. He glanced at the wall, toward Nina's room, and said emphatically, "It would be a real mistake to contact the MIA office."

"Exactly. Convince her." Broker yanked his head toward the wall.

"The MIA office is closely monitored." Trin shook his head. "Something like this . . . Everybody will," he grinned tightly, "get out of control."

"Can we do it?" asked Broker.

Trin swallowed and got the words out with difficulty. "Look at me, Phil. I'm not who I was."

"None of us are," said Broker.

Trin whispered, "Do you have a map?"

Broker knew he had him. He tapped the security belt under his waistband.

"My God. Jimmy . . ." Trin slowly shook his head. "He called me last week and said you had a present for me. I thought he meant a bonus."

"Well?" said Broker, opening his hands.

"He said something else. We were all going to play a joke on Cyrus."

"Uh-huh." Broker reached for the phone and dialed Nina's room. "I told him," he said into the receiver. "You better get over here."

55

NINA WAVED HER HANDS, CROSSED THE ROOM, AND OPENED the window. "It's smoky in here," she said. She had showered and wore the cheap plastic shower shoes the hotel provided. Her hair was still damp and stains of moisture glued her T-shirt to her collarbones.

"He told you," she said to Trin.

Trin nodded as he crossed the room to the bar area and returned with all the pony ounces of hotel booze. He sat down and lined them up. Six of them. Hands shaking, he opened two of them, held one in each hand and dribbled them into a water glass.

"You're, ah, mixing scotch and gin," said Nina, her voice and her eyebrows arched.

"Phil says you have opposite theories about how to proceed," said Trin stiffly. He raised his glass and drained it.

"I thought it might to a good idea to feel out the MIA people at the start."

"Why?" asked Trin. Methodically he began opening two more of the small bottles.

"Maybe I'm lonely for American faces," said Nina, very concerned.

"You don't trust me," said Trin, smiling wryly as he took a strong pull on the glass.

"You always drink this much, Trin?"

"Yes," said Trin emphatically. "But usually much worse stuff."

Broker sat on the bed massaging his forehead in both hands.

"Just what we need, a lush." Nina rolled her eyes.

"A woman of Hue," Trin said dryly.

"Pardon me," said Nina.

Trin did not smile. "You have the bearing of a woman of Hue." He finished his drink and began opening two more bottles. "My wife was from Hue. Aloof, smooth as silk. Like the Perfume River, not too deep, not too shallow." He smiled coldly. "A man could drown."

"Wonderful. Folk sayings," said Nina impatiently.

Trin grinned. "Here's another. What did the first water buffalo say to the second water buffalo?"

Nina's appraisal, at this point, was not kind.

"We're in deep shit." Trin downed the contents of the glass.

Nina turned to Broker. "We trust this guy?"

"We have to. He's all we've got," said Broker.

"And you told him everything?"

"I left out the dead guys in Wisconsin," said Broker.

"What dead guys?" asked Trin, swallowing.

"Jimmy shot this one guy Cyrus had tailing us. She got the other one," said Broker.

"Cyrus knows you're after him," Trin said fatally.

"It's more accurate to say that Cyrus is after us. He knows by now that Tuna told us where it is. He also thinks I'm trying to cash in on his treasure hunt."

"Aren't you?" asked Trin.

"The way I see it happening, the Vietnamese government will wind up with most of it. But we deserve a little for our trouble," said Broker.

"Is there anyone else here with you?" asked Trin.

"Just us," said Broker.

"And you have come halfway across the world to catch Cyrus LaPorte, a famous American, for looking for buried gold?"

"Look," said Nina. "I'm here because my dad took the blame for the gold incident. And Jimmy told us there's evidence on my dad's remains that proves Cyrus ordered the robbery. I thought you were friends with my father."

Trin ignored her and paced three steps, turned and paced back. "Cyrus used to be a very thorough man. Assume he had the airport watched. Possibly with the assistance of the Vietnamese police. Assume he knows we're sitting in this room right now. We must stay in public places until we make a break for the countryside. Cyrus could try anything," said Trin in nervous rapid-fire delivery.

"Listen to him all of a sudden," said Nina.

"Please sit down, Miss Pryce," said Trin in a coiled voice. His face became flat and cold as a stone adder. Nina's color rose. Broker smiled.

"What's so funny?" she demanded.

"That's the warm cuddly Trin I remember," said Broker.

Trin did not smile. "This discussion may already have cost me whatever future I have. You arrive and in two hours you put my neck on the block. Please sit down, Nina."

Nina reached in her pocket, pulled out a slip of paper, and extended her hand toward the hotel phone on the table next to the bed. "Sorry, Broker. I'm calling the MIA office to line up a little assistance, U.S. type."

Trin leaned over in a smooth motion and a slim gravity knife opened in his hand. He swept up the phone cord with the blade and held it captive. "You try to call and I'm out that door. You'll never see me again."

"Jesus," muttered Nina, stepping back.

Trin closed the knife, put it back in his pocket, and smiled, no longer coldly, now a little drunkenly, at Nina. "The MIA office is integrated at every level with the Ministry of Missing Persons. Their phones are tapped. They are not allowed to drive their own vehicles. They are under *surveillance*. Anything you tell the MIA office you tell the Vietnamese police."

"He's right, Nina," said Broker. "We can't trust the army. They screwed you, remember?"

"Like you screwed Cyrus's wife?" she said sarcastically.

"I did not," shot back Broker.

"Ah, another complication," said Trin philosophically. "You two are in love."

"You're drunk," said Nina.

"I drink," qualified Trin. "I speak English and French fluently. I can read one thousand Chinese characters. When I was twenty-five I commanded a Viet Cong battalion. At twenty-nine I commanded a South Vietnamese regiment. Then I spent five years in a reeducation camp being lectured by morons. In the camp I ate frogs and bugs. All my life I have had this problem of seeing both sides simultaneously. For that, and other reasons, I drink." He lurched from his chair, grabbed the TV remote, and snapped on the television.

"Now what?" Nina was not happy.

"The BBC world business report will quote the price of gold in New York, Hong Kong, and Zurich. It's a logical question," said Trin.

Nina flopped down in one of the chairs and folded her arms across her chest. Broker sat on the bed with his elbows resting heavily on his knees. He felt sealed in the hotel room.

Veiled in air conditioning. Outside he could feel the pressure of three million people, almost all of them poor, most of them touched roughly by war and scarcity. And the only avenue he had into this strange capital and into the countryside beyond was this bitter, and now drunken, man whose thoughts he couldn't fathom.

And he wondered how many minds in Hanoi were sorting out their anxieties in English at this precise instant. Perhaps a thousand? He struggled to comprehend the alien process going on in the surrounding ocean of Vietnamese minds.

Like what the fuck was Trin thinking right now?

With Nina he had a pretty good idea. He could read her body language, her facial expression; he had some history. He'd even been inside her body. And maybe he *was* a little bit in love with her.

She's sitting there thinking: *Am I stuck with two men I can't trust?*

Nina unfolded her arms and got up. "Phil, I want to talk to you alone." Broker pushed himself up.

"Don't worry. He didn't show it to me," said Trin.

"What?" asked Nina.

"The map. But I have a general idea where the gold is," said Trin.

"You do?" asked Broker.

"Yeah," said Trin. He eyed the bottom of his empty glass, rose from his chair in front of the TV and went to the mini-fridge and removed a can of Tiger beer. He popped the top and resumed his seat. His eyes stayed on the muted BBC news report as he lit another cigarette, sipped his beer and said, "The convalescent home is in a deserted area of dunes. Exactly where Jimmy wanted it. The coastline for ten kilometers in every direction is uninhabited. The local people call it the Graveyard of the Iron Elephants. Romantic, isn't it . . .

"In 1968—before your time, Phil—the U.S. Air Force had a plan to end what was referred to as the Ho Chi Minh Trail by Water. The North shipped supplies out of Vinh Moc above the DMZ and landed them along the coast below the zone." Trin broke into laughter.

"What's this got to do . . ." Nina interrupted.

Trin pushed himself up and reached over and plucked Broker's Zippo from the table. He tossed it at Broker and said, with a downward curve to his smile, "Read it again. You may get your wish."

Nina put out her hand for the lighter, read the inscription, and looked back to Trin. "Iron elephants?" she repeated.

Trin smiled. "When farmers dig up old U.S. mortar rounds in

their fields they refer to them as iron potatoes. Elephants imply something grander." His smile broadened. "Jimmy has played a joke inside his joke."

For a moment Trin relished the suspense of holding them in thrall.

"You see," he said, "they carpeted the beaches with two thousand–pound bombs. Hundreds and hundreds of them. They were dropped from very high so they would burrow into the sand and they were set with time delayed fuses so they would go off at random intervals . . . get it?

"Except they didn't go off as planned. They've been going off at odd times ever since. Everybody left. People avoid the place. Jimmy knew what he was doing."

Alcohol had turned Trin's nicotine-colored skin as scarlet as a chili pepper. His scars blanched. He directed this molten face at Nina.

"There are two kinds of Vietnamese. If you go out in the street and hail a cyclo and ask him to take you to the Manila Hotel he will smile and say, yes. Who cares that the Manila Hotel is in the Philippines. He will say yes and take you on a merry ride forever.

"If you call the MIA office and tell your story some smiling Vietnamese will eventually appear and say 'yes' and you will sit in this hotel until your money runs out and you will call them on the telephone and they will say 'yes' and then maybe they will give you your passports and maybe they will let you leave the country. They will be very polite."

Trin's scars bunched. Livid. "There is another kind of Vietnamese who lives in a big house and drives a late-model four-wheel-drive vehicle with a license plate with the letter A on it. This is a party official. And he will grab up your gold and then if Ray's bones are indeed under it, he will *then* call the MIA office and let the Americans dig—"

"There's evidence," protested Nina.

"But if the bureaucrats get there first there will be no crime that involves Cyrus LaPorte *today*. The remains will be turned over to the Ministry of Missing Persons for verification along with all the items found at the site. If there is evidence it will disappear between the cracks in some ministry office."

"What makes you so sure?" said Nina.

Trin fumed, gesturing brusquely. "Cyrus LaPorte is dangling millions of American dollars, talking about joint ventures. I work sometimes at the reception desk at the Century Hotel in Hue. All people talk about these days is deals. They won't jeopardize those deals on the basis of a theory."

Broker interrupted. "It's all timing. We have to catch him *stealing*. Digging it up and putting it in his boat. If we do it right, we can have all kinds of people show up."

"Correct. It is . . . policework," said Trin. "Then we call in everybody so they all arrive at the same time. The press too. There's always some Australian reporters around, and the French. CNN has an office here. If we can manage that, it will stink all the way to Washington, which is what you want, Nina."

"The three of us." Nina's voice was grim, unconvinced.

"And my men," said Trin with an enthusiasm that showed more evidence of alcohol than good sense.

"What men?" said Broker.

"The men at the home. From my old battalion in the Front. You don't think they'd let me set up a home for soldiers who backed the south, do you?" Trin said indignantly.

"How many men?" asked Nina.

"A dozen."

Nina's voice strove for patience. "Trin, I talked to Kevin Eichleay in Lansing, Michigan. He helped you set up the home—"

Trin nodded. "I know Kevin."

"Those men are paraplegics. Cripples." She made a face. "I'm sorry. I mean no disrespect, but it's laughable."

Trin scowled at her and drew himself up. "I held the flag tower in the Citadel in Hue for twenty-five days during Tet with those men." His voice dropped to a hoarse whisper. "You weren't laughing then."

"Okay," said Broker, stepping between them. "Time out. Take a break."

"Ah," yelped Trin, pointing to the TV. "Four hundred and sixty-five dollars an ounce. Twelve troy ounces to a pound. That's, ah, five thousand five hundred something to the pound times two thousand . . ."

Nina turned and stalked from the room. Broker followed her.

56

THEY FROZE IN THE HALL, PARALYZED BY THE INNOCENT SMILE of a passing Vietnamese maid. Nina unlocked her door and they quickly entered her room. She closed the door and leaned against it.

"That guy has me jumpy as a coot."

"He is a little paranoid," said Broker.

"A little? He drinks too much and he has a grandiose streak."

"True, Trin always figured there were three sides in the war: the Commies, us, and him."

"And . . ." She wagged her finger in a no-no gesture. "He pulled a knife on me."

She stomped into the room and fell backward on the bed. "No shit," she said in a disbelieving voice. "*Their* Vietnam vets are more fucked up than *our* Vietnam vets! Is that possible?"

"I need him."

"He's seriously cracked, Broker."

"Maybe. But he knows his way around."

She sat up and hugged herself. "You go out on some deserted beach with Trin and his army of cripples and dig up a fortune in gold and get your throat cut. Not me."

"We just have to wing it a little. I have a hunch Trin's all right."

"Don't be cavalier. This is serious."

Broker exhaled. "And I'm serious. Look, it would be great if Trin was sober, industrious, and reliable. But he's been pretty roughed up. That means he's had to scramble to survive." A grim smile played across Broker's lips. "He's taken a dive from regimental commander to street hustler, Nina. And I know how to handle street hustlers."

"Look out the window. I don't see the steeples of Stillwater, Minnesota . . ."

Broker waved her quiet. "I'll bet he's doing this tour guide number without a government license. The fact is, with his background, he's got more to fear from the cops right now than we do."

"It's a stretch," said Nina. Her tone was cautious but no longer adamant.

Broker shrugged, "My kind of scene. Of course it works better when you know the turf and everybody speaks the same language."

She sat up and folded her legs Indian fashion. "And what really pisses me off is that he makes some sense, especially about the MIA office. Damn." Frustrated, she sprang from the bed, paced two steps, and spun, one hip pushed out, arms hanging loosely.

Broker studied her. She was so close and eager to take her shot. Like David, she had the guts to cool it in Goliath's shadow and the murderous concentration to bet it all on one throw.

But she was young and the petticoats of her ambition were showing—as was her need to control events. She wanted to be identified officially with the project from the start; she wanted it documented.

Nina Pryce, mentioned in dispatches.

Yeah, he was probably in love with her and she was a goddamned careerist. She'd be gone the second this thing was over.

"Okay," she said reluctantly. "We'll play it by ear with Mister Trin. But if he gets funny, we head for the liaison office. Agreed?"

"Deal," said Broker.

"You have the map," she worried suddenly.

"Right here." Broker tapped his waist.

"Didn't think I'd be this jumpy," she said. "We haven't even left the hotel yet."

"We'll do better once we're in the countryside."

"Broker, I just had this really terrible image: Bevode Fret in Hanoi."

Broker grimaced. He hadn't thought about Fret for a whole continent. "Look, are you hungry or anything?"

She shook her head. "I'm clogged with airplane food. I need some sleep. About fourteen hours."

"We both do. I'll check on Trin and be right back. I'm sleeping here."

She squinted at him. "I'm not in a mood for fooling around."

"Sleep," said Broker. He left her room and unlocked his door.

Trin had taken off his shoes and sprawled, slack-jawed, passed out on the bed. Broker took the smoldering cigarette from his fingers and turned off the TV.

He returned to Nina's room with his toothbrush. She was already under the covers. He pulled the blinds against the late afternoon light and showered quickly, brushed his teeth, and slid in beside her. He dimmed the lights with a knob on the console beside the bed.

"Can you believe it," said Nina. "I'm in Vietnam and I'm freezing to death."

"I can turn down the AC."

"No, just . . . spoon with me."

He snuggled up to her back. In bed, bare skin touching, she unbuckled some of her armor.

"You two aren't planning to ditch me? Go after the gold alone?" she mused.

"No."

Her toe dug into his leg. "Get me lost somewhere?"

"No, goddammit."

"Men lie," she purred.

"Some men," said Broker.

57

IN THE MORNING TRIN WAS GONE.

Broker fingered the scrawled note he found laying in an oval impression in the bedding. "I'll be back. T." Yeah, maybe, and after doing what? Despite his protestations to the contrary, he was less certain about the conflicted character of Nguyen Van Trin in the morning than he'd been the night before. He muttered through a shower and shave and, still grumbling, went next door, informed Nina, and showed her the note.

"Why am I not surprised?" she said. But she smiled gamely and put on the silver earrings with the little jade half moons. Like a token of peace.

They went down and checked at the desk. No message. They also discovered that Trin had reserved their rooms for only one night. After they'd settled up and had their passports back, a smiling hostess seated them in the restaurant that took up one end of the lobby. Warily, they bent over their croissants and coffee. The hotel was their small fort of broken English and indecipherable smiles. Beyond the plate glass windows Hanoi looked increasingly hostile. Gray clouds hung like crepe.

Nina allowed Broker to have one cup of thick, not quite hot coffee. Then she started.

"I'm calling the MIA people. You agree?"

"Give it half an hour."

"C'mon, Broker, he was expecting something—maybe a payoff from Jimmy. When he didn't get it he made conversation, drank all the booze in sight, and passed out. Now he's bugged on us." She aimed a pointed stare. "We shouldn't have confided in him. Every bartender in Hanoi probably knows our story."

"Wrong," said Broker, gesturing toward the hotel entrance with his coffee cup.

Trin marched through the lobby carrying a shoulder bag and a small plastic attaché case. He stopped at the desk and was directed toward the restaurant by the receptionist. He had changed his black T-shirt for an ugly patterned shirt that reminded Broker of the road-killed couch in his Stillwater house. His face was scrubbed, his hair was combed, and he wore sunglasses above a brilliant Stevie Wonder smile.

Trin sat down, officiously opened his briefcase, and ordered a glass of hot tea. Nina folded her arms. Trin grinned. "I had to get my clothes and do some things," he said.

"I'll bet," said Nina.

Trin smiled. With zany enthusiasm, he countered, "But we are agreed. We all jump over the cliff together." He zipped open his case and pulled out a pile of papers. "Our itinerary, so we look official."

Broker went to the buffet and refilled his coffee. Trin and Nina leaned forward, heads and shoulders over the tablecloth, and discreetly rehashed their MIA office debate.

Broker resumed his seat and watched the intersection in front of the hotel with the professional interest of a patrol copper. Bicycles, cyclos, motor scooters, motorcycles, handcarts, left-over Russian Jeeps, military trucks, occasional cars, and even one old mamasan with ocher betel nut–stained teeth, shiny black pantaloons, and bare splayed feet carrying poles heavy with vegetables slung over her shoulder—they all convened in front of his eyes. No stop light. No stop signs. No right of way, no white lines on the pavement. A heavy volume of traffic.

Everyone in that street aimed dead center at the middle of the intersection. Even inside the air-conditioned lobby he could hear the cacophony of horns and bells. They carried a tonal range as varied as the five potential accents that could mark each vowel in the Vietnamese language.

Jesus—a Honda with a kid, maybe four years old, planted between the driver's arms, with a wife, infant in arms on the back. Headed straight into a three-way crunch with a minivan and a cyclo. The minivan leaned on its horn, the cyclo and the Honda adjusted slightly, and miraculously all three passed through the bull's-eye unscathed. The flow did not pause.

Amazing.

Nina said, "I'll just check them out. I'll be vague."

"No, no, not yet," protested Trin. "You'll be on a police list in five minutes." They resumed their argument. Broker continued to study traffic.

He was beginning to sense an underlying pattern to the rolling mayhem. Just had to knock his American road sense a little cock-eyed, recalibrate his vision a few degrees . . .

An American would create instant carnage on the street. An American would want to know the rules so he could then measure himself against them, either obey or break them. At least test them. These people moved instinctively like water, all part of the same stream. Connected.

Nina said, "How do I know you and Broker won't dig it up and load it on the fishing boat and leave me stranded?"

Trin protested, "It's not much of a boat. The fact is, it's a lousy boat. We'd have to hire a bigger seaworthy boat and men to crew it; my people couldn't do it. The minute we let anyone else in on the secret, *that's* when our throats get cut. The same problem that Cyrus has." Exasperated, Trin waved his hands. "Where would we take it? I'm no sailor."

Broker glanced at his watch. "Ten minutes," he said. "Probably two thousand people on a thousand assorted means of transport went through this intersection—no light, no signs, in constant motion and not one pile-up. Now I know why we lost the war."

"Bullshit," said Trin dryly, "accidents are common."

Broker turned back to them. "So what'd you two decide?"

"He has a kind of plan. We go to the beach and see if the stuff's there, then we go to the MIA folks, if Cyrus takes the bait," said Nina. She smiled tightly. "I presume you guys will leave some of it as bait."

Trin and Broker exchanged fast glances. "If there's a lot, we'll just set some . . . aside," speculated Broker.

"We could do that, figure out how to move it later," Trin said quickly.

"Okay. What about some guys with guns and handcuffs? Some cops?" asked Broker.

Trin nodded. "Nina was right last night. We need some assault rifles on the scene, not a bunch of disabled Viet Cong."

Nina inclined her head, accepting Trin's sop.

He went on. "But not cops. There's a militia post five kilometers from the vet's home. A platoon of local farm boys. They guard a lighthouse. I'm on good terms with them."

"How good?" asked Nina.

Trin shrugged. "I pay them regularly to look after the home. And, anyway, they respect the old fighters, my guys. They have enough firepower to deal with a band of thieves. Unless Cyrus has an army."

Broker clicked his teeth. "I doubt he has a dozen people all told. That's my job. I'll find out."

Trin smiled cautiously. "So we find it. Phil continues on to Hue. He contacts Cyrus. The timing will be tricky. If Cyrus goes for it we can't tip off the militia too soon. The whole Communist bureaucracy is just a radio call away. Once they hear buried gold . . . phew!" He tossed his hands in the air. "Many four-wheel drive vehicles with capital A on the license plates."

Broker nodded in agreement. "Ass deep in office guys . . ."

Trin nodded. "Trying simultaneously to steal it themselves and take credit for catching the American pirates."

"What do you think?" Broker asked Nina.

She leaned forward and said, "Pardon me," as she carefully removed Trin's sunglasses and peered into his eyes. "Black holes for pupils. At night he drinks, during the day he takes speed, bet you anything. We're taking our lives in our hands, Broker."

"Nina, will you let us do this damn thing?" growled Broker.

Trin smiled tightly and replaced his glasses. "She should meet my ex-wife. They'd get along."

"Are we agreed?" asked Broker.

"I don't like being isolated with a bunch of militia troops, but you're right. If we telegraph, we'll have a carnival," said Nina. "It could work. Cyrus is loading the goods, the militia hits them . . . calls in the officials." She squinted at Broker. "It's your neck. You'll be alone in Hue City with LaPorte. And you'll be on that beach with him. Could be hairy if they resist—"

"True," said Trin, smiling broadly. "The militia are good kids, but not real great shots. Hopefully, they'll loan some weapons to my men at the home. They'll be a steady influence."

Broker was not sure whether to be encouraged or to make his will. He saw spooky old bones from the past get up and walk around in Trin's smile. But it was so crazy it just might work. "So that's it," said Broker. "My end's getting Cyrus to go for it."

"One more thing," said Trin. He reached in his attaché case and produced a sheet of paper with a list in crisp, printed English. "CNN, Reuters, the Australian News Service. This afternoon, before we catch the train, you and Nina must visit these offices and get business cards from the reporters." Trin grinned broadly. "Lay groundwork. Hint that something is going to happen. Then, when Cyrus comes ashore, we get to the nearest telephone and call them in. CNN can afford a helicopter. Maybe they can film it live." Trin jammed his finger dramatically into the air. "A scoop. Video uplink! That way Cyrus LaPorte will get his face on television in America." He turned to Nina. "You like it?"

"Aw, God," groaned Broker.

"You just might have something there," said Nina, narrowing her eyes. "Put it in plain view."

"Put you in plain view," muttered Broker. Nina wrinkled her nose.

"So," said Trin, replacing his sheet of paper in his case and zipping it shut. "We have a plan. We catch the train at seven tonight; I've already called. A car is arranged for us at Quang Tri City, noon tomorrow. Tomorrow night we check the site."

"You've had a busy morning," said Nina.

"I could be the best tour guide in Vietnam if the government would let me open my own business," lamented Trin. "But I served the South. I can only moonlight. I can arrange cars and drivers and hotels. I can't handle visas or tickets in and out of the country. Maybe after we do this—"

"So what do we do until the train leaves?" asked Broker.

"Play tourist, stay surrounded by people," said Trin. "When our driver gets here we'll visit the Ho Chi Minh Mausoleum, then maybe the Dien Bien Phu Military Museum. This afternoon we visit the press."

Broker tried to sound upbeat about the thin plan. "If we pull this off, the government might buy us lunch for returning the gold."

"You mean on top of what you're planning to steal yourself?" Nina's voice was laced with sarcasm.

"First let's find out if there is gold," said Trin.

"Just a thought," said Broker.

Trin exploded with laughter. "I think a government official would give you a mathematics lesson. He would point out that you dropped more bombs on Indochina than on the armies of Germany and Japan. That we took a million dead. That we have three hundred thousand of our own missing. And then he would look you straight in the eye and say, 'Fuck you, Yankee, we won.'"

"I said it was just a thought," said Broker.

Trin lit a cigarette and stared dubiously at the smoke. "One thing bothers me," he said.

"Only one?" quipped Broker.

"Seriously," said Trin. "If ten tons of government gold would have been laying around the northern provinces in nineteen seventy-five I would have known about it. And Cyrus LaPorte is taking a hell of a risk for a hundred million dollars . . ."

Hundred million. How many zeros and commas was that? Broker sat stunned.

Trin continued. "That's the world to you or me but he's a multi-millionaire. He doesn't need it *that* much."

"He's hooked on the action. His ancestor was a famous pirate," said Broker. But he rubbed his chin. Shrewd point. He remembered Jimmy's sinister comment: *It's not just gold . . .* He and Nina exchanged fast glances. They had said nothing about Jimmy's story, the disguised pallet sitting outside the bank for a month.

Trin tapped his cigarette nervously in the ashtray and said, "Something is missing."

58

THE HOTEL FACED A TRAFFIC CIRCLE AT THE EDGE OF THE Old City. The van arrived and, as they snailed through the cramped, smoky medieval alleys, Broker began to see evidence of the strip-malling of Hanoi. Gaudy mini-hotels and satellite dishes sprouted like brick and plaster burdock among the ramshackle twelfth-century architecture. Hanoi's callused palm had been crossed with silver and hope rode a shiny new motor scooter.

All the bicycles in the world jostled the van with anthill North Vietnamese energy and aggravated Broker's jet lag. His eyes ached. He wanted to get out of the city. Into the countryside and fresh air. Get the thing moving.

Mr. Hai, the driver, turned with a sturdy grin. "Roger, wilco, wait one," he said.

Just trying to be friendly.

Broker winced as a woman on a bike scraped the side of the van. He saw his first cop: gray shirt, Kermit green trousers with a red stripe. "The cops don't carry guns," he said.

"There are lots of guns, never very far away. Just criticize the government. You'll see," said Trin.

Nina sat quietly, meditating on the street scene. She toyed with one of the silver earrings, turned and smiled. "You know. If the people doing it are crazy enough, it just might work," she said.

They came out of the dense side streets and onto a broad French boulevard on which thousands of people waited patiently in line. Trin pointed at the top of a gray stone pyre that poked through the trees. They parked and waited while Trin ran into an office. He returned with tickets and slipped a guard a U.S. dollar. The guard escorted them to the head of the line. American tourists were allowed to take cuts. Broker averted his eyes from the squints of dour peasant veterans, their shirts clanking with medals, who stood patiently in the sun.

They joined a procession of elementary school kids who wore white shirts, blue trousers and skirts, and had red scarves tied around their necks. The kids walked in orderly ranks minded by their teachers.

"Pioneers," sniffed Trin. "Communist youth movement."

The shrine rose in blocky tiers of pharaonic Russian granite. Soldiers in red-trimmed rust-brown uniforms stood mannequin-stiff at attention. White gloves. Gleaming carbines. Huge urns of bonsai flanked the carpeted entrance. Trin smiled tightly. "I've never been in here."

"Me either," said Broker. The joke died on their faces under the quiet brown gaze of the Young Pioneers. Feeling like someone being initiated into a solemn pagan ritual, Broker walked up the steps, around a corner and shuffled down a ramp into the chilled, dimly lit inner sanctum. Nina squeezed his hand. "This is our first real date," she whispered reverently. Holding hands, they filed past the glass sarcophagus that held the frail, embalmed cadaver of the little man with the goatee who had stared down the Free World.

Back in the sunlight Trin fidgeted and lit a cigarette in an explosion of nerves. He muttered in Vietnamese. Broker put a hand to his shoulder. "You all right?"

Trin bared his teeth. "We said a lot of things. He said a single thing, 'Vietnam is one.'" Trin exhaled and recited under his breath. "The mountains can be flattened, the rivers can be drained, but one truth remains: Vietnam is one." Trin shook his head ruefully. "That guy was focused."

"I know somebody like that," said Broker playfully.

Nina punched him softly on the arm, then she raised her hand. "Listen," she said.

Broker cocked his head and heard music in the trees. A PA speaker played Hanoi muzac near the tomb. The procession of Young Pioneers marched away to a twanging rendition of "Oh Susannah."

Broker stared at Trin. Trin shrugged and shook his head. "On traditional instruments, too."

Nina laughed, really starting to enjoy herself. "I'm beginning to see how this place could screw up your mind."

Trin reverted to tour guide, leading them past an opulent French Colonial building to the contrasting austere wood house on stilts where Ho had lived, pointing out the pool where the carp would come when he clapped his hands.

"There's a debate in the party," said Trin on the way back to the van. "In his will President Ho specified that he wanted to be cremated and have his ashes scattered on three mountain tops. Maybe he will finally get his wish and be liberated from that Russian meat locker."

"Now what?" asked Nina.

"The military museum," said Trin, giving directions to Mr. Hai. The museum was a few minutes away, through the swarm of bicycles. Nina sat up abruptly and said, "Hello! Is that what I think it is?"

"Absolutely," said Trin. "The last statue of Lenin in the world, I think." The statue dominated a square directly across from the museum.

"I should have brought a camera," said Nina. Trin immediately dug in his bag and produced an Instamatic.

"I want you two in front of the statue," said Nina. Trin had Mr. Hai pull over and explained the simple camera mechanism to Nina. They got out and a swirl of street kids surrounded them like blown gum wrappers. Selling postcards. Trin brushed off the kids and they walked up the shallow steps into the paved park toward the obstinate charcoal-gray statue. Paralyzed in larger than life bronze and contradictions, Lenin clasped his right lapel in one hand and knit his sooty devil's eyebrows.

Nina, camera in one hand, shooed a group of kids playing soccer out of her way. She directed Trin and Broker to stand back a few paces, took several snapshots, and then moved down the steps to get a wide-angle shot.

Broker put his arm around Trin's shoulder. It was very warm. A spoon band of cicadas clacked in gaps in the traffic. Foliage swooned in the breeze. A bright trickle of sweat ran from Trin's hairline down his temple and into his scars. Mr. Hai wove across the busy street toward the military museum ticket booth. A tall tourist meandered, adjusting his direction so as not to interfere with the picture-taking. Nina was bent forward, her purse dangling from her shoulder, camera extended, elbows out. A spear of sunlight pierced Broker's eyes from one of her earrings.

He blinked sweat.

They both sensed it ahead of conscious thought. Something in the languid summer tempo on the square showed its teeth. Trin and Broker dropped to a slight forward crouch. Broker's right hand flashed instinctively to the small of his back.

The anonymous black car angled from a cloud of bicycles and rolled over the curb. At the same moment the tall Caucasian in sunglasses, floppy shorts, and a tourist cap accelerated from his amble across the square. The car and the trotting man converged on Nina. Not fast, but very smooth. Professional.

Broker and Trin were moving. Starting to shout.

Too late.

The rear door of the car swung open and the jogging man wrapped Nina in his arms and toppled with her into the open door. The car revved its engine, the window on the driver's side rolled down. Broker, running flat out, saw Virgil Fret, patches of his sweaty scalp showing through his stringy red hair, lean out from the driver's side. Grinning like a Bicycle deck joker, Virgil flipped Broker the bird. They could make out a struggle in the back seat through the windows. The door was not quite shut. An object flew out the door and flopped on the paving stones. Then Virgil popped the clutch and the car burned a squealing double track of rubber off the cobble apron.

Broker and Trin collided in a cloud of exhaust where the car had been a second before. Broker stooped and snatched up the purse Nina had thrown from the car. Trin whipped off his sunglasses and tried to catch the license plate as the car disappeared into a tornado of traffic.

"Did you get it?" yelled Trin.

"No," panted Broker. He opened the purse and saw that it contained the copy of the U.S. Code, her passport and money. Then—

"*Wait.*" Broker's frown resembled Lenin's bronze wrinkles.

Across the street, down a block, he saw a lean rawboned man wearing a safari shirt round the corner. Hatless, his head and shoulders bobbed, fearsome as a Roman eagle, above the crowd of Vietnamese pedestrians.

"Be cool," said Broker. "They're sending someone to deal. We don't want to draw any attention to ourselves." He pulled a wad of currency from his pocket and passed fifty thousand dong notes out to the kids who had been playing soccer and who now stood wide-eyed in the vacuum of the kidnapping. The kids grabbed the bills; fifty thousand dong was the biggest denomination of Vietnamese currency, worth five bucks. They squealed and raced away.

The man paused and leaned on a wall in a patch of shade. When he saw the kids leave, he heaved his shoulders off the wall of the Dien Bien Phu Military Museum and casually raised a comb and thrust his hips in a posture that only American narcissism would strike. The long, oiled blond hair glittered in the sun.

Broker could hear Trin's tense breathing. He saw Hai coming across the street at an urgent trot.

"Send Mr. Hai back to the car," said Broker in a calm voice.

Trin barked in Vietnamese. Hai reluctantly stopped and walked back to the van, looking over his shoulder.

The American barged across the street, coming straight toward them. A bicycle skidded and overturned, brakes screeched.

Trin made a low contemptuous sound in his throat that sounded like a guttural "Meeow." Broker's memory placed the word. It was a derisive reference, an insult. The worst thing a Vietnamese could call an American.

And he remembered the traditional screens that the Vietnamese employed to block the doorways to their houses and their tombs so you had to zigzag to enter. The screens warded off evil spirits, who, like Bevode Fret, could only travel in straight lines.

59

IT WAS WINTER IN HANOI WHERE BROKER STOOD. AS BEVODE approached, he saw that the Cajun had used cosmetic base to disguise some of the bruising on his puffy lip. His face was contorted, absent its easy smile and one of its front teeth.

Broker's smile, by contrast, was chilly as an autopsy slab. "Well, I'll be dipped in shit. How you doing, Bevode?"

"You and me got some personal stuff, but it can wait," said Bevode straight-faced. He stared with fixed interest at the purse Nina had thrown out the window. Broker tightened his grip on it.

"Du ma . . ." began Trin.

"Wazzat?" asked Bevode.

"Not sure, something about your mother," said Broker.

"Tell Gunga Din to wipe the stupid grin off his face," said Bevode.

"They smile when they're nervous," said Broker.

"So why's he nervous?"

"He just saw an American citizen kidnapped in broad daylight in downtown Hanoi."

"Nah, just some friends gave her a lift," said Bevode. He glanced around the square. "Sorta hoped you'd have that big nigger along. Want to meet him again, yes I do."

"Just us," said Broker.

Bevode squinted. "You had to get tricky and bring the cunt." He shook his head. "Went and got yourself on Cyrus's shitlist." He brightened. "Lola's moved up from hind tit; she got herself off the list to make room for you. We're all just dyin' to talk with you, Broker. Now that you been to Loki fucking Wisconsin—"

"So talk."

"Get rid of the gook."

"He's with me."

Bevode shrugged, "His funeral," and despite his damaged mouth, he smiled crookedly. "I been studying the local customs. I heard the worst thing you can do to one of these dwarfs is touch their head. That true?" He reached over and playfully knuckled Trin's hair. Trin reared back and coiled in a Kung Fu snit.

"I'd watch that if I was you," said Broker.

"Aw, we know all about Gunga here. Sad story. He's come down in the world. Just a small-time smuggler and hotel pimp known to the police in Hue City. Had a little talk with them. Professional courtesy, you understand. And speaking of the police, Cyrus wants us to keep it friendly, no firearms, no rough stuff. Don't want to offend the Commies."

"We deal for Nina, is that it?" asked Broker.

Bevode sniffed and thumped his flat gut. "I'm hungry. You hungry? Hate to discuss business on an empty stomach. Tell Gunga to get us a cab."

"You tell him."

"I don't speaka da birdtalk."

"We can use the van," said Trin in icy English.

"No shit," said Bevode. "He talks American."

They followed Trin to the van and got in. "Where to?" asked Trin.

"How 'bout the hotel where you all were staying? They got a restaurant," said Bevode agreeably.

"You see that?" exclaimed Bevode. "There's a woman dropping her drawers and taking a dump right in that alley and she got black teeth. And these motherfuckers whipped the United States of America?" He shook his head and flung open the van door, pushed through a crowd of tourists in front of the hotel, and went in. Broker and Trin followed.

"That man makes me nostalgic for being a Viet Cong. Let's kill him and dump him in the Red River," hissed Trin.

"What about Nina?"

"Torture him first. He'll tell us where she is."

"Let me handle this, okay?" said Broker. They both stopped short in the lobby. Broker groaned. The giant drunken Aussie from Air Vietnam—shirt unbuttoned, barefoot, and with his fly unzipped—loomed in the entrance to the restaurant, eyeball to eyeball with Bevode Fret.

"What the fuck *is* your problem, boy?" implored Bevode, unable to pass around the besotted mountainous Australian. Deftly he inserted two fingers in the giant's nostrils, led him aside, and shoved him into a lounge chair. Showing his gap-toothed smile, Bevode summoned Broker and Trin to come on with an overhand gesture. Trin growled. Broker recalled that the Vietnamese used that particular motion to call animals; people were summoned with an underhand wave.

Bevode grinned at the Aussie, who was conversing with a member of the reception staff in hundred proof Down Under. "Thought for a minute that was one of my relatives," said Bevode, cool, showing them that he was not without humor. His muddy eyes rippled at Broker. "Speaking of relatives, I just come up shy one. You're going to have to answer for Cousin Willie."

They sat at the same table where Broker and Trin had breakfast with Nina. This time Broker didn't watch the street.

"What's good?" asked Bevode scanning the menu. "How about this? Three bowls of eel soup." He indicated an item to the waiter. "And some beer."

Trin spoke quickly to the waiter who scurried off.

Bevode studied the pair of chopsticks wrapped in a paper napkin beside his plate. He split the paper and picked one up, hefted it in his fingers, and twirled it like a miniature baton. "I heard," he said to Trin, "that at one point in your career you was a Commie. I seen in a movie where the Commies used to pound these things into little kids' ears." He squinted at the slender utensil. "Looks to me like it'd break . . ."

Trin squirmed in his chair, practically levitating. Broker put a hand on his arm. The beers arrived.

"Ah," sighed Bevode, taking a long sip. "That tastes good."

"How'd you find us?" said Broker.

"These people'd sell their mamma for the U.S. dollar. We spread some money around. Got your visas, port of entry, and your flight number. Easy. Now where were we?"

"Nina Pryce," said Broker.

"You understand I'm really doing you a favor taking her off your hands," said Bevode. "If we didn't have her, we'd have to tickle *your* gonads with a blowtorch. This way, if you don't tell us where the goddamn gold is, we just let my horny little brother fuck her till her nose bleeds. Then we use her to bait sharks. I kinda like to pop a shark now and then off the fantail of the *Lola*. Not much else to do since we're finding jack shit moving sand around by that helicopter wreck."

"Do tell," said Broker.

"Do the right thing, Broker. Just tell us where it is."

"Don't hurt that girl," warned Broker.

"No need. Just a little incentive to get negotiations going. Wow, man," said Bevode, "dig this. Eel soup. I always wanted some eel soup." The waiter expertly unloaded three steaming bowls of soup from his tray.

Bevode leaned forward and blew on the broth and inspected the ingredients. "All it needs is a few crawdaddys, eh." He picked up his chopsticks and carefully tucked them in the chest pocket of his safari jacket. Then he took up the large shoehorn-shaped spoon next to his bowl.

"Cyrus says it's a good idea to wipe down the flatware before eating. The sanitation department ain't exactly up to speed." Bevode lowered the spoon to his lap and began polishing it with the tablecloth. "You know, I told Cyrus not to trust Cousin Willie to track you down. Should have waited for me. I got there eventually. Found the county sheriff and deputies all over that swamp. Ole Jimmy Tuna's dead, Broker."

"What's to stop me from going to the local cops and blowing this thing wide open?" said Broker.

Bevode grinned, his hands busy with the tablecloth and spoon. Then he extended the spoon across the table and tipped it into Broker's soup.

The earlobe had been severed cleanly with something very sharp.

The silver and jade earring nestled in the bowl, in a swirl of noodles. The pale flap of skin attached to the jewelry was slightly sunburned. There were freckles on it. Beads of drying blood melted to crimson mist in the hot broth.

"You were saying?" said Bevode. He dug into his soup and began eating noisily.

Broker's stomach tightened. Sweat wormed on his upper lip. The wave of nausea piggybacked on a blind rage and rose to his sternum. He started to spring. A restraining forearm crossed Broker's chest like an iron bar. Trin's face was a study in napalmed ivory—two thousand years of perfect hatred.

Bevode appeared unconcerned. Between spoonfuls of the soup, he asked, "So where is it?"

"You touch her again," said Trin, "you all die."

"Go play in traffic," said Bevode, irritated. "I didn't come all around the world to talk so some itty-bitty yellow nigger." His lazy hazel eyes swung to Broker.

"You heard him," said Broker. Calm now.

Bevode shook his head and put down his spoon. "Looky here, goddammit. I got my faults. But my cokehead little brother—well, there's a word for guys like him. Slips my mind at the moment but basically he hates women, you understand. Something to do with him never fully accepting the idea that babies come from the same place he sticks his dick." He paused. "Won't be pretty."

Then he tipped the bowl up and scooped a last mouthful. "And if you go for the cops, we'll know. That's just another phone call. Cyrus is wired in tight with this crowd." He paused and pushed his bowl aside. "You, ah, going to finish your soup?" he asked.

Broker stared at him.

"Didn't think so." Bevode reached across the table and curled his knobby hand around the bowl and pulled it toward him. Casually he plucked the flap of flesh and the jewelry from the bowl and deposited it on the clean, starched white tablecloth in front of Broker. A tiny thread of blood dissolved in the spreading soup stain. Broker couldn't move. Boulders crowded his lungs. Lava spilled through his heart.

"Jesus Christ, you savage," said Bevode indignantly. "That's your girlfriend there. Least you can do is give her a fuckin' Christian burial."

Slowly, Broker folded the earlobe and the earring in his napkin and tucked it in his pocket.

Slurping, Bevode finished the soup and smacked his lips. "Not bad. I *might* even consider eating her pussy." He grinned. "After I cook it a little."

He stood up abruptly, fished his comb from his pocket, and ran it through his hair. He smoothed a hand over his ear. "Like I said. Take some time. Think it over on the train. Oh yeah, we know about that too. It's Tuesday. You got till noon the day after tomorrow. That'll be Thursday. We don't hear from you, we'll feed her to Virgil. We'll be in the Century Hotel in Hue . . . down upon the Perfume River," he sang, then winked. "Ring us up when you hit town."

Bevode Fret ambled from the restaurant and paused in the lobby at the chair where the Aussie was slouched, mouth open, head tipped, sound asleep. Very delicately he removed one of the chopsticks from his pocket and inserted it in the giant's upturned ear.

Then he gave it a casual shove with his open palm. The Aussie lurched and bellowed as his eyes popped open and his huge hands pawed at his ear. Smiling serenely, Bevode strolled away, unconcerned. The stunned doorman trembled and smiled and started to open the door. Bevode pushed him roughly aside, heaved open the door, and towered off into the crowd of Hanoians.

"I'm going to kill that guy," said Broker.

"No you're not," said Trin calmly.

60

BROKER BRACED HIS HIP AGAINST THE BUCKING WALL OF the lavatory and aimed a stream of urine at the blue enamel French pissoir set into the dirty linoleum floor. The train lurched and he hit his shoe.

He still had the piece of Nina's ear in his pocket. He had a headache. They were three hours out of Hanoi, traveling south on narrow-gauge prewar French track behind a Romanian locomotive.

The Australian tour from Air Vietnam was on board, having a party in the hall. Broker gathered that they had been to a snake village outside Hanoi that afternoon and had dined on cobra.

"Archie ate the fucking blood," crowed a feminine voice down the hall.

"Drank it. *With* a generous squirt of rice whiskey."

"Now he's virile."

"Poison dick."

Broker pushed through the revelers and eased into his compartment. Trin sat on one of the beds chatting in French with the young couple, Swiss backpackers, who shared the berth. The woman had a tour book open on her knees. Trin handed Broker a huge unlabeled bottle full of clear liquid.

"Snake wine, a gift from the Aussies," said Trin. "Go ahead. It'll help you sleep."

Broker took a slug of the concoction that tasted like fuel oil mixed with formaldehyde. A shadow fell across the compartment and the hulking Aussie filled the doorway. If his ear bothered him he didn't show it. Apparently snake wine and cobra blood had given him the gift of speech.

"Hi," he said in a sleazy high-pitched voice, plopping down on the bed across from the Swiss lady and oblivious to everyone else in the cramped space. He began pulling out a thick wad of dong, Australian currency and dollars. "I was wondering if I could buy Sheila here for the night?"

The young woman reddened and drew closer to her shocked companion. Trin exhaled. Broker took another slug of snake wine.

"You won't regret it," said the Aussie, leering. "I'm unforgettable. Whadya say . . ."

Broker reached over and cuffed him with the bottle on the ear that Bevode had pounded the chopstick in. "I think you better leave," he said.

Pain moved slowly through the dinosaur nerves. The Aussie vaguely tendered the ear with a massive left hand. "Who do you think you are?" he muttered.

"The Lone Ranger." Broker pointed to Trin. "This is my Indian companion, Tonto." Trin helpfully flicked out his gravity knife and smiled.

"Fuckin' Yank," mumbled the Aussie. He staggered to his feet and felt his way back into the hall where the party slowed down to a groan to mark his passage.

The Swiss couple thanked Broker and scurried out of sight into the upper berths. Trin and Broker sat, silent, rocking to the motion of the train. They passed the bottle back and forth. They lit cigarettes.

They'd been over it all for hours, waiting for the train. Broker said it again, "We have to involve the police."

"No. We get off at Quang Tri City, pick up the van, get some presents, and pay a visit to the militia post at Cua Viet. They'll be our reaction force."

Broker, gloomy captive to police methodology, made the routine assumption. "She could be dead already."

"No." Trin was obstinate. "She is part of the barter. We barter for the gold. I am good at bartering."

"Look, I can understand you wanting to keep this in your little circle of influence. But it's suddenly got pretty fuckin' serious."

Trin whispered. "The gold, Phil. If it's there, we can take some, hide it on the boat. It's Tuesday. We meet Cyrus at noon on Thursday—"

"You saw that guy. It's her life."

"It's my life too," Trin erupted. "You just fly in and create this . . .

situation in my life. You can fly away too. Americans are good at that. Making a big mess and then flying away. What about me? I'm stuck."

He stood up and furtively hacked the air with his hands. "Since the tourists I'm better off. In a good month with tips I can make three million dong. That's three hundred bucks. Usually it's more like two hundred. A bicycle cost thirty. Ordinary people make two million dong a year. Two hundred dollars. I lived like that, after I got out of the camp. Bartender. Laborer. Desk clerk. Dammit, Phil. I don't even own a car. This is my chance."

"We won't ditch her for the gold," Broker said emphatically.

"No. We do it all. We get some. We get her back. Get Cyrus arrested . . . we can do it. But if we go to the police—" Trin drew his finger across his throat.

Trin stood his ground in the rocking compartment, stubborn and desperate. Broker turned his head and gazed through the heavy screen on the open window into the inky Tonkinese night. He could barely hold the outline of the sadness that gripped him. Couldn't penetrate it. If he tried to picture her face and what she was going through right now he started to unravel. He ached from helpless anger. If they had gone to the MIA people she would be . . .

But he had to go with his hunch. Now he was chained to it.

"Okay," said Broker. Useless to talk. He rolled on his side and faced the compartment wall. Ghoulishly his hand crept to his pocket where the portion of Nina's ear and the earring made a tiny lump. Coil by sweaty coil the snake wine choked off the lurching light and he fell asleep to the clack of the wheels.

Broker never dreamed. Now, as he woke drenched in a cold sweat, shivering, he amended that truism.

Except in Vietnam.

He had dreamed that he and Nina and Ray Pryce and Jimmy Tuna were crossing a swift river on the back of a giant frog. Except Jimmy had the body of a scorpion. In midstream, Jimmy smiled and stung the frog and they all drowned.

He stared at his hands. His fingers itched and had broken out in a bubble of raspberry blisters. Fungus. Hadn't troubled him since 1975. Slowly he peeled the dirty bandages from his injured thumb. All but forgotten about it. Amazingly, the swelling had gone down. With a pink tickle, the stitched edges of the wound were healing. He took hydrogen peroxide and a fresh dressing from his bag and repaired the bandage.

He checked his watch. He'd slept almost nine hours. Be daylight soon. They must be getting close to the former DMZ.

The old neighborhood.

He was familiar with the slim waist of Vietnam that pinched between the Laotian mountains and the South China Sea: 60 kilometers across at its narrowest point. The Ben Hai River ran along the 17th Parallel; the old demarcation line that partitioned North and South Vietnam in the 1954 Geneva Accords. The Demilitarized Zone had buffered the river, 5 kilometers to the north and south.

Broker didn't know Saigon. He knew the province that lay below the DMZ. Quang Tri. Highway 1 linked the two main towns along the coastal plain, Dong Ha and Quang Tri City. West out of Dong Ha, Highway 9 ran the gauntlet of gory Marine firebases: Cam Lo, Camp Carroll, Ca Lu, the Rock Pile, and finally Khe Sanh. Hue City was 60 kilometers south on the highway from Quang Tri City, into the next province, Thua Thien. The large port city of Danang lay another 160 kilometers below Hue.

Quang Tri was poor and mean tough. It had lepers and bubonic plague and the temperature could hit 120 degrees in the summer. The red dirt had soaked up a lot of blood. It had been Vietnam's main killing ground for ten years. He remembered a paragraph in a guide book: seven thousand people had died digging for scrap metal in Quang Tri after the war ended. Mines. Unexploded ordnance . . .

And now Broker was back. To dig.

And his backup and main means of support lay sprawled on the opposite bunk with the empty bottle of rice wine between his knees. A book lay open on Trin's chest, *The Sorrow of War,* a novel by a disgruntled North Vietnamese veteran, a black-market English translation the Hanoi street kids hawked along with postcards.

He stared out the grated window. Steaming ground fog, hot as a kitchen stove, obscured the land. A sleepy porter trundled by the door pushing a cart. Broker croaked, "Cafe."

With a tall, almost clean, glass of thick black coffee he whipped his raw throat into shape with nicotine and watched the dawn come.

The land burned through the wet cotton mist. The ten shades of green furnace he remembered. Brilliant and still vaguely hostile, it hurt his eyes after the smoky, overpopulated inferno of Hanoi. He separated the green into shapes and marveled—not the blasted hills and craters of memory. Pine and eucalyptus trees, planted in orderly farm rows, as far as he could see. Rice fields wandering between them hemmed by dikes of rich red earth. Farmers, hoes on their shoulders, trickled into the fields.

A boy wearing a neat white shirt with a red scarf ran from a farmhouse, schoolbooks under his arm, and raced down the dirt path toward the tracks. Excited, he waved at the passing train. Broker almost smiled. So kids still did that someplace in the world.

The conductor leaned in the corridor, looking out a window. Broker fumbled in broken Vietnamese to inquire when they would cross the river that ran through the old DMZ. "Song Ben Hai khong adoi?"

The conductor pointed to his wristwatch and held up his hand, fingers spread, and said, "Five minutes," in English. He nodded to the south. "Quang Tri," he admonished solemnly. Broker leaned back and sipped his coffee.

They had planted a million pine trees in the DMZ.

The sun came up and the heat rolled over him like freeway traffic and left his bones as soggy as Cyrus's squashed cat. It was Quang Tri all right. The train chugged past a huge military cemetery and its long shadow rippled over thousands of square stone markers laid out in neat rows around a cement spire engraved with a red star.

He craned his neck, looking for reference points. He had operated on every foot of this red dirt along the train tracks between Dong Ha and the DMZ. But now, with things growing everywhere and all the new construction—the war wasn't just over: it was gone.

Except in America . . .

Broker shook Trin. "I'm lost," he said. "A sign just said Gio Linh and I can see a road that has to be Highway One. We must be coming up on Dong Ha but I don't recognize a thing. There's . . . houses." They crossed the Cam Lo River. A ticky-tacky patchwork of roofs and TV antennas everywhere. Places where he'd fought were now Vietnamese subdivisions.

Trin stared uncomprehending, crushed in the snake wine blues. He shrugged and grimaced and reached for a plastic liter of mineral water. He rinsed out his mouth, spit out the window, poured some water on his hands, and washed his face. Then he sat with his head in his hands.

Half an hour later the train stopped at Quang Tri City and they got off. A driver and another van was supposed to meet them. "Expect delays," said Trin with a weak smile. "He lives a few blocks away, we'll walk. Now we'll find out if we're being followed."

They strolled through a small lorry park and Broker saw that the boxy, thirties-style, French Renault buses were still in operation, painted bright blue and yellow. They continued on toward a small bustling open market. Several kids on bikes circled them, shouting, "Lien So."

Trin, hungover, grumbled, "They think you're a Russian."

Broker thumped his chest and said, "Co Van Mi," American adviser. The kids' hard faces broke into smiles.

"We called Russians 'Americans without dollars.' They were no fun," said Trin. He went on to explain how Quang Tri City had never recovered from 1972. Dong Ha had replaced it as the provincial capital. He stopped and pointed to four bullet- and artillery-ravaged walls. Saved as a memorial. "We call this the Lucky House," he shrugged. "The only thing left standing."

Broker gazed at the place where he'd been young. He didn't recognize it. Which was okay. He wasn't young anymore.

"You want to see where the citadel was?" asked Trin.

Broker shook his head. Looked around. "They can't use a white guy to tail us, not here," said Broker.

"More likely a Vietnamese, on a motor bike. Keep a sharp watch."

They turned down a side street past the market and Trin talked rapidly with a man who sat in the shade of his porch. Trin handed the man some money. "Our driver. I'm giving him the next two days off." Broker followed him in back of the house and they got in a gray van with Vietnam Hue Tours printed on the side.

"The van will draw attention," said Broker.

"But it will help us if we get stopped by some unfriendly militia, along with this." He tapped the travel itinerary folded in his chest pocket.

They drove to the congested market and got out. Trin marched ahead, happy at the prospect of spending Broker's money. He swaggered through the heaping stalls, yelling in Vietnamese. Broker stuffed a wad of dollars into his hand and, thus empowered, Trin seemed to grow several inches. They emerged from the market with three cases of Tiger beer, four cartons of Dunhill cigarettes, and a Polaroid camera and film. "Very important," said Trin about the camera. "You'll see." He held his index finger up in that disturbing grand gesture that now annoyed Broker.

"Before we head for the coast, there's a stop I want to make," said Trin abruptly. And Broker, with no leverage, realized that he was no longer the center of his own tragedy.

They got in the van and Trin drove north up Highway 1, toward Dong Ha. Out of their way.

Once desolate expanses of rice paddy had separated QTC from Dong Ha. Now the road was clogged with new brick buildings and worldspeak billboards: Soni, Samsung, Honda. The air was pure motorscooter exhaust. Only the red flags separated the scene from anywhere Developing World squalor. Glum, Broker held his tongue. Waited.

The road got wider, the buildings reached a three-story crescendo of pastel clutter. Trin stopped. "There," he pointed. Broker saw a vast children's playground behind a chain-link fence. Slides, swings, merry-go-rounds.

"Do you recognize where you are?" asked Trin. Broker shook his head. Trin grinned. "They built the playground on the site of my old regiment's base camp. We're at the intersection of Highway One and Highway Nine. The bridge and the river are right up there, next to the market."

Broker looked at a tall modernist structure of white concrete. The market. Dong Ha was unrecognizable, overrun with people, motorscooters, and houses. Trin made a U-turn and drove south, finally. Then he pulled a hard right and they were off, down a crowded street.

"Trin," said Broker irritably.

"This won't take long," said Trin. The road dipped and turned hilly. The homes were dense at first, wall to wall. Then they spread out, more expensive. And then Broker managed to orient himself, using their travel time from the corner of highways 1 and 9. He'd been this way before.

When Trin stopped the van and got out, Broker didn't know the place. Then he saw the stone griffin. Now it was upright, clean, the centerpiece of a carefully tended garden. Bonsai. The shapes of animals: an elephant, a deer, a lion.

The stone slab still guarded the door. And now the terraces and patios were meticulously landscaped with flowering bushes. The back of the estate was walled off and drenched in hanging vines. Broker couldn't see the small hill where the graves had been. A crushed gravel driveway meandered through the gardens and a gleaming black Toyota Land Cruiser was parked at the end of it. The letter A was prominent on the license plate.

Trin stood on his tiptoes and craned his neck. He called out in Vietnamese. Broker took his arm to lead him away.

"No," insisted Trin. "They are home. The car is here." He yelled again. There was movement on the patio, in the shade of a trellis dripping with flowers. A middle-aged man wearing gray slacks and a white shirt open at the throat stepped from the shadows. He held a newspaper in his hand. He put on sunglasses.

Trin barked at him and his musical native tongue now sounded like wooden blocks being pounded together by an angry child. This time Broker put a firm hand on Trin's arm and yanked him back.

The man on the patio responded curtly in a voice tired, but husky with authority. A lean woman in a dark pants suit joined him on the patio. She had wide cheeks and broad lips and beautiful jet-black hair. Even at a distance, Broker could feel the strike of her precise eyes. Two little Communist flags.

She made a dismissive, shooing underhanded gesture toward Trin. And went back in the house.

Now infuriated, Trin shouted and whipped a handful of American currency—Broker's unreturned change from the market—from his pocket and brandished it. The man waved his newspaper in a weary disgusted gesture and retreated inside the house.

Trin pulled away from Broker and started up the driveway. Broker was on him; from the corner of his eyes he saw people coming into the street. Trin yelled one last time, then spit on the money in his hand, and contemptuously flung it at the ground. Crumpled twenty-dollar bills, pocket change, and assorted pocket lint littered the driveway. Spent, he let Broker drag him back to the vehicle.

"Calm down, goddammit," seethed Broker. Trin sulked behind the wheel, turned the key, and drove quickly from the neighborhood.

"What was that all about?" Broker demanded.

"He's a pig," spat Trin. "They're both pigs. Big-shot Communists. He works in the customs office. She's the fucking mayor of Dong Ha. When I got out of the camps I discovered that the party had given them my house. I offered to pay if he would allow me to visit the graves."

"Trin, we have more important things to worry about." Broker's nerves were way past anxiety. He found himself riding shotgun with a time bomb of folly. He wondered if any Americans of a diplomatic stripe lived in Hue City, the nearest big town.

"I'll show him," muttered Trin with a fatal glow in his hot eyes.

They turned on Highway 1 and drove south, and Broker really began to worry. Could be worse than folly. A lot worse.

61

THEY WERE ABOUT A MILE SOUTH OF QUANG TRI CITY and Broker realized that he was looking for a bridge. A bridge that Jimmy Tuna had blown up twenty-three years ago. Trin slowed as he came up to another North Vietnamese Arlington on the right side of the highway. He pulled on to the shoulder and put the van in neutral.

Trin addressed his outburst in Dong Ha in roundabout fashion. "Look at this fancy cemetery. And these are only the northerners they couldn't identify to send home. The losers are not allowed cemeteries. We cannot look for our missing. Some of us cannot even visit our family graves. We all smile and say 'yes' but sometimes it gets very hard. Very hard," he repeated, gripping the steering wheel.

"Trin, Jesus," Broker ran his hand through his hair, "you have to control yourself."

"I will," said Trin, determined. "You saved my life that night in Hue. They were going to put me up against a wall."

"The militia? Do any of them speak English?" Broker asked gently.

Trin's eyes flashed. "I'm all right now, Phil. I can do this. I used to do things like this all the time." He closed his hand around the tiger tooth that hung around his neck and made a fist.

As Trin put the van in gear and pulled back onto the road his expression was carved in black teak. The worst possible thing had happened. He had lost face. In front of a foreigner. And, considering what Trin had been through, Broker could have accepted the mood swings in an ordinary man. But he wasn't willing to grant Trin the luxury of being ordinary.

But what if he was?

They drove on without speaking. Trin turned left before they came to Tuna's bridge and drove toward the coast on a gravel road. The cars, trucks, and hordes of motorbikes disappeared and they were in the countryside among more traditional traffic: water buffalo, bicycle, and foot.

The land now conformed more to the pictures in Broker's memory, except for the concrete struts of electric powerlines and telephone lines strung through the rice paddies. And the red flags hanging from the houses. They passed another cemetery with a bleached crop of stone under a red cement star.

Broker cranked down the window and turned off the air conditioning. "We won't have AC where we're going. I better get used to it." Trin nodded and opened his window.

The air was a swimming pool. The breeze was an itching pepper of red dust. Broker's determination to wear his sweat like a pro ran out his pores. He reached for an omnipresent liter of bottled water.

But Trin's spirits revived in the rice fields, away from the noisy highway. He worked a jigsaw on the dusty roads, weaving in and out of plodding farmers and school kids on bikes. Twice they stopped. To snack on bananas and then for some iced Huda beer. But really they paused to watch the traffic behind them. Two hours into the fields and farms Trin decided they were not being followed.

"Interesting," said Trin, more centered now. "Cyrus can't afford to trust even one Vietnamese."

Then he drove to a riverbank and they waited for a small car ferry powered by a sampan with dual outboards. Slowly they crossed the muddy river. On the other side they waited an hour. When no one else used the ferry they stopped looking over their shoulders and drove straight for the coast.

The country began to change: patchy white sand diluted the green palette of tree line and paddy and then the trees thinned out. The green and white gingham landscape became more solitary as the farmhouses and fields bordered in the reddish earth leaked away. They went by another stark grid of rectangular cement coffins guarded by a truncated pillar.

"Quang Tri," said Trin absently.

Through a veil of sweat, Broker saw thickets of traditional graves everywhere he looked. Mounded earth. Circular walls. Square walls. Painted, unpainted, weeded, unweeded. Even his unseen destination was a grave, lined with gold bars and Ray Pryce's bones. He wondered if the heat and the pressure had finally boiled away his rocky North Shore good sense. He was out here all alone in this foreign land with a tormented alcoholic for a guide. Jimmy Tuna's ghost held him captive and pointed the way. Nina's life rolled like dice.

He had crossed oceans and continents and now he wondered if he had blundered across the Buddhist frontier into a swarming landscape where the dead still cast shadows.

Quang Tri. More than bones were buried here. Empires.

And Broker, who didn't dream, except in Vietnam, reminded himself that he didn't believe in ghosts.

Except in Vietnam.

Come sundown, he mused, the Quang Tri night must draw a crowd; betel nut–chewing ghosts with big, knobby rice-paddy toes who squatted gook-fashion and haggled in their jabber talk; slim, elegant cosmopolitan city ghosts who conversed in French, or swore like legionnaires, and the Japanese and Mongol would–be conquerors and how many million Chinese grunts from the Middle Kingdom who made a one-way trip down here . . .

And the most recent members of the club, gangs of young rubbernecking American GIs who wandered through these graveyards whistling sixties' tunes. Dummies who never got the word about the Buddhist recycling program . . .

In from the sticks and utterly lost in the big city of death.

There were still occasional farms, set among meandering white furrows garnished with green.

"Sweet potatoes," explained Trin. "The only thing that really grows out here." He slowed and pointed. Two rusty teardrop-shaped projectiles lay by the side of the road, marked by a stick and strip of white cloth. Old mortar rounds.

They left the meager farms behind and entered rolling dunes patched with scrub, spindly willow trees. The desolation was interrupted only by the remnants of abandoned hamlets, their outlines softened by the shifting sand. And one more military cemetery—out all alone in the dunes.

"We're almost there. You can smell the sea," said Trin. And Broker saw it, a band of glittering blue green between the dunes. The dizzy relief of a breeze swayed the spindly willows.

"Now we walk," said Trin. They got out and Broker carried two of the beer cases. Trin hauled the other case, the smokes, and the camera. They plodded toward a red flag flying over the willows and came through the trees onto a sand beach. The sea blended placidly into a deceptively calm, baked–enamel blue sky. A buckled cement ramp poked from the sand, all that remained of the old Cua Viet Riverine base. Down the beach Broker saw a tall, new white lighthouse.

Two young men in tan shirts, brown trousers, and bare feet hailed Trin from the beach. He called back. One wore a wide-brimmed brown hat with a visor and had green epaulets on his shoulder and a red armband.

"Militia sergeant," said Trin. "He's a good guy."

Three more young soldiers were in the small headquarters tucked into the willows. On the way in Broker marked the radio cord draped from a field antennae that leaned, unsteady on its sloppy guide wires. Inside, Trin stacked the beer and handed over the cigarettes amid much deferential gab and more than a few bows.

The radio lead came in through a window and stopped. No radio. A stout, padlocked chest-high wooden bureau took up one whole wall. Maybe the radio was in there, with the guns. The militia had no apparent means of transportation besides their feet. Nobody was armed. Nobody seemed concerned. Maybe they weren't really soldiers. Maybe they just all bought their clothes at the same place.

The militia insisted they sit down for tea at a rickety table. Ho Chi Minh smiled down on them like a big-eyed alley cat from a calendar tacked to the wall. "The camera," said Trin. Broker took the camera from its cardboard box and fumbled in the heat. Sweaty fingers dripping on the instructions, he loaded the film.

All smiles, the militia straightened their tunics; one of them combed his hair; the sergeant struck a matinee idol pose. Broker hoped the camera worked.

"They *have* guns?" Broker wondered.

"Oh yes. AKs and grenades and one RPD machine gun," Trin assured him.

The camera worked. Broker continued to take pictures as more members of the militia platoon arrived. He handed over the sheets of film as they popped out. The militia boys clustered around, chatting happily as their pictures swam up from the chemistry. "Do they have a radio?" he asked.

"Yes. Locked up, with the guns."

Broker wondered if the Communist party trusted them with the key. "Do *we* have a radio? At the home?"

"No. We have a truck. We'll send somebody in the truck or the van, at the right time."

Broker clicked his teeth. They had pimples. They were kids. "What are you telling them?"

"Oh, just talk, about their families." Seeing Broker's consternation, Trin reassured him. "Don't worry. They've never been shot at before, so they'll be very eager. When we tell them that American pirates are stealing antiquities they'll be tigers."

"Antiquities?"

"Yes. There has been a big party campaign about foreigners taking our treasures, since eighty-nine."

Broker wasn't reassured. He sat in an isolation booth of language, with flies crawling on his fingers. Trin smiled. The militia smiled. Heat-induced paranoia scripted the casual conversation. *This dumb fucking American is going to show me where a fortune is buried on the beach. Some more dumb Americans have a big boat. The hole the treasure is in will be big enough to bury them all* . . .

When Trin's socializing was concluded, they left the camera and the last roll of film with the militia and walked back to the van. They backtracked up the sandy road and turned left and drove through the dunes.

"This is a long drive," said Broker after almost an hour bouncing on a rutted cow path.

"Not far," Trin minimized. "Five kilometers."

They turned again and headed back toward the sea. Trin stopped and pulled the emergency brake. "See. Not far." They left the van at the pylons of an unrepaired bridge and trudged the rest of the way, coming out of the willows onto a beach. Ribbons of breakers eased into a small cove. A decrepit fishing sampan was moored to a rickety dock, rocking gently in the surf. A baleful Chinese eye glared on the bow. A sail was furled to a boom off the mast.

"A sailboat?" Broker groaned.

"It has a motor," said Trin quickly. Immediately Broker went down to inspect the boat. He climbed over the gunwale and made a face. What looked like the rusty vertebrae of a mechanical dinosaur filled the stern of the boat. An automotive engine, off a Willis Jeep maybe, coupled to some kind of marine transmission with some kind of universal joint. A fifty-five-gallon drum served as the gas tank. He kicked it. Empty. The stirrups next to the motor were absent a battery. The boat was like the militia: unusable. He glanced at Trin dubiously.

"It runs," said Trin. Then he pointed to a whitewashed building that sat on higher ground among the willows. A different flag tossed from a pole in the sea breeze: red and blue with a yellow star. The first VC flag Broker had seen.

"He can make it run," said Trin. A scarecrow shadow in sweat-stained gray cotton separated from the shade of the porch. His left pant leg hung empty as he hobbled on a crutch down a lane between rows of vegetables. As they walked up the beach to meet him, Broker shielded the sun with his hand. The old man's skin was a mahogany shrivel over knotty muscle, his stringy gray hair was tied in a pigtail. His right eye gleamed like a Greek olive in a salad of scar tissue. A black patch covered his left eye.

"That's Trung Si, my old battalion sergeant major when I was in the Front. Welcome to Jimmy Tuna's home for down-and-out Viet Cong," said Trin with a sardonic hung-over grin.

62

TRIN INTRODUCED BROKER TO TRUNG SI, WHO WAS UNDER the initial impression that he was Jimmy Tuna, their benefactor. With that cleared up, the weathered cripple hopped off to a well and hauled up a net full of chilled beer bottles. Broker accepted a bottle. San Miguel. "Jimmy liked this beer," he said, making conversation.

Jimmy was dead.

"Yes," said Trin.

"Yes," said Trung Si.

Trin recounted how Jimmy had bought an old truck for the home. The rest of the men had driven it into Hue to have their artificial limbs reset. One man had stayed behind. A double amputee, legs gone above the knees, who remained inside, withdrawn, sitting on a sleeping platform. A set of artificial legs lay discarded on the floor by the bed. The man smiled politely when Trin introduced him and then looked away.

Back out on the porch, Broker said, "We need to get the boat running."

Trin scratched his head and seemed dazed by the sun. "It's too hard for the men to manage. They use little round wicker boats to fish."

"We aren't after fish."

"Yeah," said Trin. He barked to Trung Si, who barked back, and they had a heated discussion that Broker couldn't understand. In the end, the old man, bitching, and refusing Broker's offer of help, stalked off one-legged with a tool box, a battery, and a five-gallon tin of gasoline piled in a small wagon that he insisted on pulling all alone. His loud alien profanity carried up from the beach as he thumped down the dock. In a few minutes the engine coughed under a cloud of smoke. One by one the cylinders kicked in like fire-crackers. Trung Si threw off the lines and reversed the old boat into the cove. He piloted the tub in a circle.

"That thing won't take the sea," said Broker.

"No, it's a river boat," said Trin.

Trung Si made a dock landing, secured the boat, killed the engine, and jerked back up the beach, still swearing.

"What'd he say?" asked Broker.

"He says why fish when we have meat." Trin pointed to an old bolt action hunting rifle hanging from a peg on the wall. "They took the truck up north yesterday and got a deer in the hills. So we'll have venison tonight. Right now we should try to get some sleep. It's going to be a long night."

Broker didn't want to sleep. He wanted to keep busy. His eyes wandered up the beach, into the dunes. He'd never felt desolation like this. He didn't know what to call it. Nina's earlobe was a dry lump in the napkin in his pocket. Morbid. Didn't know what to do with it. Hang on to it until he saw her again.

"I know," said Trin gently. "You're worried about her. And you're worried about me. You're afraid to go to sleep because Trung Si and I might brain you with a skillet and take your map. There's a lot to worry about. Always."

"Don't like being this helpless," said Broker.

"We're not helpless. And she's tough. It doesn't do any good to dwell on it. We have what they want. Tonight we'll go find it." Trin paused and bit his lip. He cleared his throat. "I should have a look at that map, Phil."

Broker unzipped his security pouch and unfolded the worn laminated sheet. Trin placed it on a table on the porch and secured the edges with sea shells. "We're here," he pointed.

Broker tapped the grid square that he'd memorized. "We look for three old graves, with the curved walls."

"That puts it about four klics up the beach." Trin smiled. "That close. All these years. There's a road we can take most of the way that ends at an abandoned hamlet. Here." He pointed.

"We need a compass," said Broker.

"No problem," said Trin. "I'll line up the tools. You try to rest."

Broker looked up. Trung Si hovered over him. "You better let him look at your thumb," said Trin.

The old cripple untaped the slightly swollen, infected finger, rinsed it in rice whiskey and went back to his cook shack. He returned and applied a foul-smelling poultice and bandaged it tightly with adhesive.

"What is it?" Broker asked.

Trin shrugged. "I'm a city guy. Who knows what they do out here."

The home had one long room with a cook shack built off the back. A dozen sleeping platforms lined the walls, partitioned off for privacy. Broker lay on a hard plank platform across from the silent brooding amputee and couldn't sleep. At least the steady sea breeze fended off most of the flies. Nothing could dilute the rancid odor of years of accumulated nuoc mam sauce that smelled like dirty pussy. The dressing on his thumb itched and tingled.

Trung Si puttered and hummed in the kitchen. Trin swayed in a hammock on the porch—twelve-stepping it after his explosion in Dong Ha—drinking Pepsi-Cola from a can.

Sleep wouldn't come. Broker couldn't stop imagining, in great detail, all ways in which Nina could be dead, injured, debased, violated, and tortured. He had fifteen years of crime scenes to draw from. He didn't think restraint was part of Cyrus LaPorte's method of operation. Not with Bevode Fret for the hired help.

Mercy was not an option.

Basic desperation was a new sensation that he explored like a wild animal inspects its cage. He was stuck on this foreign spit of sand in the middle of nowhere with flies crawling over his skin. In the graveyard of the fucking iron elephants. He had lost initiative: now he was controlled by events. Cripples and barely trained kids for backup. A shipwreck named Trin for company.

The fixed eyes of the double amputee stared past him, through him, a brown study in dead ends. Broker fell asleep to escape the man's presence.

Broker woke with a start and didn't know where he was. He heard the chug of motors and faint voices. Fishing boats. A battered varnish face—the one-legged, one-eyed man loomed over him. "Nuc," said Trung Si. He made a scrubbing motion to his face with his hand. "Rua." His crutch banged a bucket of water at the foot of the platform.

Broker nodded, rolled off the plank bed, and squatted to the bucket. He stripped off his T-shirt and dashed water on his face. Something missing. The staring double amputee was gone.

Trung Si jerked energetically into the room with the pogo stick grace of a one-legged stork, both hands free, his crutch wedged in his armpit. He handed Broker a small glass bottle with a glass stopper. Broker opened the bottle and smelled moonshine, home-brewed million-proof rice whiskey. Then the old man pointed at Broker's trousers and raised his hand to the side of his head and tugged on his ear.

After several demonstrations Broker understood. Trin must have told him. He removed the napkin from his pocket. Trung Si unpacked the shriveling ear part and earring and cleaned off clinging bits of thread and dirt. Then he dropped the grisly memento into the glass jar, which he plugged tight. He set the bottle on a shelf.

Then he brought a charcoal brazier from the kitchen shack and set it on the table on the porch. He put a screen over it and laid out strips of meat.

"Trin?" asked Broker.

"Yes," said Trung Si, smiling, and going back to his kitchen. He hopped back with a tall glass of steaming black coffee.

"Where's Trin?" asked Broker, blanking out on even the simplest Vietnamese.

"Yes," said Trung Si, again smiling politely. He gave Broker the glass and pointed to the porch. Broker went out on the porch and sat down, lit a cigarette, and watched the afternoon shadows lengthen down the beach. A rattle of metal preceded Trin, who came around the corner of the house looking like the Tin Man in *The Wizard of Oz*, loaded down with a fuel oil lantern, a tin of fuel, two short shovels, a longer-handled shovel, two mattocks, a coil of rope, and two huge banging buckets.

Trung Si muttered something.

Trin held up one of the short snub-nosed shovels. An old surplus North Vietnamese army shovel. It was worn from use and the wooden handle had been shined smooth by sweat and callus. He laughed. "Trung Si says this shovel won the war."

They sat down to eat, picking strips of meat off the brazier and mixing it with rice and raw vegetables laced with cilantro and chopped chilies and garlic. Flies settled on the table. Trung Si grumbled and shooed them with his chopsticks. The slender sticks flicked; he shot out a hand and plucked a single fly from midair. He flashed a grin at Broker and tossed the crushed insect aside.

The sound startled Broker. At first, lulled by the surf, he thought it was the call of a loon. Then he located the source and saw the double amputee sitting on a dune up the beach, bent over a bamboo flute. His wide face shone in the muzzy light, fiery with music.

Trin smiled. "It is a very old song. For us."

The notes were a sinuous blend of pastoral and savage and Broker, who came from a place where old didn't really mean "old," asked, "How old?"

"Oh, a thousand years. It's a village song. A young man takes a wife but then he must go to the mountains to fight the invaders." The cripple's breath soared through the wooden flute like adrenaline in a fighting man's blood.

"Do you live here?" Broker asked.

"Sometimes. I have a room in Hue. A bed, a desk, a chair, and some books." Trin squinted in the failing light. "Don't worry. I'm good." He held up his Pepsi can as evidence.

Then it was time to go. Trin handed Broker a bucket packed with a tall Chinese Thermos, two flashlights, six liters of bottled water, and some kind of lunch wrapped in bamboo leaves. Trin picked up a similarly packed bucket. They both grabbed a shovel and a mattock.

"Compass," said Broker.

"In my pocket."

Trung Si took the hunting rifle off the peg on the wall and loaded it. Trin said, "We'll post Trung Si up the trail from the beach. If anybody comes he'll signal."

Trung Si shouldered his ancient rifle. The flute marched them through the long shadows as they walked up the sandy track to the van. Without speaking, Trin guided the van through the dunes keeping to a faint trail. He stopped twice to consult the map. The third time he stopped for good by the skeletons of abandoned houses, foundations, and one wall that framed a solitary window. "Trung Si waits here. Now we walk," he said. "It should be up there, in the willows."

Silently, Trung Si hobbled over to a block of cement sticking from an old foundation and sat down with his rifle. With their tools and loaded buckets Trin and Broker headed toward the slosh of breakers rolling on the beach. Except for the bang of tin on steel and the rhythm of the sea it was perfectly still.

"Are we walking on bombs?" asked Broker.

"Iron elephants," grinned Trin. "A whole herd of them sleeping below us."

Broker stopped and stared. Just ahead. Hundreds of raised rectangular stone markers slept in the wind-rippled dunes. The low walls of the military cemetery were irregular, slurred in the sand. The central monument was shorter, squatter than the others he'd seen. The sand and salt wind had eaten the color from the pitted stone star. It sparkled, a gritty molten ocher, in the rays of the dying sun.

He picked his way carefully through the field of stone and sand, and suddenly he stopped and cocked an ear at the vast silence. It occurred to him. He hadn't heard a single helicopter since he'd arrived in Vietnam.

They left the boneyard behind and walked up a slight rise, ankle deep in sand. Trin stopped, studied Jimmy Tuna's map and pointed. "There are your graves."

Just like Jimmy said. Three old graves. Gray and embroidered with moss and big around as wrestling rings. A masonry screen blocked the entry to each tomb. Inside the walls, a simple circular cairn of rock.

"Jimmy chose well," said Trin. Below the graves the beach tucked in a gentle sloped ravine for two hundred yards down to the waterline. The sea in front of them was quiet, shielded on either side by natural breakwaters.

You could see how it happened. The encircling arms of the cove would catch the eye from a helicopter, the inviting fold of the ravine, probably with higher walls twenty years ago. Drop the sling into the ravine, set the charges and drop several tons of sand over the load.

Pirate cove.

Broker walked around the screen and entered the center grave. Trin tossed him the compass. Broker shot his azimuth and extended his arm down the beach. "Eighty-two paces," he said. Trin took the long-handled shovel and Broker called out adjustments as he walked it off.

Trin stopped and thrust the shovel into the sand about fifty yards from the water's edge. He trudged back up the slope. "Now we wait for dark," said Trin.

They sat down in the shadow of the tombs and waited. Broker opened the Thermos from his bucket and poured a cup of coffee. Trin opened his Thermos. Broker steered it under his nose. Sniffed it.

"Hot tea," said Trin.

The desolation was deceptive. The surf breaking on either side of the cove sounded like a Superbowl crowd. He said, "Ray's down there."

"His bones are. They should be returned to his family." Trin rubbed his chin and looked around. "Do you think she'll talk?"

"She'd die first."

"Do you love her?"

"I came here with her. And that's crazy—"

"Love is yes or no," said Trin.

"I'm afraid to be in love with her," admitted Broker.

"I know what you mean. Once I bit into a chili pepper that was really hot. My wife said, 'But not as hot as me.'"

"I thought you were divorced?"

"We are used to long struggles in Vietnam," said Trin dramatically. "She has been very arrogant the last twenty years. But things are changing and I will come back into fashion."

Trin's grandiose words sounded like more folly. Broker leaned into the warm sand and sifted it through his fingers; dry damn featherbed where hundreds of unknown North Vietnamese soldiers slept with the iron elephants and stood sentinel over a cache of buried gold. Nina's life . . . trickling away through his fingers.

Sunset bronzed the sand dunes one last time and boiled the blue out of the sea. Dark soon. Broker cashed in his single chip of hope.

"We have one chance," he said. "Cyrus's wife."

Trin squinted. "Something you didn't tell me?"

"She may help us. She'd like to be a rich widow."

Trin grinned. "You have an agent in their camp."

"Maybe. She'll swing to whoever wins."

"God, this is so crazy." Trin's face glowed in the last sputter of sunset. "I've wanted to do something like this all my life."

He pulled the gold tiger tooth from his pocket and held it in both hands. Shoulders touching, they laughed and leaned forward. Down below, the long shadow of the shovel planted in the sand crept slowly toward the sea.

63

WHEN IT WAS DARK THEY RUBBED ON MOSQUITO REPELLENT, picked up their tools, and walked down to the beach. Like the flute player's march, the night was older here, blacker. Looking up, Broker did not know the stars. A steady breeze came off the sea.

Trin stamped a circle around the shovel and pulled it from the sand. A lopsided moon delineated their faces. Trin drove the shovel into the sand.

Broker hefted the mattock and gauged the ache in his taped thumb. He swung into the packed sand and grunted. He'd be all right.

Besides the sea, the only sounds were the thud of the mattock loosening the sand and the sigh of sand on steel as Trin's shovel moved it aside. When they had made a hole six feet in diameter they both worked on their knees with the short shovels. Sweat and sand made a sodden paste of Broker's T-shirt and their breath came in short, regular bursts. Giddy, Broker imagined a grown elephant frozen, tusks extended, in full rampant charge just below his feet. He calculated the circumference of a B-52 crater, about thirty feet across. *Poof.* A powder of crimson ash would sprinkle down on the South China Sea.

"Remember how Jimmy loved booby traps?" said Broker.

"Dig," said Trin.

After a while they passed a slippery water bottle and fell back, resting their dripping backs against the damp sand. Shoulder deep in the pit and bugs had started to find them. Trin reached up into his bucket and jammed a bundle of incense sticks into a shelf of sand. Lit them. The smoke sought them out and curled, tickling their drenched bodies and seeped into the dark.

Broker wondered if Mama Pryce was really down there, below his feet, and if he could read smoke after twenty years.

It was getting impossible for both of them to work in the pit. Trin stayed in the hole. Broker lowered a bucket on a rope and hauled out loads of sand. The hole was now six feet deep, narrower at the bottom. Trin had hacked a place for the lantern and looked like a copper cave dweller toiling in the weak light.

Exhausted, they took a break and staggered down to the sea and fell in. Back on the beach, they sat, gobbling the rice balls Trung Si had prepared for them as they dried off. Washed them down with bottled water.

"Beach could have shifted," said Broker. "It could be anywhere."

"Start another hole," said Trin.

They were getting slap-happy. But they started a second pit. It was close to midnight. They had been digging for almost four hours. An hour into the second site Trin decided to return to the first pit. Broker resumed hauling up the buckets.

Ludicrous. The waves breaking on the sand chanted, cynical—*Yo ho ho and a bottle of rum.* Broker dug on the desperate word of a dead man who his whole life had loved to play jokes. The veins had turned to acid wires in his arms, his tendons were yanking out of his joints; fingers were webbed, cramped, fusing together.

Trin had stopped digging and sprawled back on his haunches, arms dead at his sides. Spent. The pit angled now, back toward the three graves like evidence of slipping focus. The walls kept caving in. The lantern sputtered and died. Trin refilled it. Broker sprawled with his head hanging over the edge.

"I think we've had it," said Broker deliriously. Below him, Trin giggled. Broker pushed up on his elbows and rolled over and stared up at the stars. Low in the south he thought he saw the Southern Cross.

He'd always been a working-stiff existentialist. Attuned to the buttons and unbuttonings of the absurd. He and Sisyphus were asshole buddies. Digging up beaches, pushing boulders. Same same. Just keep moving it down the line. He fumbled for a cigarette. His cramped fingers snapped the fragile paper cylinder. Shreds of flying tobacco tickled his nose. His Zippo spun from his grasp and dropped into the pit.

Trin giggled louder. Broker heard the Zippo click open, heard Trin thumb the wheel. A flicker. Flame danced in the hole.

Broker hunched his head. Something flew out of the pit. It fell into the sand at his feet with a heavy thud. His hips and lower back protested, but he forced himself up. Carefully. His spine was a balancing act. A precarious stack of rocks. He crawled for the object. An oblong piece of wood. Dense. Intact, with screws in it.

"Huh?"

Trin giggled again.

Broker pawed for a flashlight and switched it on. He saw fragments of stenciled letters under a coating like a transparent tar-like substance, crusted with sand. Numbers: 155.

"Wha?" he muttered, pawing at the panel of wood.

"Ammo case. For artillery rounds. The wood looks like it's been treated with preservative. Creosote maybe," panted Trin. He giggled hysterically again.

Broker crawled furiously on all fours to the edge of the hole and squinted down his flashlight beam. Trin's eyes and teeth glowed in a mask of dirt and sweat. His right hand was snarled in metal that dazzled chrome-yellow in the electric light.

"It's gold!" shouted Trin. He tried to scramble up the walls of the pit, one hand extended with his fistful of trophies, the other trying to clamp a long, shallow sand-packed wooden box to his side.

Broker almost pitched in. Reaching, clawing at Trin's wrist. Exhaustion evaporated. Weight was nothing. He almost catapulted Trin and the crate into the air. They rolled over on the lip of the pit and laughed like boys. Up off all fours they danced on their knees as Trin waved his right hand under Broker's eyes. Dozens of gold circles dripped from the damp sand in his fingers. Hundreds more winked in the sandy box.

"What are they?" yelled Broker.

"Vietnamese credit cards," yelled Trin. "Gold rings!"

He pawed the sand in the ammo box. Everywhere his fingers moved the sand, metal gleamed. "Thousands of gold rings." He plucked out a thin sheet, then a wafer that looked like a yellow domino. "Leaves," he said. "Taels. There must be a hundred pounds of gold in this box!"

Suddenly Trin went rigid. "Listen," he hissed. They killed the flashlights. Broker strained his ears. Trin's eyes bulged. Mercury saucers in the dark. Instinctively they both hunched forward and absurdly threw their arms protectively around the heap of gold. A distinct, sharp clacking, above them, on the slope, by the graves. From a carefully stored inventory of nightmare sounds, Broker specified: the click of bamboo on bamboo. VC semaphore in the night.

Trin's chest heaved in relief. "Trung Si signaling. He's coming in."

Gingerly, they struggled up on rubber knees. The darkness shuffled above them and the old sergeant swung down the beach on his crutch. The hunting rifle was slung over his shoulder.

A moment of sheer paranoid panic that was as old as pirates and buried treasure and betrayal knifed Broker as Trung Si unlimbered the rifle. But the old man was just easing his back. Trung Si muttered to Trin.

Trin began to laugh and then he cupped his hand over his mouth. In a quiet controlled voice he said, "He could hear us yelling halfway to Quang Tri City. He says we should shut the fuck up. Sound carries out here."

Grumbling, Trung Si braced on his crutch and lowered himself to the edge of the pit. Carefully he laid the rifle and the crutch across his lap. He massaged his leg. Trin switched on his flashlight and played the beam across glitter at his feet.

Trung Si coughed and hawked a wad of phlegm. Then he put a cheroot-looking cigarette, rolled from raw homegrown tobacco, to his lips. He took a cheap plastic lighter from his tunic and lit the fag. He blew a stream of smoke and grumbled something.

"What?" asked Broker.

"It's a saying," said Trin. "You find gold, you pay with blood."

"Back home we call that a curse," said Broker. The intoxication had subsided. He squatted and sifted his fingers through the golden trinkets. "Rings?"

"People don't trust banks or currency; those rings are the basic denomination. Easy to carry. We don't deal in dong for big items, it's too clumsy. A television set is, say, eight gold rings." He picked up the tael. "Ten gold rings."

"That's today," said Broker. "The stuff we're looking for was buried twenty years ago." Broker shook his head. "This isn't it."

"So? It's loot. A lot of robbery took place on the roads when the war ended. It's gold," protested Trin. "That's only one box. There's lots more . . . stacks."

"The pieces I saw were bigger."

"You saw?"

"Yeah, at Cyrus's house in New Orleans."

"You never told me—" Trin moved closer.

"I'm telling you now. A lot bigger, about six, seven pounds, with Chinese writing on them."

Trin seized Broker's elbow. "Writing?" The flashlight illuminated their faces from below, pocketing their features. Halloween masks.

"Chinese characters, you know . . ." Broker made a tangled ideogram with his finger in the dark.

"Fuck me dead," gasped Trin in perfect sixties slang. He leaped back into the pit.

64

TRIN'S VOICE RODE A HYSTERICAL BATSHIT VIETNAMESE bobsled down in the pit. The silica flew. Above ground, Trung Si totally lost his phlegmatic peasant reserve. He scrambled to his foot and his crutch and, despite his earlier cautions about keeping it quiet, jabbered in the night.

Broker was double lost. Strange land. Strange tongue. Stuck in the dark with crazy people. One of whom was armed. He strobed his flashlight back and forth between the pit and the agitated old man who now had gone peg-leg wild and was stumping in the sand, swinging the rifle at the ready in all directions.

Trin's shovel hacked with manic energy at sodden wood and sand. Crazy man here, chopping down a beach. The sound carried hollowly up from the pit. His excited voice exceeded all previous pitch, close now to the tonal frenzy of the flute player's music.

In a stab of light Trung Si dropped his rifle and waved his arms, covering his face, warning Broker. Objects flew out of the hole, thick, oblong. One. Two. Trin's voice maxed out on a triumphant fever shriek. Broker stepped back as another dark shape lobbed through the dark.

Panting, greased with sweat and dirt, Trin scrambled up from the hole. Trung Si had plopped back down on the sand and yelled, crawling one-legged, collecting the three sand-gummed ingots that Trin had thrown from the pit. Trin yanked him upright and arm in arm, clutching the heavy bars, they did a three-legged race down to the edge of the sea. Broker followed them as their electric torches swung like giddy miniature searchlights. They continued to rave as they collapsed in the water and scrubbed at the ingots. Then they crabbed their way to the edge of the surf.

Kneeling in the wet sand, Broker shook them by the shoulders. Trin went down on all fours. He lined the three ingots up in a row in the soft smooth sand and bent, his flashlight held over them like a caricature of Sherlock Holmes with his magnifying glass. Trung Si protested and picked up the center bar, moved the left one in and put the bar down at the end of the row. Broker gathered that they were arguing about an ordering sequence.

"Speak English, goddammit!" he shouted.

Like an Asian Laurel and Hardy, Trin and Trung Si comically hushed their voices. Trin rocked back on his heels and grinned. "French would be more appropriate," he crowed in a whisper.

"That's them," said Broker, pointing at the ingots. Both flashlight beams now pinned the yellow rectangles to the inky sand. The indestructible sheen of gold perfectly complemented the desperate night. Gleaming, wrapped in soft ribbons of surf and nervous muscular brown hands sluiced by sea water, the ingots were about seven inches long, three to four inches wide and more than an inch thick. A panel was stamped in a decorative border with stacked Chinese characters, three on two of the ingots, four on the third.

Trin shook himself, fell on his back and fluttered a hand on his chest. "It's too big for me," he said.

"It's gold, like I told you," said Broker.

"It's not just gold," said Trin in wonder.

"Okay, it's old Chinese gold," said Broker.

Trin jackknifed up into a sitting position, pounded the sand with his fist and declared, "Not Chinese. Ours!"

Broker, weary of dramatic outbursts, got up. "I'm going back to the hole to get some coffee and my cigarettes. You calm down."

Trin and Trung Si commenced a brusque debate in Vietnamese. Broker helped Trung Si return to the pit and reunited him with his crutch and his rifle. Muttering to himself, the old man hobbled back up the slope and disappeared into the dark. Broker then returned to the beach. He poured a cup of coffee and tried to take its comfort. He faced Trin. They sat cross-legged, the ingots between them.

In the distance they heard an engine start. The van.

"What's going on? Can that old guy drive?" asked Broker.

"He uses the crutch on the clutch, he's fine. Phil—he's going for the boat," said Trin in a grim voice.

"So we're going to do it," said Broker.

"How many boxes should we take? Ten? Fifteen?"

"As many as we can. How many are there?"

"A lot."

They lowered their eyes. No flashlights. The metal picked up a faint iridescence from the moon, pecked by tiny points of starlight. Like the moving lines of surf.

Calm now, Trin composed himself. "That hole is a lot deeper than you think," he said. He tapped the first ingot. "Gia Long, third year, eighteen oh-three." His finger moved to the second bar. "Minh Mang, fifth year, eighteen twenty-five." The third. "Tu Duc, tenth year, eighteen fifty-eight."

"Emperors," said Broker slowly as he recognized the names and placed them in context. A shuttle of magic moved in the night. Hemming them in. His skin shrunk two sizes and prickled and cinched around the testicles. "No shit!"

"No shit. This wasn't stolen from a bank. It isn't just . . . money. This is Imperial gold. Part of the treasure of the Nguyen emperors. No one has seen gold like this for over a hundred years except in a museum in Paris."

"Goddamn, Trin. I thought the French took it all . . ."

Trin nodded. "When they looted the Hue Citadel in eighteen eighty-five. Looks like they missed some." Trin shook his head. His hands groped the air. "You see. It's . . . big." He clicked his teeth. "Bigger than us."

"Real treasure," said Broker, now understanding Cyrus's morbid obsession. And he saw how, in his fractured way, Jimmy Tuna was making his amends.

"If they knew about this in nineteen seventy-five Hanoi would have parked a division of tanks on it," said Trin slowly.

"Okay," Broker blurted. "Jimmy and Cyrus found the stuff and got it as far the bank. They phonied it up as a pallet of ammo. It just sat there after Hue fell."

Trin exhaled. "God, I probably walked by it a dozen times myself. Just sat there for over a month?"

"Fuck, man, I don't know. Ask Cyrus."

Trin struggled to his feet. Broker joined him. They wobbled, supporting each other.

"So," said Broker.

"So, we have to keep Highway One open for one more day." Trin's voice threw a resonating thespian echo down the empty beach. "We just get Nina away from Cyrus and then draw Cyrus here and call the militia when he's digging it up." It was three in the morning. The plan had the teeth of a butterfly assault on Mount Rushmore.

"That's all," said Broker, reeling. They both had the gold delirium tremens.

"C'mon. We've got to haul some boxes down to the water. And they're heavy. Then we have to fill in that hole," said Trin. "And meet Cyrus at noon in Hue. And not tell anybody else."

"Trung Si knows," said Broker.

Trin wearily brushed sand from his shirt. "Trung Si will keep his mouth shut. He's more worried about the curse of found gold."

"Once we load the boat, where we going to hide it?"

Trin shrugged. "Let Trung Si worry about that. He was a guerrilla all his life. He's hid stuff from the Japanese, the French, the Americans . . ."

Arm in arm, they staggered back up the beach.

65

TRIN'S LATEST MOOD SWING TOOK HIM, TARZAN FASHION, clear across his personal jungle. When he spoke to Trung Si and Broker as they loaded the gold, he sounded just a little bit like he was talking to more than two people. Like maybe he caught glimmers of his entire old VC battalion lined up there on the beach. And this weird light came in his eye, like he was communing with the whole mystic Vietnamese nation: living, dead, and unborn. All convened there by the sea, as numerous and without end as the faded stars.

It was just a little weird, and maybe it was just being balls-out exhausted, but it put Broker a tad on edge. Not that he could tell for sure in the shape he was in. Working like maniacs, they had filled in the pit.

It was midmorning when they finally got underway to the hallucinatory Rube Goldberg thump and fart of the improbable sampan motor. They slumped on the smelly deck. They had loaded thirteen heavy crates into the boat, using a winch that Trung Si had rigged from the mast. Now the old peasant sat at the tiller, his pigtail snapping in the wind, a cheroot clamped in his teeth throwing sparks, his one eye fixed off the bow.

It might work if they could get Nina clear. And Lola was the only hope of that. On the other hand, they'd just found ten tons of gold. They weren't thinking that clearly. Broker tried to hold the plan in his head. The militia post was a good hour's drive on a bad road. No telephones. And once they involved those guys it could get, like Nina had said, hairy. A bunch of teenage farmboys let loose with automatic weapons.

Broker had one ingot in a burlap sack along with the top to the first ammo box Trin had dug up. Chips. To bargain for Nina.

They unloaded the first box they found, the one with rings, gold leaf, and taels, at the vet's home. Trin told Broker and Trung Si, with that faraway look in his eye, that the stuff in the pit belonged to the People of Vietnam, and the People of Vietnam would not begrudge them setting aside an additional hundred pounds of gold rings for their trouble.

Then Trung Si chugged off to hide the boat and their piece of the treasure. They cleaned up, sort of, washing in the sea, pulling on a change of clothing. Tripping with fatigue, they got in the van and headed for Hue City. They left the treasure of the Nguyen emperors in the keeping of a one-legged, half-blind, ex–Viet Cong peasant sergeant who had one old French bolt-action rifle and eight rounds of ammunition. And an uncommunicative, legless flute player. The rest of Trin's vets still had not returned with the truck.

Trin sped down the sandy track looking out at the dunes. He grumbled, "I knew we should have buried some weapons out there, in Vietnam it just makes sense to have some weapons buried out there . . ."

Then Trin launched into an impromptu discussion of Trung Si's curse. Dramatically, he thrust the tiger tooth under Broker's nose. "It's like your native Indians. Except with us it's the Chams. In the fifteenth century we conquered and annihilated them, our Manifest Destiny. The March to the South.

"One of my ancestors rode an elephant through the Emperor's Gate in the Hai Van Pass on that invasion. He brought this tooth back among his booty. The gold in Vietnam was mined in Champa, south of Danang. Still is. So if you find gold it's probably Cham gold. Therefore cursed with their blood."

Broker shrugged, he was way past curses. And things like reasonable doubt and probable cause, not to mention consequences. They were inappropriate Western concepts anyway. His dad always said he didn't have the sense that God gave a goose, so he wasn't particularly afraid. He liked the . . . velocity.

Trin, who probably had acquired the wisdom in middle age to be afraid and who had probably waltzed, a few times, with little green men on various bar counters, hunched over with his eyes level with the top of the wheel like a ninth-grader, elbows raised and driving sixty, sometimes seventy, miles an hour, sending bicycles and water buffaloes scurrying toward the ditch.

They sped through Quang Tri City. In the market, the sun ricocheted off a thousand conical straw hats and pounded platinum knitting needles into the raw sun spots Broker had on loan for eyes. He had never been so tired in his whole life. He had ten tons of gold on one shoulder and Nina Pryce's life on the other.

Trin looked just as crushed and Broker hoped he was carrying the same load but he wasn't 100 percent sure. Not even close. And for today's work they needed 120 percent.

Trin skidded onto Highway 1 and aimed the van south, toward Hue City, down the center of the road, and stepped on the gas. He did not budge for anything on wheels.

"You got any speed?" asked Broker.

"All out," said Trin.

They turned and grinned at each other. They had always been unsuited for ordinary life. They were probably rushing headlong toward doom.

They were probably happy.

Broker must have fallen asleep with his eyes wide open because suddenly a huge Tiger Beer billboard leaped in the windshield and Trin swerved left. Vaguely he noticed the dusty russet limestone walls of the Imperial Citadel rise across a muddy lotus-choked moat. Different now, masked by new houses.

> Hue. The Nguyen emperors had made it their Imperial capital for a hundred and fifty years. Had to be here to understand the romance of the city and the war. A feudal castle, the hills upriver studded with Imperial tombs.
>
> The Perfume River divided the town. The citadel complex took up the left bank; moated and surrounded by thick ramparts it contained the Forbidden City, the palaces and offices of the mandarins. Across the river, the right bank housed the Colonial facade of the old French administration, universities, and medical schools. A college town, a cultural icon: everyone had thought that the city was untouchable. In the late afternoons flocks of schoolgirls in their flowing white au dais rode their bicycles down Le Loi Street past the old French buildings. In 1968 the Communists chose it for their most dramatic battleground: Tet.

Broker blinked back the reverie when he saw a red flag the size of a fucking basketball court flutter from the citadel's famous flag tower.

> Trin's battalion died on that tower during Tet, left behind to burn in the bombs. That's when Trin quit the revolution. And when he discovered that the Communists had rounded up three thousand of Hue's intellectuals and officials, and their fami-

lies, including his own father and mother, and marched them into the jungle. Beat them to death with shovels after forcing them to dig their own graves.

My Lai had been worth a Pulitzer. The Hue massacre never made the front pages.

It was 11:30 A.M.

Trin turned again. An exuberant cluster of hammers and sickles burst on another billboard. Happy Worker, Happy Soldier, Happy Student, Happy Farmer. Oh boy.

They roared across the bridge toward the right bank. Trin pointed to a floating restaurant. "Cafard," he said. Their old hangout. Used to be on the shore. Now on the water. Where Broker hid in the cellar. They ran the stoplight on the other side, whipped another right onto Le Loi Street. Trin scattered bicycles and leaned on his horn. Little pops of recognition struggled in the swampy fatigue behind Broker's eyes. Colonial gingerbread along riverfront. The grassy promenade along the river. A monument to Annamite troops who served in World War I. That's where he and Trin had hid on that rainy night twenty years ago and took their swim in the river. Now stands were set up and women were selling stuffed animals, videos, postcards.

They pulled through a gate and stopped amid the carefully tended gardens of a Colonial monstrosity. Trin smiled. "Five Le Loi. The last stop on Jimmy Tuna's itinerary. C'mon."

Smiling, they confirmed reservations. Broker handed over his passport and for fifty bucks, U.S., Trin got it right back. No sense letting the cops know they were in town. They were led to the single round room on the third floor. Broker tipped the bellboy who had nothing to carry and sat on the bed and stared at the phone. It was 11:49.

His numb filthy fingers pawed his wallet from his jeans and smeared the snowy white card Lola LaPorte had given him in New Orleans a million years ago. He dialed the switchboard at the Century Hotel. Trin opened the icebox and found it stocked with Huda beers. He tossed one to Broker.

"Connect me to the Imperial Room," said Broker.

He opened the can and took a swig and didn't miss a beat when the cool, husky voice of Lola LaPorte came on the line like magic.

"Hi, Morticia, kiss any alligators lately?"

"It's him," she said, aside. Then, directly into the receiver, "Where are you?"

"Wherever it is it's hotter'n shit and they go in for really big red flags with yellow stars."

"I'm looking at the same flag." She paused. "Broker, we had to detain Nina. We didn't know what you were up to. She's . . . all right."

"Sure she is."

"Okay. Bevode got carried away as usual. Cyrus has apologized to her and even discussed plastic surgery. She's here. Okay."

"At the hotel?"

"In Hue."

"Where's Bevode?"

"Cyrus thought it would be a good idea to keep you and him separated so he sent him . . . away. On the boat. You'll be dealing with us."

"Uh-huh."

"Do you have anything to tell us?" She sounded like she was holding her breath.

"Tell Cyrus I got something with sand on it, not salt water."

"He says he found it," she said, offstage again. Her voice was like being on the beach again, Pandora's box springing open: imprisoned Cham curses fluttering out like monarch butterflies.

Cyrus LaPorte came on the line, breathless with excitement. "Just what have you got?"

"Ming Mang's mad money, in a hole in the sand on the beach," said Broker.

"How?" Incredulous.

"Easy, we followed the map."

"What map?"

"The one we got from Jimmy, dummy," said Broker.

"You didn't need to kill those boys," Cyrus said hotly. "I don't buy this story the Wisconsin cops put out. Jimmy Tuna in his last gasp nails two men."

Broker yawned. "Fuck you, Cyrus. You should have stayed home."

"He's dead, Jimmy, the cancer got him," said Cyrus.

"Yeah, well. Look, we have to work out some ground rules," said Broker. "I want to see Nina, then you can have a look."

"When?"

"Thirty minutes."

"Jesus. Where?"

"Right under that big red flag across the river. Bring Nina. And bring a shopping bag. We'll do a switch." Broker hung up the phone. He didn't like not knowing where Bevode Fret was.

"Now . . ." said Trin, intently inspecting the pop top in his beer can.

"It all depends on Lola LaPorte. If she won't give up Nina, we're screwed. Cyrus'll probably try an approach, to feel us out," said Broker.

"Try and split us up."

"Yeah," Broker squinted, "try to get you to betray me."

Trin smiled. He looked like a Vietnamese Dead End Kid with a partially washed face. But it was still an exquisite Vietnamese smile that masked Vietnamese thoughts and it didn't reassure Broker one bit.

The Imperial Citadel was overrun with foreign devils. French, Germans, Aussies, Kiwis, Americans, Canadians: unloading from vans like retarded, wrinkled children in Bermuda shorts and herded by tour guide terriers. Mostly they headed through the gate to the Forbidden City. The direction Broker and Trin took smelled like shit. Someone had taken a dump next to the paved ramp that led to the flag tower. A squalor of pop cans and paper wrappers fouled the patchy grass. Trin handed him a blue baseball cap with Hue Tours printed on the crown and pointed to the sun. A fresh wave of sweat streaked the dirt on Broker's arms. They'd done a poor job cleaning up. How many other things had they overlooked in their condition?

What was probably the only rental Mercedes in Hue City screeched to a halt perpendicular to the ramp. A blue van almost rear-ended it.

Trin and Broker started down the ramp. A rangy six-foot-two redneck in an absurd Save the Whales T-shirt got out from the sliding side door of the van. He could have been the tourist who had snatched Nina in Hanoi. With the help of another guy inside he held Nina Pryce up in the door. A white dot of tape marked her left ear. She was dressed in the same jeans and white blouse she'd worn in Hanoi. Save the Whales had to brace her shoulders to keep her upright. Cadaver pale in the bright sunlight, she stared ahead unblinking. Her hair was wet-cat damp and stuck to her temples, like someone had run a clumsy comb through it.

"A look," cautioned Save the Whales. He had turpentine eyes under a painter's cap, flat muscles, and the golden hair on his corded forearms looked like wood shavings. He raised a hand.

"She's drugged." Broker started to come closer.

"Better'n tying her up. She's feisty, this one."

Nina swooned on rubbery legs and tried to open her mouth. Broker wondered if she recognized him. Save the Whales eased her back in the van, got in himself, and closed the door. The van backed up, lurched, and accelerated. A chalky arm poked from the driver's side, middle finger extended. Fuckin' Virgil.

The passenger door on the Mercedes swung open. One smooth beige fashion model leg swung out, then the other. Lola popped from the gleaming German metal. An American Beauty thorn.

Okay. Bevode Fret was nowhere in sight.

"Remember Madame Nhu? That's her big sister," Broker said. "They'll sell out anybody, including each other. A real happy couple."

They exchanged grim smiles. All they had was sheer bluff. It all depended on Lola. The main thing was Nina was still alive. "You go off with Cyrus and talk business. Get me alone with her," said Trin.

Broker didn't like it. Trin strutted the Imperial grounds as though *he* was planning to ride an elephant into Champa. But it was happening.

Lola looked cool and poolside in her long dark hair and a white cotton skirt, blouse, and a broad straw sunhat. Sunglasses hid her eyes. She raised a big shopping bag in her left hand. Cyrus, tanned to perfection and wearing a blue yachting cap, a desert shirt and a rakish red bandanna around his throat, emerged from behind the wheel.

They came up the ramp. Matching black sunglasses gave their smiling faces a shiny praying mantis warmth.

"Goddamn, Trin. How you been, boy?" Cyrus, always smooth, extended a leathery hand.

"Watch your step, Cyrus." Trin sniffed, pointing to the side of the walkway. "Don't step in the shit." So much for old home week.

"Same old Trin, suckled by a tarantula. Lola, honey, this is the famous Nguyen Van Trin I've told you so much about." Trin and Lola merely stared at each other. "How you doing, partner?" Cyrus aimed his hand at Broker.

"I told you not to come," said Broker, refusing the handshake.

Cyrus withdrew the hand and cocked his head. "Be a realist. We knew you'd find it for us. Now it can only end one way . . ."

Broker's bloodshot eyes snapped on Lola.

"Let's hear it, Broker," she said, tipping her sunglasses down on her nose and revealing her champagne eyes. "This is turning out to be . . . exhausting."

Broker hefted the heavy bag in his right hand and said, "Let's walk." He turned and led then up the limestone ramp and stopped at a parapet that overlooked a strip of grass, the moat, a grassy park, and the street along the river. Some kids kicked a soccer ball directly below them.

"If I remember right, the Nguyen emperors used to stage exhibition fights in that pagoda," said Cyrus, leaning his heavy forearms on the parapet. "Tigers against elephants. Fixed fights. They declawed the tigers." He grinned. "How about we put you and Bevode in there." He turned to his wife. "You'd probably get off on that."

"I don't particularly like to see men fight, but then, I've never really seen them do anything else," she replied in a bored voice.

Broker reached into his bag, withdrew the ingot, and slapped it, blazing in the sun, down on the parapet wall.

"Holy God, son, not out here." Cyrus covered the bar with his hands and stirred nervously, looking around. The shadow of the huge flag rippled his arid features.

"Why not? It came from here," said Broker as he slid the bar back in the bag.

Cyrus cleared his throat and wrung his hands. "Ah, Lola, why don't you and Trin take a little walk and let me and Phil talk some business."

Trin smiled his exquisite smile. With a cynical dapper bow that was in extreme contrast to his shabby clothing, he extended his hand, guiding the way. Lola grinned and they sauntered off down the wall. Smiles all around. A convention of pirate flags.

Cyrus wheeled and grabbed Broker by the arm. "I don't know, son. Trin on the play."

"Jimmy found him."

"I wouldn't trust the fucker." Cyrus squinted. "He has a history of changing sides."

Broker roughly removed Cyrus's hand. "I'll worry about Trin."

"Do that," said Cyrus. "So, talk."

"You give us Nina. Nina stays with Trin, out of the way. I take you to the gold. We get a tenth. Finder's fee."

"The girl will talk," said Cyrus, shaking his head.

"Best I can do. Take it or leave it."

"How long's your visa good for, Phil?"

"What?"

"Twenty days, thirty at most. Then they'll throw you out of the country. I'll still be here." Cyrus smiled. "And so will Trin."

Broker needed some kind of edge. And fast. He leaned over the rampart and called down to the kids playing below, "Hey!"

They skidded on the grass and looked up. Broker's hand came out of the sack and heaved the ingot over their heads. It glittered, turning end over end and went slurp in the moat. Bull's-eye in a puddle of lotus and lily pads.

"Jesus," LaPorte gasped.

Broker stepped in close and snatched Cyrus LaPorte's left earlobe and twisted. "Jimmy told me in great detail all about that night. Nina's the only thing keeping you alive, old man." He released his hold. LaPorte staggered back, massaging his ear.

"Think about it," admonished Broker as he brought the piece of ammo box lid out of his bag and slapped it into Cyrus's stomach with a loud whack. "Meet me again. Tonight. Cafard's still there, on the river. Seven o'clock." He grinned. "For old times' sake."

Then he swept up the shopping bag Lola had left and walked away, motioning to Trin to join him.

"How did it go?" Trin asked.

"I played crazy. I'm meeting him at Cafard's at seven for another round. It don't look good." As they descended the ramp he opened Lola's bag. It contained a gray T-shirt with the slogan Good Morning, Vietnam printed across a red Communist flag.

"Nice touch," said Trin, inspecting the shirt. "She's . . . big." He sighed thoughtfully. "Screwing an American woman must be like separating a pile of bacon that's been left out in the sun." He curdled his lips. "Sticky."

"You must have had a great conversation."

Trin nodded. "I told her about my life-long ambition to open a big combination liquor and video store in Los Angeles."

"What'd she say?"

"She knows where Nina is. She asked, if she helps us free Nina and runs from Cyrus, will we take care of her. I told her yes. She left a note in the bag on the shirt receipt."

"Keep walking," said Broker.

66

"IT'S A TRAP," SAID BROKER.

"Of course it's a trap, but what kind of trap?" said Trin, who had once been a connoisseur of traps and was now a guzzler of Huda beer. He tapped the hurried, scrawled note: "My Thong Kiet Villa, 21 My Thong. Rm 102. I take her a meal, 8 or 9. Try to get guards to break for supper. Get me out of here. When Bevode back. We're all dead."

"We're" was underlined.

"I know that street. It's secluded."

The note lay on the cramped table between Broker's tonic water and Trin's beer. They'd stopped near the Citadel Gate to eat in a restaurant that looked like a garage with the door pulled up. A tiny fan was screwed to the wall and moved the heat around like a toy airplane propeller.

A cat so emaciated that it had to be HIV positive dragged a huge, fat, dead rat across the dirty floor. Broker sat up. He had seen that cat and that rat before. Their great, great grandfathers . . .

He looked around. "This is the pancake place. We used to come here in seventy-two," he said.

Trin smiled. "The same. Still the best banh khoai in Hue." Broker ate four of the pleasure cakes with rice, chili peppers, garlic, and raw vegetables, some of which he could identify. The peanut sauce he did remember. He pushed his plate away and felt stronger.

Trin's second beer arrived and he said, "Since we could both be dead tonight it's time to tell me everything." He leaned across the table. "Nina is after more than just having the militia arrest Cyrus for stealing antiquities, correct?"

Broker nodded. "Remember that cigarette case Ray had? Jimmy says Ray made Cyrus put the order to go after the gold and ditch us in writing. And sign it. Ray put it in the case. Ray's under the pallet with the orders that can implicate Cyrus. Cyrus still thinks Ray is on the bottom of the ocean."

"What fate would Nina like for Cyrus?" Trin asked solemnly.

The beer talking. Pumping up his grandiose bent. Broker exhaled. "She wants him tried by the U.S. military for murdering her father."

"More likely he'll wind up in a Vietnamese prison."

"I think she has her heart set on Leavenworth Penitentiary. Or a firing squad."

"That makes it harder. She's very demanding." Trin nodded profoundly and his dark eyes were merry with alcohol and mystery. "I like the way this woman thinks. She must be saved."

Back on the street the motorscooters darted, edgy in the fierce afternoon heat. Broker looked longingly at a husky, sober traffic cop, neatly turned out in his crisp uniform and whistle. He turned to Trin.

"Why don't we go to your place, I'd like to see it."

Trin shook his head and stared straight ahead. "It's nothing, not worth your time."

Broker leaned back, uneasy. Translation: There was no apartment in Hue.

They cruised the back streets and found the address on My Thoung Street. It was perfect. Like Lola's hair. And her offer of help.

The villa was screened by a six-foot hedge that continued out on either side of the driveway. Peeking up the drive they could see the blue van parked in the yard. The lot next to the villa was under construction and there was room for a vehicle to slip in and hide between the walls of the new building and the hedge.

"A government-run tourist villa," said Trin. "Probably one housekeeper on duty. I doubt there are any other guests. Cyrus has probably taken all four rooms."

"If there's a guard, and he's armed, we have a problem."

Trin protested. "A gunshot in Hue? There would suddenly be so many police . . . No, I think if there's a guard he's a sacrificial offering. Expendable."

Trin seemed to know a whole lot all of a sudden. Since his chat with Lola. Broker ran the possibilities. Trin and Lola against the world. Trin, Lola, and Cyrus against him. "What if it's Bevode Fret?"

"That man has no finesse. Cyrus wants to bring off something smooth. That man would ruin everything."

They drove the streets to eat up time. They paused at the ViaCom Bank and inspected the cement apron in the back where the pallet of gold had sat from March 19, when the Communists took the city, until Jimmy Tuna and Ray Pryce choppered in on April 30, 1975.

The former MACV compound, where Trin had been held prisoner, was two blocks away. Painted smartly in government brown it was now a military hotel. Back on Le Loi, they stopped so Broker could confirm the location of the new La Cafard. Now La Cafard floated, two brightly lit donuts connected by planks and gangways. Sampans docked next to it.

They returned to the guest house and walked out on the broad veranda that overlooked the Perfume River. Trin swung his beer and pointed below them. "This used to be corps headquarters. That's the tennis court where General Troung used to play with Westmoreland."

Broker was now seriously worried about Trin's alcohol intake as well as his reliability. His face had reddened to a permanent pepper flush a few shades hotter than the huge Communist flag that tossed in the breeze across the river. The flag kept time to a disco on Le Loi Street that blared "Hotel California" in the foundry heat. Trin grinned and toasted him with his beer can.

What if Trin *was* dying to stir his crank in a pile of round-eyed bacon grease? Or maybe he wanted to get all the concerned Americans in one place and then let the militia shoot them all on the beach. It was possible that he really wanted to open a liquor store in California . . .

Broker's head hurt. "It's a trap," he repeated.

"For sure. That's given. They know we're at the same game," Trin said jovially. "We're in Vietnam, where traps were invented." He waved the beer can dramatically. "The question is what kind of a trap and is it better than our trap."

"They could jump us when we go for Nina—"

"That would still leave the messy business of getting us to talk. We might stand up under torture," Trin said in a detached voice. "Or die under it. That's not a lock. Cyrus used to like things sewn up. No. Lola is the key. If she helps us get Nina out and wants to *come with us* . . . We could show her the gold in gratitude. Then use her to signal them in. If she wants to go with us, then we'll know!" Trin jabbed his index finger oratorically in the air. "Better for us. It saves us the trouble of having to reestablish contact after we get Nina."

"I forgot what a devious guy you are," said Broker.

Trin collapsed back on a lawn chair and took a long swig of beer. "You have no idea," he sighed.

"Cool it on the booze."

"It's just beer. I know what I'm doing."

"Yeah, but I'm not sure I know what you're doing."

Trin's laugh was intricate with fascination. "Imagine that we're all jumping off a balcony over a swimming pool. We all have ropes around our necks. All the ropes are different lengths. Some of us will splash harmlessly into the water. Some of us will hang. We won't know until we take the dive." Trin smiled and drained his beer.

Broker wished he had Ed Ryan, J.T. Merryweather, and an ATF entry team.

But he didn't.

He had Trin.

Across the street, "Hotel California" started to play again.

They went into the room and Trin called the desk and requested a six o'clock wake-up call. They were asleep the minute their heads hit the pillows.

At six the telephone woke them. Broker, cinder-eyed, stumbled to the bathroom and climbed in the tub and sprayed away grime with tepid water from the hand-held shower. He rubbed his chin whiskers. No shaving kit. He put on the T-shirt Lola had given him at the citadel. It was the only article of clean clothing in sight. He was glad for his short hair, which he combed with his fingers.

At six-thirty they split up. Trin took the van to scout the villa again during Broker's meeting with LaPorte. He'd pick Broker up in front of the restaurant at eight sharp. Then they'd hit the villa.

Broker joined the strollers on Le Loi. A cyclo driver rose lizard-like from his cab and approached. "Buddha cigarette?" he offered in a casual voice.

"Didi mau—fuck off," said Broker. Apparently smoking grass had survived the revolution. The disco across the street was still playing the same damn song. Maybe it was the new Communist anthem. He hailed a cyclo. The driver nodded when he said La Cafard and they set off.

Hue was still a city of bicycles and some of the old Le Loi ambience lingered; except, now, the clouds of female students on their bikes were dingy from exhaust from all the motorbikes. Now the bursts of flowering frangipani, flamboyants, and the tall old tamarinds squeezed between the new billboards. The same bleached Colonial buildings lined the avenue like the mustard and ivory bones of France and somewhere in the city, according to Trin, the last Vietnamese mandarin sat in the dark behind shuttered windows and chain-smoked and guarded his dusty Imperial mementos.

The cyclo driver's sturdy legs propelled Broker beneath gaudy neon tiaras strung from light poles. Across the river, the ramparts of the flag tower were decked in more lights that were layered like a wedding cake. The lights popped like flash cubes for the eyes and blunted the dragon teeth in the sunset forming over the Annamite Mountains.

Rock and roll pumped from the cafes and a group of teenage girls strutted to the beat in designer jeans. Some of them wore red pins with little yellow stars.

The rosy early evening air was sticky as cotton candy and Hue swung its ass in American denim and sweated to American music and Broker, way past irony, stared straight ahead as he trundled down the midway of Coney Island Communism.

67

Cyrus Laporte waited on the gangplank to La Cafard dressed in a beige desert shirt, khakis, and Teva sandals over cotton socks. He smelled of talc and shaving lotion and he had the red bandanna tied around his tanned throat. He was smiling. Lola was not with him.

"So what's going to be, another tantrum. Or can we talk?" asked Cyrus.

"Talk," said Broker. His shoulders slumped. He didn't have to act exhausted.

"Good. Let's have a drink at the bar," said Cyrus. "They resurrected some of the old decor as part of the open door policy." They both pulled up stools. "Try a Huda beer, they bottle it here in town," he said.

Behind the bar three mildewed movie posters were framed under glass. They harkened back to the war, when the old restaurant had been on the riverbank and was an American haunt. *Cafard* was an expression the French had used to convey being far from home in all this heat. The Blues.

The first poster advertised *The Quiet American* with Audie Murphy. Then came Marlon Brando in *The Ugly American*. The third had John Wayne with his love handles on parade in the *Green Berets*.

Cyrus raised his glass to the posters and proposed an old toast: "From quiet to ugly to stupid in one generation." He took a sip of beer and glanced around. "Remember how Gaston, the old proprietor, liked the movies. He used to say 'America is a movie the rest of the world watches in the dark.'" Cyrus LaPorte smiled. "Not anymore."

Broker stared into his glass of beer. They were getting ready to

kill him, and Trin and Nina. Maybe Lola was going to help. Maybe
she was in harm's way herself. Maybe Trin was being bought off by
Cyrus and Lola. Trin was right about one thing: They all had ropes
around their necks. Apparently LaPorte thought he had the longest
rope, so he was indulging his charming raconteur side.

Where was Bevode?

"How did you get onto this stuff? Jimmy wouldn't say," Broker
asked finally.

"Pure accident," said Cyrus. "In seventy-three an ARVN captain
brought me a gold ingot he'd found in the river bed near the mouth
of the Perfume. He wanted help getting his family to the States.

"We spent the next year combing the river location that captain
gave me, just Jimmy and I. And we found it. Maybe when the
French looted the citadel one ship sunk, got buried when the river
changed course. Or maybe the Vietnamese had hidden it. Who
knows?

"We dug it out and crated it, box by box. Bringing in a boat
would involve other people. But I could get a helicopter. With
Jimmy, and a couple of Air America guys I trusted, I was going to
sling it out. Hide it in Laos. Then activity in the sector picked up. We
had to move it. We snuck it into Hue. Then we disguised it as an
ammo pallet. I was in Danang arranging for the helicopter when the
Commies came down and took the city."

LaPorte pursed his lips. "So I was only taking back what was
mine by right of discovery. On hindsight, my method was regret-
table."

Perhaps he meant that as an apology. Broker used it as a cue. He
let his shoulders sag, ground his teeth, and gave in.

"Can you keep Bevode under control?"

Cyrus toyed with his glass. "Can you keep Nina Pryce quiet?"

The questions passed each other in the soft evening air.
Unanswered. LaPorte said, "Meet me at seven in the morning, in
front of the Century Hotel. I'll be sitting there alone, in the car with
Nina. She gets out. You get in."

"A trade," said Broker.

"That way if she talks—"

"If she doesn't, what happens to me?"

"That depends. The girl is a problem. But maybe we can work it
out. Cheer up. You might wind up liking hanging out with us."

They ordered coffee.

"So how'd Jimmy do it?" asked Cyrus.

Broker shrugged. "The chopper set down on the coast and they stashed the load in a ravine, blew a small hillside to cover it, and took off again."

Cyrus's pale ice eyes did not waver. He didn't care. Nothing mattered except getting closer to the gold.

"It's worth a lot more than its weight, isn't it?" said Broker.

LaPorte nodded. "You have no idea. There are Cham artifacts mixed in with the gold that are a thousand years old. They're priceless. The trick is to keep it off the market, release it bit by bit to museums all over the world. That's how you make the money. What about the bars I found in the water?"

Broker said, "Jimmy caused the crash at sea. The other crew members drowned because they were weighted down with gold souvenirs."

"Jimmy always was tricky," said Cyrus in an appraising voice. "I could never get into his banking records. That was the key." Cyrus nodded.

"Jimmy thought it should be returned to the Vietnamese."

"Big of him," said Cyrus.

"I thought so too," said Broker.

"What about Trin?"

"Trin's screwed here. But he went through the reeducation camps, that makes him eligible to immigrate to America if he has a sponsor. I promised to help him get out," Broker ad-libbed.

"So why'd you bring the girl?" Cyrus was moving right along.

"Once I found out what we were on to I thought it was best to keep her close."

LaPorte nodded. "Loose cannon."

Broker paused. "One last question. You've already got it all: wealth, position, a reputation. Why take the chance on losing it all? It's not like you need it."

LaPorte chuckled. "It's not just gold to be exchanged on the market. It's a national treasure. It's going to *make* my reputation."

"There'll be an international stink."

LaPorte drummed his fingers on the bar. "What the hell, whatever they write on my tombstone, it won't be: He showed up on time for work every day."

Broker raised an eyebrow.

"Somebody owes me," LaPorte said with conviction. Some of that old flintlock look came into his eyes. "All the time I put in here. Hell, I would have used that gold to keep fighting from the hills."

Maybe he really believed that once. Maybe he still did. It didn't matter.

Cyrus LaPorte reached across the bar and took one of Broker's cigarettes. He studied the inscription on Broker's lighter. Then he lit the cigarette, inhaled, exhaled, and studied the smoldering tobacco.

Over his shoulders the clouds, at sunset, looked like a forest fire in the mountains. Sampans with groups of traditional musicians cruised on the Perfume River. Voices and the tremble of stringed instruments carried on the breeze. The boatmen placed paper lanterns, illuminated by candles, in the water. They bobbed in the soft, warm night.

"Nineteen sixty-nine," Cyrus ruminated. "I flew back home between tours. Braniff flight out of old Saigon. We were coming in, making the approach on Oakland.

"Pilot announced that we were coming up on the coastline of the States. Suddenly it became silent on that airplane. And the pilot took some liberties; he swung that big bird, banking left and right so everybody on both sides could get a look of the coast . . ."

Cyrus took a deep drag on the cigarette, screwed up his lips and blew out the smoke.

"The stewardesses knew. They must of been pros on those flights. They all took their posts in the aisles and every one of them looked down those rows of young guys who were wearing that green with the red dirt fade. They could read the shoulder patches . . . see the CIBs."

He curled his lower lip. "Nina Pryce thinks she deserves a CIB. Hell, there was more combat experience on that one airplane than in the whole goddamn Gulf War. Those stews knew they were hauling infantry. All those young American men, sitting up, looking straight ahead. Absolutely quiet. Polite.

"And every one of those women began to cry. Silent men, crying women standing at their posts like statues. I pity those girls for the weight they carried. They were sin eaters for the whole damn nation. And the plane landed and nobody would get out. Nobody moved from their seats."

Cyrus lowered his voice. "There'd been this incident, see. A mother of a boy killed in the war had greeted a returning flight at Oakland, right out on the runway. According to the story she'd shot the first guy who got off that plane. It was really much more than that. It was . . . everything.

"Well, I had the rank so I had to get off that plane and walk around. Make sure it was safe. Then I come back in and I go down that aisle and I talked to those kids, told them it was all right . . . each of them. Face to face."

Cyrus LaPorte let the cigarette drop, like the greatness that had once been at his fingertips. "But it wasn't all right, was it? I never commanded American troops again. From then on I *advised* the Vietnamese." He ground the butt under his sandal. His pale eyes drifted over toward the lights strung on the citadel. "Before your time, son."

Broker stood up and said, "Thanks for the beer. Seven tomorrow morning." For that moment only, they exchanged oddly sincere smiles.

What might have been.

He left Cyrus LaPorte sitting at the bar, staring through the floating lanterns into the past. Broker crossed the gangplank and sprinted across the dark parking lot. The van was waiting. Trin held open the door. He dived in.

68

"So?" ASKED TRIN.

"Let's do it," said Broker.

Hue was a small place. It was a five-minute drive to the villa. Trin turned into the shadow of the lot next door. They got out and crept to the hedge and waited. After a few minutes, Save the Whales and another man, with the rugged build of a salvage diver, came out on the front steps. A third guy joined them. He wasn't wearing a shirt. Broker recognized the anemic, sunken-chest muscularity, the red hair.

"You hear that car?" said one of them.

"It's a street, numbnuts, cars go by all the time."

"I think I'll stick around," said Virgil.

"You idiot, want to be in there? After what you did? Let Lola clean her up, for Chrissake."

"Bevode wouldn't want me to leave them alone, you understand."

Broker surged on the balls of his feet, hearing the punk mimic his older brother's voice. Virgil turned and went back in the door. *Shit.* Broker started to go. Trin held him back until LaPorte's two men ambled off the steps, headed for the gate, and disappeared down the driveway. A moment later an engine turned over and a car drove away.

Trin clamped his hand on Broker's forearm. "It could be bad in there. Be prepared for anything. And no blood. It'll take time to clean up. We have to take the guard with us. Get rid of him in the countryside."

Broker didn't hear. He was through the hedge. Moving with

silent springing steps. He mounted the steps where the Cajuns had been a moment before. The double front doors were open. An office was tucked under the porch to the right and was empty. There was a living room area with a couch and two chairs. Beyond that a long dinner table. Two rooms to a side. The second door on the left was 102. It was open. He could see Lola LaPorte with her hands on her hips, dressed in white. Her chin jutted combatively, furious.

"Virgil, goddammit. Look what you did. I have to get her cleaned up to travel in the morning. Now get out of here."

"Hey, I just want to watch." Virgil's smirky nasal voice.

Broker had a bad moment going through the door. *Bevode?* Then Virgil looked up and Broker was past Lola and hit him like a linebacker.

Virgil's red hair bobbed and his skinny white ribs convulsed as he flew back across the room. He was barefoot, shirtless. The buttons on his jeans weren't done up right. Nina sprawled on one of the two beds, carelessly covered by a sheet that did not entirely cover her bare right hip. Her mouth was open and her eyes rolled in their sockets.

Virgil backpedaled, trying to find his balance. His stoned popcorn punk grin stayed on his sallow face as Broker moved right in on him. Broker, the street student of anatomy, calculated at onrushing synapse speed, what would stun, what would cripple and what would *kill slowly*. His right fist smashed deep into Virgil's throat like a pile driver seeking the hyoid bone at the base of the tongue. There was a soft cartilaginous snap.

Virgil traveled horizontally through the air, went over the bed and crashed into the wall. Without breaking stride Broker skirted the bed and caught Virgil as he flopped off the wall with a pinpoint kick, again in the throat, that would have scored a field goal.

Broker spun and realized that Trin was trying to hold him back and he was swinging Trin through the air like a kid's game. "No blood," hissed Trin.

Virgil's dirty hazel eyes were cranked wide and he had both hands at his throat clawing at the knot of mangled tendon and muscle that was shutting down his windpipe.

"Jesus Christ," muttered Broker, going to the bed, throwing back the sheet. Nina's skin had the pallor of a trout dragged in the mud. Her left ear was red with festered pus. Her hips lay in a stale stain of urine. Cigarette burns dotted her chest and made little circles of ash in the copper curls of her pubic hair.

The other earring was still pierced through her right ear.

"Oh my God," someone said. Not Trin. Broker turned and saw Lola supporting herself, knees staggered, one hand on the doorjamb. "That poor kid."

"We knew it could be bad," said Trin as he came out of the bathroom with a wet washcloth and efficiently wiped Nina down. The cool cloth revived her a little. She moaned and her eyelids fluttered. Trin grabbed a bottle of prescription capsules on the bedside table. "We have to take this," he said.

Broker shook his head.

"We don't know how much they gave her. We may have to use small doses if she gets sick." Trin pounded Broker's shoulder. "Find her clothes. And his."

"See how they are," said Lola. "That poor damn kid . . ."

The second "poor kid" did it. And her tanned perfection and the fucking precision-combed hair and the clean white slacks and the white Topsiders and the white silk blouse.

Broker started for her. Trin, the thespian, was on him. "No. She helped us," he pleaded.

Slumped against the wall like a comic suicide who was attempting to choke himself to death, Virgil Fret did a pasty jig on his butt while caw-hiss sounds—part bird, part snake—squeezed from his strangling throat.

Lola was in front of Broker. "Are you all right?" she asked. Her alarm and shock were palpable, real. And every hair was in place.

"Help," Trin yelled at her. "Put a shirt on him." He pointed to Virgil. "We can't leave him here. Hurry." Trin was wrapping Nina in a clean sheet from the other bed. "Find her clothes."

Broker checked his watch. It was thirteen after eight. He tore open the bureau and found Nina's clothes in a cast-off pile. He put the tennis shoes in her jeans, threw her underthings and shirt on top, and tied the jeans in a knot. He looked across the room.

Lola efficiently yanked a T-shirt on Virgil, batting her way around his struggling arms and hands. She had tears in her eyes. Two lines of mascara dripped down her cheeks. She found one of Virgil's shoes and began beating him with it. "You hurt her, you bad—"

"Caw-hiss," sputtered Virgil and Broker saw with satisfaction that the veins had swelled up like worms in his popped eyes. Lola's voice failed but she continued to hit him with the shoe, like he was a bad dog who had soiled the living room carpet. Susan Sarandon was shit out of luck. Lola was going to win the Oscar.

They really think we're this dumb? Doesn't matter how it looks as long as they keep getting closer to the gold. Or what the cost. Sorry about that, Virgil.

Trin lifted Nina without apparent effort and jogged from the room. They were alone with Virgil Fret, who continued to die in breathy slow stages.

"I couldn't talk today, Phillip. He was having me watched," said Lola, stepping back from Virgil, who was now madly pumping his elbows. "Caw." Pump, pump. Maybe he was going to fly away and save them the trouble of disposing of his worthless ass.

Trin dashed back in the room with a horrible grin on his flushed face. "Grab him, quick." Trin rushed for Virgil. He seized a fifth of whiskey from the night table.

"What now?" said Broker, going with him.

"Inspiration," said Trin, grinning, taking a quick slug of whiskey and holding the bottle out to Broker. Broker shook his head. Trin shook a dollop of whiskey on Broker's shirt and then splashed some on Virgil's inflated face. They yanked him to his feet.

"Quick, he'll get away," yelped Trin, dragging Virgil toward the door. They had him upright, his flailing arms over their shoulders, running now down the steps, Broker following Trin's lead. "You stay here." Trin waved the whiskey bottle in his free hand at Lola.

Rock and roll spooled in the inky night, neon spun behind dark trees. They galloped down the driveway and burst into the street. Tight lipped, Broker said, "I didn't see a gun in there—"

"I checked the whole place, no gun," said Trin.

"This punk would have a gun."

"They don't want *us* to have one. It's a trap. This piece of shit is a throwaway."

Several snoozing cyclo drivers spotted them and rose from their cabs. "There," panted Trin. Down the block Broker saw the bear-walking drunken Aussie. His broad back was naked, streaked with sweat over a sarong. He stumbled down the street, staying upright mainly by the support of his right shoulder bumping on a cement wall. Patient as jackals, several cyclos padded on silent rubber tires, trailing his slow progress.

"Hey, buddy," shouted Trin as they pulled abreast. "Have a drink." He thrust out the bottle. "Let's party."

The giant yawned and pawed the bottle. Trin quickly analyzed the cyclo situation and selected the oldest driver, who also had the widest seat. He heaved Virgil in. The driver inspected Virgil and began to protest.

"What's he say?" said Broker.

"He says this American is dying and he won't ride him. We need dollars." Broker dug in his pocket. Trin tugged the staggering Aussie and pulled him toward the cyclo. He pointed to Virgil whose protruding tongue was deep purple in the bounce of neon and who was feebly inching his hands back toward his throat. "Hey, mate, he knows where the girls are. Number one boom-boom."

"Caw," said Virgil. A newly hatched vulture chick mouthing the air.

The Aussie lit up, having found kin who talked his twittering dialect. Trin steered the giant into the cyclo and grabbed the handful of twenties from Broker. He turned to the agitated driver.

"I'm telling him he's only had too much to drink," said Trin who then broke into machine-gun Vietnamese as he counted out bills into the driver's wrinkled hand.

The driver continued to protest, but his posture and voice had turned sly. The other cyclo drivers craned forward, crowding in as Trin and the older driver argued. Trin turned back to Broker.

"He's a hard sell. He says, bullshit, he knows a dying American when he sees one." Trin grinned insanely. "He says he was a fucking guerrilla in the fucking jungle for fifteen fucking years. Give me a hundred-dollar bill."

Broker handed over Mr. Franklin.

"He says," said Trin, "that's the drunkest goddamn American he has ever seen in his life."

In the cab, the Aussie tenderly poured whiskey into Virgil's weakly moving mouth. With an evil smile creasing his leathery face, the former Viet Cong bent to his pedals and moved the bike cab out into the street. Virgil Fret disappeared into the teeming bicycles and motorbikes of Hue, wrapped in the meaty embrace of the cooing Aussie, who bent over him like a mama feeding her first child.

Trin spun on his heels and marched back toward the villa. "I told him to dump them in a rice paddy halfway to the coast." They jogged back to the van parked in the shadows next to the villa. Lola's outfit made a voluptuous, unmistakable fashion statement in the humid buzzing night.

"White," said Broker.

"So nobody will shoot her by accident, say in the dark on a confused beach," said Trin.

"I can't stay now. I'm coming with you. That was our deal . . ." Lola, breathless with excitement, coming to meet them.

"I'm satisfied. You satisfied?" said Trin.

"Roger," said Broker. He pivoted and his sand-busted tennis shoes crunched in the gravel as he put his left fist on stun and popped Lola LaPorte with a short left jab, hard enough to knock her cold, not quite hard enough to cave in her surgically enhanced, gorgeous right cheek.

They dragged Lola into the van and stretched her out in the aisle perpendicular to Nina. Trin picked up her purse and threw it in after her. Then he dug under the seats and pulled something out and grinned. "Duct tape. The only good thing the American army brought to Vietnam."

Quickly he taped Lola's ankles, hands, and ran two strips around her mouth. Then he scrambled to the wheel. "Now, we run like hell."

69

"IT'S ALL RIGHT," SOOTHED BROKER AS HE CRADLED NINA IN the backseat. She opened one eye.

"Don't bullshit me, Broker," she croaked.

"It's better," he allowed.

He had sponged her off and opened Trin's first-aid kit and had attempted to clean up the ear. Then he'd wrapped her in a blanket. Like a morbid footnote to the mad night, he remembered that the rest of her ear resided in a little glass jar, pickled in rice alcohol, in the house on the coast.

He dribbled mineral water on her caked lips and used his bandanna to clean more of the ugliness from her face. He didn't know what to use to medicate the emotional wounds on the inside.

Unconditional love, maybe.

Fitfully, Lola stirred against her binds and moaned from the floor. Trin drove Highway 1 north out of Hue with agonizing restraint, cautious, now, of drawing attention. The headlights made a weaving tunnel of illumination that was regularly invaded by impassive Vietnamese crouched over handlebars. Occasionally a truck. It took forever to get to the turnoff to the coast. As the black farmland closed around them, Broker entertained paranoid fragments of the past: driving through the countryside at night with the lights on. Unarmed.

They were in the paddies now, going slow. Shadowy bicycles jostled the van. Nina turned in his arms, dug her face against his chest, and used her forehead for leverage to push herself up.

"She's coming around," said Broker.

With her face still buried in his chest, her marble cold hand worked up his throat and chin and felt his face. "Just barely," she said in a hoarse voice.

"How you doing?"

"Sloe gin," she muttered. "First time I had a horrible hangover, was sloe gin. I feel like sloe gin. 'Scuse me, open a window. I gotta puke."

Broker quickly pulled back the sliding side window and helped her lean out. Her ribcage heaved and she retched down the side of the car. He pulled her back in and wrapped her in the blanket. "Got anything to drink?" she said in a dry voice.

"Water."

"That Trin up there?"

"Uh-huh."

"Give us a drink, Trin," said Nina. "Got this horrible taste in my mouth."

Trin reached under the front seat and handed back an unlabeled bottle of clear liquid. "Watch it. That's homemade rice whiskey, it might not mix with what they gave you," he cautioned.

"Gimme," said Nina. She fastened her hand around the bottle. Broker smiled. A dicey smile. He'd been afraid she'd be in shock. Trauma. By the thin light of the moon he could see the set of her jaw. She was one pissed female human.

Nina gagged on the first swallow of whiskey and lurched toward the window. But she kept it down and went back for a second jolt. She handed the bottle to Broker. "Drink with me," she said. He did. The moonshine brought tears to his eyes. He handed the bottle back to Trin, who took a long swig, corked it, and stuffed it back under the seat.

"Who's that on the floor?" said Nina, arching her neck.

"Madame LaPorte. She led us to you. We're not real sure we trust her so she's not traveling first class."

"You found it."

Broker nodded. "It's something."

Nina shuddered and Broker took her in his arms again. "You all right?" he asked foolishly.

"Hell, no, I'm not all right. Got a cigarette?"

He put a cigarette in her lips and popped his Zippo. She steadied on the tobacco, drawing it deep into her lungs. Exhaled.

"You remember anything?" asked Broker.

"The bad parts. There weren't any good parts."

"Knock on wood. We might have a fighting chance now."

"I'm for fighting," said Nina. She smoked and gazed out the window. They were into the sand now and moonlight twinkled on the dunes. Willows spun crepuscular shadows around the stark geometry of a North Vietnamese cemetery.

She said slowly, "They burned me with cigarettes. I didn't tell them shit. Gave 'em a lecture on the fucking Code of Conduct." Gingerly her hand went to her festered left ear.

"I saved it for you," said Broker absurdly.

"What?"

"You know."

"Fuckers." Her voice was still hoarse, but stronger. He could feel her cinching herself by an act of will into a tight knot of leather and stitched canvas and buckles.

"That red-headed creep tried to rape me." She shook her head ruefully and dragged on the cigarette. By the flare of the cigarette tip she saw the expression on Broker's face. "Don't worry, fire base cervix didn't get overrun . . . here." She tried to smile. "Might have in Minnesota, though." She turned and gazed out the window. "Little shit tried to rape me," she said, forcefully this time. "But the only thing he could get up was cocaine up his nose. I laughed at him. That's when he burned me."

"That was Bevode's little brother. We took care of him."

"Fuck him and his limp little dick," she muttered.

Broker winced at her truculent vulgarity. But she needed it now. If there was a part of her childhood left that remembered playing with dolls it had died in that room.

They drove on in silence broken only but Lola LaPorte's gagged protests. Nina used Broker's bandanna to give herself a quick catwash. She excused herself and crawled over Lola to the back of the van with the bottle of water and performed a crude douche. She returned at least ritually cleansed. Broker helped her into her clothes.

A farmhouse up ahead was illuminated by an improbable glow. When they went past, they saw a family gathered on a sleeping platform in front of a big color TV.

"Huh," said Nina. "Is there electricity out here?"

"Batteries," said Trin.

"*That's* the beginning of the end of Vietnamese culture," pronounced Nina dryly and they all laughed. Shaky. But a laugh. She was trying to let them know she was all right. Not a burden. They drove for a long time in silence and there were no more houses.

Then Trin arched in the front seat and yelled. "Oh-oh." Just before he killed the headlights Broker saw the tree felled across the road.

The barrel of a rifle poked through the open driver's window. The van was surrounded by limping side-slanting shadows, crabwalkers.

A low discussion commenced in Vietnamese. "It's all right," Broker told Nina, recognizing Trung Si behind the rifle.

"It's not all right," said Trin very coldly.

Trin cut the tape on Lola's feet so she could walk and pushed her toward Broker. She tried to pull away, the whites of her eyes bulging in the moonlight, mummified protests coming from her gagged lips. Nina shoved her roughly ahead.

Formed in Indian file, they went off the track and snaked through the dunes, toward the sea. Trin and Trung Si were in the lead. Then five hard-faced middle-aged men in softly straining artificial limbs. Broker saw at least one empty sleeve among them. They all carried primitive weapons: machetes, rice sickles, butcher knives. Despite their handicaps they moved with precision, instinctively keeping an interval. Stopping every few steps to listen. Broker pushed Lola in front of him as he and Nina fell into the rhythm of the night discipline.

As they neared the beach they halted at the clack of bamboo. Another paraplegic hobbled from the shadows. He conversed tensely with Trin and Trung Si. When Nina started to ask a question Broker warned her to be silent. The stony intonation of Trin's whispers informed him that, for better or worse, this was now a Vietnamese show.

Slowly they approached the house on the slope over the beach. The cripples sprawled carefully in the cover of the dunes while Trung Si hopped spry and silent on his crutch to a covering position and leaned over his rifle. Trin crept down to the house.

Five tense minutes passed. Then a low whistle sounded from the beach. Trung Si swung up on his crutch and waved his rifle. The cripples pushed themselves up and went down on line. Broker and Nina followed.

The place had been trashed. Shards of crockery and utensils were strewn in the trampled vegetable garden. Trin and his men gathered at the flagpole next to the porch.

Nina's fingers spasmed on Broker's biceps. Her nails broke the skin.

In the moonlight they could make out the legless mass of the flute player's body. Trin held up a fuel oil lantern and Trung Si lit the wick. The soft yellow light revealed that the dead man's neck was grotesquely stretched in a noose knotted in the flagpole lanyard. A chopstick had been pounded almost out of sight into his left ear.

"Meeow." A low growl thickened the inflection of the voices around the flagpole. Smoldering dark eyes swung toward the three white people in the yard. Lola shied back, straining against the tape on her wrists. Nina grabbed her by the hair and shoved her forward and forced her to her knees in front of the flagpole.

Flies stormed around Lola's face and she averted her head from the barnyard stench. Trung Si swore. They saw that the Viet Cong flag had been taken down. It lay in the dirt, filled with feces. More flies clustered in black twitching furrows on the dead man's body. Among the crawling insects they saw patches of skin upbraided, hanging in flaps.

One of the vets began brushing the flies away. Another steadied the corpse while another cripple cut the rope with a machete. Slowly they lowered the body to the earth.

Broker exhaled. Whipped and lynched. *You find gold, you pay in blood.* The flute player and Billie Holiday could have played a duet.

Trung Si tapped Broker on the shoulder and pointed out to sea. At first Broker thought he was pointing at the stars and then he picked out the faint regular line of electric lights hugging the horizon. A boat lay off the coast.

Then Trung Si spoke to Trin and Trin swore vehemently in his native tongue. Not in the heat of anger, but out of something much deeper and deliberate and sinister.

"That man. Trung Si was on his way back from hiding our boat. He saw them leave. Six white men in a powerboat. They carried AR-15s. That man had a whip."

Then he moved in a certain scary way and Broker, who believed that Vietnamese all hid deadly stingers under their friendly smiles, braced himself.

The gravity knife appeared in his hand and the long blade pressed against Lola's cheek, snaked it up under her gag, and cut it. He ripped the tape from Lola's face.

"Jesus Christ," gasped Lola. "Do something about the smell."

"Lying bitch!" Trin slapped her face. Then he placed his tennis shoe in her back and pushed her off her knees, face forward into the reeking flag. Her neat white outfit wasn't white anymore.

Trin squatted and yanked Lola's hair, bringing her face up level with his. "Talk. Fast."

Lola struggled to her knees and shook off Trin's hand with an arrogant toss of her head. She stared at the murderous circle of faces that ringed her.

"I don't know."

"How'd they find this place?" demanded Broker.

Lola, finding herself in close proximity to excrement and the cloying bronze-sweetness of human blood, screamed it this time, "I don't know!"

An angry debate erupted among the vets in Vietnamese. Trung Si shouted at Trin. Trin shouted back. They had formed a circle around Lola.

Nina shivered through another spasm of delayed shock, clinging involuntarily to Broker's arm. In a hoarse whisper, she said, "Something's wrong."

Broker nodded. They were in the dark, outside the circle. There were times when body language said it all. They overheard Trin seethe at Lola in English, "People are dead, that changes things."

Broker and Nina shifted uneasily.

Trin issued crisp orders in Vietnamese. Two of the vets pulled Lola away. Trin turned to Broker and Nina. "We have to get out of here."

"Your turn to talk," Broker said pointedly to Trin.

He regarded him through lidded eyes. "You wanted to lure them in. I told her that if she'd give us Nina back, we'd bring her along and show her where it is. She didn't say anything about this." He curled his lips at the carnage surrounding them. His face was utterly cold and foreign. He'd locked them out.

Nina and Broker remained silent while the vets tended to their dead comrade. The lantern light caught on a now familiar glint. His mouth had been stuffed with gold rings. Several of the glittering circles dropped from his lips like round, dead words.

With peasant practicality the vets held the body upside down and shook it gently, cleaning the gold from his mouth.

"This is my fault. I let them get a step ahead of us," said Trin slowly.

Across the yard Trung Si was talking in a steady intense voice to his housemates.

"It's time to wake up that militia post," said Broker.

Trin nodded. "Trung Si will take the van. We'll go ahead and wait near the site. On foot. We can't take the truck, we'd need the lights and lights would give us away." Trin went into the house as they talked. One of the vets stuffed items in two roomy backpacks. Broker saw the little glass vial, undisturbed, on the shelf. He put it in his pocket.

Trin slung one of the packs to his back. He tapped Broker on the arm and pointed to the other one. Broker put it on.

"Food. Water," said Trin.

"We need weapons," said Nina.

Trin did not respond. He held Trung Si's deer rifle, the butt resting on his hip. He made hurry-up motions with his free hand. Just before they extinguished the lantern, he turned to Broker. He did not make eye contact.

"Lola has a radio to direct them in."

"What?"

"In her purse. I'm sorry, Phil." Trin pulled his shirt aside and drew a shiny 9mm pistol. So Virgil had had a gun after all. "Do as I say and it will turn out all right."

Broker glanced out to the sea, to the faint running lights on the vessel. The lights looked back like multiple all-knowing eyes. He sagged. He had violated Trin's basic rule . . .

He had trusted Trin.

They left Trung Si at the van. Trin removed Lola's purse from the back. Slowly Trung Si turned the vehicle around and drove away with the lights out. Broker and Nina filed off through the dunes. Trin walked behind them, the pistol hanging in his hand.

70

THE MARCH THROUGH THE DUNES TOOK FOREVER. THEY HAD to stop frequently. Artificial legs weren't meant to go cross-country. Broker didn't like it. The silence. Lola had been gagged again. Her two guards walled her off. Trin trod at the back of the tiny column with the rifle and the pistol.

"What the fuck's going on with him?" whispered Nina.

"I don't know. Are you strong enough to run if you have to?" asked Broker.

He could feel her wince in the dark. "That bad?" she said.

"It's possible," said Broker. He shifted the pack to ease the straps cutting into his shoulders.

The man hobbling behind them muttered something. Broker heard his machete blade zing casually against some brush. The sound made the tiny hairs alert on his neck. Under guard, along with Lola.

He wondered if Trin had decided to fuck a bunch of white people. Lure Cyrus in. And then dump all the honkeys in one hole. Broker's mind raced. Christ, *he's after Cyrus's boat? He wants it all.*

Paranoia gamboled from the stunted shadowy trees and brush and joined the line of march. They hobbled past familiar landmarks. The abandoned hamlet and then the Spartan ranks of North Vietnamese headstones. Not far ahead they heard the waves breaking on the sand.

Communication was now exclusively in Vietnamese.

Machetes and wickedly curved rice sickles very much in evidence, the vets indicated that they should stop and rest in the cover of the three old round graves on the bluff above the cove. The packs were opened and food and water were doled out.

Trin stayed aloof. Not speaking. A shadow in the moonlight, he'd handed off the rifle to one of the vets and kept the pistol handy.

"It's down there?" asked Nina.

"About a hundred and fifty yards," said Broker.

"Maybe we shouldn't get spooked. It could work," said Nina, speaking with her mouth full. They scooped rice and fish from banana leaves with greasy fingers and washed it down with bottled water. Fuel. Their eyes had totally adjusted to the dark. The moon cast the surrounding terrain in silver relief.

"If he puts the militia up here, they have a perfect field of fire down that beach." Her voice was absent, practical.

"Yeah," said Broker. "But will we be up on the bluff here or down on that beach when the shooting starts?" He focused on Trin's shadow. He'd freed Lola's hands. And returned her purse. Now they were walking together down to the beach.

The man with the rifle hobbled over to them and casually tapped the muzzle against Broker's knee.

"Watch it," said Broker.

"Yes," said the man politely, his smile delineated in the moonlight. Then he chided them in Vietnamese, "Ngu. Ngu." For emphasis, he transferred the rifle to one hand and reclined his cheek in the palm of the other. "Ngu."

Broker nodded. Exhaustion took precedence over anxiety. "Whatever happens, we need some rest."

As the man with the rifle stood guard or watch over them—or both—they squirmed, getting comfortable in the warm sand at the base of the old cement wall.

"How're you making out?" he asked.

"I'm hurting some," she said frankly, "and I still have those downers in my veins, but I can hack it."

Anger snaked in his chest. "I've done everything . . . wrong," he blurted.

"Shhh," she said, touching her finger to his dry lips.

He threw his arm protectively around her and she curled into his chest. Physical necessity almost immediately plunged them into a deep sleep . . .

Beside a grave, on the pirate beach, in the graveyard of the iron elephants.

71

THEY WOKE UP TO A DAMP WHITE WORLD OF SAND AND FOG and the tang of burning wood. The vets had a cookfire going. A larger fire crackled on the beach. No one seemed particularly concerned about concealing themselves.

Nina squinted and made a face. "Doesn't look like our numbers have increased during the night."

Broker busied himself with pouring sand from his filthy socks. He put his busted-up tennis shoes back on and laced them tightly. Amazingly, the pain in his thumb had diminished since Trung Si had applied his gunk.

Trin was nowhere in sight.

Through his stiffness, Broker smelled the blessing of brewing coffee. They were fed steamed rice and dirty glasses of coffee. The coffee was good. Nothing else was.

They sat and shared a cigarette in the cover of the willows, ragamuffins behind a clean sand dune.

Where was the militia?

Somewhere, away from their beach, there were governments and courts of law and the police. All of which Broker had avoided in order to deal directly with Nguyen Van Trin. On the beach there was only their pounding hearts, sweat, the itch of sand fleas, and the stink of betrayal. A fiery salmon sky streaked with lavender started to burn through the mist.

Two hundred yards away they could now see Lola LaPorte wander up and down the beach, picking up driftwood and adding it to the fire. A short compact figure walked the water's edge and that was Trin. Gradually the mist lifted and then the sun broke the line of the sea like the blazing helmet of an approaching giant. They could see the boat, a white blur on the horizon.

"The *Lola*," said Nina with cold pride at her retention of detail. "She's a hundred-five footer. Norwegian steel pilothouse research vessel. Built in 1960. She has a fancy yacht interior, heated and air-conditioned cabins for a crew of ten. Caterpillar diesels. Two generators, an emergency backup. She has a seven-thousand-mile range at ten knots. She cost LaPorte seven hundred and fifty thousand dollars five years ago."

"Subtract Virgil and he could still have a dozen guys counting Bevode," speculated Broker.

"They drove me down from Hanoi in the Mercedes and I was blitzed. Never saw more than two or three at a time," said Nina.

"You know," said Broker, glancing around, "we're real exposed out here. Where the hell is the militia?"

"I'm not a big fan of AK-47s, but we could use a couple dozen about now," said Nina, gnawing her cracked lip.

"I don't think we should stick around to find out." Broker stubbed out his cigarette and dusted sand from his palms. They stood up and stretched. The silent, walnut-faced cripple with the rifle motioned them toward the beach. Trin stood a hundred yards away. Lola was closer.

She looked up, smiled, and called out, "Good morning, Vietnam." It was written across his chest.

"Trin's out of pistol range. I think I can get that rifle. Then we head for the trees. Fast," said Broker under his breath to Nina.

"Just say when."

Because Lola had spoken, Broker steered toward her. She watched him approach, hands on her hips, with the wind in her hair, like a tarnished stainless-steel madonna. She had marvelous recuperative powers. The spot under her right eye where he'd hit her was hardly bruised.

Broker stopped ten feet from her. Nina lagged a little behind. The guard labored to keep up on his artificial leg. He came up on Broker's left side. The rifle hung casually in his hands at arm's length. Not real alert, this guy.

Lola folded her arms and smiled. "Well, how do you like the big time, Minnesota?" she said with a confident edge to her voice.

"You know, I almost trusted you," said Broker.

"You didn't really hope to take down Cyrus and Bevode . . . with these scarecrows? And *that*?" She jerked her head at Trin who stood at the water's edge regularly checking his wristwatch and shooting impatient looks up the slope at the trees near the three old graves.

"So now what?" said Broker, edging slightly toward the man with the rifle.

She smiled indulgently. "We're really not bad people once you get to know us. You just caught us in an extreme situation."

The urgent growl of an approaching motor vehicle carried to the beach. Behind them in the dunes. Broker saw that Trin heard it too. He snapped his head in a self-important gesture. Agreeing with something he had just said to himself.

"Okay," he yelled to Lola.

She grinned at Broker. "Mr. Trin is about to get the surprise of his life." She withdrew a compact, solid-state radio from her purse, whipped up the antennae, pushed the transmit button, and said, "Come to Mama."

Nina had moved beside Broker. Her eyes trailed back toward the dunes. "You think . . . ?"

But Broker was watching the guard, who was momentarily distracted, fascinated with the shiny radio. Broker swept out his foot, hooking the man's good leg and wrenching the rifle away as he toppled.

He hefted the rifle, covering Trin for a moment. Then they turned and sprinted up the slope. Broker heard Trin's warning yell, "Don't do it, Phil . . ." But they'd gained the crest and pounded past the surprised vets, who knocked over their pot of rice as they struggled to rise from their cookfire.

The trees were thickest a hundred yards away. That's where they headed. From the corner of his eye Broker spotted the gray van: Vietnam Hue Tours. Parked at the edge of the woods. He shot out his left hand, cautioning Nina, slowed his pace, and shifted the old bolt-action rifle up in his right hand, holding it like a long dueling pistol. His thumb fumbled on the unfamiliar safety. Breath coming in long ragged gasps. Nina not doing much better.

"Broker!" Nina.

Cyrus LaPorte stepped from the shadow of the trees. Red pirate bandanna. Real nonchalant in his pukka sahib desert duds. Another guy appeared. Hard-looking guy. Blue tank-top shirt, lots of muscle, no hat, short-cropped black hair. Had a rifle slung on his shoulder. The guy reached into the trees and pulled Trung Si into the sunlight. Not rough, like, C'mon . . .

What the fuck . . .

"Militia my ass. We've been had," Broker panted, lurching to a full stop in the sand, rifle coming up smooth. Blue shirt first. Seventy yards. Couldn't miss. Casually, Blue Shirt unlimbered his AR-15. Why did they just stand there?

Broker found out why when he squeezed the trigger and the bolt snapped on an empty chamber. He yanked back the bolt and stared into an empty breech.

LaPorte came toward him, smiling, with his hands clasped behind his back. "You're not having a very good vacation, are you, Phil?"

72

BROKER DIDN'T THINK IT COULD GET ANY WORSE. THEN IT DID.

As they were marched back to the beach they heard more motors, loud, snarling, coming in over the water. Two sturdy rubber cargo dinghies cut through a lingering bank of mist, propelled by huge outboards. Lola jumped up and down on the beach like a cheerleader and waved them in.

Bevode stood in the prow of the lead boat, hatless, his oiled hair streamed in the sun. A mean black AR-15 was balanced casually on his hip and he had one foot up on the gunwale in a conqueror's pose. Tall, gleaming brown leather boots, jeans tucked in. Safari shirt. A thick braid of leather wrapped his shoulder. LaPorte's heirloom whip. He was smiling.

Trin's vets weren't. Seeing Bevode, they clustered in a group and jabbered among themselves. Trin, the motherfucking traitor, was trying to calm them.

Intuitively Broker and Nina joined hands.

Before the first boat ran up on the beach, three men rolled out and dashed through the surf with AR-15s at the ready. Not Cajuns. More related to the Blue Shirt. The same cropped hair. They vibrated a pumped-up military narcissism that wouldn't be tolerated in veteran soldiers.

"Mercenaries," said Nina in a flat voice.

Their rifles covered Trin. Virgil's pistol had been his brief marshal's baton. Now he was forced to drop it. One of the mercs shoved Trung Si into the group of cripples. Trin began to protest at the rough treatment. The merc swiftly butt-stroked him in the stomach and sent him sprawling. Fluent Vietnamese rippled from his lips.

Under his direction, Trin and his men spread out and put their hands behind their heads.

"How'd I do?" Lola shouted to her husband.

"You were great," said Cyrus LaPorte. His eyes were fixed on the horizon over her shoulder.

She was grinning, but she also read something in Cyrus's cold manner. In the way Bevode ambled up the beach.

"Oh God," whispered Nina under her breath, going rigid. Her fingernails cut into Broker's hand.

"What?" said Lola. Cyrus had turned his back on her. He walked away, down the beach with his hands cupped meditatively behind his back. Lola spun and confronted Bevode. "Hey," she protested.

"Ain't personal, you understand," said Bevode.

Broker struggled with an inappropriate, disassociative thought. The day was too beautiful for this. Only Bevode looked inspired.

Lola started toward Cyrus. Bevode cut her off, and shoved her back with his rifle.

"Knock it off," insisted Lola, still smiling. "Jesus Christ, I did everything you wanted."

"You did fine," said Bevode conversationally as the rifle swung up. "Only problem is, Cyrus has enough maids. What he needs is a wife."

Crack. The rifle bucked. Broker jumped back. The shock of the gunshot pierced him like cordite needles. Bevode shot Lola at close range, between the ribs. She plopped straight back and down, heavily on her rump. It had happened so abruptly that her facial muscles were still untangling from a smile. Bevode pushed her over with his boot and, hardly looking, laid the muzzle into her thick black hair.

Broker turned his body to shield Nina when the rifle cracked again and Lola's head made a thump-dribble up and down on the sand.

Nina tore away from Broker and charged. Bevode watched her come. "Stay put, you," he joshed. "I mean it." A rifle barrel pinned Broker in place, jammed deep into his neck, up under his chin. It spoke English with a European accent. Belgian. French? "Don't even breathe."

Bevode danced back, taunting Nina, and giving himself time to drop one shoulder and uncoil the whip in a move he probably practiced in front of a mirror. Nina went in on instinct, her hands coming up, tendons raised, fingers arched.

Expertly, with perfect timing, Bevode let the whip snake out toward her and flicked his wrist. The lash snapped somewhere around her hips. She went down like a singed spider and Broker saw blood against her bare flank through the rent in her blue jeans.

"Told you to stay put," said Bevode.

Broker searched across the bloody beach for Trin's eyes. Trin had his head bowed. Did not raise it.

Bevode caught the eye play as he casually coiled up his whip. He sauntered toward Broker and stepped over Lola's body, careful not to dirty his boots.

"Broker, man, you should'a listened to Cyrus. He told you that ole Gunga had a habit of changing sides . . ."

Broker sat in the sand with his hands clasped behind his neck. Shock manacled his ankles, turning them to wood. He was having trouble breathing. His eyes took pictures that his brain wouldn't accept and the oxygen in his blood had gone on strike.

Bevode dragged Lola's corpse into the surf by the hair, swearing loudly when he lost his grip because part of the skull wobbled loose. Still swearing, he heaved the dead weight over the rubber gunwale of a dinghy so the legs dangled, feet in the water.

Then he pawed around inside the boat and came up with a long, plastic-hafted diver's knife. Swiftly he slashed the muscular clay of hamstrings and calves.

"Draw the fishies," he said, fastidiously stooping and washing his hands in the surf. He nodded to the green-faced Cajun at the tiller, who was striving to keep his breakfast down. "Take it a couple miles out and dump it."

The Cajun reversed the powerful motor and backed the boat into the gentle swells. The torn white trousers swayed over the gunwale and leaked twisted crimson stripes like a wet, dirty American flag.

Casually, Bevode nodded at the bloody drag trail at his feet and said to one of the mercs, "Rake up this sand. Cyrus don't need to see this shit."

Then he walked up the beach and towered over Broker. Save the Whales had come ashore in the second boat. He knelt a few feet away, with Nina, opening a first-aid kit.

Nina pitched on her back, supported on her elbows, trembling the full length of her body. And that was shock.

Save the Whales shook his head and eased down Nina's jeans. "Between you and Virgil you sure put some miles on this girl," he said laconically.

Bevode winked at Broker. "Don't worry, she's all right. I just nicked her. So what'd you do with my little brother?" he asked.

"He's gone into rice farming," said Broker, fighting to get the words from his dry mouth. "Organic farming. You know, where you dump human shit in the fields."

"Well, he always had a problem, you understand. Drugs. I told him he should clean up his act. Wouldn't listen. So we found a way for him to be useful."

Bevode was totally relaxed, standing there, enjoying watching Broker appreciate the situation. He reached in his pocket and brought out a plastic flask of sun lotion. SPF 30. He dabbed it assiduously on his face.

Broker braced himself, he was starting to shake. Bevode just smiled and walked away. He was in control. And Bevode knew that was harder for Broker than dying, knowing that Bevode was in control.

Slowly, pensively, Cyrus LaPorte walked back up the beach.

Trin was separated from the other Vietnamese and sat alone in the shade of a willow. Hands in his lap, he was lightly guarded, if at all. Bevode squatted and patted him on the head, got up, and walked back to where Nina sat sullenly trying to beat the shaking—bleeding, handled, filthy jeans pulled to her knees.

Save the Whales ordered Nina to remove her underpants. She refused so he did and she began to shiver while he inspected the laceration. He splashed on some iodine. She seemed to embrace the reality of the sting. Bevode ordered her to stand up. She pulled up her panties and stood. Then he told her to walk. She took a few steps. Blood and iodine trickled down her thigh and around her knee like veins in marble.

"See," he said, "she's just fine." In a gesture of crude possession Bevode laid the whip handle between her legs. With venom eyes, she drove her will into the sand and refused to shake. Bevode waited patiently, toying. She tried to spit, but she was too dry. He smiled. Despite all her conviction, she trembled uncontrollably.

Broker got to a crouch. One of the mercs put him down with a rifle butt.

Save the Whales stepped forward and peeled down her pants again and slapped a tape compress along the ragged red pencil that ran below her hip up into her left buttocks. Nina modestly pulled up her underpants and went to reach for her pants and Bevode, playfully, snagged them with the front sight of his rifle and held them from her.

"Uh-uh, I kinda like to watch you walk with blood on your ass."

Broker's sight was fractured. More brilliant than normal but cracked. Trin still wouldn't meet his eyes. Fucking Trin. *Make a deal with the maggots eating your corpse.*

Bevode was saying, "Now I got me a whole work crew of people who mostly walk funny."

Save the Whales tied Broker's hands behind his back. Then Nina's. Trin sat in the shade, his face a fixed mask, averted, unreadable. They didn't tie him up.

LaPorte came up the beach dragging his feet through the surf like General MacArthur, his hands still clasped behind his back. "Everything all right?" he asked Bevode crisply.

"Yes, sir."

"Take one of the boats. Run the gimps back to the house and clean it up. Take Louis along for the translating. I'll keep Trin here with me."

It was absolutely quiet on the beach. Just the lulling swish of the waves. LaPorte's men unloaded the remaining dinghy. They set up a camp table, chairs, and an umbrella and brought several large coolers ashore. One of them unfolded the tripod of a surveyor's sextant.

The normal-sounding cadence of profanity carried from the water line. Men working in hot, humid conditions and bitching. The sound pecked at walls of shock.

LaPorte walked over to Broker. "Pardon our little act. We *are* scouting hotel sites on the coast. You'll rest as long as it's light and be fed. Tonight, after we're reasonably sure no one is going to wander through, we'll get down to business."

He started to walk away, paused, and turned.

"I would have given her a divorce, you know. But she was . . . well, greedy," said LaPorte, slowly shaking his head. "And there was something else. She lied to me. Don't lie to me, Phil, and render service. You and the girl just might come out of this."

The vets were loaded into the boat and Bevode and one of the mercs motored them off up the coast. LaPorte sat with Blue Shirt and Trin at the camp table. They talked and drank from glistening green bottles they took from one of the coolers. LaPorte talked on a radio, presumably to someone on the *Lola.*

Nina's voice muttered, striving for control, "He's going . . . to have to change . . . the name . . . of his fucking boat."

Broker looked away. Every muscle fiber in her body struggled to contain the uncontrollable shivering. Patches of her skin shuddered.

Sick dog jerky. Broker discovered that he couldn't look her in the eye.

Not physical. Pain she could take. No. He glanced at the pit site. The loose sand had settled into a slight concave depression. He'd brought her to within fifty yards of where her father lay . . .

He looked out to sea. *His* father had said that death approached with a slow deliberate tread. Gradually you got to see its features, know its habits.

Death wiggled on Bevode's leash, smack in his face, so close that he had to wait for it to back up a few feet to get a good look at it. Broker was ashamed that, in these first moments, he thought only of himself.

73

Broker confronted the paradox of hope during the benign interval of planning that followed in the aftermath of Lola's murder. Hope played hide and seek in the hot sun. Hope was fickle enough to root on the gallows steps.

Why were they allowed to live?

He and Nina were handled efficiently, like important merchandise. They were frisked and Broker was allowed to keep the glass vial. Then they were positioned apart so they couldn't communicate. But they were hand-fed water and energy bars by Save the Whales.

Snatches of conversation carried to him. They would lay low for the day and see if there was a local reaction to Bevode's shooting. LaPorte sounded better informed now about the deserted nature of the place.

Trin.

Broker was blindfolded and was marched off the beach. His hands brushed the baking masonry of one of the old graves, where he was stored in the shade so he wouldn't spoil.

He lost track of time. The day broke down into simple experiences. When he sat, his tired body ached. When he lay down, it didn't hurt as much. He found himself creeping after the shade along the round walls, staying ahead of the sun. He was fed and watered and allowed to relieve himself. His bound hands were checked and loosened slightly. They needed him for his hands and his back.

To dig it up? They had more men, in better condition.

One of the European mercenaries gave him a cigarette. Communication was practical, without animosity, conducted on the level of skilled animal handlers. He waited, kenneled in his blindfold.

For Bevode, who would come out at dark.

Later, afternoon maybe, Broker heard LaPorte's voice getting louder, casually discussing his manpower problem. His tone had changed. Less anxious. In practical matters he consulted the one he called Marc, Blue Shirt: How close could they hazard bringing the vessel in to shore? How long would it take to ferry loads? How many men to hoist them with the winch into the cargo hold? The weather was always a worry.

Then Broker learned why he was being kept alive. LaPorte was concerned that, given Jimmy Tuna's fascination with demolition and practical jokes, the gold pit could be booby trapped.

Footsteps in the sand. Broker was so sensitive to the blister of the sun that he could feel a man's shadow. He smelled fresh, hot coffee, not the soupy Vietnamese stuff. American.

"I thought you might like some coffee, Phil." The relaxed, deep voice had a slight drawl, not enough to be regional, just enough to be interesting. LaPorte. Talking with macabre nonchalance while he tracked blood. Did he learn that from Bevode? Or did Bevode learn it from him?

The lip of a cup touched Broker's cracked lips. Even hot, the coffee was wonderful and tasted like home. He felt a cigarette tuck in the corner of his mouth. Heard the flare of a lighter. After one drag the cigarette was removed, Broker wondering what he had to do to get it back. The cup returned and then the smoke.

His throat and senses lubricated, he asked, "How did you get to Trin?"

Sounds. The sand stirring. LaPorte was sitting down, getting comfortable. His voice was practical.

"Don't underestimate Bevode. He wasn't in Wisconsin because he tarried in Lansing, Michigan. Lucky for him . . . I guess."

"Kevin Eichleay." Broker winced. He got a picture of yellow police tape strung at a charity relief office.

LaPorte chuckled. Broker was allowed another sip of coffee. This time the cigarette was left in his mouth. "Oh, Kevin still has all his fingers and toes," said LaPorte. "Fingers are probably in a cast by now, though. Bevode motivated him to give us Jimmy's Vietnam connection. I guess he was pretty tough. All Bevode got was Trin's name and a phone number. I damn near shit when I heard *that*."

LaPorte's voice took on an absent quality, ruminating, "You know, Bevode grew up in one of those Christian cults, way back in the swamp. Snake handlers. He used to suffer in this moral quandary. He drank a lot when he was a cop. I guess the problem of evil really bothered him. He's been sober since I revealed to him that he really was just a sadistic sociopath."

Broker had another sip of coffee. LaPorte continued. "Bevode has been here with me before. One of the things he does is run security checks with the police on potential employees. So he ran Trin with the cops in Hue. To set up his gimp day care he needed permits. Our Communist brethren are sticklers for paperwork. It left a trail. From People's Committees, the district, the province on up to the state. He followed the trail out here."

"Still doesn't tell me how you turned him," said Broker.

LaPorte's baritone shook with laughter. "Turned him? From what? Hell, he was using you and he meant to use me. Your buddy has been picked up for vagrancy, drunkenness, petty theft, and pimping in the new hotels. He's suspected of smuggling and running scams on tourists. I just gave him his head."

Broker grimaced. LaPorte continued. "Oh, we made him an offer, manager of the hotel I'm building, threw in a new car . . ." LaPorte laughed. "These people are nuts about new cars. Do you know the Koreans have the inside track on widening Highway One into a four-lane freeway? The way these guys drive, I'm thinking of investing in a national ambulance service."

"Why'd you string up that poor dude on the flagpole?"

"I didn't. Bevode got a little carried away. But to answer the question: Trin was thinking bigger than hotel manager. The Hue cops suspect that he's been bribing the local militia post for years. Uses this stretch of beach for smuggling."

Broker winced. The cigarette had burned down and the paper was stuck to his lip. LaPorte plucked it away.

"So," said LaPorte, "figuring Trin might be up to his old tricks, I sent Bevode and all the boys in early to have a visit with the militia. Caught them at dinner. Dumb shits had their guns locked up. With a little persuasion, they talked. Trin planned his trap for tomorrow morning. We would have come ashore into twenty AKs and a machine gun. He even tried to delay me and tipped the customs police. They showed up at our hotel and combed through our luggage. Looking for art objects. Fortunately, bribery is a way of life in the Orient."

"What did you do with the militia?" Broker asked grimly.

"Paid them off. Got two men watching them way back in the dunes. Don't worry, we won't hurt them," LaPorte added. "In fact, they wanted to be tied up for appearance's sake. They're ignorant kids out to make a buck."

"He was after the boat, and the whole thing," Broker said grudgingly.

"There you go. Why would he break cover and come into Hue after he had the jackpot? Certainly not just for the girl. But she was an excuse to deal with me. He needed a method of *moving the stuff*. He was going to ambush us with his rag-tag militia, rip me off, and sail off with a vessel full of gold."

Broker exhaled carefully. "I thought the militia was coming to arrest you. Next time I'll learn the language."

"I figured you to be a better judge of character, Phil. Trin's a drunk, with delusions of grandeur."

Broker heard LaPorte stand up. Dust off his pants. After a moment, LaPorte said softly, "Trin makes sense. And I can understand you blundering in here and him taking advantage of you. But the girl still doesn't fit. We leaned on her hard and she didn't even peep."

Broker sat, head bowed. Silent.

"It's ironic," mused LaPorte. "But my being here has saved you and the Pryce kid." He paused. "He was going to cut your throat, Phil."

Another cigarette was placed between Broker's lips. And lit. "Give you some advice. Don't piss Bevode off. He's got the idea you're trying to wipe out his family."

LaPorte's footsteps faded in the sand. And Broker puffed on the cigarette and tried not to think of last smokes and firing squads. LaPorte was just toying with him. He and Nina had witnessed Lola's murder. He wondered why Trin hadn't tried to cop a plea about Ray Pryce's incriminating skeleton being in that hole. Maybe he didn't believe it.

The sun gradually changed on Broker's skin. He could hear the shadows stretch longer. Fatigue took priority over waiting. He slept on a sand pillow.

Then the moment came and the blindfold was ripped off. Broker's eyes exploded, almost blinded by the indifferent glory of the sunset. He saw . . .

Bevode Fret. Powerful, rested, smiling.

Bevode cracked his whip and the rational energy of Dachau and the homespun industry of the Old South convened on a deserted beach in central Vietnam.

74

THEY WERE REUNITED WITH TRIN AT THE PIT. TRIN'S HANDS were not tied. LaPorte gave them a little pep talk. "Right now I own this beach," he said. "I can grant absolution. You can still get out of this." LaPorte walked away.

Two of the Europeans untied Nina and Broker. The second that Broker's hands were free they flew like springs to Trin's throat.

Blue Shirt and two of his comrades jumped in and pried them apart. Blue Shirt explained patiently. "Work together and you live. Keep this up and we shoot the girl. More work for you two."

He threw them three shovels, a net sack full of water in plastic liter bottles, a pack of Gauloises and a book of matches.

"*Arbeit macht frei,*" he said without irony.

Bevode had not returned Nina's jeans. Her bare shanks were streaked with sand, dried blood, and mosquito bites. Bevode came for a visit and slowly dragged his coiled whip up the front of her body, raising her dirty T-shirt, ending with the harsh braid distorting her cheek. He leaned over and whispered in her ear, "Before the sun comes up you'll beg me for it."

Nina's face tightened and found a sticking point. She had dispensed with shaking and was now composed. She now had something to measure the rest of her life against.

"You'll understand," said Bevode, "if we stay back aways in case it's rigged to blow." He walked away.

They stood alone in the escaping light, blinking, massaging their wrists, painfully shuffling their feet to get the circulation going. Trin's hands shook as he tore open the cigarettes. He held the pack to Broker, who craved one. Broker curled his lip. With trembling fingers Trin manipulated the matches and lit a Gauloises. His dark eyes burned with a disturbing fix in the twilight. He stooped, picked up the shovels and handed one to Broker, then to Nina.

"I told them it might be set with explosives," he said under his breath.

"Fuck you," said Broker.

"If we dig and load it and last till dawn, we live," said Trin. "It's that simple."

"Cyrus tell you that." Broker spat contemptuously.

"*I'm* telling *you* that," he countered, grandiose to the end. And he smelled of dementia, sweat, exhaustion, garlic and onions and sour, leftover alcohol. But strangely not of fear. With psychotic energy, he tore into the sand with his shovel.

"You wanted it for yourself," Broker accused. "You were going to kill us all—Cyrus, her, me. Then you could take the boat. But Cyrus foxed you."

Nina grimaced. Her eyes tightened. Broker wanted to touch her face. He'd never see her again in the light.

Not much light left.

"Nobody begs," she said in a barren implacable voice. She set her mouth. Okay, she had her epitaph to go out on. But it sounded like fatalism. Surrender. Broker wondered what she was thinking right now, standing nine or ten feet over her father's bones. She drove her shovel into the sand. Maybe she had to see if they were really there.

Even if it meant digging her own grave.

Broker set his thresholds. He would not talk to Trin. He would not beg. His life was a few tons of sand running through his fingers. He wished he had a cigarette. Trin had the cigarettes and matches in his pocket.

There was pain and fear and fatigue. There was no adrenaline to run with it. Broker's muscles balked, cold taffy. He discovered that he wanted to dig to warm his blood.

To feel alive.

He had the shovel. He could use it as a weapon if Bevode got close enough. At the right time. Swing it like an ax. Take his fuckin' head off.

They worked side by side, each in their private bargaining with what comes next. Trin giggled. "This is the second time I've dug up this damn hole."

Broker felt Nina's irritation at Trin spike the night.

And now, in total darkness, there were practical demands. "We

need some light," yelled Broker. Blue Shirt came over with two battery bar lights. Broker hacked shelves in the sand. The widening pit
filled with soft illumination. They could see each other's faces.
Seeing the mad expression on Trin's dripping face, it was a mixed
blessing.

He had never looked so foreign. Digging. He was spawned from a
tribe of resolute diggers. In his chromosomes, Broker supposed,
thousands of years of piling up the dikes to control the water to
grow the rice to keep the circle of the seasons turning. One of the
great warrior-digger races of history. They dug at Dien Bien Phu, at
Cu Chi, at Khe Sanh . . .

Were Ray's bones really down there? All the graves in this damn
country. You'd hit skeletons anywhere you dug. Bone City. Stacked
up for millennia and cross-fertilizing a culture of ancestor worship
and reincarnation and pretty soon there'd be no room left.

Nothing but graves.

Nice thing about a big young country. You could travel for days
and never see a grave . . .

Fuck this. Broker threw down his shovel, pushed Trin aside, and
grabbed at the cigarettes in his chest pocket. He was so tense he bit
right through the first one and had to light another. With a loony
smile, Trin advised him, "Relax."

They worked. Drank water. And worked some more. Trin kept
widening the hole and at first Broker fought a flush of petty resent-
ment. Making more work. But a bigger hole meant more time. Time
was what they had. They emptied it, shovel by shovel, out of the
hourglass of their lives.

Deep in his own bones he began to hear the whispers of childhood.

Our father, who art in Heaven . . .

He looked up. Great damn stars. He didn't recognize any of them.
His torn tennis shoe slipped off the shovel and he almost fell.
Stumble-footed. He kicked at the empty plastic bottles. They
bumped and staggered like sleepwalkers.

Too done in to do the work. Out of time.

Trin read their fatigue. "We must finish what we started," he
panted. Nina fell to her knees and yanked at her T-shirt. Sodden
with sweat and wet sand, it interfered with her movement. She tore
at the cloth, ripping a two-foot piece above the hem. Freer in the
abbreviated shirt she wiped her face with the ripped cloth. Trin
extended his hand for the rag. She threw it at him. He wiped sweat

from his face and then handed it to Broker. "We work slow and steady," Trin insisted.

Nina glared at Trin. A copper wraith, her bare stomach was coated with a sugar of sand and sweat. She sucked in a harsh breath and spit, "How could you deal with them?"

Trin's smile was pure gook insane. "If we finish the work we live. That's the deal. Now don't quit on me!" he snarled at her.

"Fuck you," she hissed and drove her shovel into the sand. Trin smiled. A Vietnamese smile. Two thousand years old. Broker tried to decipher the expression on the short man's square face. He was keeping them going.

And so they dug with a new bizarre agenda within the grim prospect that waited. They would not fall down on the job. A credo Broker was raised with. He was a machine stuffed full of bullets. The bullets popped out as sweat.

Six feet into the pit. Even with the already loosened sand from their previous labors, Broker's arms burned with every lift of the shovel. Each time it became harder to clear the lip of the hole. Nina's breath was a dry rattle.

Scoop, swing, toss.

Trin's shovel stabbed into wood with a hollow thunk. Again.

Loose ingots appeared haphazardly, as brilliant in the electric light as details from a Van Gogh. Must have spilled them in their haste their first time in this goddamn hole. Nina cradled one of them in her hands like a small flat loaf of bread. She put the bar down and touched the moldy webbing of the cargo sling that twisted around the pallet. The sling had not been treated with preservative and it crumbled in her hand.

One by one Broker heaved the gold ingots up into the night, twenty, thirty of them.

A flurry of flashlight beams played above the pit. LaPorte and his crew still stayed back, wary of their imagined booby trap. But they were no longer silent. The night animated with their excited voices.

"We've hit the pallet. We're taking a break," Broker yelled, throwing down his shovel and collapsing in the sand.

"That's fair. We're sending over some food." LaPorte's voice sounded in the night. His reasonable, collector's voice. Trin slowly climbed to get it.

He scrambled back down into the pit with a handful of candy bars, energy bars, some donuts, and more water bottles. They squatted like cave dwellers, tearing at the cellophane wrappers with hooked grave-digger fingers. Broker chewed sand along with mouthfuls of an energy bar. Trin bent over a wrapper near one of the lights: brain-dead, he read the list of ingredients.

Nina averted her eyes from this weird normal moment and chewed methodically. Sand cascaded into the pit. Looking up, they saw Bevode's shadow loom over them, outlined against the stars, catching enough spill from the lanterns to define the leer on his face.

In leisurely stages, Bevode unzipped his fly and eased out his dick. For a long time he massaged himself pleasurably and then he let a thick stream of urine splatter down. The piss steadied in one spot and splashed on the wooden lid of one of the ammo boxes.

"Break's over," said Bevode. He zipped his pants and slowly uncoiled his bullwhip.

75

THE YEAR 2000 WAS FIVE YEARS AWAY AND BROKER WAS building the pyramids in reverse, in the dark. Cyrus's pyramid.

Grunt and heave. His leg muscles coiled and nearly cracked. He was growing into his injured thumb. His thumb screamed as he dragged a box up the long sand ramp that Trin had stamped and shoveled into the side of the pit.

He had lost track of time since the leather eye of the whip started watching him in the night. He was bleeding from the right shoulder now, where the whip saw something it didn't like. Just him and the whip and the ramp and the Imperial weight of Ming Mang's gold.

Long fucking way up that ramp. Rope handles on the ammo boxes. Like a wire brush, stiff with tar. Ripped his hands. He'd torn the pockets from his pants and tried to use the blood-stained tatters as makeshift gloves. Trin was barechested, his sweaty torso muscled like a bantamweight. Lost his tiger tooth? He'd torn his shirt up and shared it with Nina to use on the cutting ropes.

Broker stared at the ammo crate. Weighed anywhere from a hundred to two hundred pounds apiece. The rough wooden box had waited twenty years in its chrysalis of sand for him. This must be what slavery was like. Suffering doled out one drop of sweat at a time. Gimme water, gimme rest, gimme food, gimme another hour . . .

History was turning backward in the pit.

It's a wheel. No wheels on the sand ramp though. Just muscle. And all his muscles were braced—not just with the obstinate weight of the box. With anticipation.

For the whip.

He cleared the top of the pit and the benediction of the sea breeze made his sweat sing. Up here in the fresh air there was organization. Purpose. A future.

Men who owned the future stood with guns. And a whip. Making plans. They had a system. Broker, Nina, and Trin dragged the boxes up the ramp and another twenty yards down the beach. LaPorte had decided this was the danger close zone. If there was an explosive device in the pit they should be protected by the walls of the hole and the distance. In teams of three, the crippled vets were hitched to the boxes and dragged them to the surf. Trung Si and the other three struggled with the boxes and loaded them into the dinghy.

Hire the handicapped.

Broker dropped the rope handle and plodded back toward the pit. Nina's head inched up, then her corded shoulders and arms appeared, straining at the terrible weight. Couldn't look her in the eye. Hadn't been able to for hours. Supposed to protect her.

"Don't be eyeballing that woman," shouted Bevode. The whip winked with a leather hiss. A light, flesh-clipping butterfly kiss on the shoulder blade.

"Bevode," chided Cyrus LaPorte. He sat in a chair, at the folding camp table, near the waterline. He was reading a copy of *USA Today* by the light of a battery bar. He was drinking fresh-brewed coffee. A dinghy brought it on a return trip from the boat. Broker could smell it. For the next hour all he could think about was the smell of coffee.

In the morning.

Because morning was coming. The texture of the dark had changed. From drenched canvas to velvet to gauze.

The pit had started to look familiar, like an apartment they lived in and were remodeling. Broker lurched back down the ramp. Every time they dragged a box their bleeding hands left a little trail. He winced when he heard the whip crack. Bevode's voice gloated in an epiphany of power and contempt. "C'mon, you split-tail nigger; tote that bale, bitch."

Trin met him halfway up the ramp, struggling with another box. No one had spoken for hours. What was the use? Trin continued to struggle on. Steady. Determined. With what? Nothing left.

After hours on the ramp it had become familiar. A routine. Broker dropped to his knees and blinked. But now the remaining boxes were countable. A finite number. Six of them. He saw the rotting wood of the pallet base protrude from the sand. What was it Jimmy said. How many words . . .

Well, Jimmy, how many boxes you think I got left?

Nina stumbled back down the ramp. Face set. Hammered copper. Mycenaean death mask face. Won't talk. Setting an example. Don't show emotion in uniform. Whatever. He could tell by the way she stared at the broken pallet. She's going all the way, to the bottom. Like a kid playing a rough game of tag. Going to touch home.

But first there were six boxes. Broker wrapped his bloody hands around the rope and yanked, tried to straighten up. Trin stood above him on the lip of the hole, surrounded by cottony gray light. He studied the sky. "That's it, you're done," he called down.

Done. Him up above. With Bevode and the whip. Them in the pit.

Nina was on her knees, wrestling boxes aside. She began to claw at the bottom of the hole. Her hands left bloody smears on the powdery wood. Losing it. Broker reached for something inside to brace on. Found nothing but pain. It'd do.

"I said, that's it," Trin repeated. A crazy man, forming iron words of command in his mouth. Dumb fuck. In a few minutes his mouth would be full of sand.

Broker had to try. He flung his shovel ahead, out of the hole. And went up the damn ramp with a box. Bevode watched him come across the sand, scuttling like a cockroach dragging its broken legs. Broker dropped the rope, grabbed at the shovel, set his feet to charge. The whip caught him across the chest and took his wind, and he had become so acute in his understanding of pain that he heard the skin split open when the lash snapped. Heard his own blood leak like a spigot.

"Come on, you sorry piece of Yankee shit," taunted Bevode. He cracked the whip in a popping circle, like a lion tamer. "C'mon."

Broker struggled up, vaguely menacing with the shovel. His will had turned to ash. A soft breeze blew it away. I can't die this way, he thought. Not with that bastard winning. He lurched to his feet. Gotta. Try.

Trin was there, with considerable reserves of strength in his short compact body. He dragged Broker back toward the pit. Pushed him down into the hole.

"What's going on?" muttered Nina, on her knees among the five remaining boxes.

"Give me your shirt," Trin shouted down to Broker.

"What the fuck?" blurted Broker.

"Give it!"

Maybe it was the whip. The myopia of sweat and pain. Broker had learned in one night to respond to authority. He peeled off the torn rag and tossed it up. Trin held it and smiled as he read the ironic caption printed over the sand- and sweat-stained Commie flag. "Good morning, Vietnam," he said quietly.

"Hey, who told you to take a break," yelled Bevode.

"Meeow," growled Trin. Then he waved the rag three times over his head. A crisp circular platoon leader's hand signal: *Gather on me.* Impossibly, he sprinted down the ramp.

He went immediately to Nina and put his arm around her. "Hold it in. Just a little longer," he said gently. Then Broker heard Save the Whales yell, down by the beach. "Bevode, we got us a sit-down strike here."

Trin smiled and fished a Gauloises from the crumpled pack stuck in the sand. He put it to his lips and offered the pack to Broker. Something in that smile, thought Broker. Maybe hope does grow on gallows trees.

Broker took a cigarette. Trin found the book of matches and struck one. "What?" Nina yelled. "What?" They lit their cigarettes as a blinding band of sunlight cut a hot bar across the wall of the pit. Just above their heads.

Bevode was yelling and cracking his whip down by the water line. "Get up, get up."

Then LaPorte's voice. "Bevode, check the pit." There was just a hint of apprehension in that voice. Broker started to rise, to take a look. Trin pulled him back and smiled broadly.

Broker blinked, fought off a blackout, and brushed at shadows that were suddenly flitting around his face. The air was full of dragonflies. They had materialized out of the sunlight. Must be hallucinating. He heard dragonflies swarming. The ghosts of a thousand helicopters.

"What's going on?" Broker rasped.

"We are taking cover," said Trin calmly. "This hole is the only protection for three hundred meters on a wide-open beach."

The swaggering shadow of Bevode Fret's head and shoulders jutted up in the band of sunlight on the wall of the pit. Growing larger as he approached with dawn at his back.

"Hey," he yelled. Then, "You hear . . ."

Broker would never remember what he heard first, the shrill whistle from back in the dunes or the rifle volley. But he could tell that the gunshots were deliberate. Sparse. Aimed fire. He couldn't tell who was screaming in pain or in panic. But they were all screaming up there.

Nina sprung at the sand wall and clawed her way up until her eyes were level with the top of the pit.

"Soldiers," she muttered. Then she reared up, head and shoulders into the sunlight, and pumped her bloody fist in ferocious double-time glee. Her voice swelled into a hoarse cheer, "*Soldiers!*"

76

*T*RIN'S RULES.

Broker burst out laughing.

There were twenty of them, maybe more. Hard-faced young men in green camouflage tunics. Some carried AK-47s. Others toted deadly customized sniper rifles. They sprinted from the willows in the dunes, spreading out. Field radios crackled as they ran past.

Of their former tormentors, only LaPorte was still on his feet, running down the beach. Broker could see the sunlight catch the water that filled his footprints. Nina's eyes marked him like iron bolts. She sprung from the pit, shucked her fatigue, and pounded after him.

Avenger. No angel about it.

"Let her go," said Trin. Then he spoke curtly in Vietnamese to one of the soldiers, who, with two of his comrades, took off after Nina.

Broker kept laughing. Maybe he would never stop. He continued to laugh when he saw Bevode Fret crumpled over, clutching his right knee in both hands. Bevode appeared to be amazed that a bullet could go through his flesh and bone. "Jeez Louise," he gasped through bloodless jerky lips. "You didn't have to shoot me."

Near one half-loaded dinghy, Save the Whales was also down, pushing hard on his thigh with both palms, applying pressure. Blue Shirt lay crumpled, unmoving. Two more of the Europeans made motionless rag piles on the sand. The rest of Cyrus's men crouched behind the other dinghy with raised hands.

Broker had not been hallucinating. Three helicopters came in a line from the north, dots over the sea. Two fast patrol boats bracketed the *Lola.*

Then Broker saw two, three more soldiers who sat erect in spider holes in the sand a hundred yards up the slope where the dunes petered out. They were almost invisible in sandy folds of netting. Wads of sand-colored cloth hung from their helmets and tunics. They held heavy-barreled, scooped rifles. Snipers.

"Were they there all night?" he asked.

"I'm not sure exactly when they moved into position. The timing got all screwed up," said Trin.

"These guys aren't militia," said Broker.

"Army Special Forces," said Trin quietly. "The militia's fine. They were a throw-away plan, for Cyrus to figure out."

A lean Vietnamese woman in jeans and a military tunic ran from the last knot of soldiers and veered toward them, long black hair streaming. She had a pistol belt strapped on her waist with a red star on the holster.

"Who's that?" asked Broker.

"A real bitch. The mayor of Dong Ha."

She started screaming at Trin as soon as she slowed her pace. Just when Broker thought she was going to haul off and slug him, she hugged him instead.

Broker had seen those resilient lava eyes before. He stared as she unbuckled the pistol belt and handed it to Trin. She continued her harangue as Trin cinched on the gun with his torn hands.

"Speak English," he shot back.

She took a haughty breath. Her thoroughbred nostrils quivered. "You said it would happen today. In daylight. Not *last* night! We couldn't chance a fight in the dark. We might have hit you. Goddammit." Her eyes flashed, taking in Broker, Nina.

Trin nodded. "They got ahead of me. But it was right you waited. They had to be caught transporting it away."

"The house in Dong Ha, you were the woman," said Broker.

"Correct, Mr. Broker, and I'm married to a real bastard who likes to take too many chances. He thinks he's hot stuff, but he's just a colonel in the border police."

Trin smiled tightly. "Phil, meet Mai Linh, my wife."

With flowering understanding, Broker inclined his head. He couldn't shake. His hand was a mess. She nodded back. Then Trin conversed with her in rapid Vietnamese. She switched back to English. "You still insist on doing this thing?"

Trin nodded curtly. "Get them all out, except those two." He pointed first to Bevode, then down the beach. Nina had cornered

LaPorte, who stood waist-deep in the ocean. Soldiers closed in on him and motioned to him with their rifles. Trin turned to Mai Linh. "You can't be here," he said flatly.

"I don't approve of this," she insisted.

"You're not going to see this. Go." She turned and jogged toward the beach. She stopped at Blue Shirt's body and spoke to two soldiers who were starting to drag it up the slope. One of them bent, got up, and sprinted back to where Trin and Broker stood. He handed Trin the gold tiger tooth. Trin closed his hand around it in a bloody fist and glared at Bevode Fret, who squirmed in the sand thirty feet away.

Then he turned and shouted at the snipers who popped from their holes and jogged down to join their comrades at the waterline.

A truck rumbled down through the dunes and most of the soldiers gathered up the dead, the wounded, and the prisoners and loaded them aboard. Trin's wife joined them. The truck gunned back up the slope and out of sight.

"What was that scene at the house about in Dong Ha?" asked Broker.

"I wanted her personally to see you. She photographed you through the window. To be able to identify you if it came to this."

"Who was the guy at the house with her that day?"

"Our driver. I'm a cop." A thin smile crossed his mouth as he aped Pidgin English. "How you say—undercover."

"You could have let me in on it."

Trin shook his head. "You might have tipped them off."

"Cut it kind of fine, didn't you?"

"You're the one who kept insisting we had to catch him loading it into the boat." Then he glanced up and his face could have been a rock on Broker's beach. In a tight group, Trung Si and the six cripples slogged up the beach toward them. "Don't interfere, Phil," Trin admonished.

Bevode Fret was situated between them and the approaching Viet Cong veterans. He began to scramble painfully toward Broker and Trin. He crawled over his whip and left it behind like a molted skin.

"Hey, Broker. Okay, man. I'm your prisoner . . ."

"Talk to the guy in charge," said Broker.

Bevode's eyes were brilliant yellow with pain. They swiveled to Trin. But Trin's gaze was fixed ahead, behind him. Slowly Bevode turned his head and saw Trung Si pause, balance on his good foot, and use his crutch to scoop up the whip and toss it in the air. He caught the whip by the handle and let it uncoil in a nasty twitch.

"Okay, you caught me. Quit fuckin' around," said Bevode.

The cripples filed past Bevode and walked to a stack of loose ingots—the first ones Broker had tossed out. Wobbling on their artificial legs, they reached down and loaded their arms.

Trung Si tested the whip in the air.

Crack! The sound echoed away down the beach. It took all emotions except hate with it.

The lash whipped across Bevode's legs. He shivered with an involuntary cringe and scuttled to escape. The cripples formed a gauntlet and funneled him toward the pit.

"Hey, knock it off!" Bevode's eyes were indignant. Still no fear. No remorse. Not quite getting it. But then that's where he got his dark energy: Not quite getting it.

Trung Si let the whip sway menacingly. Waiting. Broker saw Nina limping up the beach pushing LaPorte in front of her. A soldier had given her a pair of baggy fatigue trousers to cover her dirty underwear. She looked like Charlie Chaplin.

Two soldiers walked on either side, herding LaPorte with their AKs. Nina collared LaPorte by the scruff of the neck and pushed him to his knees in front of Broker and Trin. The soldiers stepped back.

"You're a . . . soldier?" She stared at Trin's pistol belt, numb, bewildered, definitely happy.

"He's a fuckin' cop," said Broker. "Don't ask me how."

In the distance, the three helicopters, blocky Russian Hinds, circled the *Lola*.

Trin reached and roughly seized LaPorte by the ear. He nodded to Trung Si. The whip feinted left, circled, and snapped into Bevode's face. Bevode bellowed, scrambled, and tumbled backward into the hole.

One of the cripples immediately drew back his arm and fired one of the heavy ingots. A howl of pain rose from the pit. "Cut that out!"

"Who are you? You can't do this," whispered LaPorte.

"I could shoot you right now for stealing Vietnamese antiquities; we take that very seriously," said Trin without emotion. He kicked LaPorte and dragged him forward by the ear and tipped him forward over the pit.

The cripples now hobbled around the edge of the hole. Down below, Bevode had torn a piece of the rotted planking from the pallet. Instinct. Grasping a weapon. An ingot drew a glittering arc and smashed through the moldy wood. Bevode roared in pain and scrambled on his hands and one knee, scooting in a circuit of the pit, dragging his wounded leg. Taking their time, the cripples talked among themselves, altering their stances around the circumference of the hole.

Tiger in a pit came to mind. Other analogies would fit. Maybe it was the war. If Bevode could get his hands on them he could tear them apart. But then, they had position on him . . .

On a command they all hurled their missiles. One of the bars scored a solid hit on Bevode's skull. At least two hit him in the arms and trunk. He fell forward roaring, smashing blindly with his fists. He gathered himself and attempted a staggering charge up the ramp. A volley of ingots chopped him to his knees. He was badly hurt now. Blinded. Parts not working. With the awkward jerky tempo of a squashed bug, he crept back into the hole and began to claw at the rotted wood. Digging. Trying to hide.

Trin yanked LaPorte to his feet. LaPorte came partway up, reluctant to rise to his full height. Knees bent, he stayed with his head below Trin's.

"Run," said Trin.

"Wait a minute," protested Nina. Broker touched her arm. Shook his head, warned her off.

"Run," repeated Trin. "You have money? Your passport?"

LaPorte hunched over, his wild pale eyes fixed on the pit where the cripples were taunting Bevode with feints, preparing to throw another volley.

"Go that way." Trin pointed across the dunes. "Get to the road. Someone will run you into Hue for a few bucks. Then you can catch a plane. Go quick before I change my mind. Before *they* get here . . ." He yanked his head at the helicopters that still circled the boat.

A flurry at the pit. Another volley. Bevode's impaired voice, "Come down here . . . try that, chickenshit lil' fuck . . ."

One of the cripples held out his right hand. He didn't have a left one. He bent his index finger back with his second finger into a crude oval. And Broker remembered that one too. Right up there with "Meeow." Calling Bevode a pussy.

Trin pointed to the helicopters again.

"Office guys, Cyrus," said Broker helpfully. "No sense of humor whatsoever."

"He's right," said Trin. "When they get here it becomes official in a stuffy way. Right now I have some discretion."

LaPorte's eyes locked wide open. *Flight.* Trung Si snaked the whip across the sand and let it skitter, undulating next to LaPorte's desert boots. The cripples hurled another shower of gold. LaPorte heard the broken wet squeal from the hole. He looked around once and bolted, running in long strides across the sand. Some soldiers, who had stayed to picket the top of the slope, chased him, yelling insults. Laughing.

"You let him *get away*?" Nina's voice was confused.

Trin smiled grimly. "If you find what you're looking for down there, let the U.S. Army catch him when he gets back to America." Softly, he added, "One last joke on Cyrus."

Nina drew herself up. "You are really something, mister."

Then, pitiless, they turned their attention back to the pit.

Bevode was losing a lot of blood from his face and scalp. One arm hung, smashed and useless. His crouch had deteriorated into a fetal curl. With his good hand he pawed through the punky wood and scooped feeble handfuls of sand.

"Jesus," gasped Nina in a harsh release of emotion.

Bevode, blinded by blood, raised a shard of chalky bone in his functioning hand, trying to protect his face.

Trin snapped an order.

The cripples dropped the gold of Ming Mang and Trieu Tru and Gia Long and Tu Duc. Slowly they lurched and tottered and staggered down the sand ramp. They dragged Bevode to the side of the pit. Carefully, remorselessly, they pried the bone from his twitching hand and reverently placed it aside. Then they formed a semicircle and, arm-in-arm for stability, balancing on their artificial limbs, using their good legs, they kicked Bevode Fret to death.

77

AMERICAN ROCK-AND-ROLL DRIFTED DOWN THE BEACH from a portable radio that some of the troops played under the shade of a poncho liner. Four-wheel-drive vehicles were parked hubcap to hubcap along the edge of the dunes. Some of the fiercest old faces in the Politburo had arrived by chopper. They didn't seem to mind the music.

A cooling sea breeze rippled through the camouflage silk of a parachute that had been strung between the rotors of the square Russian helicopters. Like half-time in the Roman arena, sand had been kicked over the pools of blood after Bevode's carcass had been dragged away. Nina, Broker, and Trin sat in the shade on camp stools and waited. Army medics had cleaned their wounds. Now a doctor was coming.

Two young troopers in white gloves, with carved bronze faces and bayoneted assault rifles held at the ready, guarded a carefully stacked pile of ammo boxes. The loose gold ingots formed a solid cube on top. They had been carefully washed in the sea to expunge all traces of Bevode Fret. Apparently saltwater was the natural thing to spruce up gold. Broker tried to remember where he'd heard that before. Shook his head. It sure dazzled in the sun.

Older Vietnamese men in white shirts, straw hats, and gray trousers lingered near the gold. Ponderous Marxist-Leninist pressure ridges plowed their foreheads and they had lots of pens in their chest pockets. Very senior office guys, Commie type, figured Broker. Occasionally one of them would reach out with perverse pleasure and steal a touch at an ingot.

An orderly brought around a tray with chilled bottles of Huda beer. Trin reached for one. Then withdrew his hand. Broker, who took one, raised an eyebrow.

"I drink too much," Trin admitted as the orderly returned with a cold can of Pepsi. Nina, who sat quietly between them, raised her hand to touch his shoulder. But her hand was raw hamburger waiting for the doctor and she lowered it. She pronounced his name fondly, "Trin," and resumed her silence.

He gestured with the pop can. "See all these big wigs? Most of them fought the war in offices." He gestured down the beach to where Trung Si and his men sat in the dunes, in the sun. Poor country cousins. They had been given food, drink, and cigarettes. And had been moved downwind. Trin exhaled. "I changed sides and, now, because of Mai Linh's protection, I have status again. They won the war and they're fucked. Everything's rotten. So I drink."

Broker and Nina offered no comment to the complicated and bitter observation.

Trin kicked at the sand and inclined his head at Nina. "Maybe the young people . . ." His voice trailed off.

In the shade of the parachute, an army doctor set up shop and muttered indignantly as he cleaned and bandaged torn hands and whip lacerations. First Nina's, then Trin's, then Broker's. A sloe-eyed nurse with beautiful black Annamite hair swabbed Broker's face with a cool scented towel. His thumb had gone on a rampage and conquered both his hands. They were a stiff study in gauze and adhesive tape.

He had been given a clean pair of Army fatigues. Extra, extra large. But he couldn't put them on with his bandaged hands. Soldiers who had watched without expression as Bevode died now wore easy boyish smiles and helped him. Vietnamese are fastidiously clean people. They insisted that he wash in the ocean first.

They were given inoculations. Tetanus and vitamin boosters. A field kitchen had been set up. The nurse spooned hot pho-beef soup and hand-fed Broker warm fragments of baguette, piece by fluffy piece. In rifts of wind change he caught a whiff of electronic circuits and radio crackle from the interior of the choppers. Trin and Broker were no longer the center of their adventure. The office guys had taken over. The office guys clustered around Nina.

She stood at the edge of the pit wearing a baggy pair of clean, olive green Vietnamese army fatigues and a soft army cap. She had also bathed in the sea and washed her hair. A lot of Americans had arrived on the choppers. Some of them talked and postured to her nonstop. A few feet away, a husky black man in jeans and a Hawaiian shirt, who had the blue-collar aloof presence of a senior NCO, spoke in deliberate Vietnamese sentences. A Vietnamese officer listened patiently. A team of Americans and Vietnamese waited with boxes of equipment. Another American took a reading with a Global Positioning System.

Broker gathered that one of the Americans talking with Nina was from the State Department. Part of an advance team that was setting up the U.S. Embassy in Hanoi. The other was Department of Defense. A senior member of the MIA mission. More helicopters dotted the horizon. Words: "Should have been a combined effort. Phobic about security. A little too close to the edge if you ask me . . ."

Nina raised a hand, mittened in tape, in a feminine reflex, to touch her hair, to smooth it down to cover her deformed ear, which the doctor had scrupulously cleaned and left exposed. Too short. Stiffly she dropped the hand. After that she stood with her bandaged hands clasped behind her, listening. Appropriately austere and under control, her eyes never wandered toward the pit.

Broker asked Trin, "You put all this in motion?"

Trin nodded. "Right from the time you landed in Hanoi. Mr. Hai, the driver, was one of my men. The cyclo driver outside the villa in Hue, who took Virgil away, also my guy." Trin knit his brows. "I made two big mistakes. I didn't expect they'd be so bold as to grab Nina in Hanoi. And not putting security around the vets' house. That cost a life."

"You in trouble?"

"Probably not. Tot, the dead man, was just an ex–Viet Cong rifleman. Not a party member. He won't cast a shadow in Hanoi."

Broker clicked his teeth. "Fuckin' office guys, look at them, crawling all over the place. They even brought their own kitchen."

Trin smiled back. "I've been working this thing for years, since Jimmy sent Kevin Eichleay. Waiting to see who would come. But I didn't really know what we had until we dug it up. Now they'll get the credit."

Broker grinned. "That whole story about the reeducation camps?"

"All true. I ate frogs, little goddamn birds," Trin protested ruefully. "But . . . things changed. When the door opened to the West I was resurrected in slow stages. I had the language skills and the background to fit in with the tourist trade. And antiquities are being looted." He shrugged. "And I was lucky. I had a sponsor in the party."

"With a big letter A on her license plate," said Broker.

Trin sighed and inclined his head. "She kept a lid on the operation. She kept them at arm's length in Hanoi. She took charge of bringing in the force on the beach last night. Without her . . ." he shook his head, "catastrophe."

Mai Linh stood in the crowd of dignitaries, at ease now in a tailored gray Hanoi power suit and sunglasses. With her arms folded, she chatted with Nina, who also had her arms folded across her chest. Broker recalled seeing female executives taking up those defensive stances talking to each other in American offices. Despite Nina's bandages, she and Mai Linh shook hands. Nina resumed talking to the guys from State.

Mai Linh turned her head, lowered one lens of her sunglasses with a crooked finger, and winked at Trin. They exchanged curt sentences in Vietnamese. Then she walked away. "Great," said Trin. "She has to go to Hanoi."

Broker grinned. "I think you can afford the fare."

"Shhh," said Trin. "Let's, ah, take a walk on the beach."

They wandered away from the crowd around the helicopters and the pit. "Just checking," said Broker. "Am I going to get arrested for stealing antiquities too?"

"I have a feeling my wife and I will need a sponsor in America in the near future," said Trin from the side of his mouth. "If I don't get killed by my own border guards sneaking thirteen crates of rare gold across the mountains into Laos, I don't know exactly how to exchange it yet, but I'll figure it out. Half and half."

"Okay," said Broker.

They started back toward the gathering. Nina came out, alone, to meet them. "Excuse me, Trin. Phil, would you walk with me?"

They went down the beach, away from the pit and the crates of gold and the blood drying under the sand.

"You know what happens now, what I get back there," she said. He nodded. She took a deep breath. "I can't cry," she said. "Audie fucking Murphy wouldn't cry."

"Forget Audie fucking Murphy. You're Nina fucking Pryce."

"Aw shoot." She threw her arms, bandaged hands and all, around his neck and burst into tears.

"Hey, knock it off, Jesus—hey, here, I have something that belongs to you," he protested.

She sniffed and wiped her nose on her baggy sleeve. "Okay. I'm better now. What?"

Broker carefully worked the small glass bottle from his hip pocket with his taped hands. Somehow he had kept it intact during the ordeal in the pit. She stared at her earlobe and earring, an exotic sea creature swimming in rice whiskey.

"It's how we ghouls profess our love," he said, proud of the line, which he had rehearsed for an hour.

She closed her adhesive plastered knuckles around it and backed away, uncertain. "Thanks," she said, lowering her eyes. She turned and ran back down the beach to where they were all waiting for her.

And Broker figured what the hell—they could travel side by side for a little longer, but they were in different lanes and pretty soon she'd turn off toward the big time, where she'd been headed all along.

Trin joined him and they wandered back to the crowd. Another helicopter was landing. "That's not a Russian," said Broker.

"No, commercial. French make, I think."

Wide-eyed Westerners with electronic gear piled out. Boxes, wires, cables. A television camera with letters on it. The TV crew literally slipped on their own drool when they saw the pile of gold ingots glittering in the sun.

"Oh good." Trin laughed. "CNN is here."

Broker watched the black American approach Nina and introduce himself. "Chief Warrant Officer Holly, Mam." He lowered his voice and recited stiffly, "Ah, for the record, I think you got a raw deal in the Gulf."

"Thank you, chief," said Nina diplomatically.

"Now," said Chief Holly, "if you'll step over here, we're about to get started excavating this site."

It became very quiet on the beach as the recovery team made their measurements and took their pictures and very slowly began to remove buckets of sand and wood fragments from the bottom of the pit. The buckets were shifted through screened boxes. Artifacts were carefully set aside and labeled.

They sectioned off the dig with twine and labeled each segment. Nina stood very soberly, concerned. She had dusted the chip off her shoulder. No more defiant Jericho eyes. Broker figured she was calibrating herself. Video cameras were all ready recording the event. CNN was getting ready to tape.

She did not show emotion when the outlines of a human skeleton began to emerge from the sand. A hush fell at a rusty jungle . . .

Dog tags.

Nor did she wall herself off. She asked appropriate questions. Brief, to the point, about the procedure.

For the last time gold glinted in the pit.

Photographs were taken from all angles. Notes were made. People spoke into tape recorders in two languages. The team passed the cigarette case in gloved hands to Chief Holly who handed it to his Vietnamese counterpart. The Vietnamese carried it to the ramp and turned it over to another older Vietnamese who, walking in step with the American from the diplomatic service, carried it up and presented it to Nina.

There was a discussion among the technical people and they decided to open the cigarette case inside a large plastic bag, shielded from sun and wind. Very slowly, wearing transparent plastic gloves, a technical assistant pried the case open with something that resembled a dental tool.

A dirty lump of smoky gray plastic was folded inside. The tech very carefully peeled it open. The note was faint but legible, bazen tinged:

Over his protest, here noted, I order Major Raymond Pryce to command a helo extraction of materials vital to United States security from the National Bank of Hue. 0200 hours, 30 April, 1975,
    Signed,
    Cyrus LaPorte, Colonel, commanding

Tape ran. Camera shutters snapped like a piranha feeding frenzy. With a deft sixth sense, Nina Pryce anticipated it and tilted her face from profile to a more flattering three-quarter view that didn't show her bad ear.

78

September, Devil's Rock, Minnesota

They were supposed to go fishing. First J.T. called and canceled, then Ed Ryan. Tom Jeffords said some idiot backpacker from the Cities had gone missing, so count him out.

And John Eisenhower couldn't even claim police work as an excuse. He was giving a speech at a banquet in Stillwater. Broker shook his head. You just couldn't rely on cops.

A framed letter from the Premier of the Socialist Republic of Vietnam hung on his cabin wall and thanked him for his aid in restoring a National Treasure to the People of Vietnam.

The letter did not mention the seven bars of imperial gold that he had been quietly awarded for his services. The back channel deal had been arranged by Col. Nguyen Van Trin of the Vietnamese Border Police. Equally quietly, Trin and his wife and their two children were about to become American citizens.

Fatty Naslund had negotiated the sale of the seven Imperial ingots to the Smithsonian Institute. The gold would go on display in the fall. The amount of money that changed hands exceeded the gold's weight-based market value. Now Fatty was off on his first real-life clandestine mission. He was in Vientiane, Laos, outfitted in a whole Patagonia catalog, to bargain secretly on behalf of a small, discreet group of gold collectors. One of the crates that Trin and Broker had sneaked off had been full of the really old Cham relics.

The stuff of curses.

Broker's Beach was rebuilding on unlimited credit from Fatty's bank, retired Det. Phil Broker installed as manager. Mike had moved up from ballpeen hammers. He could carry out the garbage now.

Irene was debating giving up painting loons and trying sunsets.

Jimmy Tuna had succumbed to cancer just about the time that Cyrus LaPorte said he had.

Nina . . .

Broker pushed the taped CNN broadcast in the VCR and watched it again. A dreary Air Force runway pecked by rain, a Pacific mountain range in the background. Color guard. The band playing. The camera zoomed in at a stately pace and focused on the lumbering C-130 that had just landed from Hanoi. The reporter's voice-over tried for dignity but was breathles. ". . . Part of the cere- mony accepting the return of her father's remains from Vietnam." The goddamn media. Ray Pryce was taking second billing at his own funeral.

Broker had been invited. He'd declined. Not really his kind of scene.

Ray finally got his flag. It draped the coffin being rolled from the back of the transport. And then the camera moved in on the color guard and framed Maj. Nina Pryce, reinstated in the army and pro- moted on a wave of publicity that she had not honored with a single comment. Major Pryce just stood at attention.

Her hair was longer now and the camera stayed on her face, which had filled out in a way that Broker liked, especially the color in her cheeks. But she showed no expression. Dry eyed. The slick under her eyes came from the rain.

Then, slowly, the camera moved off and then roamed up the left front chest portion of her uniform, over the Silver Star and the Purple Heart and jump wings and paused on the blue rectangle with the silver Kentucky rifle and the silver wreath.

Then they showed the film clip of the Chairman of the Joint Chiefs pinning the Combat Infantry Badge on her. Under presiden- tial pressure, the secretary of the army, an appointed civilian, had crafted the citation to hurdle over the Army regs. ". . . retroactive award to an *individual* for performance of exceptional duty . . ."

The Little Dutch Girl had poked her finger through the dike.

Then came the panel of legal experts giving background. Cyrus LaPorte, who had been recalled to active duty for his impending courts-martial, had his own CNN logo and his own theme music.

Next came the clip from the round table of talking heads. Cut to the sound bite of a talcum-smooth conservative Republican, a mil- lion perfect teeth: "This trick that the president forced down the mil- itary's throat will cost him the election."

Political commentator Mark Shields bounced up and down, laughing.

Switch to Bob Dole shaking his head.

Then the news anchors came back on and anchor-talked and the female one enunciated like a drama student, "A recent CNN poll conducted among army personnel predicts by a wide margin that men won't accept this history-making precedent."

"Some men," said Broker. Then he yawned and rewound the tape to the shot of Nina that framed her from hips to chest. He noted that her uniform skirt was fitting rather snug around the middle.

"Broker, you sonofabitch," she had yelled on the phone in an amazed voice when she'd received the results. "Now what?"